If I Had You

If I Had You

The Grand Russe Hotel

Heather Hiestand

LYRICAL PRESS
Kensington Publishing Corp.
www.kensingtonbooks.com

LYRICAL PRESS BOOKS are published by

Kensington Publishing Corp.
119 West 40th Street
New York, NY 10018

All Kensington titles, imprints, and distributed lines are available at special quantity discounts for bulk purchases for sales promotion, premiums, fund-raising, educational, or institutional use.

Special book excerpts or customized printings can also be created to fit specific needs. For details, write or phone the office of the Kensington Sales Manager: Kensington Publishing Corp., 119 West 40th Street, New York, NY 10018. Attn. Sales Department. Phone: 1-800-221-2647.

Lyrical Press and Lyrical Press logo Reg. U.S. Pat. & TM Off.

First Electronic Edition: September 2016
eISBN-13: 978-1-60183-579-6
eISBN-10: 1-60183-579-5

First Print Edition: September 2016
ISBN-13: 978-1-60183-580-2
ISBN-10: 1-60183-580-9

Printed in the United States of America

For anyone who feels like a wallflower and wants to join in on the party of life, Alecia's story is for you. Reach out, turn on some music, get help. There are people out there who will love you. You aren't alone.

ACKNOWLEDGMENTS

Eilis Flynn once suggested I write a novel set around a hotel. My editor, Peter Senftleben, suggested I set a book in the 1920s. Without those suggestions, this book wouldn't exist. Thank you to Judy Di Canio, Mary Jo Hiestand, David Hiestand, Delle Jacobs, Melissa McClone, Peggy Bird, Marilyn Hull, and Madeline Pruett for your assistance and support. Also I'd like to thank production editor Rebecca Cremonese, copy editor Tory Groshong, cover designer Elle Rossi, the rest of the Kensington team, and my agent, Laurie McLean, and the Fuse Literary team for their support of the Grand Russe series.

Chapter One

London, midnight, December 28, 1924

J*azz.*
The saxophone wailed and screeched over the piano. A trombone blared in, deepening the rollicking sound. Alecia Loudon's foot tapped as a female singer sang the words to the newest tune from America. Underneath the music beat the sounds of the nightclub: cups rattling on plates, champagne glasses clinking, and matches being struck for innumerable cigarettes.

Alecia longed to see the action, but it was hidden from her on the other side of the nightclub's rear door. Cocooned in the luxury hotel that shared the club's wall, she couldn't see the dancing. Styles changed so fast, and she wished she knew the current fads. Of course, the song had about as much relevance to her sex-free life as the dancing. "'My baby don't love nobody but me . . .'"

No, the life behind that door bore no resemblance to hers. She was a questionably modern secretary of twenty-two who'd never been kissed. Oh, but she'd thought about kissing, fantasized about kissing, daydreamed about kissing one certain handsome man here at the Grand Russe Hotel . . .

She pushed the thought away and tried the handle of the door. One inch to the right, two inches . . . it caught. Frustrated, she turned the knob again but it only rattled, metal against metal. Securely locked. She considered leaving the safety of the hotel, darting onto busy Park Lane at Hyde Park Corner, going into the alley where the main nightclub door was. But she wasn't dressed for the nightclub.

Giggles emanating from a dark corner on the far side of the door stole her away from her thoughts. She peeled away from the wall where she'd been leaning, in what was little more than a service corridor between the nightclub and the newly reopened hotel. Even back here, the opulence of the Grand Russe Hotel continued undiminished. The tops of the walls were stenciled in a forest green and red-brown geometric pattern that reminded her of teeth. Colorful paintings of ballet scenes done by itinerant Russian artists dotted the walls every six feet, uniform in size and frame.

The hotel's decorations had been inspired by *The Sleeping Princess* ballet performed at the Alhambra in Leicester Square a few years ago, but for sure, the couple on the dark velvet sofa in the corner were no Sleeping Beauty and her Prince Charming. The man in the clinch did not meet any masculine ideal. She'd seen a man who did, though, late at night here at the hotel. Alecia ghosted her way through the somnolent hotel in the wee hours, escaping her ever-present nightmares, while he protected it. A night watchman. She'd never spoken to him.

Dark waves of hair gave him a rakish edge. He possessed eyes of a brown that were closer to amber. Thick chocolate brows overshadowed his eye sockets, making for a fiercely probing gaze. Sculpted, full lips, the rosy bottom just slightly larger than the top. A nose almost too expansive for the face, but imposingly masculine. Angular cheekbones and triangular jaw with a mildly cleft chin. Golden sand-colored skin. A real sheik, though she was no sheba to find herself bent back over his arm and ravished. How she wished.

Oh God. The mere thought of that man, those broad shoulders and trim hips, six feet of masculine perfection, made her weak in the knees and damp in places her late grandmother had told her never to think about. She ought to set her sights on the kind of man who could take her to the nightclub, but her imagination hadn't released the night watchman yet.

The man on the sofa though, leaning over the woman in the revealing champagne-colored French dancing frock, was the type to be able to afford London nightlife. Unfortunately, he was young, balding, stoop-shouldered, and tending to embonpoint around his midsection. The expensive clothes did not make up for this. The gleaming gold bands on the couples' ring fingers told the tale. A Christmas season wedding, followed by a honeymoon in the most scandalous hotel in London.

The hotel owners no doubt hoped the complete refurbishment of the place, and the name change, would rescue their investment from the ignominy it suffered as the location of the infamous Starlet Murders of 1922, but even she, living then with her vicar grandfather and younger sister in Bagshot, Surrey, had heard the stories. With all the inns nearby, the London news could not help filtering in. Rumors of gin and cocaine and sex and sex and sex and, well, death.

Nothing like the quiet life her employers, Richard and Sybil Marvin, had introduced her to when they took up residence here at the hotel, though they, like the rouged and lipstick-wearing murder victims, were actors.

The bride giggled again as her new husband kissed her décolletage. The man ran his tongue along his wife's collarbone. Alecia's eyes widened as his hand went up her knee-length skirt. Were they actually going to have sex, right there on the sofa?

She cleared her throat loudly, but they didn't hear her, or didn't care. The silver tray holding two empty champagne bottles and two overturned glasses explained why these two were in their own world. Drunk as lords. What should she do now?

When she glanced away, she saw *him*. The handsome night watchman wore his uniform of gold coat and deep ruby trousers. Black chevrons were appliquéd on his sleeves. All the buttons were gold, matching the trim on his ruby cap. Underneath the bill, his eyes narrowed as he saw her. He heard the moan behind her at the same time she did. They both turned to see the couple on the sofa. The woman's marcel-waved hair was crushed against the armrest as her husband knelt between her splayed legs and fumbled with his trousers.

"*Hvatit*," the night watchman ordered.

Alecia didn't know what the word meant exactly, but knew his intent. *Stop that, you sex-starved just-marrieds.*

Her dream lover moved past her. She smelled birch oil. This was the closest she'd ever been to him. Though his coat went almost to his knees, she could see the contours of his well-muscled backside underneath the fine wool.

"You must return to your room," he said in a Russian accent. His Rs rolled in a way that set Alecia's heart to fluttering.

The woman screamed when she opened her eyes and saw the watchman standing not three feet away from her. Her husband scrambled to his feet, still fumbling under his jacket. Alecia could see the tops of the woman's stockings, the lace edging on her camiknickers.

She was too drunk to close her legs properly. Her husband finished fumbling and hauled her to her feet. Without speaking, the duo stumbled down the hall, past the night watchman, their gazes downcast.

Alecia still didn't know if they'd ever noticed she was there. When she lifted her gaze, the night watchman was regarding her steadily.

"Voyeurism is not polite, even at the Grand Russe." He said "is" like "ees," so sexy. The word "polite" rolled off his tongue in a drawl. *Heaven.* Oh, he was the cat's meow to be sure.

"I didn't know they were there at first. I've been listening to the music." She nodded at the nightclub door and tried to channel her flirtatious sister. "What is your name?"

"Ivan." He paused. "Salter."

"I'm Miss Loudon," she said. "I work for the Marvins on the fifth floor."

"I know who you are," he said, each word clipped and disapproving. "If you want to hear the music, you can go into the nightclub."

"I don't have the right clothing," she said, pointing to the long, shapeless gray frock she'd sewn herself.

"Mrs. Marvin must have trunks full of suitable garments."

"Not for me. I'm just the secretary."

"*Myshka*," he said, his eyebrows coming together. "That is what you are."

"I don't know any Russian," she said. "What does that mean? Are you really from Russia, or are you playing a role?"

He narrowed his eyes. "Do I seem false to you?"

"No, of course not, but you know how it is. Ladies' maids and cooks and shopgirls pretending to be French, actresses pretending to be Russian. It's all the rage."

"The rage," he growled. "Such a funny expression. When you've seen true rage, it does not seem so fashionable." His gaze wandered to a painting of peasants in a yellow field, before returning to her.

She wondered if he'd been in the Russian army. "At any rate, Salter doesn't sound very Russian."

"It wasn't always my name," he said evenly.

"Ah." She cast about for something to say, but words failed her. How could she stay with him, keep him talking, so she could watch the way his sensual mouth formed each word? "I fancied that staff was given a handbook of Russian phrases and an accent coach, that you're really from Islington or someplace."

He shook his head. His shoulders relaxed. "I was born in Moscow. But I am English for three years now."

"There must be quite a story there," she ventured.

A whistle blew in the distance. A summons? His gaze shifted back to the corridor. "I must go. Return to your room, please. It is late for a young lady to be wandering alone."

She knew she wandered too much, late at night, but she had to wear herself out completely or she saw the submarine approach in her dreams, the *Lusitania* sinking, her parents' drowned faces. He stood, unmoving, until she began to walk again, quick, nervous little steps. He escorted her as far as the bank of lifts, then continued his path toward the Grand Hall at the front of the hotel.

The lift operator let her out on the fifth floor. She could never remember which direction to turn. The pattern on the wall here, a thick red-brown line underscored by a sharply jagged stripe of forest green, had dots around it, like tiny green berries. A distracting pattern. Staring at it, she nearly stumbled into a fern. She blew a frond out of her face, then noticed the elderly woman standing behind it.

"What are you doing?" Alecia asked.

"Good afternoon," the woman said. She wore a frightfully Edwardian costume, much too rich and decorated for 1924. And a straw boater. And galoshes.

"It is the middle of the night," Alecia said carefully, not wanting to frighten the woman.

"Is it? I seem to have lost my way. On a garden path, are we?" She touched a frond.

"No, at a hotel. Is there someone I can fetch for you?"

The elder's heavily-lidded eyes drooped even further. "Oh dear. A hotel?"

"The Grand Russe."

She made a congested noise in the back of her throat. "Never heard of it."

"It used to be the Grand Haldene."

"Very dreadful place. One hears things." She sniffed.

"Yes, well, it's been rather quiet lately."

"My daughter is a bit of an adventuress," the woman said. "Too old for it, though."

Alecia's interest pricked. "Is she staying here?"

"With me. Daft girl. The younger set, all frivolity."

"Can I see you to your room?" Alecia asked, since the woman seemed to be making more sense now.

"It's just down the hall, ducks. Not to worry. Room 502." The elder's gaze lost focus. "Don't know why I was standing outside. Probably didn't want to listen to all that tee-heeing. And the cigarette smoke. So vulgar."

Her daughter must be having a party. "Yes, ma'am."

"Well"—she nodded—"good morning to you."

Alecia didn't correct the woman. At least she had her key out now. Alecia waited until she shut the door, then went down the hall to her own room. She had been housed in the valet's chamber attached to Mr. Marvin's room, since he didn't have a man with him. Mrs. Marvin, however, had a maid, a grumbling, poorly-used person named Ethel.

Her room held none of the decorations of the public spaces. Only three pieces of furniture were present: a bed, a dressing table, and a chest of drawers. The chair at the dressing table had splinters in the seat, and a door connected her room with Mr. Marvin's, which was not proper. She kept her side bolted at night and hoped never to hear him knock in the wee hours. Aside from marital fidelity, something she was not sure applied to actors, he was fifty-one, almost thirty years older than her, and had a luxuriant mustache that all too frequently had food in it.

Nothing like Ivan Salter. She sat down on her bed and removed her shoes, replaying their conversation in her head, reveling in his voice, just as sexy as she'd imagined.

Greetings from Peter Eyre.

The next evening, Ivan stood in front of a notice pinned to the employee board in the hotel's basement. The place was a dank, groaning hive of activity. He suspected the scarred furnishings of the employee dining hall had been in place since the hotel was first opened in the 1890s, but the daily notices from the fastidious general manager were always crisp and clean.

29 December! The increase in petty theft is alarming. Watch for pilferers of ashtrays, glasses, furniture cushions. If you see any Gypsies entering the premises, please escort them out right away. We don't want them stealing our rugs and chairs. Please report any concerns, or concerning persons, in full detail to your supervisor. Your servant, Peter Eyre.

"Now we are to man all the doors and still make our rounds to the second?" complained Ivan's fellow night watchman, Norman Johnson, tucking his pocket watch away.

"Not you," Ivan said, pointing to the day's roster. "You've been assigned the top floors. Extra security."

Norman squinted at the roster. The habitual expression had left premature lines around his eyes. "Who is in residence?"

"Some American businessman. A film actress. Lady Cubult," Ivan recalled.

"Who is the actress?"

"I don't remember. I don't go to the movies."

"You should. What else is there to do?"

Ivan shrugged. "Family, friends."

"You have some? I thought you were from Russia." Norman straightened his cap and licked his teeth.

"I came here with my sister."

"The rest of your family still there, then?"

"Dead," Ivan said through clenched teeth. He didn't like speaking of them.

"Awful thing, the wars. My little brother died in the trenches, you know. Don't know why I survived." Norman sniffed.

"I should not have survived either. But we go on. We remember our dead." *Catherine. My parents.*

Norman nodded. "I'm off to prowl the halls. Maybe I'll be invited in for a drink. Someone must know who that actress is." Whistling jauntily, he strode off.

Ivan went to start his rounds on the main floor. It was still terribly busy at ten P.M. because Peter Eyre was holding court in the glittering, silver-and-blue Coffee Room. The real draw, despite the gorgeous geometric wallpaper and stunning parquet floor, could be said to be the glamorous Eyre himself, wandering through most evenings, greeting the anointed, glaring at the out of favor. His eyes would narrow at times as he decided who would be paying the champagne bill for everyone that night, as if mentally calculating the worth of each visitor.

Eyre was an obscure fellow, about the same age as Ivan, and much whispered about in the dens where the maids and valets waited for summonses. He might be an offshoot of some German royal family. Or the son of an Irish peasant. No one knew. He hadn't been to Eton or Harrow, but that crowd adored him as much as they were adored by gossip columnists. He'd sprung whole from the hotel the day it had been reopened. Who knew? He might even be the owner.

But Eyre wasn't the ever-present figure that most intrigued Ivan as he left the Coffee Room and made his way through the web of corridors on the main floor. Miss Loudon, the little mouse who had not run away when that dreadful twosome were coupling on the sofa behind the nightclub. A woman who would not avert her eyes from sex and insisted on listening to jazz.

It would not take much to turn her from a mouse to a cat. She had the very English peaches-and-cream skin, large bright-blue eyes, and yellow hair. Classic beauty, hiding in a dress that was too large. A boyish figure that was all the rage. She could be in style if she wore red lipstick and cut her hair. A little paint, some money for better clothes, and she might be on the arm of some man, entering the club instead of skulking behind it.

He made his way past the Salon, the Reception Room, the Ballroom, the Restaurant, the Reading Room. The only trouble he found was a damp wad of chewing gum decorating the armrest of a chair, and two occasional tables that were missing their ashtrays. He made a note in his book and moved on.

By eleven P.M., he had done a full round of the two main floors of the hotel and had circled the outside of the building. Part of the duties of the night watchman downstairs was to keep an eye on the nightclub. Drunken dramatics tended to spill into the hotel.

After the previous night, he decided he'd better check the service corridor where the honeymooners had been canoodling the night before. He also felt duty-bound to make sure the carpet had been cleaned where champagne had been spilled.

"Excuse me," said a man Ivan recognized as being in sales, stopping him by the lifts. The man had taken one of the rooms with a parlor set up with a display area for his wares. Garden products. "Can you recommend a place where I can get a plate of kippers this time of night?"

"The Restaurant is closed, sir, but if you go into the alley around the block, Maystone's, our nightclub, is still serving."

"But will it be edible? I know these places have to serve food to keep the champagne flowing, but I want a meal."

"You can ask the hall porter to have sandwiches delivered to your room," Ivan suggested.

"No. I don't like to eat alone."

"Flash your money around inside Maystone's and you'll have companionship soon enough," Ivan said.

The man winked and moved off. Ivan wove deeper into the maze of service corridors. Rarely did he find guests, but when he did, they were usually up to no good.

And there she was, the *myshka*. Leaning up against the back door of the nightclub again, still in that same foul dress. Did she not know the Grand Russe Hotel was an elegant place?

"It isn't midnight yet," Alecia said when she spotted Ivan Salter coming toward her. She told her traitorous heart rate to slow. While he might be handsome, he wasn't kind. She'd asked the Russian chambermaid who cleaned her room what *myshka* meant. Little mouse, indeed. An insult. She had thought him a creature out of a fairy tale.

As he approached, not speaking, she lifted herself from her slouched pose along the wall and straightened her shoulders. Pins holding her too heavy hair in its prim bun dug into her scalp. She needed to take it down and go to bed, but the music had drawn her. Better than a lumpy mattress, the *Lusitania* sinking.

When he was two feet from her, he stopped. His gaze wandered the space, taking in the empty sofa, and, oddly enough, the carpet.

"What?" she demanded, very un-mouselike. She had resolved to be as belligerent as a maiden aunt. "There isn't a sign saying hotel guests are not allowed back here."

He cocked his head. She wilted when he sucked in his cheeks, highlighting the magnificent structure of his cheekbones. No. He may have every blessing God might offer a man, but he was only a night watchman. She was just a secretary. Unless she was breaking a rule, he had no right to intimidate her. She would not be cowed.

"Say something," she said very crisply, as if she was dressing down a young nephew.

His lips curved. She felt a sinking sensation in her midsection. How dare he look so knowing?

"Young ladies wandering about unchaperoned are looking to be kissed."

"By you?" How stupid she was, to say this.

His teeth were exposed by his widening smile. The top row was perfect, but his two lower front teeth were just a little crooked. She fell in love even more. In lust?

"You knew you would see me tonight. I am the watchman."

"Very well then." She lifted her chin. "It is unlikely that I am looking to be kissed. I like to wander and have never been kissed."

"Never, *myshka*? Such a pity. You are somewhat pretty."

"How dare you!" Outrage bubbled in her lungs. She could not find any other words.

But the truth was, she could find another thought, even if she couldn't say it aloud. She wanted to be kissed. By him.

Chapter Two

Somewhat pretty? What a thing for a man to say, especially when he was the most attractive fellow she'd ever come across. Alecia had been in London for two weeks. No one had been remotely as handsome, despite the high-flying celebrities who came to the hotel. And he thought she was a mouse.

"Do you want me to dare?" he asked, his cap sliding slightly to the right as he tilted his head.

She stopped breathing. Was he teasing her? What if he said yes to kissing her? This had been a most scandalous hotel. Maybe the employees were meant to be suggestive. No no, of course not. They wanted respectability now, here at the Grand Russe. She studied him.

One eyebrow was slightly uplifted. His lips were so plush, so kissable. Sadie, her racy younger sister, would say he was born to come to a petting party.

"Mr. Salter." She didn't know where to put her hands. They fluttered at her sides like a pair of dying peahens.

"It's closing in on midnight. Don't you want to be Cinderella?" he asked, straightening his cap.

"Why would you ask me such a thing?" She'd lost all hope of belligerence now. Her voice had gone soft, betraying her.

"For all that I'm proud to be British now, we Russians have a passionate nature. We don't always think before we act."

Before she could say another word, he stepped so close to her that she could smell the cucumber on his breath. One hand went around the nape of her neck, just below her carefully coiled bun. She tilted her chin, her eyes closing instinctively. His thumb rubbed across her lip.

"Wind-chapped, *myshka*," he chided. "You must take better care of yourself."

Her eyes opened just as his lips touched hers. Electricity sizzled. She shuddered, pressing against him as the shock went through her body, feeling the heat of his mouth. His lips parted slightly and he stole her breath, inhaling her, as she thought, *Yes, mine.*

His eyes were still closed. He angled his mouth, deepening the kiss. Her hands went into that glorious hair, as soft as she'd imagined, but she accidentally dislodged his cap in her desire to have more of him against her skin. It canted sideways and he stepped back, righting it. His hands dropped away and released her. She panted as if they'd had a necking session, instead of little more than a peck.

His upper lip pressed against his teeth. "I am sorry I shocked you. It must be my boots on the carpet."

"It was memorable," she said, then chuckled in a way that sounded crazy even to her own ears. She blinked. "I'm sorry. You meant to be sweet."

He didn't answer her. Was he still tingling from the shock? "I will call you Cinderella now, instead of *myshka*. You had better leave the ball before your clothing turns to rags."

She glanced down at her serviceable dress. "It won't take much. I hope to buy better clothes soon."

"You should be dressed to dance in that nightclub, not clean it." He inclined his head to her and strode away from her, down the corridor, whistling.

She still didn't know what to do with her hands. They twisted at the wrists. She put them to her lips. Finally, a story to write Sadie about, something her sister would actually appreciate. Alecia Loudon, twenty-two, had finally been kissed. Even if it had not been a fairy-tale moment of bliss. Still, he'd been gallant enough. If only she hadn't pushed his cap out of place.

Greetings from Peter Eyre, Ivan read the next day on the notice board.

> *Looking ahead. Just confirmed, arriving on 17 January: Russian diplomat George Ovolensky and staff. Our first high-profile international guest will be meeting with the prime minister while he is here on a trade mission. Let us ensure he gives Mr. Baldwin a good report. Best uniforms, prompt service, and all courtesy on offer.*

Ivan's eyes scanned the notice, but his brain had disconnected. Georgy Ovolensky was his distant cousin. Nearly seven years before, Georgy had been the betrayer of his sister, his parents. He might as well have been at the head of the firing squad that executed them after Fanny Kaplan's failed attempt to assassinate Lenin. Ivan could see his cousin had used his betrayal to further his position with the present government. He had turned himself into Stalin's lapdog. It had only taken him six years to shed any vestiges of his aristocratic background and become the model Bolshevik.

Did Georgy care that Ivan and his last surviving sister, Vera, had escaped Russia? It had taken them three years to make it to London and a new, more secure lifestyle. He'd just found work again after being sacked a few months ago from a failing, less prestigious hotel than the Grand Russe. Vera was engaged to another Russian émigré, and was catering in the Russian community.

"What's brought that sour face on?" Norman asked, coming up behind him. He peered over Ivan's shoulder. "No haranguing today, eh?"

Ivan nodded stiffly. "The Grand Russe is honored to have such an important visitor so soon after reopening."

Norman flexed his upper lip. "If you say so. I'd rather have the film stars. You should have seen the number of bottles being delivered to Miss Dare's suite last night. I had a little chat with her maid. Might have an in there."

"Good luck," Ivan said.

"Maybe she has a friend. Think we'll be allowed into the nightclub on our night off if we dress properly?" Norman elbowed him.

"Maybe. The man at the door wouldn't recognize us from the hotel."

"Let's keep it that way. A pity to lose access to such a prime spot, just because we work next door."

"Yes."

Norman peered at him. "Everything all right?"

"Right as rain," Ivan said. His mood elevated slightly when he realized he'd used British slang. While he'd learned English in the schoolroom, his tutor had been much too proper to teach him any slang. It had been a process to unlearn aristocratic speech and talk like a man from the East End.

He wished it were the end of his shift already, instead of the start, so he could tell Vera what was happening. Should he quit his job?

Should they leave London for a time? Given Georgy's legendary bitterness toward their father, would he attempt to obliterate the last of the Saltykov line?

Alecia handed Richard Marvin the next sheet of newsprint. Her employer had wanted to catch up on yesterday's final edition of the *Evening News*. After he grunted his thanks, she chose another piece of toast from the rack and spread it with marmalade.

Before she could put teeth to toast, Sybil arrived, trailing her fox stole carelessly on the floor. Her glittering headpiece might have made sense at Maystone's, but not in the Coffee Room at eleven in the morning, even on New Year's Eve.

"Oh, darling, how very sweet of you," Sybil drawled, sweeping the toast and jam from Alecia's hand and taking a large bite. She cast herself into a chair dramatically, then looked around to see who might be watching.

Alecia poured Sybil a cup of coffee, then added a generous helping of cream, before reaching for the last piece of toast. She bit into the bread before Sybil or Richard could commandeer it.

"Anything left for me, darlings?" Max Parker said cheerfully, weaving his way through the tables. He wore gray tweed plus fours and a long driving coat, and smelled of the cold, rainy outdoors. Unlike the Marvins, who had no fixed address in London, their agent had rooms in town. He had to keep the pulse on the theater district. The Marvins were his most important clients, but he had others.

Alecia smiled at him and tilted the coffeepot over the last empty cup. Half of the cup filled with the dark fluid. "That's all, I'm afraid."

"Add cream and sugar and I'll be happy," Max said with a wink.

She found Max quite attractive, with his twin wings of black hair parted across the length of his head, graying just the slightest bit at the temples. His skin was unlined for a man of thirty-seven, and he had a ready smile, especially for someone who'd spent four years in the trenches, but he did have a few scars, especially on his hands. Powder burns, he'd said, when he caught her looking at them.

The biggest problem with Max was you were never sure if he liked girls and was merely theatrical, or went the other way.

Alecia complied, then waved a waiter over to take their pot and refill it from a larger urn. "More toast too, please," she requested.

"Oh, my dear, you'll make us fat," Sybil demurred.

"Never, Sybil," Max said smoothly. "You are incapable of being anything less than perfect."

Sybil simpered and laughed, tossing her head back like a girl without a care in the world, instead of a thirty-nine-year-old woman.

"How have your first two weeks of employment been, Miss Loudon?" Max asked.

Alecia knew if Max really wanted to know, he'd have asked her in private. "Very good, thank you. It's been such a treat living here at the Grand Russe."

"A far cry from the vicarage?" he queried.

"How you ever survived that, a pretty girl like you," Richard said from behind his paper. "How did you escape the yoke of marriage?"

Alecia thought of the boy she'd thought she loved at fourteen, who had died at Ypres, only eighteen years old. She thought somewhat less fondly of the curate she thought might propose last year, only to confess he was in love with her sister. "I thought I'd be a modern girl and take up nursing," she admitted. "But it turned out I did not do so well with blood."

"You're too young to have had anything to do with nursing in the war," Sybil commented.

"True, but I thought it a noble calling nonetheless. And I'm an orphan, you know. I wanted to make my own way, so my grandfather wouldn't be concerned about my future."

"Should have found a husband," Richard said.

"She's doing fine as a professional girl," Max opined. "A lovely job like this, working for a prestigious theatrical couple. Which brings me to the point, my darlings. I have work!"

Sybil sat up very straight. Richard set down his newsprint and folded his glasses on top of them. His hair was blond, blonder than it should be at fifty-one, but thinning. He had very dramatic blue eyes, an expressive mouth, and a stern, square jawline. Altogether, he looked the part of the stalwart hero. He'd been cast as Henry V many times. Now he did a lot of drawing-room comedy. He'd been cast in a prestigious production of a new Noel Coward play, but rehearsals didn't start until mid-spring. Alecia had questioned the viability of her own position if neither of them worked for the rest of the winter.

Richard folded his hands on top of the newspaper. "Please explain, old friend."

"A diplomat is arriving here in London in three weeks. He'll be meeting with the prime minister on Russia's behalf. Since you toured Russia so famously in '13, the office in charge of the visit contacted me to request an evening's entertainment."

"The prime minister will be watching?" Richard said.

"A command performance for the prime minister?" Sybil said at the same time.

"I'll be directing?" Richard inquired.

Max nodded. "I can't say who will be there precisely, but important people."

The waiter arrived with the refreshed coffeepot. Alecia poured for everyone, then set down the pot and picked up the cream jug.

Richard pulled a flask from an inside pocket of his jacket. "This calls for a little something more." He poured a dash of amber fluid into his cup, then offered the flask around. Sybil waved it away with an air of distaste.

"Just a capful, darling," Max said. "Of course, our little Alecia won't want any."

Alecia pressed her lips together. It was true, but one of these days, she just might.

"Do you know, there are rumors coming out of Berlin that one of the Grand Duchesses might be alive in Germany?" Sybil said. "That poor, dear family. I am so glad we could play for them in happier times."

"What did we perform?" Richard said. "It's been almost a dozen years."

"*A Doll's House*," Sybil said quickly.

"Of course." Richard sniffed.

"You did some *Hamlet* as well, I believe," Max said.

"Ah, that's right," Richard said. "I wonder if we could do Chekov."

"A Russian playwright for a Russian? How about some Oscar Wilde?" Max asked.

"How Victorian," Sybil moaned. "We should do something modern. Do you have the script for your new play yet, Richard, dear?"

"No," Richard said. "How about *The Colleen Bawn*? I had some lovely speeches."

"Victorian again," Sybil said.

"*Dracula*," Richard said, with a waggle of his eyebrows. "The play is new, even if the story isn't."

"Not much of a role for me," Sybil said. "This isn't just about you. We toured Russia *together*."

"You'd have lines," he said.

Sybil made a face. "*Juno and the Paycock?*"

"Too Irish," Max said. "No, it had better be Shakespeare."

The coffee cups were empty again. Alecia lifted the pot, but Max waved it away. "I have to see someone about the O'Neill play Mrs. Marvin read for. Rumor has it that the theater censor might ban it, and I need to keep an ear in."

"Dreadful," Sybil said. "The lord chamberlain has too much power right now."

Max kissed her cheek. "Chin up, old girl. If this production falls apart, I'll pitch you as the understudy for Binnie Hale in *No, No, Nannette*. It's opening in March."

"Understudy?" Sybil's expression was blank.

"It's money," Max coaxed.

"I've heard it's doing well in Chicago," Richard said. "You should take it, Sybil. A singing part would be good for you."

Sybil moaned. "I need to be on stage."

"How about the moving pictures?" Max said. "I know someone at Gainsborough Pictures."

Sybil shook her head sadly. "It must be the stage. Darling Max, you do try."

"I'll see about this O'Neill project then," Max said, standing. "Richard, Alecia." He strode off, and was not more than a few feet away when he started to hum jauntily.

"At least something is brewing," Richard said when Max was out of earshot. "He never sings when things are going badly."

"I wonder if he wants us in film," Sybil said, toying with her coffee spoon.

"If we are offered the right part, either of us, it is worth consideration," Richard said. "The money can be good."

"If we wanted money, we should have gone to America. Look at how well Leslie Howard has done for himself."

"Do you want to start all this again?" Richard asked.

"No, I want to think about what I'm going to wear at Maystone's tonight," Sybil said. "What fun we will have."

"You should come," Richard said to Alecia as he picked up his paper again.

"What? Me?" Alecia said, shocked.

"Yes. Borrow something of Sybil's. You make her look younger when you are together."

Sybil and Alecia stared at each other.

"I-I don't understand," Alecia stammered.

"Don't say you are her employee, but her friend," Richard said, snapping his paper. "A young friend makes a woman look younger. Sybil turns forty next year, unfortunately."

"Thirty," Sybil shrieked. "I turn thirty."

Richard held the paper up to his nose and rolled his eyes over the top of it. "With Alecia in tow, you might just get away with it."

Sybil patted Alecia's hand. "We'll do our makeup the same way and call ourselves sisters."

"I've never worn makeup," Alecia admitted, intrigued.

Sybil clapped her hands. "How exciting. What fun we are going to have!"

"Very well," Lionel Dew, the night manager, said to the assembled watchmen at six that evening. "It is all hands on deck tonight. New Year's Eve is always chaotic in the hospitality business. Until ten P.M. we'll be following our regular assignments. At that point, I want Salter and Johnson to move to the nightclub. Tonight we need to keep a particular eye on it."

Ivan eyed Norman, who looked positively twinkly-eyed at the notion of standing guard inside the nightclub.

"Johnson, you'll patrol the outside of the club. Salter, I want you inside. Your face won't scare the guests."

Norman's jaw clenched as he heard what he'd be doing. No watching the band and the flappers. He'd be wandering around outside in the cold.

"Sorry," Ivan whispered.

"Lucky you." Norman sighed. "I want to look at the scantily clad ladies."

"Stay above the fray tonight, Salter. I've got my eye on you," Lionel said.

"Yes, sir," Ivan said, saluting. "I'll start my rounds now."

"Take Swankle with you and show him the trouble spots," Lionel said.

Ivan nodded at the gangly youth in his brand-new uniform. "First night?"

"Yes, sir," Swankle said, displaying a mouthful of crooked teeth. "Been working at a factory before this."

Ivan pointed his chin toward the door. "I've the easy floors, so I can show you around."

"Where are you from?" Swankle asked as they left the room. "Not from around here, with that accent."

"Moscow."

"A Bolshie, are you?" Swankle's head swiveled on his scrawny neck as he took in the dank basement corridor. "Aiming to help the workers rise up?"

"I'm no Bolshevik. My great-grandfather was a Russian prince." All his legacy as an oldest son, long lost now.

Swankle whistled. "How'd you get out, then?"

"Fled in '18." It had cost them everything but their lives.

"Better than where you left, I suppose," Swankle said.

"I'm afraid it is, these days." Russia was for Cousin Georgy and his ilk now.

The service-lift operator let them come aboard. "Third floor tonight," Ivan said.

The operator nodded and closed the door. "Not your usual patch."

"Showing young Swankle the ropes. It's his first night."

"New Year's Eve?" The operator whistled. "What a time to start."

"It's when I was needed," Swankle said composedly. "I'm just happy not to be starting 1925 hauling tires about all day. I'm twenty-four and already having pain in me back."

"I thought you were younger," Ivan admitted.

Swankle shook his head. "It's me baby face. Same as me grand-dad, they say. Went to his grave still looking like a schoolboy."

"Maybe it will be of use. Help people to trust you," Ivan said as they exited the lift. "This is a standard floor. Single rooms, doubles, valet den to the east, supplies to the west. If you see anything in need of cleaning, make a note. You've five floors a shift, or two if you have the main floor, since there is so much more to watch."

"What's the worst thing you've seen?"

"Drugs, sex, fights." Ivan shrugged. "We've only been open a month."

"Did you work here before? Back when them murders happened?"

"I'm new as well. I started on the first night the hotel reopened."

"Made any friends among the staff?"

"I pay attention to my work. That's why I normally have the first two floors." Ahead of them, he saw one of the chambermaids, bucket at her feet, talking to someone. Some of the girls loved a gossip, but this was the lead chambermaid and was more likely to need rescuing from a guest than to be a problem herself.

"Let's liberate Her Serene Highness from our guest," he said to Swankle, and strode down the hall.

"What? Who?" Swankle's shorter legs sped up.

"That chambermaid is a Russian princess fallen on hard times," Ivan said. "This is what my countrymen have come to since the war."

"Crikey," muttered Swankle. "What do I say to her?"

"As little as possible," advised Ivan.

"I have not been to the theater since I lived in Saint Petersburg. They are calling the city Petrograd now," the princess chambermaid said as they walked up to her.

Ivan had to peer around her to see who she spoke to, and was surprised to discover Miss Loudon. "About time for your dinner break, isn't it, Olga?" he said in Russian. She'd forbidden him to use her title at the hotel.

The maid froze. "Yes, of course." She strode away, ignoring Swankle's friendly grin.

Ivan shook his head. "Return her bucket to the maid's closet, will you, Swankle? Down the hall there, you'll see the Staff Only sign."

"Yes, Mr. Salter." Swankle picked up the bucket.

"A bit early for you to be prowling, isn't it?" Ivan asked Miss Loudon. At least she wasn't dressed in baggy gray this time. Her dress was navy and the fabric draped better. For the first time he could see the shape of her body, not quite as boyish as current fashion preferred. The lady had curves, more generous in the bosom than the hips. Delicate bones. His body responded in predictable fashion. She really was a beauty, with Cinderella potential.

"I had questions for the Russian employees," she said.

"Trying to find me? Looking for more kisses?" he teased.

Her eyes widened and her nose went pink. "M-my employers will be doing a command performance when a Russian diplomat comes to London, and I wanted to find out what plays a Russian might like."

"How disappointing," Ivan drawled. "Will you not ask me the same question to prove you are telling the truth?"

"I don't need to prove anything. It's true. I work for the Marvins. They are quite famous."

He waited.

"I've only worked for them for two weeks," she admitted. "I'm allowed to speak to the hotel staff, aren't I?"

"The maids need to stay on their schedule."

Miss Loudon bit her lip. "Is anyone in management Russian?"

"No. You can ask me your question." He leaned in.

She soothed her lip with her tongue. His body tightened further. He wished he could touch her lips with his tongue, see what she tasted like. "What plays do you like?" she asked.

"I like to see tragedies, where Fate plays out," he said.

"Very dark stuff. Are you political?"

He tore his gaze from her lush, bitten lips with difficulty. "I can assure you that whatever side Georgy Ovolensky is on, you will find me on the opposite side," he said.

Her eyes sparkled. "You know about his coming, then. Do you know him?"

"He is my cousin."

Miss Loudon tilted her head. "You must be joking."

"No," he growled.

She blinked. "I dare say you are not looking forward to the family reunion."

He spoke very precisely. "He's a very bad man. Stay away from him."

She straightened her shoulders, which made her chest press out from her dress. "I won't have any reason to interact with him. Of course I won't. But I do need to help select a play. Do you think he'll like Shakespeare?"

"Why not? I don't," Ivan said, tearing his gaze away from her breasts.

Her expression softened. "My goodness, you really do hate him. Why?"

He kept his eyes on her face, her pretty blue eyes. "You shouldn't ask such questions. You know nothing of what we've suffered. The revolution, the war."

Her chin went up. "I lost my parents almost a decade ago, when the *Lusitania* went down. I'm an orphan. My two uncles died in the war. Russians aren't the only ones who've suffered."

"I'm sorry for that, but Georgy Ovolensky is responsible for the deaths of much of my family, Miss Loudon. Stay away from him."

Instead of fleeing as he expected, she stood taller. "You already warned me. An unnecessary warning, as I pointed out. Perhaps you should be the one to flee."

"I'm considering it," he told her.

That took the fire from her. "Oh. I see. How dreadful. Are you considered a criminal in Russia?"

He frowned. "No. I was too young. But my oldest sister, she was a revolutionary and Georgy took advantage of that to annihilate my family. Only Vera and I survived."

"Who is that?" Her voice faltered. "Your wife?"

"Another sister."

"I see. Such a sad conversation, when it started with kisses," she said. She should have smiled with such flirtatious words on her lips, but she did not. "I'm sorry about your family."

Ivan saw Swankle appear at the top of the corridor. He'd been talking too long. "Kisses are never a waste," he said. "Maybe next time."

As her mouth rounded with surprise, he stepped forward, too close, and blew her a kiss. She gasped. He saw Swankle staring at them both. His cheerful gaze narrowed.

Ivan swore. Would Swankle report him for his familiarity?

Chapter Three

Peter Eyre checked the clock in his office behind the hotel's registration desk. Ten P.M. New Year's Eve. He'd better make an appearance at the nightclub.

"Everything in order?" he said to Lionel Dew as he passed through Registration.

His night manager glanced up with a smile. "Every room is full tonight."

Peter surveyed the throng in front of the desk. A janitor was on duty to keep the blue, black, and white marble floor spotless. Every spot on the plush, circular seating arrangements was taken by flappers and their beaus, flirting and trading quips. He could hear the music of upper class drawls, money in the bank. "Try to keep nonguests out of the Grand Hall. It is crowded enough in here. All of these people cannot be waiting for a table at the Restaurant."

"There is a private party in the Ballroom."

"It's for an older crowd. Discreetly deal with those persons not in the best attire."

He passed by the white and blue walls of the Coffee Room with regret, brushing a minute speck of lint off the lapel of his tailcoat. When he reached the service corridor, he straightened his bow tie and pulled a ring of keys from his pocket so that he could unlock the rear door between his hotel and his club. After he went through the dark space, he carefully relocked everything again. It wouldn't do to let just any guest through. Recently, he'd had enough reports of bad behavior in the service corridor to consider locking the entire area off from guests, but then, he didn't want to destroy every opportunity for sin at the Grand Russe.

The modern age required a modern hotelier, and people deliberately came to places like this hotel to let off some steam. He didn't expect Victorian behavior in the Jazz Age, far from it. Murder, on the other hand, he could do without. Another situation like the Starlet Murders and he and his silent partners would be out of business for good.

He had debated allowing theatrical folk into the hotel as guests for just that reason. Drugs, illegitimate liaisons, and other drama seemed to follow such people like clockwork. But they brought fame, élan, and the Grand Russe needed that too. Not just well-heeled politicians and middle-aged aristocrats.

He spotted Cuddy Friend, the nightclub manager, hovering behind the bar. "Who is here tonight?"

"Tallulah Bankhead, Duff Cooper's crowd, and a very junior royal with a lady not his wife," Cuddy reported.

"Excellent. Celebrity, aristocrats, and royalty. Is Lady Diana here with her husband? No Bright Young Things?"

"Yes, she is. A few members of Elizabeth Ponsonby's crowd are here."

He smiled. "Lady Diana is far more exciting than her MP husband. I think we've covered all the bases."

"We have. I'm not sure Tallulah has. She's not wearing much more than a few strings of pearls."

"She's an eccentric, but London loves her. As long as her body is beautiful, I'm all for it. Are we making any money?"

"When the waitresses can get around to the tables," Cuddy said. "It's overcrowded. We've already had to start turning people away at the door."

"The band sounds good." Peter listened to the piano player play his version of "King Porter Stomp," one of this year's big new songs. "Do they know *Rhapsody in Blue*? I'd like to hear it."

"Oh sure, Judd knows his stuff. Gets all the latest sheet music from America."

The piano tune ended, and the full band came together for a song Peter didn't recognize. A couple of the flappers on the dance floor screamed and began to shimmy as it began, though, kicking out splayed legs as their partners whirled them around. Crystal dress beads caught the overhead chandeliers' illumination and the floor picked up the dazzling lights, creating a display as dizzying as the music. Some of the dancers attempted to hold cocktail glasses. The floor would be sticky by the end of the long celebration.

"The crowd seems to like the piano player." The band leader was standing now, blowing insistent notes over the crowd on his cornet.

"Has his share of followers. I had to kick a couple of girls out of his dressing room this afternoon before he even arrived."

"That's a good sign." Peter pulled out his new gold cigarette case from Asprey of Bond Street, a Christmas gift from his mistress, and selected a Pall Mall, then lit it with his Dunhill lighter.

"Are you going to wade in? Or are you going to hold court in the Coffee Room?"

"Wade in," Peter said. "I have to make an appearance at May-stone's on New Year's Eve."

"Building that cult of personality?" Cuddy winked at him.

"We need all the advantages we can, to save this hotel."

"In that case, find yourself a more intriguing mistress than Miss Plash. She's nobody special. Or be more obviously unencumbered."

Peter winced. "She's rich and convenient, an old family friend."

"She's a decade older than you, shrill, and not exciting. You can do better."

Peter picked a speck of tobacco off his tongue while he considered what to say. "You may be right, though she isn't as old as you think. I'm tiring of her anyway. Any suggestions?"

"I'll think about it."

Peter spotted a girl he'd never seen before, acting like a wallflower even though she was dressed like a real biscuit. He recognized her sparkling green and cream dress as a Vionnet. Calf-length at the front, it showed her shapely lower legs. Since it draped low in the back, he could see her creamy skin. Slender, but had just enough meat on her to hide her bones. The ropes of sequins and beads that hung down her back, right down to the floor, would sway as she danced, drawing the eye. "There's my berry patch." He pointed his chin at the blonde. "Who is she?"

"She came in with the Marvins. Staying on the fifth floor. Theatrical couple of some renown."

He blew a smoke ring. "So she's an actress. Ought to be fun for the night."

"Emmeline will kill you." Cuddy smiled.

"That's one way to end a liaison." Peter ground out his cigarette in an ashtray at the end of the bar and made his move toward the curtain-draped wall where the young beauty stood. His interest increased as he saw her sexy shoes, green velvet with silver details. They weren't hers though. Her feet were tiny and narrow and the shoes were meant for a larger woman.

As he walked toward her, he sensed someone staring daggers at him, and glanced around. He recognized one of the night watchmen, the Russian one, with his gaze now trained directly on the young blonde. He hoped his employee didn't plan to flirt while he was keeping an eye out for trouble.

Grabbing two glasses of champagne off a tray held by a passing waiter, he handed one to the young blonde with a flourish. "Peter Eyre, hotel manager. Are you staying with us?"

She gave him a steady blue-eyed gaze, but her quiet voice belied the confidence of her expression. "I'm Miss Loudon, from the fifth floor."

"Ah, yes." He took a sip of the champagne. Not their best brand. He wondered whom he'd stolen it off of. "How are you connected to the Marvins?"

"I'm their new secretary."

He regarded her. Not promising. The only thing she had to offer him was youth and beauty. She wouldn't have any money. The shoes were obviously borrowed. The dress was a signpost down the wrong path. But she was certainly lovely. If she was fast, he'd take her for a spin, but she wasn't worth throwing Emmeline over for, not when he considered his new top-of-the-line cigarette case, and their shared history.

One of Miss Loudon's feet tapped as the band began a new number. He didn't think she noticed. "Jazz fan?" he asked.

Her smile lit up her face, accentuating her perfect cheekbones. "Oh yes. I have to admit I sneak downstairs late at night just to hear the band through the service door."

This was exactly why he hated to lock down the service corridor. He liked offering opportunities for pretty young things to misbehave. "Why don't you come into the nightclub?"

"Oh, I just want to hear the music, not dress up and all this," she said, blushing. "This isn't my dress. Mrs. Marvin lent it to me."

She was precious. Like a ripe fruit ready to be plucked.

"You must dance," he said, setting his empty glass on a waiting table. He took hers from her unresisting hand. "Oh, here's an oldie. 'Maple Leaf Rag.' Do you fox-trot?"

"You have a wonderful piano player," she said, her eyes sparkling as he held out his hand.

"Yes, that's our own Judd Anderson. Let's take advantage."

She took his hand delicately, like a fawn taking a first trembling step into adulthood, and he pulled her onto the floor. The horn section joined in on the tune as they began to dance.

This precious girl had a wonderful sense of rhythm. They finished the first dance, her beads swaying behind them as they did the fast steps, then the band struck up a tango number. Peter had no intention of letting her return to propping up the wall. He pulled her toward him, her supple body flowing against his torso.

A tap came on his shoulder just as they started dancing side to side.

"May I?" asked a man of fifty or so years, with a luxurious graying mustache.

Peter recognized Richard Marvin. He'd seen him in *Antony and Cleopatra* a decade before. His wife must be the woman in his arms. Mrs. Marvin wore a black, Chinese-style Patou, almost floor-length, covered in a silver fantasy scene picked out in thread. The dress was entirely sleeveless, showing off the woman's slender arms. A jangle of silver and paste bracelets decorated her slim wrists. The middle-aged spread almost hidden under the long column of her dress told the real story of her age, however.

"Of course," he said, resigned. Marvin stole his partner and began to lift her.

Mrs. Marvin giggled. "I hope you don't plan to do that to me."

"No, we'll execute a more basic step," Peter promised her.

"Mr. Marvin has always enjoyed showing off," his wife said, as Peter turned her on the floor.

In more ways than one. He'd plucked his pretty secretary right out of Peter's arms. Peter wondered what else he planned to do with the girl. He knew with absolute certainty that she was a virgin. An experienced woman didn't tremble in a man's arms like she did.

Across the floor, he could see the Russian night watchman following the tango with a heated gaze. Peter imagined he wanted to break into the athletic dance exhibition and exit stage right with his prize.

It wouldn't do to have his employees distracted by lust. He sensed it was time to send staff another memo about interacting with guests. When the dance ended, another fox-trot–worthy tune began. He handed Mrs. Marvin back to her husband and inclined his head to Miss Loudon.

He walked off the dance floor, wondering where Emmeline had gone.

"There you are," said Edith Plash, Emmeline's mother, coming alongside him.

Mrs. Plash had given birth to her lovely daughter at an advanced age. She had to be in her late seventies, at least, with a cataract making one eye filmy. However, she clutched at his sleeve with strong fingers.

"You haven't been up to see me in a couple of days," she said, pursing her carmine-coated lips into a pout.

He pulled out his cigarette case, gently extracting his sleeve from her fingers. "I've been busy, Mrs. Plash. Where is Emmeline?"

"Oh, her, never you mind," Mrs. Plash said with a surprisingly girlish giggle. "I'm sure she'll be out all night. It's New Year's Eve, you know."

"Yes, I know."

"Why don't we swipe a bottle of bubbly and go upstairs?" She winked. "Have ourselves a different kind of celebration?"

He kept his expression impassive only with great effort. "Madam, I'm afraid you have the wrong idea."

An expression of confusion crossed her face. "I often do, dear. Do you come here often?"

"To the nightclub? When I must."

"I know I've seen you before. With my daughter?"

The abrupt change of conversation had him as confused as he was concerned. Thankfully, he saw Emmeline coming toward him, dressed in low-cut red silk without enough identifying markers to show what designer it came from. She wasn't showy like Mrs. Marvin, but much more beautiful, regardless.

His mistress took her mother's arm.

"I think it is time Mrs. Plash went to bed," he told her.

"Oh, Peter, no," she protested.

"She stopped recognizing me," he said gently.

Mrs. Plash smiled at her daughter. "Is he one of my beaus?"

"Oh, good Lord," Emmeline said, her lips pinching. "Come along, Mother. And happy New Year to you," she said over her shoulder, dragging the older woman away.

Mrs. Plash's head went down and she walked with a shuffle, cowed like a young child. Peter winced as he lit up his cigarette. It looked like a lonely New Year's Eve was in store for him, unless he wanted to make an effort.

"Butt me?"

He turned to see Tallulah Bankhead, half naked, as advertised, her long dark waves caressing her creamy shoulders. She held out an empty cigarette holder to him.

"Of course, Miss Bankhead. Happy to," he said with a roguish smile at the notoriously promiscuous American actress.

Greetings from Peter Eyre. January 1, 1925. Happy New Year! Everything goes a little soft over the holidays, but the first day of the New Year is an excellent time to remind you to keep your employee rule book in mind. No fraternizing with our guests, either inside or outside of the hotel or nightclub. Be polite, be professional. We know all of our guests' little secrets and idiosyncrasies. They need our discretion, not offers of friendship.

Ivan made a face. As if everyone didn't know that Mr. Eyre was having an affair with a resident. He'd come out of room 502 twice when Ivan was making his rounds. The problem was, he was the man in charge. The rules didn't apply to him.

Ivan could only hope the hotel manager's attention didn't continue to wander through the fifth floor and alight on Miss Loudon. He'd seen how they danced together. People said how you danced was how you made love. If that was true, Miss Loudon would be a veritable goddess in bed.

But, he wasn't about to lose his job over a secretary, even if she was beautiful when she came out of her shell and put on a rich lady's dress. He'd had trouble walking when she'd left the dance floor, all but stunned to his knees. The rest of the night he'd imagined himself tangoing with her, a sheik to her sheba, the beads of her dress flying behind her as they took quick turns on the dance floor. Only discipline had kept him focused on his work. He'd stopped one fight over a woman near the nightclub bathrooms and removed a known pickpocket from the premises.

Neither of them had a glamorous life, despite the previous evening. The closest they had to that illusion was the Grande Russe and the unusual opportunities it afforded. Little did Miss Loudon know what his life had been like years ago, before the war. But all that was long gone now, all the glitter of his childhood, his parents' world, swept away by war and revolution, Lenin and Ovolensky.

"Busy day ahead of us?" Swankle asked, coming to the notice board.

"Bad-tempered, more like. The entire hotel has a hangover."

"And no surprise. But the staff cleaned up so well you'd never know the place was covered with bunting and confetti and wine bottles last night."

"It's amazing that such a high-caliber staff could be recruited, given the hotel's reputation," Ivan commented.

"Unemployment. People will take anything," Norman Johnson said, joining them. "Most of the younger staff probably didn't know about the murders and the ghosties when they applied for a position."

Ivan snorted. "I've never spoken to anyone who has seen these supposed ghosties."

Swankle smiled. "You don't spend any time chatting with the chambermaids. I've only worked here a day and I've heard two stories."

"Attempting to scare the new hire," Ivan said dismissively.

"A very effective attempt. I won't be wandering around in the ballroom at night with the lights out, I'll tell you that."

"They say the actresses were killed in a demonic ritual," Johnson said with a leer.

Swankle shuddered. "You Russians are a superstitious lot, right? You think that sort of thing is for real?"

Ivan shrugged. "I've never seen a ghost."

Sybil dabbed scent on her wrists. "Help me with my Chanel, will you, darling?"

Sybil lifted her arms over her head, and Alecia climbed on a chair with the heavy, beaded dress and helped Sybil shimmy into it. Her maid had the day off.

"Do you think I should still reveal so much skin at my age?" Sybil said, after looking at herself critically in the mirror.

"I would never have believed you were thirty-nine if I hadn't seen your papers," Alecia said. This wasn't entirely untrue. Certain aspects of Sybil's figure had become a bit middle-aged, but not her arms, legs, or face.

"Thank you. My grandmother always looked very young. Cucumbers. That's what she believed in. Like the Russians."

"Russians believe in cucumbers?"

"They adore them, darling, simply adore them." Sybil sat in front of her dressing table and applied her lipstick. "We're going to dinner with the *No, No, Nanette* people tonight. Let's hope it turns into a job for me."

"Yes, ma'am."

"Pray Binnie Hale breaks her nose or something," Sybil said. "That's the break we need."

"Oh, I can't pray for that. I'm a vicar's granddaughter, you know. How about a bad case of bunions?" Alecia said, only half joking.

Sybil whistled in response. "Then you really aren't going to like what I have to say next. This needs to stay strictly confidential, but you're a good girl and I think we'll be able to keep you employed for a long time."

Alecia put her hands to her temples. She knew that tone. It was a threatening kind of tone. She remembered it well from her less than successful attempt to study nursing. Sybil was about to say something that could cost her this job, her room in the Grand Russe, and her view of the entrancing but infuriating Ivan Salter.

"What do you mean, Sybil?"

Sybil sang a few notes.

The words "lover's oasis" caught Alecia's ear and gave her a clue as to what was coming. "What is that from?"

"'Tea for Two.' From *No, No, Nanette*, you see. I'm practicing so I can break out in song for this evening."

"It's a nice lyric."

"And appropriate for the Grand Russe. So many handsome men here. It does turn a girl's head."

"It's the uniforms. They make all the men look so broad-shouldered and fit," Alecia said.

Sybil raised an eyebrow in the mirror. "Uniforms? Oh no, darling, the man I have in mind was in white tie and tails."

Alecia met her employer's gaze. "If you mean Peter Eyre, he already has a mistress. Miss Plash. She lives on this floor."

"Why is she still a miss, I wonder, at her age? Did she revert to her old name after a divorce?"

"Fiancé killed very early in the war. Or so the rumor goes."

"Oh, she's not so much younger than I am. She should have been married before that."

"That's all I know. Our chambermaid told me. I was asking questions because I was concerned about Mrs. Plash. She was very confused the other night. Talking to a fern, that sort of thing."

"Goodness," Sybil said. "With such distractions as that, it should not be too hard to knock Miss Plash out of the running."

"But how old is Mr. Eyre?" She thought him to be about the same age as Ivan. Much too young for Sybil.

Sybil set down her lipstick. "It hardly matters. I'm not looking for a husband. But I'll need you to lie for me, whenever I'm missing."

Alecia chose her words carefully. "What do you want me to say?"

"That I'm beautifying. Men always believe that. It's so often true."

"I should say something like you are having a manicure somewhere new?" She opened Sybil's manicure case and set the tools to rights.

"Or I'm on a quest for the newest lipstick shade. Only inexpensive things. Do not panic my husband."

"Of course not."

Sybil picked up a gold and red enamel bracelet and slipped it on one arm, then held it up for admiration. "I must say, I'm surprised you are going along with this so easily."

"I knew theatrical folk were different," Alecia said. "And London isn't Bagshot."

"Steer clear of Mr. Marvin at any rate. You don't have to think he'll need a substitute for me. I'll keep my end up in my marriage. I just want to have a little fun. Being married to an older man can be such a bore at times."

"Yes, of course." Alecia took the jewel case that Sybil handed her. "I'll take this down to the safe."

"Thank you." Sybil looked up with a broad, happy smile as the door to the adjoining room opened and Richard came in. She accepted his kiss on her cheek.

"Very nice, poppet. You'll be a shoo-in for the part."

"The understudy part." Faint wrinkles showed on Sybil's upper lip as she pouted.

"You'll have your chance to go on stage. Meanwhile, we have this command performance to consider." Richard checked his arms in the mirror and turned one of his square gold cuff links.

Alecia left the room as silently as she dared. She'd thought the pair completely attuned. Perhaps they were, but only in matters of business. They did have separate bedrooms, even in an expensive hotel, and had been married for seventeen years. Did all marriages go this way?

She did wonder, though, what would happen to her position if the affair was discovered, along with her part in helping it along. She might end up returning to Bagshot sooner than she'd like.

While she went down the five flights of stairs to the lobby, she had time to think. In general, long marriage or not, she was horrified by Sybil's behavior, or at least how she planned to behave. Alecia's cheeks heated at the thought. She didn't know much about sex, but at least she knew a little about kissing now. She suspected Ivan was good at it. Did he have a sex life?

Oh, don't think about that. Once she started she wouldn't be able to think about anything else. Some modern girl she was. But what lay underneath that handsome uniform? A broad chest? Muscled arms? Toned thighs?

She swallowed hard as she reached the door to the main floor, panting audibly. It was the stairs. She needed to take more exercise. A long walk every day. Yes, that was the ticket. Or dancing.

She breathed slowly until both her body and her mind were calm, then put her hand to the doorknob just as it began to turn. She stepped back, clutching Sybil's jewel case.

When the door opened, she saw Ivan, just as if he'd been summoned by her thoughts.

"Hello, Mr. Salter." She smiled, not even a little bit shy. More acting. Cinderella, not a mouse.

Instead of speaking to her, much less teasing her like he had before, he scarcely nodded in her direction before starting his climb upstairs.

"No kiss?" she asked bravely.

"No, miss." He didn't even turn around.

Tears pricked her eyes as she rushed into the lobby. It was as if he hadn't even recognized her.

A bellboy ran past, almost colliding with her as he called, "Mr. Hiram. Mr. Hiram!"

Two fashionable girls in fur coats slipped by next, their hats dotted with snow. A nanny hauled along her charge, his dimpled knees red with cold below his short pants.

They could have been ghosts for all she cared. Her lovely fantasy, destroyed. What a little nothing she was. Why had she thought their flirtation meant something?

Chapter Four

Ivan walked past the crates of late winter greens at the greengrocer's on the ground floor of the building he and his sister lived in. At nine A.M. the local women were busily shopping, scooping up watercress and dandelion leaves and everything else that was edible. The grocer's daughter smiled brightly at him, and her father scowled. But, dead on his feet, he ignored them both and went through the shop, then unlocked the weather-beaten door in the back that led to the two-room flat above, and slowly climbed the steps.

He finally had his day off. He planned to sleep and sleep and maybe dream about Miss Loudon in her borrowed Vionnet dress and sexy shoes. Perhaps his dreams would put him in Peter Eyre's place, his hand on her bare back while the beaded strands belled out behind her on the dance floor. At the very least, he hoped he would hear the tinkling ivories of that talented pianist the nightclub employed and remember the gorgeous smile of music-loving Miss Loudon.

He and Vera had been saving up for a camera record player. They could get one for about four pounds. Not nearly as fancy as a nice cabinet Victrola, of course, but Vera could take it to parties when she catered her Russian specialties. She might even be able to charge for it, if they had the newest records. They figured they could budget for a new recording a week and build up a nice little collection rather quickly.

In fact, he'd given her a first record as a Christmas present. He'd bought "It Had to Be You" by Isham Jones and his Orchestra, an instrumental recording that any budding singer at a party could sing over. That would not be Vera, who, as much as she loved music, could not sing. The sentiments of the song, being sad and glad together, fit how he felt about his sister and their lost family. He was glad he and his sister had a chance to start over, but wished the rest of them could have been there too, even if they'd had to stay in Russia. Damn that Ovolensky and his evil denunciation. He wondered if his cousin enjoyed the art and collectibles he'd no doubt plundered from the family dacha. Servants had taken everything portable, but that had mostly been their mother's jewelry.

Sergei Bakunin, Vera's fiancé, greeted him at the top of the stairs. They had known each other as children in Moscow. One day fifteen months ago, Sergei had shown up at their door here in London. In a little while, it seemed as if no time had passed, and he easily fit into their little Russian-centered lives in the East End.

Over time, though, Ivan had noticed Sergei was political, as political as his sister Catherine had been, though they did not share beliefs. Vera's views had been changing too, to match Sergei's. Sergei identified with the White Russians, who wanted a tsar back. No one really knew what had happened to Tsar Nicholas, though by now, it was assumed he had been executed in 1918 along with his family. But Sergei expressed a longing to go on a pilgrimage to Berlin to see if the reputed Grand Duchess Anastasia was real. Even though, as a female, she could never have the throne, she was a useful rallying point for the Russian exiles.

The true tsar in Sergei's mind was Grand Duke Kyrill Vladimirovich. He dreamed of infiltrating the small circle of Romanovs who lived in England, but had no entry into the circle. His affectations and dandified wardrobe, which he could ill afford, irritated Ivan, but he loved Sergei for his sister's sake, and for the nostalgia of their shared childhood.

"You look tired," Sergei said in Russian, the only language they spoke at home.

"Six days on, one day off," Ivan said.

"But it's mostly standing. Not hard labor." He pushed the bridge of his glasses more firmly against his nose.

"Walking, forever walking," Ivan said. "That has its own form of exhaustion. No letting your mind rest while your body works."

"But it is so glamorous," Sergei exclaimed. He eked out a living driving a cart at a train station. "I imagine you spend most of your time paying attention to lovely ladies."

"Some of the time," Ivan said with a smile. "But it hurts to look and not be able to touch."

Sergei let out a guffaw and slapped Ivan on the back. "It is hard to walk for ten hours with an iron rod in your trousers. Come, have a few glasses of vodka."

"Why don't we work on your English, instead? So you can find a better job?"

"Vera wants to speak to you."

"Not now. If you don't want to practice, I'll have a sandwich first," Ivan said. "Then sleep."

"No time for sleep, *bratishka*," Vera said, appearing in the doorway of their front room, where they cooked, sat, and Ivan slept. "We have big news."

Ivan looked at his sister with eyes that felt full of sand. "Unless you have recovered Mother's diamond bracelet that went missing in Hungary, I cannot imagine I care right now."

"Oh, but you do," Vera said, taking his hand and pulling him toward a plate of cheese and cucumber sandwiches she had placed on the battered table in the corner.

Ivan sat, observing the way Sergei put his arm around Vera's thin shoulder and caressed it. He hoped they were going to marry soon. She had lost weight recently, as if worry had been whittling her to the bone. Her neck looked too thin to hold her elegant skull upright. Picking up a glass of milk, he said, "What, then?"

Vera looked up at Sergei, then leaned her head into his shoulder. "Georgy is coming to London."

"Ovolensky, you mean?" Ivan said, snatching half a sandwich. On rye, just as he liked. He took a drink of milk then a bite of his sandwich. "Yes, he's staying at the Grand Russe."

"You knew?" Vera shrieked.

Ivan nodded, his mouth full of food.

"The Grand Russe, of course," Sergei said, stroking his small, pointed beard.

Vera smiled with satisfaction. "That will make it even easier. We will have no trouble avenging our parents with his murder."

"Let's work on act three, scene four," Richard Marvin said, settling back onto the sofa.

Alecia sat in the matching armchair—though he'd suggested they share the sofa—holding a script. "It's Macbeth's line first."

"Right." Richard gazed at the ceiling. "Hmm, I always forget this part. The dull bits tend to escape me without a daily review."

"'You know your own degrees,'" she prompted.

"Ah, yes." He gave the rest of the short speech with no problem, and they made it through the next exchange in the script.

"Where is Lady Macbeth?" Richard asked, since her line was up next.

Alecia couldn't believe that Sybil had already begun her disappearing act. She'd hoped Mr. Eyre would turn down the aging actress and everything would go back to the way it had been during the first couple of weeks of her employment.

"I believe she said she'd chipped a nail last night," she said cautiously.

"Manicure, eh? Can't anyone at the hotel do it? There is a salon."

"I don't know where she found an appointment."

"No doubt my Sybil had to attend the most fashionable manicurist in London, with matching wait times and costs," Richard said. "Ah, well. You can read all the parts, except Macbeth of course."

"Yes, sir. 'Pronounce it for me,'" Alecia said, finding her place in the script again. She wondered how long it would be before she had the Marvins' bread-and-butter plays memorized just like they did. Mr. Marvin had known the first two acts of the Scottish play perfectly.

A knock came at the door. When Richard nodded, Alecia stood up and went to answer.

"Mr. Eyre," she said, when their guest was revealed.

"Don't look so shocked, Miss Loudon," said the hotel manager.

She wondered how he had managed to escape Sybil's clutches. Perhaps she had gone for a manicure after all. "I'm simply surprised to see you for a second time so soon, sir."

He smiled, making an already handsome face devastating. A lock of golden hair had fallen over his brow. He pushed it against the darker hair at his temples. "Does it please you to see me?"

She curled her fingers around the door, willing herself not to blush. "Of course, unless there is some trouble with the suite bill."

He chuckled. "Not at all, Miss Loudon. I hope you will come down to the Coffee Room some evening. You are often about late at night. As am I."

She inclined her head. "I have seen your crowd in the Coffee Room. All Bright Young Things. I would not fit in."

His gaze raked her from top to bottom. "Not in that rag," he murmured. "Why don't you visit our dress shop? They can smarten you up."

"M-maybe when I'm paid next," she stammered.

"A young lady like you, freshly arrived in London. You owe it to yourself to dress as the person you want to become," he said. "Do you have any artistic leanings of your own?"

"I just wanted to be in London." Alecia heard steps behind her. Then Richard came up, almost against her, his body heat radiating onto her back.

"Who is this then, Miss Loudon? A beau?" Richard peered over her shoulder. "Oh, it's you, Eyre. What brings you to our digs?"

"I need to discuss the command performance."

"Excellent. Come in. I'll have Miss Loudon fix us a little drinkie and then she can go about her business."

Alecia had no idea what he meant. She shifted her weight away from him. "Business?"

Richard inclined his head to Peter Eyre and pulled Alecia aside so he could enter. "Have a seat. Don't mind the scripts. You can see we chose the Scottish play for our Russian guest."

"Excellent," Peter Eyre murmured.

Alecia followed Richard out of the sitting room. She balked when she saw he meant to have her enter his bedroom, but she was in a pickle now. Rubbing her hands together, she followed him into his room. He closed the door and pointed to his bureau.

"Mix us up some manhattans, will you?"

While she didn't know how the drinks cart had landed in his bedroom, when it normally belonged in the main part of the suite, this routine was familiar. Alecia nodded and chose vermouth, whisky, and bitters bottles. She'd learned to make the cocktail for her parents when she was twelve. They never indulged in the maraschino cherries, though, that Richard and Sybil insisted on. Drinks-making had been one of the reasons she'd been hired. She'd had to prove she could make a manhattan, a martini, and a sidecar. Sybil had opined that Alecia's sidecar was as good as any Ritz bartender could make, and thus, she found herself employed.

While she poured the liquors into a cocktail shaker, Richard rummaged around in his wardrobe. She had the drinks on a tray by the time he came back, holding a small jewelry case.

"Have a look at this," he said, thrusting the case at her.

She opened it to find an achingly lovely bird brooch. "It's exquisite."

"Sapphire, diamond, abalone, and platinum," he said. "Quite out of date, of course. Some Russian admirer gave it to Sybil on our tour."

She stroked the abalone belly of the bird. The iridescent blue shimmered. "What am I to do with it?"

"Ask the concierge for a reputable pawnshop and pawn it," he instructed.

She frowned. "How sad. He's such a pretty bird."

"He came from Russia, and he can be used to buy us better costumes," Richard said. "I have some ideas for new staging."

"Why do you have to pay?"

"They won't give us a budget commensurate with the way I want to do things," Richard said. "I won't do anything by half. We'll sort it out, and we'll retrieve the bird later. Off you go now, I want to speak to Mr. Eyre in private."

"I'll gather my coat then, and go. If I could have taxicab fare?"

He grunted and found her some coins. She took the brooch and walked out of the door in his room that led to the corridor, not wanting him to even notice that doors connected their rooms.

She was attempting to cultivate subtlety, something the nursing sisters in her failed program claimed she lacked entirely. They had let her go after she made a third patient cry. Now, however, she hovered between utter silence and complete outspokenness in her personal life, not sure what subtlety was, precisely. She went downstairs, telling herself she was thrilled to be having an adventure, not terrified of venturing into London alone.

The concierge told her to try Poplar High Street in the East End. She was to look for the characteristic three balls hanging on the brick wall above the side entrance. In the taxicab, she drank up the metropolitan sights as best she could through a heavy downpour as the streets became steadily grittier.

On Poplar High Street, the shop the concierge had recommended looked rather prosperous, more so than she'd expected, with a nice clock inlaid above the door, gaslights hanging over the crowded display windows, and even some ladies looking into those windows at the assortment of wares less fortunate families had made available.

The rest of the street made her well-ordered soul quail, however. While a couple of public houses, out of several choices, were in equally excellent condition, the rest of the shops were in ill repair, and many of the windows were boarded up. Being near the Billingsgate fish market, the air had a generally marine feel to it. While she wanted to explore London, this did not seem the place to begin. She suspected this was the street where dockworkers came to drink.

She entered the shop quickly and nervously, but the clerk seemed to be the standard London man of business, and Richard had told her the amount she had to obtain for the brooch. Thankfully, the clerk said he could probably give her more than Richard had demanded, so she didn't need to negotiate.

"Satisfied?" he asked.

"Yes, sir." It seemed her adventure would scarcely be worth writing to Sadie about.

He nodded. "I'll just gather the owner then. Wait 'ere a minute." He disappeared behind a curtain waving in the wall.

"Did any new seventy-eights come in today?" Ivan asked Boris Grinberg, his best friend in London.

Boris, a florid-faced forty-nine-year-old who had left his Jewish faith for atheism, put down the polishing cloth he'd been using on a delicate samovar. "No, none of your bubkes today." He softened the insult with a smile.

"Keep an eye out. Vera's birthday is coming up." Ivan took a battered iron kettle off Boris's spirit burner and poured water over the tea leaves in Boris's own silver-plated teapot. Despite his second-hand business, Boris liked modern things.

"This must be new," Ivan commented.

Boris touched the ornate cream jug with a blunt-tipped finger. "Lovely work, isn't it? A Christmas gift to myself."

"If you don't believe in religion, why do you give yourself holiday gifts?"

Boris shrugged. "Why not?" He leaned forward and rubbed the space between Ivan's eyebrows.

"What are you doing?" Ivan flinched.

"Ah, boychick, you came in with a line between your brows. I think you are having some trouble."

"With Vera and Sergei."

"Nothing you can't fix over the samovar."

"Dear samovar," Ivan said sarcastically. A time-honored tradition had disputes being settled over a cup of tea, using the family samovar as an intermediary. "Not much good, when we couldn't possibly have a samovar in our flat."

"This just came in," a clerk said, pushing his way through the curtain. "I thought you might want it, Ivan."

"Thank you." Ivan took the record and read the label. "Bebe, a fox-trot, from Victor Talking Machine. Yes, this is exactly what I want. It's quite new."

"Mr. Grinberg, a young lady is out front with an expensive brooch she wants to pawn for her employers, so she says."

"I'll be out in a bit. Let her stew. If she's dishonest, she'll probably leave." Boris leaned back in his chair.

The clerk nodded and went back through the curtain.

Boris stared at the record and put his hand to his heart in dramatic fashion. "A rejected holiday present. Did a swain present this as a gift to his lady love, and now she has spurned him?"

"You and your fantasies," Ivan said. He held up the record. "What do you want for it?"

Boris tilted his head. "For you, my gonif, two shillings."

"Now who is the thief? This wouldn't sell for three, new."

Boris lifted his hands to the sky. "How would I know this? Very well. One and six, but you are robbing me blind."

Ivan fished in his pocket and tossed him the coins. "There, we are both happy now." He set his new find aside and poured the tea.

"What is the problem with your sister and her swain?" Boris chose a lemon slice to squeeze into his tea.

"They want to kill Georgy Ovolensky when he comes to London."

Boris's fist convulsed, spraying lemon juice all over the table. Ivan snatched up his new record and wiped it carefully.

Boris pulled a handkerchief from his pocket and tidied his hand and the table, then squeezed what was left of the lemon into his cup. "Kill, you say?"

"I'm afraid so."

"I thought only your sister Catherine was involved in that sort of thing."

"Yes, until our family was murdered. Vera understands hatred all too well."

"Ah. This is the cousin of yours who turned them in."

"Yes." Ivan dropped a sugar lump into his tea and watched it dissolve.

"I thought Sergei was White Army?"

"Yes, but he's willing to do this for Vera. Besides, Georgy has betrayed his aristocratic past to become a Bolshevik. He wouldn't be worth protecting from a White perspective any longer."

Boris rubbed his chin. "Why don't you want him dead?"

Ivan clenched his jaw until his cheeks hurt. "Oh, I want him dead, I just can't be a part of it. I was out of work. I'm just getting back on my feet again. Vera doesn't make much. And Ovolensky is going to be at my hotel. There is no way I'll keep my job in the aftermath. Given the hotel's shady reputation, it might not even survive another murder."

Boris lifted his cup and regarded Ivan over the rim. "So you choose money over family honor?"

"I have no room in my life for family honor," Ivan said. "I miss Catherine and my parents dreadfully, but killing Ovolensky won't bring them back. It might, however, destroy our lives now."

"How old were you when your family died?"

"Nineteen. They were executed by firing squad, all of them. Vera and I were out of town, visiting former neighbors who had moved to Narva, when our parents and sister were taken. A servant came with the news and such portable valuables as she could carry. When we heard the news, I insisted we head for Finland, to escape Russia. While Narva was going to be part of the independent Estonia, Russia still controlled the area at that time. I thought it was my duty to keep Vera safe as best as I could. I was afraid we'd be executed too, if we returned." Ivan's hand shook slightly. Tea sloshed over the rim of his cup.

"Will Ovolensky recognize you at the hotel? Can he do anything to you?"

It was an unanswerable question. "I would prefer he not see me, not recognize me. We've committed no crimes, and Lenin is dead now. Why would Stalin care about me or Vera?"

"He'll care about you if Ovolensky dies." With a flourish, Boris lifted his cup and poured the contents down his throat.

Ivan pounded his fist on the table, rattling the tea set. "Exactly. You see why we cannot do this."

"Do you have any revolutionary ties back in Russia? Someone who could end the threat there?"

"No. No contact with Mother Russia since the day we left," Ivan said. "Georgy used my family's deaths to rise in the party. We lost everything. Friends, family, possessions. All we had was some jewelry of Mother's that she had lent Vera because we were attending a wedding, and what the servant brought. We worked our way across Europe to land here."

"What do you have to lose now?"

Ivan flexed his fingers, stared at the worn cuffs poking out from his coat sleeves. "Not much in material possessions. But our lives, our freedom. Any chance we have to continue our family line. Vera should be married, having a baby, not planning death."

"Is Sergei the wrong man for her?"

"I did not think so until now." Ivan frowned. Such thoughts made his head hurt.

In contrast, Boris looked benevolent. "Instead of trying to talk them out of this emotional crime, you might best work on your sister."

Ivan smiled. "I like how you are thinking, Boris. It is wise counsel."

"She might be best off marrying an Englishman," Boris said.

"I could introduce her to one of my fellow employees," Ivan said, rubbing his chin.

"Give it a try. Try everything. The less she is with Sergei, the less they can plan."

"Very well." Ivan drained his teacup. "Thank you for the hospitality."

Boris rose. "I should see to the young lady with the brooch."

"I'll walk out with you."

Boris tucked Ivan's record money into a cash box on top of his safe, and they both went through the curtain into the main part of the shop.

Alecia's feet hurt in her cheap, heeled shoes, and she was pretty sure she had a ladder on the foot of her stocking. Her first excursion in London had not amounted to much. She'd enjoyed the taxicab from the hotel to Poplar High Street, but she'd come to London searching for music and color and the high life, not poverty. And sleep, it had continued to elude her. It seemed every time she closed her eyes the four funnel stacks of the *Lusitania* came into view, just like they had for nearly a decade now.

She lifted one foot and rubbed the back of her other calf with it. Her muscles were cramping, unused to standing in heeled shoes. Her grandfather didn't hold with anything fashionable. She stared at the brooch, shining and glamorous amidst the relative squalor of the shop.

Then, finally, the curtains parted. A rotund middle-aged man came out, followed by a tall, handsome fellow with soft-looking black hair that fell around his face. The brooding expression reminded her of someone, and then it hit her. It was Ivan Salter, in the back of an East End pawnshop.

"Mr. Salter," she said, delighted to see a familiar face.

His expression remained impassive, not matching her smile. "Miss Loudon."

"What a treat to see you outside of the hotel," she said. Her nerves jangled uneasily amid his continuing unfriendliness. Had she offended him somehow? "Russell told me to come here."

He didn't respond.

"The concierge?"

Mr. Salter looked at the little man behind the counter. He shrugged, then took a loupe out of his pocket and bent to examine the brooch.

Alecia noticed the record under Ivan's arm. "Are you a music lover?"

"Not like you," he replied dryly. "This is for my sister."

He spoke! "How nice. Is it a dance record?"

"A fox-trot, yes."

"I know how to do that, at least." She lifted her arms. "I want to learn some of the other dances, like the Charleston."

"I don't dance," he said.

She didn't like to see his beautifully molded lips thinning, those lips that had once kissed her so generously. "I see."

"I'm not supposed to be speaking to you," he said.

His words startled her. "Why not?"

He looked above her head instead of at her face. "Mr. Eyre sent out a notice."

She remembered his familiarity earlier. Was he laying a claim to her? How shocking. She'd read of such things in novels. "Not to speak to me?"

"Not to be familiar with the residents," he explained. "Not just you."

"I see." Not so glamorous then. "Well, better that than something against me specifically." She worried at her lip. "I was afraid I had hurt your feelings somehow, the way you so pointedly cut me on the stairs."

"I must do my job," he said in a stiff tone.

"We aren't at work now. We could even have a cup of tea together." Her daring thrilled her.

"There are no nice little tea shops in this part of town," he said blandly. "Just public houses."

"A glass of ale, then," she suggested.

"You aren't meant to be sitting around sailors and traders and hopeless drunks," he said. "You shouldn't even be in the East End."

She wanted to shake the smile back into him and then kiss that sensual mouth. "You don't know anything about me."

"I don't need to. You are a woman with no past."

She stepped back involuntarily, stung deeply by his remark. "That's no longer true, as you well know."

"Was that kiss so important to you?" He leaned forward, voice low, and brushed her lower lip with his thumb.

"Ivan!" shouted the little man with an air of command. He spoke rapidly in a language that Alecia didn't understand.

Ivan stepped away from her. "You needn't worry. She's just a secretary."

"I thought she was from the hotel," the pawnshop owner said.

"I live in a valet's room," Alecia said, feeling the humiliation acutely. "I work for a married couple who reside at the hotel."

"And this is their brooch?" the man said.

Ivan glanced at the brooch. Alecia saw his eyes widen, his face pale.

"Yes," she said, frowning. "They want the money for a project, then they want to retrieve the brooch."

"That's what everyone says," the man murmured.

"I'll be going," Ivan announced unexpectedly.

"No," the owner said. "You will wait and escort this young lady back to the Grand Russe. She shouldn't be in this neighborhood alone, especially with money."

Alecia saw Ivan's jaw shift. He was probably grinding his teeth, and no wonder. She must be ruining his day off. "I'm sorry."

He shrugged. "I'm in no hurry to return home."

She felt a traitorous thrill. "Do you live nearby?"

"Yes, above the greengrocer's down the block."

This wasn't a peaceful neighborhood. "How do you get any sleep?" she asked.

"I have dark curtains. And no one to kiss me awake." He was still pale, but his mouth twisted into a slight smile after he spoke.

Her mouth dropped open just as the little man put his loupe away and wrote a number on a piece of paper. "It's a good piece. I'll give you this for it, since you are a friend of Ivan's."

The amount was better than she'd been told to expect. "I accept."

He nodded and picked up the brooch. "I'll write you a ticket and get you the money. Look sharp, boy."

"Keep that brooch handy, will you?" Ivan asked. "It looks familiar."

The man nodded and went behind the curtain. "Boris, Mr. Grinberg, is a good man," Ivan said.

"It doesn't seem like the sort of shop that can handle nice jewelry."

"Looks can be deceiving. But he doesn't keep such things here."

"Why did you ask him to then?"

"It looked familiar, like something my mother used to own."

Could she have offered him a glimpse at his mysterious past? She spoke eagerly. "Richard said it was a gift from a Russian aristocrat. From when they toured Moscow in '13."

Ivan's brow furrowed. "So much of her jewelry was lost. It is probably just a similar piece."

She stroked a finger over the countertop, wishing she could smooth his brow. "Or she gave it to the Marvins. Was she a theater lover?"

Ivan scrubbed his face with his hands. "I don't know if she loved it any more than the next person."

Alecia could feel his unease, palpable in the crowded shop. She changed the subject. "You are friends with the pawnshop owner? Does he live above this shop?"

"Yes, we've been friends for years. He has a nice flat elsewhere. Four rooms instead of two. He would be a good catch, if you want a Jewish widower old enough to be your father."

Alecia opened her mouth but couldn't come up with anything clever to say. "I wasn't looking for a husband."

He lifted one of those forbidding dark brows. "Girls like you tend to marry the first boy they kiss."

"That would be you," she pointed out. "But you don't want to marry me."

He chuckled, his mood shifting. "A wife would only keep me from my sleep."

Chapter Five

Alecia couldn't figure Ivan out. Were all Russians so changeable? Unable to think of a response to his teasing, she just stood there in front of the pawnshop's counter like a statue, fuming. He wandered away from her, perusing the full shelves. The clerk had vanished. Her head swam a bit, both from hunger and from the exchange with Ivan.

Not interesting. Doesn't know how to talk to men. She could hear her younger sister's voice in her head. How would she ever find a husband? But that wasn't why she'd come to London, was it? She wanted adventure, a taste of the flapper life, not a dreary life in East End poverty with the first boy she kissed, no matter how handsome. No matter how good a kisser.

Marriage could be an adventure, but there was no point in having a bad adventure, just for the sake of having one.

"Who are you arguing with?" Ivan asked, having circled back around to her.

"What do you mean?"

"You have a very intense expression on your face."

"Oh. My sister. She's much more modern than I am. And prettier."

"Older?" He took out a packet of Wrigley's chewing gum and offered her a piece.

She shook her head and watched him put a piece in his mouth, as elegant as if he were lighting a cigarette. "Younger."

"Huh."

"Where did you get the gum?"

"American who is staying on the fifth floor. Likes to tip with gum. I suppose he works for a candy company or something." He grinned. "I'm developing a taste for the stuff."

"I guess people can treat you however they like." She paused. "At work, I mean."

"Yes, but the uniform commands respect from most people." He shrugged. "Anyway, you are quite pretty when you make an effort. I doubt your sister is more attractive, but if she is . . ." He made a fanning motion with his hand.

She dismissed his words. He didn't find her pretty, whatever he said. She'd seen how men treated girls they fancied, with care and consideration. Not dismissiveness. "Don't worry, she's safe in Bagshot."

"One of you has to be sacrificed to the greater good?"

"I don't see it that way. Our grandmother is gone, and our mother. Grandfather is all we have."

"What happened to your parents?"

"My father was an antiquarian bookseller. He took my mother out to Boston to see Charles Lauriat Jr., who was a famous bookstore owner. He had an old-book room at the store and lots of the stock came from English estates."

Ivan leaned against the counter and crossed his arms over his broad chest. "Your father procured for him?"

"Yes, though Mr. Lauriat spent months each year in England himself. He kept doing business throughout the early days of the war, and nothing went wrong. The passenger steamers were supposed to be immune from attack."

"But they weren't."

"No. My mother had been ill and my father wanted her to rest. They chose a sea voyage. So they went to Boston, hand delivering some lovely sixteenth-century books, and then came back on the *Lusitania* with Mr. Lauriat."

"They died in the submarine attack."

He said it so flatly. She wondered what he'd seen when he fled Russia, to find spectacular deaths in a famous shipwreck so uninteresting. And she wondered why he had fled his homeland in the first place. "Yes. My grandmother's death was of the mundane variety. Pneumonia after a long bout of influenza."

The curtain parted and Mr. Grinberg came out with an envelope for her. "The ticket is inside as well. Make sure you get her directly back to her employers, Ivan. It wouldn't do to lose her now."

"I'll take good care of her," Ivan said, straightening. He snapped his gum.

"Filthy habit." Mr. Grinberg sighed to Alecia. "I quite despair of this boychick."

"He thinks the brooch might have belonged to his mother," she said.

Mr. Grinberg put both hands over his waistcoat. "He'll have to bring his sister in for a look. But you need to take that money to your employer, first." He made a shooing motion. "Find a cab, Ivan."

With a half smile, Ivan shook his head and went outside.

"I despair," Mr. Grinberg repeated. "He should be fawning all over a pretty treat like you."

"Such applesauce." She smiled politely but without much warmth, as she would with a parishioner of her grandfather's that she didn't enjoy very much.

"If I had a living daughter, I would treat her like a princess, not set her loose on London in clothing like that," Mr. Grinberg said softly. "Why are you so alone?"

"I'm making my way," she replied. "But I've only just come here."

"I hope to see you transformed when you retrieve the brooch," he said.

"I hope to be transformed." They nodded at each other.

In a crack between objects in the crowded window display, she saw a taxicab pull up next to Ivan. "That's me. Thank you, Mr. Grinberg."

"You are welcome. I will see you back soon."

"Hopefully in about three weeks," she said. "After the command performance."

"For Ovolensky?"

"Yes."

He clucked his teeth. "A very bad man, that Ovolensky. A cousin of young Ivan's, did you know? But he is light. Ovolensky is dark."

Alecia nodded as if she understood, but she knew nothing of the Russian diplomat. She went out the front door. Seagulls were circling overhead, cawing, a reminder of the river nearby.

Ivan held the door of the cab for her, like an experienced door-man, then climbed in himself. The Grand Russe had a black-skinned man from America as the doorman. He was much nicer than Ivan, al-ways smiling and friendly. But he'd never tried to kiss her. Her shoulder touched Ivan's arm. She felt feminine and petite next to his large, masculine form, and longed for him to put his arm around her, though she knew he wouldn't. In a moment, the cab started down the road.

"Are you always going to be a secretary?" he asked abruptly, as if they'd already been having a conversation.

She couldn't decipher the reason for his question, so could only answer with the truth. "I don't know. I've only been one for two weeks, but it is better than nursing."

"You don't want to live with your grandfather?"

He shifted, his arm rubbing against hers. She could smell tea on him, as if he'd rubbed leaves between his fingers. Also dust, as if the suit he wore did not leave his wardrobe often. She wondered if he would spark electricity with her again. Would the flirtatious Ivan re-turn, or was he too intent on the secret of the brooch to pay attention to her? "Part of living with him involved secretarial work. I suppose I was his secretary. It's how I learned to use a typewriter. I typed up his sermons, handled his correspondence."

Ivan continued to stare straight ahead. "Is he well-known?"

Alecia glanced out the window, trying to soak in London, though this poorer part didn't offer much of a view. Just soot-stained build-ings and rain-soaked pavement and tired people in dark coats. Still, she wanted to see as many ladies as possible, so she would know what to buy when she had money for clothes. She suspected Sybil's taste was far too theatrical for the average person. "Well respected. Very conservative views."

"That explains your dresses," Ivan said.

"I haven't had time to do any London shopping," she admitted. "I've worked every day."

"You should have days off." He finally looked at her, a bit sullen-looking due to that full lower lip. But strength was evident too, in the strong jaw.

She looked away from him. "I want to go to C&A, the department store. But Sybil is very demanding, and I don't like to put on airs, being so new, demanding a full afternoon off or such."

"So you work seven days a week?"

"Because of my grandfather, they assume I want Sunday morning off to attend services. I have Saturday morning too. They are always hungover."

"You don't like these hours."

"My grandfather expects me to write home every week with commentary on the sermon I heard on Sunday. So I haven't a choice. But it doesn't feel like a proper half day, I'll tell you that."

"No, it doesn't. And you should have a full day, at least one."

She stared down at her gloves. "I'm happy as long as I can creep downstairs and listen to the music at night."

His tongue touched his upper lip for a fraction of a second. "You go on a little holiday every evening?"

She smiled. "I suppose. I do love the music. I think my situation will change when the Marvins are working again, properly, in a theater. Right now they have too much time on their hands and we're really just trying to get to know each other."

"At least, for your sake, theatrical people are late risers," he mused.

"Yes, and I don't sleep well. It works in my favor."

"Unless I'm specifically told not to allow anyone near the nightclub door, I won't trouble you," he promised. "Now that I know what it means to you."

"That's very kind," she said. "Decent of you."

"Until the rules change again," he said. "I must do as I'm told. I can't be seen being flirtatious."

"I would never ask you to risk your job for the sake of me listening to hot jazz," she said. "Or flirting with me."

His slight smile pronounced his cheekbones. "It's Friday. The club should be on fire tonight."

She felt like they were flirting now. Bittersweet that he'd be cold to her again when they arrived. "Do you often work inside it?"

"No, New Year's was the only time. Did you enjoy dancing with Mr. Eyre?" His tongue darted out again.

"Not as much as Mrs. Marvin did," Alecia said without thinking.

Ivan grinned. This close to him, it was hard not to stare, not to wish he would kiss her again.

The cab stopped with a jerk. She glanced out the window and was keenly disappointed with the sight she'd adored just two weeks ago. "Back to the hotel so soon? I hadn't realized."

Ivan was already stepping out. He helped her down, then paid the driver.

"You shouldn't, you should take the taxicab back to your flat. You don't need to be here today."

He hesitated. She could see he really didn't want to be at his workplace. He probably wanted to take his sister to see the brooch. "Take the taxicab, Ivan. Mr. Marvin gave me enough money for the fare."

"Very well." He nodded brusquely, lifted a hand to the doorman who had been hovering nearby, then climbed back in.

Through the window, she could see Ivan sitting very straight, as if he were uncomfortable. Mindful of the money she carried, she went through the hotel speedily, though she would have loved to dawdle at the dress shop, or even sit on the banquette seating arrangement across from the salon to watch the ladies as they exited with new hairstyles. Her own hair was a heavy, neatly tucked coil against her neck.

She asked the lift operator to take her to the fifth floor and was so focused on putting money into Richard's hands that she almost missed the elderly hand waving to her from behind the fern across from the lift door.

She recognized Mrs. Plash. When the old woman stepped out from behind the large plant, Alecia saw she held an old apron in a bundle.

"What do you have there?" she asked.

Mrs. Plash looked down, confused.

"Here, let me assist you," Alecia said, moving to take the bundle. It rattled, its unwieldy burden shifting. She took it to the chair next to the lift door and unwrapped it. Crystal ashtrays, all with the distinctive GR logo in the middle.

"Oh dear," Mrs. Plash murmured.

"You have quite a collection here," Alecia said. "Do you know where you found them?"

"Did you know a woman recently officiated at a wedding for the first time in London?" Mrs. Plash said, averting her gaze from the ashtrays. "A Miss Dorothy Haldane, in Bloomsbury. I'm not surprised, really. Bloomsbury, you understand."

"Where did you hear that?" Alecia said, attempting to follow the conversation.

Mrs. Plash's gaze was vague, focused on her mind's eye. "*The Vote*, my dear. My daughter is a member of the Women's Freedom League."

"Oh?"

"She believes in equality of morality," Mrs. Plash said.

"I see," Alecia said, assuming that was why the woman was unmarried and having an affair. "I do find that tidbit fascinating, but I did wonder about the ashtrays?"

"What ashtrays?" Mrs. Plash patted her arm. "You shouldn't smoke, dear. Makes wrinkles around the mouth. So unattractive." She tottered down the hall to her room, Alecia and the apron of ashtrays quite forgotten.

Alecia hefted the apron, hoping Mrs. Plash wouldn't miss it later, and took the ashtrays to her room. Then she went into the sitting room. Mr. Eyre had gone but Richard sat at the table, drinking a cup of tea and reviewing *Macbeth*.

"I think you'll be pleased," she said, handing him the pawnshop envelope.

He opened it with a grunt, and flipped through the banknotes. "You did well. Used to fleecing your flock, I suppose?"

"That was never my job, except at the annual bazaar," she said.

"Hmm." He regarded her with a speculative gleam.

She found it discomforting. "If you don't mind, I need to return something to the front desk. I found it in the hallway, but I wanted to get the money to you as soon as possible."

"Take a letter for me first, will you?" Richard said.

She held back an urge to sigh. She'd wanted to use the time to review her afternoon with Ivan as she made her way downstairs. "Of course. I'll find my pen."

He dictated a letter to Dolly Tree, a very prominent costume designer for stage and film, asking her to create the costumes for the command performance. "She'll be very dear, especially in this time frame, but with such a distinguished audience she might be swayed. Send this off immediately so we can have a response Monday. We'll have a lot of letters to write then if she says no."

"Yes, sir." Alecia stood. "I'll just do a proper copy of this for your signature."

"Use the hotel stationery," he said.

She nodded and went to the writing table next to the picture window. Ten minutes later she had a clean letter and Richard signed it. "I'll post this and run my little errand, then be back."

"No sign of Sybil yet?" he asked.

"No. Do you want me to check the salon?"

"No, she wouldn't still be there," he said, returning to his book. "Make a dinner reservation for me downstairs, will you? If she turns up she can join me."

"Yes, I will." She poised expectantly on the balls of her feet. When he said nothing more she went out the main door of the suite and down the hall to her own door. Inside her room, she blew on the envelope to dry the ink and tucked it into the pocket of her dress, then hefted the apron of ashtrays, hoping she wouldn't chip any of them on the journey downstairs.

The man at the front desk had a tag on his red uniform jacket identifying him as Lionel Dew, Night Manager. Alecia felt oddly relieved when she realized she wouldn't have to see Mr. Eyre.

"Good evening," she said, hefting her apron full of contraband onto the desk. "I found these behind a plant on the fifth floor and they appear to belong to the hotel."

Mr. Dew, a blond with a barely discernible unibrow, given his unusually light hair for a man of middle years, opened the bundle with an air of professional indifference. "Where did you find them?"

"Near the lift," she said, not convinced she should give away Mrs. Plash's secret. Mr. Eyre had to know the poor woman had her troubles, given his relationship with the daughter.

"I'd like you to speak to Mr. Eyre, the manager."

"Of course," Alecia said, her midsection turning to butterflies. "I'll find him tomorrow."

"He's here now, miss. In the Coffee Room. He's there most hours after I come on duty at seven."

A couple, dusty and road weary, but dressed respectively in a Poiret driving costume and custom plus fours, walked up to the counter. Alecia had a feeling she ought to know who they were, if for no other reason than the woman had an unworldly beauty, from her carefully lacquered black hair, almost geometrically arranged around her face, and her perfect, thin black brows, to her oversized carmine lips. The man had a ruddy, squashed face and ginger hair. He matched the lady not in beauty but in distinction and individuality.

When he saw Alecia's perusal, he doffed his hat with a grin. "Yes, dear, of course you can have my autograph. But Miss Page, you know, never signs them."

The beauty gave them both a bored stare, and Mr. Dew began to fuss over her.

"Oh, you're Teddy Fortress," Alecia said, finally placing the man. A well-known movie comedian, one of many Brits who'd attempted to replicate Charlie Chaplin's success in Hollywood. Miss Page was his wife, and an actress too.

He chuckled. "I'm pleased such a beauty recognized me."

"He needs your John Hancock, Teddy," his wife said in an unpolished American accent.

"Of course, of course," Teddy said, giving Alecia a wink and stepping around her. "Catch you later, doll."

She walked briskly away, realizing she preferred Mr. Eyre's unsettling urbanity to Mr. Fortress's gangster-speak and teasing, especially in front of his wife, who must be very used to it, given her demeanor.

The Coffee Room was considered by many to be the most beautiful room at the Grand Russe. The most up-to-date, certainly, with its stunning navy and silver geometric wallpaper. The parquet floor's dizzying pattern could make a girl's head spin a bit, even more than the champagne that flowed between eight and eleven P.M.

Even though the champagne hour had not yet begun, the room had filled with Bright Young Things of the sort who drank their evening meal instead of eating it. The law insisted food must be available when alcohol was served, so a buffet was ever present along the side wall. Alecia had never investigated it in the evening, and wouldn't now, since Mr. Dew had gestured at her apron-wrapped package with disdain.

Instead, she walked across the floor with her eyes focused on her package, trying to ignore how she might appear in her black dress—her newest frock, sewn to wear to her grandmother's funeral initially—and hoping she channeled the bored attitude of Miss Page, though she was no actress.

When Mr. Eyre saw her though, he treated her as a special guest and not a bedraggled supplicant. He rose from his chair, holding his cigarette, and inclined his head, smoke spiraling around his carefully combed sandy hair. "Why, Miss Loudon, what a treat."

"I found these upstairs," she said.

Mr. Eyre smiled and took the bundle from her.

"It's ashtrays," she explained. "I attempted to leave them with Mr. Dew, but he was busy with new arrivals."

"Have Mr. Fortress and his lovely wife entered stage right?" he asked.

"Yes, sir."

"I'll have to welcome them personally," he murmured, taking a peek in her bundle. His expression seemed to sharpen, though his face didn't move.

"What are you doing with my mother's apron?" A brassy blonde with dark eyebrows that didn't match approached, holding a long, empty cigarette holder. Her slinky, sleeveless navy dress, spangled with silver, matched the walls. This was Emmeline Plash, Fallen Woman. "Peter?"

"Miss Loudon found it," Mr. Eyre murmured. "Have you made the acquaintance of Miss Plash, Miss Loudon?"

"No." She nodded at the woman.

"A pleasure," Miss Plash said, lifting her nose. "Butt me, will you, Peter? My case is empty."

Mr. Eyre snapped his fingers, and a liveried bellboy appeared from behind Alecia with all the speed of a genie exiting a bottle. "Take this bundle to my office," he ordered.

"My mother's apron," Emmeline said impatiently.

"Leave the ashtrays there, and return the apron to me," he said. "Unless you'd like me to have it washed and ironed for you."

"No, it's one of my mother's prize possessions," Emmeline said, snatching at Mr. Eyre's gleaming cigarette case as he pulled it from an inner pocket. She rubbed at it. "Honestly, Peter, it's all smudged."

Mr. Eyre smiled at Alecia. She felt like he'd let her in on his private joke, and was warmed by it, instead of made nervous, as she had been with Teddy Fortress.

"If you'll excuse me, ladies, I had better see to the Fortresses." Mr. Eyre inclined his head and strode off behind the bellboy.

Emmeline shook her head angrily. "Who is supposed to light me up?"

A waiter appeared at her elbow, holding a lighter. "Miss, if I may?"

Another genie. Alecia watched as their transaction was completed.

"Efficient, I'll give them that." Emmeline blew smoke out of the side of her mouth in businesslike fashion. "Now, I know you didn't just find those ashtrays. My mother took them, right?"

"I found her with them, and she gave me the bundle. I don't know how she came to have them."

Emmeline blew out smoke again and stared at the wall. "I don't know what to do with that woman. What a mess."

"I'm sorry."

Emmeline smirked nastily. "It's you I feel sorry for. A pretty girl who dresses like a fright and has to play fetch and carry for those theater people." She waved her cigarette holder around the room. "You're always going to be on the outside. It will get worse as your employers age. I've heard they are both past their prime as it is. The hotels will become shabbier, your pay will reduce. Although I don't know how you could dress any worse."

"I only started working for them last month, Miss Plash," Alecia said, swallowing her anger. "And the Marvins have all kinds of prospects. I have faith in my employers. Besides, this hotel isn't the least bit shabby."

"You shouldn't have faith in employers. You should find yourself a rich boyfriend and enjoy being young. How old are you? Twenty?"

"Twenty-two."

Emmeline rolled her eyes. "To be twenty-two. You have the look of a just-born fawn. I'd claim to be younger, if I were you. This is the age of youth, and you can get away with it." Her gaze wandered. "I wonder if we can open a bottle early tonight."

Alecia felt as though she'd been sucked into the genie's bottle herself, the way Emmeline suddenly stopped recognizing her presence, and took a step away. She knew she didn't fit in. Oddly enough, given her London fantasies, she didn't even want to, not with this bored, heavily imbibing crowd with the high-pitched drawls and "sick-making" talk.

A string quartet had come in and were setting up in a corner, music to keep the beast at bay until the nightclub opened later. A young man in full evening kit approached them, mouse-brown hair, center parted and gleaming with oil, a bored expression in his heavy-lidded eyes. "Will you dance, ladies?" he drawled.

Emmeline rolled her eyes.

"Both of us?" Alecia said, momentarily distracted from her plan to exit by the notion of dancing.

Another young man approached. They were mirror images of each other. Twins.

"Goodness," Alecia said, trying to flirt. "Which of you is nicer?"

"Harold," said the first.

"Gerald," said the newcomer.

She had no idea whether they were saying their own names or each other's, but the string quartet finished checking their instruments and began a Tchaikovsky waltz. No, she couldn't resist. "I'd love to dance."

The first man bowed and took her hand. In an instant, they were in the center of the floor, twirling around as half a dozen others joined them. The size of the room compared to the number of couples meant they could command the floor. Alecia had never been spun so fast or moved so far, being used to church tea dances where the music was sedate and the floor crowded. But this, this was living, despite the man's practiced boredom and her own inappropriate attire. She forgot him, and her clothes, and not fitting in, and let him spin her until she was dizzy, until she couldn't see him clearly. He might have been Ivan Salter, or Richard Marvin, or Peter Eyre. Anyone, really.

When the music ended, the quartet paused. Alecia saw a group of Bright Young Things had entered the room. She heard the high, tittering laugh of one of the men.

"I should go," she said to her partner. "This isn't my party. But thank you for the dance."

"Who are you?" he asked. "You're a very good dancer."

She touched her flushed cheeks. "Thank you. I've never danced like that. It was heaven. Which one are you? Harold or Gerald?"

"Gerald." His gaze had wandered away from her.

"I'm Miss Loudon."

"A pleasure, I'm sure." His gaze tracked a boyishly built young woman in her late teens, dressed in a Chanel evening gown, who'd just entered with a large party. She wore diamonds like they were paste.

For a moment Alecia wished Harold would ask her to dance now, but he was opening a bottle of champagne for Emmeline. No, she needed to escape. For this crowd, you had to be rich or artistic, and she was neither.

She walked away from Gerald and darted through the broad, quadruple-doored entrance to the room.

"Leaving so soon, Miss Loudon?" Peter Eyre asked, reappearing just outside. He lifted his cigarette to his mouth. He'd obviously found more, though he'd given his case to his mistress. The band started up again.

She nodded. "I'm more a hot jazz kind of girl." She smiled as she walked away.

Chapter Six

Ivan felt like he hadn't had enough of a break from the Grand Russe, with only one day off. Not that home was a refuge, with Vera's fevered rantings about Cousin Georgy and what he'd done to their family. But the air on the ground floor of the hotel that Saturday night seemed particularly smoky and heavy. Perfume, perspiration, wet wool, and cold air from the doors mixed with the blasts from the heat vents, all left a foggy atmosphere, putting him in a dreamlike state.

People and objects seemed farther away than they truly were. He spotted a woman moving, murkily, far down the service corridor leading to the nightclub's rear door. Following, he knocked into a short pillar and caught the plant that rested on top of it just in time. The woman, careless or not hearing him, kept walking away.

Eventually, he could see the far wall. The art framed there began to take shape, dancers cavorting brightly, captured in sharp strokes of thick, colorful paint. The woman stopped, her ear pressed to the bright crack between the door and the lintel. Now he could hear it too, the band. They played "Red Hot Mamma," a fox-trot he liked.

He could see the woman did too. Her hips swayed, followed by her shoulders. When she tossed her head he recognized her, as if the smoke around her had suddenly cleared. Until that moment, she might as well have been a ghost, one of those murdered starlets.

As if they were in a film, he took Miss Loudon's hand and pulled her to him. She stumbled for half a second when her heel caught on the carpet, then righted herself as he apologized.

She shook her head and smiled, as caught up in the moment as he was, then put her hands into position with perfect geometry, and they began to dance. One hand on his shoulder, the other in his gloved hand. He spun her in a tight hold around the corridor, her body light as air in his arms, their torsos molded together. His heavy uniform coat kept him from feeling the shape of her breasts against him, but he could feel the warmth of her body nonetheless.

His hand pressed against her back. He could feel the delicate curves of her bones. She hid a lot under these shapeless dresses. Tonight's was some off shade of taupe, the third of her dresses that he'd seen. He wished she could have kept some of Boris's money from the pawning of what might have been his mother's brooch, and bought herself a new dress.

When the music ended, she sighed happily. "I feel like Barbara Miles."

"Who?" He waited, poised to dance again when the next number began.

"She won the world's professional dancing championship last year. I don't remember her partner's name."

"I see." But the music didn't start again. The band must be taking a break. Reluctantly, he let her hand go.

Her other hand left his shoulder and she stepped back. "Why did you dance with me? We aren't supposed to fraternize."

"I am sorry for everything that happened yesterday." He caught her gaze with his. "I was still thinking about Mr. Eyre's edict, and I had heard some bad news at home. It made me surly."

She nodded. "I am sorry you had to deal with me on your day off."

"It wasn't you. If we had met somewhere, to dance like this, I would not have minded it. You are a good dancer."

She blushed. "I could feel the music skipping across my skin. When the cymbals clashed it made me shiver." She demonstrated with a roll of her shoulders. "Have you heard 'Snakes Hips'? It's almost as good."

He couldn't help but notice the sway of her breasts. Could he kiss her again? Of course not. Not only would she feel the heavy heat between his legs and become nervous, he would risk losing his job. What he wouldn't give to make love while a jazz record played. How he longed for those carefree days of wealth and privilege sometimes.

"And the trombone," she continued. "Is there anything better?"

His gaze fixed upon her lips, her tongue flashing between them as she sang the tune, "La, lala, lala . . ."

"I can't kiss you," he said.

She stopped singing. "What?"

"No kissing."

Her eyebrows lowered, wispy, delicate arches of blond. "I didn't ask you to."

"Yes, you did."

She shook her head. "No. You're hallucinating."

He fanned out his fingers. "Look at yourself, this sensual creature. You're made of kisses."

Her brows lifted.

"When you speak of music, your eyes are as hungry as Theda Bara's," he continued.

She blushed. "Such applesauce. You've never spoken to me like this before."

"I'm serious. Music brings you to life."

"Not always. I was in the Coffee Room yesterday evening. I don't fit in there, though I did dance once. It wasn't jazzy though, not like in the nightclub."

"Someone asked you to dance?" He was obscurely dissatisfied that he hadn't been the first to dance with her in the hotel.

"One of the twins." She smiled. "I don't know if they are regulars."

"Yes, I know who they are. Cousins of Miss Plash."

She nodded. "That makes a great deal of sense. They came up to us when I was speaking to her."

He suddenly understood. "Oh! Was it you who returned the ashtrays?" That evening's notice had been about the return of purloined articles. He'd solved the problem of the missing newspapers, when he found that one of the long-term residents' valets had been taking them to the den on the seventh floor as soon as they were fanned out in the Reading Room. Then a cache of coffee spoons had turned up in a laundry sack in a storage room on the fourth floor. He'd found those too, during his rounds.

"Yes, Mrs. Plash had them, I'm afraid. But I don't know if she collected them or found them already together."

It could be either way. "Poor woman."

"Do you know?" she asked. "Well, it's an indelicate question."

"What?"

"Are Mr. Eyre and Miss Plash still keeping company?"

Irrational anger surged through him. Did Miss Loudon think

Peter Eyre would take her on, make her over in his mysterious, stylish image? Maybe he could. Maybe, just. This sensuality was a new side of her; one he'd imagined, however momentarily, that she'd shown only him. Maybe it was Eyre bringing it out in her, not the music.

"I have to make my rounds," he said stiffly. "You should return to your room."

"Why?"

"Because the ghosts might get you." He stomped away without answering her question about Eyre. He didn't know the answer anyway.

Alecia rolled her eyes at Ivan's back as he stomped away. Ghosts were unlikely to be much of a nuisance here. Drunken lads from the Coffee Room, those who stayed there to drink themselves into a stupor instead of moving on to the nightclub, were much more trouble.

She wished she'd been able to determine what Sybil was up to. Ivan might know, but he didn't seem inclined to help her.

Did Ivan realize she was as traumatized by her parents' fate as he was by his? That her ghosts were inside her own head? She wished she were a man. They seemed to be able to compartmentalize better, spend less time in their own heads. She doubted he saw his equivalent of the *Lusitania*'s four smokestacks every time he laid his head down on his pillow.

Or maybe he did. He worked nights for a reason.

Ivan opened the door to his flat, exhausted after a long night on his feet. One of the kitchen maids at the hotel had given him a bag of bread rolls when he'd drifted through the kitchens hoping to grab a cup of coffee, and he munched on one of the yeasty treats as he walked in. As he began to toe off his shoes, he realized there were more voices than usual. Vera and Sergei had been joined by their White Russian friends. Ivan knew the speaker only as Pavel. Another man, Anatoly Smirnov, who never spoke in Ivan's presence, sat in the corner on Vera's footstool.

"What did you bring us today?" Vera asked, holding out her hand for the bag.

Ivan didn't give it to her. He didn't mind Sergei, but he loathed the others. Nothing good came of their presence. They'd spend hours here, debating the fate of the Romanovs, filling the air with smoke and eating every morsel of food, drinking every drop of vodka in the flat. He had no interest in supporting whatever they were. Not working men. Imperialists? Revolutionaries? He had no label for their activities, and didn't care.

Ignoring them, he went to the icebox. Of course, his cider was long gone. He poured himself a glass of water and walked past the group into the bedroom, his chin itching when he saw Pavel's untidy beard. Maybe he'd shave before he slept, but then he'd have to take his rolls into the untidy shared lavatory on the landing.

Not worth it.

"Ivan!" Vera shrieked in Russian as he opened the bedroom door. "Don't disappear. We need your guidance."

"I need to sleep."

She rose from the arm of the chair where she was resting against Sergei and slapped him on the chest. "You need to hear this. We're going to take down Ovolensky at the command performance of *Macbeth*."

He felt stupid and slow. "*Macbeth*? How do you know about that?"

Anatoly smirked, but as always, said nothing.

Oh God. Were Miss Loudon's employers involved in this travesty somehow? He stared at his sister, her eyes glittering with excitement.

Gritting his teeth, he said, "Are the Marvins involved with your little conspiracy?"

"Want in?" she challenged.

"You know I don't."

"Then I won't tell you anything." She flounced away and went back to her seat. Anatoly's close-set black eyes bored into Ivan's for a moment, before he tossed back the contents of his glass.

"Why don't you both go back to Russia, instead of making trouble here?" Ivan said.

"The battle must be fought on all fronts," Pavel said. "We have formed a Special Punitive Group as required by the circumstances."

"I think you are too much of a coward to go back," Ivan responded. "There is no good in killing a man. You think the British government will want Russians here if you bring fear to these shores? What about all the charities that have helped us? If the common people see us as murderers, we are finished."

"Our committee has passed a sentence of death upon Ovolensky," Pavel said calmly.

"Now you sound like a Bolshevik, not a White," Ivan jeered. "I don't think the tsar had committees. He was an autocrat."

Pavel sneered. "You know nothing."

"What were you before the war? You are older than me. Were you in the army? I know you couldn't have been an aristocrat. What then? Some humble schoolmaster, in love with a Grand Duchess? Do you think to bring the dead back now?"

"Stop it!" Vera shouted. She rose again and snatched his bag from his hand, then slapped his face.

"Do not push me," he said to his sister, refusing to touch his stinging cheek. "You need me more than you are willing to admit."

She stared at him, saying nothing. He looked up at the cracked ceiling, then walked back through the sitting room and out the door. Boris would let him nap on the old sofa in the back of the pawnshop.

He stayed away from the flat until he had to wash and be back at the hotel. Thankfully Vera and her Special Punitive Committee had gone elsewhere. He had yet to see her alone to ask her about the brooch.

When he arrived at the hotel that evening, he found a notice requesting him to appear in Mr. Eyre's office before he started his rounds. While he felt gritty-eyed from the lack of sleep in a proper bed, at least his appearance was impeccable. He wouldn't let the bloody Special Punitive Group cost him his position. What would those bastards do without people like him who were conned into keeping them going, providing spaces for their meetings, food for them to steal, vodka to fuel their idiocy?

On a Sunday night, the hotel was quieter than usual. Even the Coffee Room seemed subdued, though it was after eight P.M., a prime time for the usual crowd who couldn't afford to dine in a restaurant and were killing time until the clubs opened.

"Mr. Salter," said Peter Eyre, rising from behind his desk and holding out his hand when he walked in.

Ivan took it, confused. He saw Lionel Dew was present as well. At least the handshake seemed friendly. Would Mr. Eyre have shaken his hand if he were about to be sacked?

"I wanted to thank you for finding those spoons and solving the newspaper dilemma," Mr. Eyre said. "You are doing good work."

"Just my job, sir," he said eagerly. "I try to keep an eye on all the nooks and crannies of the hotel."

"Excellent. You are my eyes and ears, you night watchmen," Eyre said.

"Yes, sir."

"You'll find a gesture of gratitude in your next paycheck," Lionel Dew added.

"Thank you, sir," Ivan said. "That is very welcome."

"You were unemployed for a time before you came to us, correct?" Dew continued.

"Yes. Work is scarce."

"Especially for immigrants," Eyre said, lighting a cigarette.

Ivan watched the unconscious grace of the man as he went through the motions. No wonder women found him so attractive. Masculine poetry in every movement, none of this effete nonsense upper-class young men were affecting right now. "Speaking of immigrants," he began.

"Yes?"

"I have some concerns about certain elements of the Russian community where our visit from Georgy Ovolensky is concerned. He is a controversial figure in some circles." How he hated even saying the name.

Eyre picked a piece of tobacco off his lip. "I imagine any part of the present government is, among those who fled."

"Very true, sir." He chose his words carefully. "I have heard there might be some manufactured unrest at the Marvins' command performance."

Eyre's eyes narrowed. "From who?"

Ivan shrugged. "Those who hate Stalin's government."

"Plenty of those." Eyre sat back, regarding him.

Ivan didn't know what to do with his hands. He locked them together behind his back, his palms feeling hot underneath his gloves. "I might be able to learn more about it."

"How?" Eyre elongated the simple word.

Ivan cleared his throat. "I can keep my ears open around the Russian community, but I'm also concerned that someone in the Marvins' world could be helping."

"You don't say," Eyre drawled.

"Yes, but I can't learn more about that."

"No?"

He felt he had to explain. "You've told us not to fraternize with guests."

Eyre nodded. "What do you have in mind?"

"Miss Loudon, the Marvins' secretary, is often underfoot late at night. I've attempted to follow orders not to speak to her since you explicitly ordered us to refrain from fraternizing, but if I was allowed to continue our initial conversations, I might be able to learn who is feeding information about the performance to the Russian community."

"Do you think she is the problem?"

"No, sir. She's newly come to London, but she's always on duty, so she has access to everyone the Marvins do."

Eyre steepled his fingers together under his chin. "How much trouble do you think these elements are going to make?"

"I think it is going to be bad, sir, very bad."

Mr. Dew's eyebrows rose. Eyre looked even calmer.

"We don't want any trouble." A thin trail of smoke rose to the ceiling from Eyre's forgotten cigarette.

"No, sir, we can't afford it."

Eyre nodded. "I know of whom you speak. She does tend to wander, that one. Go ahead and do your worst with her, as long as she seems of value to the greater enterprise. But I'm going to want to know what you're hearing among your people. That seems more important to me."

Ivan nodded, sadness warring with elation.

A knock came at the door. The night concierge poked his head in after Eyre called, "Enter."

"Miss Plash is outside, sir. Says her mother is missing?"

Eyre ground out his cigarette in a battered brass ashtray, not one of the Grand Russe's, and stood. "Do we know for how long?"

"She didn't tell me. Shall I send her in?"

Eyre nodded.

"Why don't you request a date with this Miss Loudon?" Mr. Dew suggested. "That will flatter her."

Eyre stood. "There's stationery in the credenza, Mr. Salter. Ah, here you are, Emmeline."

Ivan went to the credenza and took paper and an envelope to the corner of Mr. Eyre's desk and wrote a note under Mr. Dew's watchful eye, while Miss Plash fretted about her mother.

"I'll take it upstairs," Mr. Dew said. "You start the search for Mrs. Plash."

Ivan nodded. "It really isn't necessary for you to take the note. I'm sure I'll see her around midnight."

"You need to make a young lady feel desired." Dew reached into his pocket. "Here." Dew handed several half-crown coins to Ivan.

"I can't take your money," Ivan protested.

"I'll get it from petty cash. Show her a good time."

Images of Miss Loudon's mouth, brushing softly against his, came to mind. "Doing what?"

"Go to the pictures. Buy her lunch." He winked. "You know the sort of thing."

He didn't, not really. "I'll start looking for Mrs. Plash."

"Do you know what she looks like?" demanded Miss Plash.

"Tone, Emmeline," Eyre said gently.

"I do, Miss Plash," Ivan said, as Mr. Dew left the office. "We'll fetch her back to her room. Don't you worry." He nodded at the upset woman and left, wondering if her smeared mascara was evidence of real emotion or if she was simply being dramatic.

"Make me a sidecar, will you, darling?" Sybil asked from her perch next to her husband on their sitting room sofa.

Alecia glanced in despair at the framed print on the wall depicting "The Chinese," a character from *The Sleeping Princess* ballet that had inspired the name of this Chinese Suite. "Help me," she implored silently. The gold and white striped pattern on the ballerina's hat was echoed on the walls, and the bathroom wallpaper resembled the blue and white floral pattern of her skirt.

Alecia had been shut up with the Marvins all afternoon, making endless drinks. How Sybil remained relatively sober was beyond her. She'd been utterly unrepentant about the concern she'd caused by being missing for hours the day before. Alecia had to admit her nails had been freshly varnished, so a manicure had been part of the day's proceedings.

"A sidecar for you as well, Richard?" Alecia asked.

"No," Richard said absently, turning a page in his script.

Alecia had just finished squeezing a lemon when a knock came on the door. She went to open it and found the night manager there. He held out an envelope. She smiled and took it. "Thank you."

"Good night." Mr. Dew winked at her as she closed the door.

"Bring it here," Richard said.

"Actually, it's for me," Alecia admitted after examining the envelope. She set it down and finished preparing the drink.

"Something from the vicar?" Sybil asked, an air of malice flavoring her words.

Alecia went back to the drinks cart and retrieved the envelope, then sat across from her employers. "No, it's not from my family."

"Well, don't keep us in suspense," Sybil said. "Read it out loud."

"What if it's private?" Richard wondered.

"Alecia is such a baby, it couldn't possibly be anything that interesting," Sybil said archly, and took a sip of her drink. "Oh, this is heaven, darling. You do have a career ahead of you as a bartender."

Alecia slid her finger underneath the lightly sealed envelope and flipped it open. She pulled out a single sheet of notepaper. "It's on hotel stationery." She read, then an "oh" escaped her before she reread it.

"What?" Sybil said.

"That night watchman I keep seeing about has asked me to spend tomorrow afternoon with him."

Sybil blinked. Richard's brow furrowed.

Alecia put the note back in the envelope. She'd never been asked on a date before, had certainly never expected Ivan Salter to do so. What had changed? Was he still attempting to apologize for his behavior on Friday? Her face felt hot as she remembered their dance.

"She's blushing, poor baby," Sybil said to her husband. "Do you think we should let her go on this date?"

"We are in loco parentis," Richard said. "I do not like the idea."

"But she must have a life," Sybil said grandly. "Yes, I think she should go. It's just the afternoon. Daylight. No trouble there."

"Just the afternoon," Richard repeated.

"But a Monday," Alecia said.

"Is that his day off?" Sybil asked.

"No. But his shift starts at eight. They work twelve-hour shifts, six days a week."

"Immigrants," Richard said. "They are used to hard work. Need to get ahead."

Alecia suspected Ivan didn't come from a poor background. He seemed educated, well mannered, and too well-spoken for that. But she wanted the conversation to end before the Marvins talked themselves out of letting her have Monday afternoon free.

Sybil set her glass on the table next to her. She missed the coaster, and Alecia's fingers itched to right the glass before it left a stain on the beautiful wood.

Sybil rose. "Let's investigate your wardrobe, Alecia, darling. You must dress suitably for such an important occasion."

"You've seen all my clothes." As had Ivan Salter.

Sybil's head wobbled on her neck. "Then let's investigate my wardrobe and see what can be done." Her eyes half closed as she held out her arm.

Alecia glanced at Richard, who shrugged, so she rose to her feet. What was the harm?

Ivan spent two hours searching every nook and cranny of the main floor. Either Mrs. Plash wasn't there or she was one step ahead of him at every moment. However, it was past ten thirty at night and the old woman must be tiring. Might she be napping somewhere?

He went down the dank stairwell to the basement. For the most part, this area wasn't open to the public, but he didn't want to admit defeat to Mr. Eyre, and there were lavatories down here, left from when the hotel first opened and private rooms didn't have their own.

He'd check in with the night manager after investigating there, not bothering to go into the area marked Staff Only, just past the public lavatories.

The light down here was feeble and flickering, the corridors uncarpeted. The Russian fantasy of upstairs was missing here, but the four lavatories, though plain and functional, were still occasionally used by guests. He opened first one door, then the second, peeking in. When he rattled the knob of the third door, it refused to turn in his hand.

"Mrs. Plash?" he called.

Shocked, he heard a response. "Yes?"

"Mrs. Plash?" he said again, disbelieving.

"Yes," said the elderly female voice again.

"Your daughter wants you," he said.

"Thank you."

He stood bemused as the door opened. "My goodness, it is you," he said.

"I don't know you." The elderly woman frowned and clutched at a rope of pearls.

"Mr. Salter, ma'am. I'm a night watchman here at the Grand Russe."

"My daughter sent you to collect me?" The creases around her eyes deepened.

"Yes, ma'am."

"How odd. I wouldn't have thought she knew where I was."

He held back his commentary. "Have you been here all evening?"

She didn't answer, merely sidled out of the door, around him, then began trudging down the hall toward the stairs.

"We could go up in the lift," he suggested. "It comes down here."

She paused. "That would be lovely."

"May I take your arm?"

She nodded, and leaned heavily against him as he walked her toward the service lift, intended mostly for moving laundry from the basement washing facilities to the guest floors.

They found the front door to the Duchess One, the Plash's large, two-bedroom suite, open. Miss Plash paced alone, looking small and plain against the gold-and-black striped walls and oversized russet furniture. Ivan expected Mr. Eyre to be with her, but the manager must be tending his flock in the Coffee Room.

"Mother!" Miss Plash shrieked, her hand going up as if she wanted to slap the elderly woman, before descending to her rouged cheek. "Where did you go this time?"

The elderly lady glanced uncertainly at Ivan. He didn't want to reveal any secrets, whatever the situation, so he smiled politely.

"Good evening, ladies," he said, in his best imitation of Mr. Eyre's smooth manner.

"Not so fast," Miss Plash said, coming toward him.

Would she offer him a tip? He deserved one, but he'd never known the woman to be generous.

Instead of finding her purse, however, the woman fixed her hands around his upper arm and leaned into him, batting her eyes, which had been freshly made up.

"How can I ever repay you for finding my darling mother?" she cooed.

He couldn't wrench out of her grip, but he did take a step back. "It was no trouble, Miss Plash," he said.

"When is your shift over?" she whispered.

"Eight in the morning."

"Oh, how ghastly," she said. "Why don't you come in early tomorrow and I'll give you tea? We'll get to know each other better. I really must express my appreciation."

One hand left his biceps to drift into her cleavage. He used the opportunity to break away.

"Thank you, Miss Plash, but there is no need, and I am not free then in any case. Hotel business."

He waited for her to suggest she would persuade Mr. Eyre to free him, but she said nothing. Had she fought with the manager after he'd gone on his search? He'd best alert the male hotel employees that she was on the prowl, though he wondered how long the woman could afford her suite without her protector.

Chapter Seven

"What do you want?" Richard Marvin leaned his cheek against the door but still looked hostile.

Ivan held his ground despite the heavy scent of alcohol wafting off Marvin's breath, but he did wonder if he should have knocked on Miss Loudon's private door rather than the main entrance to the Chinese Suite. "I'm here to see Miss Loudon."

"Oh, you're the boy who wants to date her." Marvin sneered, his bushy, gray-blond mustache riding up on one side.

Ivan smiled politely. He would not dispute mere terminology. "I thought we could stroll toward Piccadilly, and then maybe go into Hyde Park, take a walk along the Serpentine. Just a walk."

"Good weather for it," Richard allowed, "but she's here to work, not play."

"Yes, sir," Ivan said, wondering if this idea cooked up by the hotel managers was a good one. If he created a rift between Miss Loudon and her employers, how would he learn anything about the link between them and the Russian conspiracy? "I'll have her back before dark."

"In January?" Marvin scoffed, changing his tune. "You don't offer a girl a very good time. You can't even manage an early tea before dark."

"I didn't want to have her out very late," Ivan said, backpedaling. "Out of respect to her employers."

Marvin's eyes narrowed. "You don't seem very keen on the girl."

"We're both working people. I'm realistic."

Marvin's sneer turned to a grin as he puffed out his chest and slid one hand into the opening of his coat. "You'll never win a girl's heart by being realistic. Did not Shakespeare write,

'So on the tip of his subduing tongue
All kind of arguments and question deep,
All replication prompt, and reason strong,
For his advantage still did wake and sleep.
To make the weeper laugh, the laugher weep,
He had the dialect and different skill,
Catching all passions in his craft of will.' "

"If that is the case, sir," Ivan, who had been forced to read Shakespeare in his entirety, said, "it doesn't matter what we do or how long it takes, just that I persuade the lady she had a good time."

Marvin chuckled. "Well said, young man. I suppose a night watchman is a suitable beau for a secretary. Why not? Come in."

Ivan stepped in, acutely feeling the shabbiness of his clothing in the opulence of the room. Places like this were once his birthright, but all that was long lost now. And his sister wanted to destroy his access to what he had left. At least he could walk these halls in comfort and watch the doings of luckier folks. What about him and Vera though? When did they start to live for themselves and not for the dead?

Mr. Marvin pointed to his wife then left the room.

"Hello, there!" Sybil Marvin lounged on a sofa in front of the painting of the costumed ballerina that provided the theme for the room. The actress showed to good effect in plain ivory pajamas against the Chinese floral-patterned upholstery.

"Mrs. Marvin." He inclined his head.

"I hope you don't mind taking out a girl in nice clothes," she said, perusing him with a tiny wrinkle between her eyes. "I've lent Alecia some of mine."

So that was Miss Loudon's first name. He liked it. "She is already nicer-looking than me, so it hardly signifies."

Her laugh sounded full and theatrical. "My dear boy, you know better than that. The Grand Russe hires night watchmen like great ladies of old used to hire footmen. It's all about looks. What did you do before?"

"I was a night watchman before, at a hotel that failed."

"And before that you were in Russia?"

"Before that I was in Paris, then Berlin, then Helsinki. I haven't seen Russia since 1918."

Her voice dropped gravely. "You've been away from home for a long time."

"Yes." He didn't want to dwell on it. "Where are you from originally?"

"Exeter. My father was a tram operator there. Humble beginnings."

"You had talent that took you from a conventional life." He felt like this was the line she wanted to hear next.

"Yes, I suppose I did." She tilted her head. "What are your dreams?"

"To be able to provide for myself and my family, I suppose." He shifted from one foot to the other.

"Now there is a humble dream, dear boy. Were you someone quite unimportant in Russia?"

"My family had connections, but no, we weren't important."

"Wealthy?" she guessed. "You made it this far."

He was saved from responding by a door opening. Miss Loudon walked in, followed by Mr. Marvin. She wore a blue cloth coat with fur around the collar and cuffs, in a very current style. Her close-fitting hat matched, and her blond hair curled around her cheeks. He checked her shoes, and they were sensible ones that she could walk in, not quite in step with the rest of her outfit.

Mrs. Marvin gave him an expectant look.

"Very glamorous," he said, holding his hands stiffly at his side, along the threadbare, elbow-patched winter coat that he'd had since Berlin.

"I like your tie," Miss Loudon said shyly.

He ran his hand down the red silk self-consciously. It had been a holiday gift from Boris and was the nicest piece of his wardrobe by a long shot, if he didn't count his uniform.

"Thank you. You remember Mr. Grinberg? He gave it to me."

"He has good taste."

"Who is that, darling?" Mrs. Marvin asked.

"A pawnshop owner," Miss Loudon said.

"The night watchman is friends with a pawnshop owner?" Mr. Marvin said crossly. "That seems like a recipe for trouble."

Ivan didn't want the man's temper to go south again. "His shop is on the street where I live. He took your brooch."

"I see." Marvin clicked his tongue against his upper teeth. "Well, Alecia, have a good afternoon with your swain."

She smiled politely, then looked at Ivan. He was glad to have a cue to exit and made his goodbyes.

"I couldn't wait to leave," he admitted as they reached the lift.

She spoke haltingly. "Was Sybil making you uncomfortable? I wish she hadn't told you I was wearing her clothing, but then you've seen everything I own." When she twisted her hands together, he could see she was nervous.

"We're young and we don't have any money, either of us. Still, you weren't at Boris's pawnshop for your own benefit."

She giggled as the lift operator gestured them in. "True. Where are we going?"

He liked the cheerful sound. "To the park, I think. It's a nice day for the season."

She nodded.

Was she enthusiastic enough? "Unless you wanted to go to the pictures? Or there might be a tea dance somewhere. We could ask the concierge."

"No, I'm dressed for the outdoors." She tucked her hands into her borrowed coat's pockets. "This coat is smarter than my dress anyway."

Alecia perused Ivan as they left the hotel on the Park Lane side. His clothing was shabby but it didn't matter. His shoulders were heroically broad and the lean body underneath gave the impression of coiled strength. He had the face of a film star, and his tilted black fedora made him look broody. She was glad he didn't sport a cap. She liked men in proper men's hats. His tie's pop of color gave the hint of what burned underneath, the fiery heart of a Russian.

"Why did you invite me out?" she asked, as they passed by the end of the hotel. She wanted to break Ivan's habit of silence, not to mention her own. A trio of boys ran by, chasing a dog. They nearly spun an older lady around in a full circle. The woman grabbed her chest and puffed.

Ivan reached for the woman's arm. "Are you well?"

The woman coughed. "Yes, dear boy, thank you."

Ivan let go of the woman and regained his position next to Alecia. "Do you mind?"

She admired how casually he'd helped the woman. But given that they were all but on hotel property, he probably had to for the sake of his position. "No, I've just never been on a proper city date before. I don't know what one does."

"This, I suppose." He thrust his hands into his pockets.

Was he uncomfortable? Shy? "Shall we look at the magazines?" she asked, pointing to a news stall.

"If you like." They ambled toward it. He picked up a newspaper and she reached for *Punch*.

They read for a couple of minutes, her shoulder touching his arm. She was acutely aware of him, that scent of cucumber and birch already so familiar. A cartoon struck her as funny and she giggled.

"What?"

She showed him the page, reading aloud. "'Pavement Winter Sports. For those who cannot get away to Switzerland.'"

"Roller skates," he said, looking at the drawing. "I've never done that. We ice-skated as children, of course."

"In Russia, how could you not?" she agreed. "Oh, look at this. An article called 'This Green Winter.' It's true, isn't it? London is all water and mud right now."

"We won't be skating on the Serpentine, that's for certain," he agreed. "Would you like the magazine? I'll buy it for you."

"Oh, you know I'll find it lying around the hotel somewhere this week. And anyhow, I wouldn't want to carry it while we're walking."

"Very well. Shall we go to the coffee stand and then walk down to the water?"

"Coffee sounds wonderful. Your nose isn't even red, but I imagine mine is a fright."

"No. I like what winter does to girls' faces. Red cheeks, a little sparkle in the eye. Very appealing." He glanced at her, then looked away.

"And all bundled up," she reminded him as she set down the magazine.

"In fur," he retorted, with a smile.

"It's stunning, isn't it?" She caressed the fox collar of Sybil's coat.

"You want luxury?"

"I want new clothes. I'm tired of my drab homemade rags."

"Do you want to be an actress?" he asked. "Is that why you took the job, to have an in?"

"No, I didn't really have an ambition, other than to be a modern girl, not a Victorian relic. It would be so easy to stay with my grandfather and be his helper and live like that."

He took a moment before he spoke again. "So you want to go to the pictures and dance all night?"

"It's not the worst idea," she said. "We're young. Being young doesn't last very long. I feel like I've already wasted most of my time. I'm twenty-two."

He stared at the wall of magazines, but she didn't think he saw any of it. "I'm twenty-six."

"Your life was dreadfully interrupted by the war," she said.

"Yours too. It sounds as if your parents were rather different from your grandfather. What was your life like before?"

"Books, conversation. Rather thrilling ones, sometimes, about ideas. But I was only twelve when they died, so I didn't understand much of it. Lots of dinner parties with writers. Nothing to do with theater or artists or anything. It wasn't like Bloomsbury or Chelsea, but still, a lot different from life in a vicarage."

"I'm sorry. It sounds like you were happy." He tilted his head toward the street and she followed him.

"Oh, very. What about you?"

"We mostly lived a country life. My mother's lungs were weak, so we didn't spend that much time in Moscow. We had tutors and played outdoors."

They walked up to the wheeled caravan that comprised the coffee stall. Ivan paid for two coffees and dispensed the hot drink from the large urn.

"This will take the red out of my cheeks," she teased.

"Oh, don't say that, Miss Loudon." He winked.

She couldn't help repeating her question. "You didn't really say why you wanted to take me out. I would think you'd be sleeping still, at this time of day."

"It's about three now, I think." He sipped at his coffee. "You're right. I would be, for another hour or two. It's hard, sharing with my sister. When her friends are around they make a lot of noise."

"You need to stop up your ears."

"I go and sleep on the sofa in the back of the pawnshop," he told her.

She made a noise to suggest he continue.

"As for you, miss, I simply wanted to speak to you outside of the hotel, get to know you better when we weren't under the eye of my fellow employees. Or employers. I wanted to know about you and Mr. Eyre . . ." He trailed off suggestively.

"There's nothing to tell," she protested. "Goodness, one dance on New Year's Eve. And he has a girl."

"I think that is over," he said. "I had that impression yesterday."

"Ah." She remembered Sybil's long disappearance and couldn't help but agree.

"What?"

"Oh, nothing." She put her cup to her lips.

He lifted his eyebrows. "Are you interested?"

If Ivan only knew how she'd ogled him. "In Mr. Eyre? No. He's a wonderful dancer. I'd dance with him again, but I was playing a role, in a way, that night. I don't normally go to nightclubs; in fact, that was the first time. And I wore Sybil's clothes."

"A lot of girls wouldn't care. They'd just be happy to be at Maystone's."

"I'm too self-conscious, maybe," she said. "Too ordinary."

He shook his head slowly. "I don't think so. Much too pretty."

She put her free hand to her cheek. "Now you're going to make me blush."

"You know you look your best with red cheeks," he said, leaning closer. She could smell the coffee on his warm breath.

Mesmerized by his mouth, she forgot her coffee cup, only righting it as it was about to spill. "I need to finish this before it gets cold," she said quickly, then lifted the cup.

He drank his as well, then offered her his arm. She took it with alacrity, never having walked any street on a man's arm before. It felt daring and freeing and young, something her sister might do, not herself. She loved it, picturing the image she made to others: a handsome man, a girl in the latest fashion, at Hyde Park Corner. Yes, she could have hugged herself, and did her best to memorize every detail. The feel of his strong arm underneath her glove, the faintest hint of beard on his cheek, the patch on the elbow of his coat. The passersby, not as fashionable as one might expect, but everyday Londoners out for a midwinter walk in the park before it grew dark. Not freezing, no rain, no fog. What else could you ask for in early January?

"Shall we go into the park?" he asked.

She hesitated, still memorizing the scene.

"What are you waiting for?"

"I was just thinking this is a perfect moment."

His arm twitched. "How could it be?"

She didn't understand how he could think otherwise. Had London ceased to impress him after everything he'd been through to come here? "What do you mean?"

"There hasn't been a kiss. It's not romantic without a kiss."

Her skin tingled. She focused on his mouth. "You don't think so?"

His smile was sly. "You haven't been kissed enough to learn that, I suppose."

He was teasing her. "How many girls have you kissed?"

His gaze drifted over her head. "More than I can remember, back home. Between sixteen and eighteen I kissed as many pretty girls as I could. I thought of little else."

"Wartime," she commented.

"I suppose. We were all desperate for distraction as our world fell apart. I was too young for any serious thoughts, not like my father, or my oldest sister."

"So it was your parents and two older sisters."

"By then."

She sensed a world of sorrow in that remark. Had he an older brother who died in the war? So many did. She thought of the Latin-cross memorial on High Street in Bagshot, and the forty-nine names listed. One family had lost three of their young men. Others had lost two. She had been lucky to only have a sister, she supposed. The deaths of her parents had come early in the war, before everyone was numb to loss and there was no point talking about grief anymore.

He put his free hand over the hand that still loosely clasped his arm. "I've lost you, Miss Loudon. Where did you go?"

Four smokestacks, always four smokestacks. Had she slept at all last night? The dream had come again. She shook the remembered nightmare away. "I wish it was colder and we could skate on the Serpentine. It does happen some years, I believe."

"There are indoor rinks. Do you want to go to one?"

"No. Let's walk."

He nodded. They crossed the busy street into the park and found a path through elms and chestnut trees, leading to the man-made river.

"It's a good thing hemlines are higher these days, with all of this mud," she commented.

"It's hard to imagine snow," he agreed. He slid her hand down his arm onto the palm of his glove and laced their fingers together.

Wind rustled through the leafless trees. Branches crackled and she shivered. "If my grandfather could see this, I would receive such a talking-to," she told him, because she didn't think Ivan was at all serious about her.

"At least I could say, quite sincerely, that no matter how wayward my youth was, I've been an angel since." He sounded glib, despite the Russian accent that made most of his pronouncements seem so serious.

She moved a little closer to him, feeling his heat radiating through her body. Her neck was warm because of the fur collar, but she needed more layers under the coat. "No girls in Berlin or Paris?"

"Or Helsinki. Definitely not there."

"Nor London? No girls in eight years?"

"Girls don't like boys with heavy accents and no money. If I'd had a title, count or prince or such, I could have changed my fate."

She liked his accent very well. Silly, prejudiced girls. "You aren't secretly Count Ivan?" she teased.

"My grandfather was a count," he said, surprising her. "But I'm two generations a younger son, and it's all gone now, that world."

Such sad words. They had both lost their childhood certainties completely. "Will you ever return to Russia?"

"Never." They turned onto the path along the river. "That cousin of mine, the Russian diplomat who is coming to the Grand Russe?"

"Yes?"

"I cannot feel my sister and I would ever be safe in a place where he has power."

She didn't understand his point. "Why do you blame him for killing your family?"

"He informed on them. My parents had done nothing wrong, but you can be sure Georgy enjoyed stealing their possessions."

"It is unfortunate that diplomats move around."

"Indeed they do. I hope he does not hold his post long. He's not an honest or honorable man, which makes me even more certain that the present government of my homeland is not good."

She couldn't help but think such a topic was not a wise one for this occasion. How could she lighten up the conversation? "I came down here on Christmas morning to see the Peter Pan Cup swimming competition at the Serpentine," Alecia said.

"I did too," Ivan said, after a pause. "It was just after my shift ended. I was happy to be a spectator rather than a participant."

She grinned at him. Without thinking, she squeezed his hand.

Ivan felt the pressure of Miss Loudon's small hand in his and took it as an invitation. He sought to remember his techniques for kissing girls, back in the old days. Did the actions of a callow boy have any value to a sober man of twenty-six?

He pulled his pretty blond date off the path, leading her to a large tree, skeletal in its winter nudity, but wide enough to hide them from the passersby on the path. She leaned against it without prompting, and lifted her chin.

Was she hoping to be kissed? Her soft pink lips were gently parted, but her eyes were still open. The girls he remembered always closed their eyes, a clear signal. He licked his wind-chapped lips, still tasting the coffee on them. Her gaze fixed there, then she bit her own lip.

He groaned at her unconscious sensuality, unable to help himself, and leaned in.

Crack! A noise over his head startled Ivan into action. He grabbed Alecia's arm and hauled her into the clearing between the trees. A heavy branch hung down on the tree she'd been leaning against. He heard a scraping sound as the many-fingered tip of the branch bounced against the tree trunk. The entire branch collapsed, plummeting to where Miss Loudon had been standing a second before.

"What?" she whispered breathlessly. Her eyes were huge on his, then she swiveled around and saw what had happened. She shrieked, putting her hand to her lips. Another gust of wind tore through the stand of trees.

"We had better go back to the bank of the river and stay on the footpath," he said.

"You saved me," she gasped.

To his shock, she flung her arms around his neck. His hands went up instinctively, cradling her cheek and the back of her close-fitting hat. Their lips met, and he forgot about the danger.

She had an untutored kind of passion. He knew she'd never kissed anyone but him, and the thought made him bold. He would teach her. His lips moved against hers, forgetting the dangers. He changed angles, realigned his hands, teaching her the tastes and touches of open-air necking. Breeze danced across the bare back of his neck and whipped tendrils of her hair from its bun. She showed no signs of fear. Her fingers moved up and down his arms. Growing impatient for a touch of her fingers, he released her mouth and, staring at her, pulled off one of her gloves and set her fingers against his cheek. Openmouthed, with puffy, rosy lips, she stroked his cheekbone with flattering intentness.

"I feel so warm," she said, then dipped her index finger into the tiny indent on his chin. When she touched his lower lip, he nibbled at her finger, making her giggle.

Bolder now, he sucked her finger in. When she didn't protest, he used his tongue, swirling it around her long, slim digit, their gazes locked.

Wind buffeted them, but he scarcely noticed. He wrapped his arms around her, pulled her close, dipped in for another kiss. This time, he offered her a more overt carnality. When her mouth opened beneath his, with all the sweetness of new beginnings, he gently explored her with his tongue.

"Oh!" She bent her head back, disengaging. "You did that with my finger."

"Yes. Did you like it?" Lower down, his erection raged. He wanted to press against her. Her coat was as much armor as any pre-war fashion from a Russian winter. She probably couldn't even tell how excited he was by her taste and touch. Did she know what it meant for a man to be fiery hot and hard?

"I-I don't know, exactly." Her bare hand went to her lips. Then she pressed it against his. "I'm overwhelmed."

Disappointment warred with arousal. "We should move away from these trees."

"I could have been killed."

He nodded.

"That would be a story for the papers. Young woman dies on her first date." Her expression became solemn. "You'd be a bad luck man."

"Doomed to wander London alone forever?" he asked.

She pressed stray locks of hair back under her hat. "Someday, we'd haunt the hotel. At least I would. They'd tell our legend late at night. Some other girl listening to the nightclub music would come across some other night watchman and they'd shiver together."

"You're a funny girl. Maybe you are a storyteller."

"I don't know what I am, really, except a girl with a little more experience of life than I had previously."

"One near-death experience," he prompted.

"And kisses. Real kisses." She smiled. "I'd like you to do that with your tongue again."

He smiled back, but then the wind gusted. The coiled hair at the back of her neck, just peeping out from her hat, lost its battle with gravity and looped over the fur collar of her coat. A pin dropped to the damp grass. The bottom of her coat waved. She had to shift to keep her balance.

"Maybe the river is the wrong place to go," he said, picking up her pin.

"We don't want to go back to the hotel," she protested.

"No, it's early yet." He still had nearly all the money that Mr. Dew had given him. "How about a movie? We could have popcorn."

"What is playing?"

"I wanted to see *The Sea Hawk* if it is still in a theater. I remember the poster because the boat looked almost Russian." He handed her the pin and she started coiling her thick hair, trying to get it back into order.

Such old-fashioned hair. Not practical for a secretary. He'd tell her to get it cut, but he liked the look of it too much. "I read about that. They used real ships."

Movies weren't an indulgence he usually set money aside for. But they had to get out of this wind.

"You don't have to pay for me," she said.

He felt bad for hesitating. He wanted to show Miss Loudon a good time, but so far, she was more interested in him than politics, and he needed to find out what side she—and more importantly, her employers—were on. "I had a bonus," he said, thinking quickly. "For finding a petty thief's cache at the hotel."

"How nice," she exclaimed, as another gust of wind came through. "Goodness, it's getting worse."

He took her arm. "Let's go quickly then."

They returned to one of the main paths and walked out of the park with rapid steps. He glanced up at the sky and saw the clouds were coming in, thick and gray. Would they bring rain or snow? They weren't expecting snow. Maybe it was just the wind.

"This reminds me of a really terrible day."

"It does?" she asked.

"Sorry. I didn't realize I said that out loud." He sighed.

"What happened?"

"First of all we had better decide where to go."

"There are a lot of movie palaces, but I haven't been to any in London. Which is your favorite?"

He laughed. "There is the Rivoli. It's grandiose, enormous. I took my sister there for her birthday. They even have a café and the uniforms rival ours at the hotel."

"Really?"

"Yes, you'd fit right in, a pretty little blonde like you. They wear blue pageboy tunics, short skirts, and patent-leather leggings, with white gauntlets on their arms and jaunty peak caps on their blond heads. All girls. They open the doors."

"It sounds very smart."

"Yes, it's in the East End, though. We don't have time to go there before I have to be at work."

"Why don't we go to a café? You should eat before you have to work."

He thought he'd like a nap in some disused corner of the hotel before he started his shift, one of the valet dens. If only he could persuade Miss Loudon to lend him her bed.

"You have a funny kind of look on your face," she observed.

Little did the untutored girl know what he had on his mind. His first time dating an English girl and she just had to have been raised by a vicar.

Chapter Eight

"Let's go to the closest A.B.C.," Alecia said, "and warm up."

"Yes, we should be indoors," Ivan agreed after a glance at her wind-pale skin and very pink cheeks. He took her arm to pull her along, trying to shield the remnants of her hairstyle from collapsing.

They walked from the park to Piccadilly Circus, buffeted by wind, and were blown into the busy tea shop. Soon, they were huddled over hot chocolate and scrambled eggs.

"Such luxury," she said happily. "I know the service at the hotel is superior, but this is fun. I used to dream about this sort of thing."

He smiled. "I lived a very country life in Russia for the most part. Nothing like this industrialization."

"What was your terrible day that you remembered?" she asked. "Was it in Russia?"

He could feel a frown line appear between his brows. "Yes. There, of course, the rivers freeze every year and we used to skate every day. Skate, sled, all sorts of winter fun. I was the oldest boy in the family, but I had a younger brother."

She set her fork down. "Oh, I didn't realize."

"His name was Sergei, just like my sister's fiancé." He smiled wistfully. "We were skating one day in early spring. We thought we understood the ice, but I guess we weren't paying attention."

She winced. "It broke?"

His hand trembled as he reached for his cup. "I saw the cracks. I called out. But he was an athlete, a daredevil. Far away from me. He was gone before I could fall on my belly and reach out my hand."

"Were you all alone?"

All his breath expelled. His answer came out in mere a whisper of sound. "Yes."

"How old were you?"

"Sixteen. He was thirteen." He put his mouth to his cup, then set it down without drinking.

"And after that you started kissing all those girls."

She sounded so wise. "I needed a distraction."

"What are you trying to distract yourself from now?"

Her gaze was keen, now. How had she picked up on a subtext he hadn't realized? "I'm worried about Ovolensky coming."

She leaned forward. "Do you think he can hurt you or your sister?"

"Maybe."

"My employers are going to be entertaining that dreadful man." She sighed and picked up her fork again.

The top of his hot chocolate had gone scummy. He forked up the rest of his eggs quickly before they went cold and greasy. "It's nothing to do with you."

"I pawned that brooch to get money for costumes," she said. "I'm sorry to be any part of it."

He hadn't had the time to ask Vera about it yet. "They are just the entertainers, right? It's not like they support Stalin."

"No, I wouldn't think so. They are very proud of having played for Romanovs before the war."

"I am glad to hear it." He didn't think she had any knowledge of what was going on with his sister and her group. Surely she wasn't the inside person. Nor did it sound like the Marvins, in her opinion, would be likely conspirators. He needed to learn more about their colleagues involved in the project, and also about hotel staff who were involved in the performance.

But if she wasn't knowledgeable, he had no reason to court her, and he wanted to see her again. She was sweet and sexy.

"What?" she asked.

He realized he'd been staring. "My next day off is Friday."

"A long time from now."

"You don't have any days off at all," he pointed out.

"Sybil won't be difficult."

"I wouldn't be so sure about her husband."

"No," she agreed. "Sybil promised me he wouldn't cause me any trouble, but I'm not sure I believe it."

He considered her words, a sense of unease building as he thought it through. "He has a strong personality and a lot of charisma. She may not know what he's up to, if he intimidates people into following his orders."

She blinked. "Truly, it's all been fine so far."

He nodded, hoping it stayed that way. "I do have a genuine interest in your well-being now."

"That's nice to hear. London is a lonely place for someone with no friends."

"You have one now."

They smiled at each other.

"Let's plan to meet every night around midnight in the service corridor," he suggested. "As long as my assignment doesn't change, I can easily see you then."

She licked her upper lip. "What will we do?"

He wanted to reach for her hand across the table, but they were in the middle of a crowded café, full of respectable ladies, and he didn't want dirty looks. "Well, there was that night, with that married couple on the sofa near the door."

Her face went crimson. "You want to do that?"

Yes. Luckily the word did not pass his lips. "I simply meant we can sit there."

Her eyes narrowed. "I'm not sure I believe you." The tip of her tongue darted out to lick her lips again.

He wondered if she was as aroused as he was, or did she simply have chocolate on her mouth? How far would she be willing to enter into the flapper lifestyle? Sadly, with their work responsibilities, it would be hard to find out. In one way, they had the benefit of being able to see each other often, but there was no real privacy in the situation.

"You want to hear the music." He shrugged. "I want to see you. We'll pass a few minutes together each night. Meanwhile, you can work on Sybil to give you some free time on Friday."

"After just having given me Monday afternoon."

"Try to have the evening off," he suggested, holding back a yawn. "That's fair. You can't be expected to work sixteen hours a day."

"Do you have time to go home and take a nap before you have to work?"

He looked at the clock on the wall. It was past five already. Somehow he'd lost more than an hour, sitting here with her. "There are rarely any valets or maids on the fourth floor. I'll nap in one of the hotel dens."

"Then I'll see you tonight," she said.

"Midnight. It's a date," he said, wishing she was the sort of girl who would invite him back to her room.

As Alecia waited for Ivan deep in the night, she realized she had hoped for more than yet another midnight hallway assignation from a man who'd taken her on a proper date and kissed her so thoroughly. But Ivan had been in a rush when he'd seen her the night before. He'd said a pack of Gypsies were roaming the main floor and who knew what they were planning to steal. She told him to go, not wanting him to risk his position by staying with her when there was mischief afoot.

Tonight, though, she'd borrowed one of Sybil's dresses, with her approval. Black, like the night, but with silver embroidery and crystals that made the dress seem like a starry sky. It was loose and flowy and it made her want to dance. Sybil and Richard were out to dinner with a director they knew. They hoped to drum up some more work for one or both of them, and she knew they planned to give the director an invitation to the command performance. She'd picked up their share of the engraved invitation cards today and they had argued all afternoon about who would be best to invite. The decision was between people who might give them work and people who might increase their general prestige.

She had listened carefully and hadn't heard any Russian names bandied about. It didn't seem like they had any ties to people who might want to do the diplomat any harm. After Richard had gone to take a bath, she'd asked Sybil about every name she didn't recognize on their guest list, assuming the woman would think she was trying to learn more for her work. Sybil answered all of her questions, and now she was gaining insight into the theatrical personalities of London.

She heard the tinkle of the piano start up behind the nightclub door and rose from the sofa to hear the music better. Listening to the entire band was more fun, but this piano player was extremely talented. Maybe she should learn how to play jazz piano. She pressed her ear to the door as she tried to identify the tune.

"May I have this dance, miss?"

She smiled and turned around. Here was her brave Cossack. "How much does that coat weigh?" she asked.

He pulled her into a fox-trot hold. "Why?"

"I've been working on costumes all afternoon with Sybil. Weight is important. It can help you embody, or ruin, a character because it changes how you move as an actor."

"Ah. I need to look imposing as a night guard." He puffed up his chest.

She giggled. "I happen to know these shoulders are broad, even without this beautiful coat on them."

"All the better to lead you." He danced her down the corridor, then moved the few paces to the opposite wall to dance her back toward the music.

"Such masculine shoulders," she murmured, wishing she could run her hands over them. She missed a step and tripped before righting herself.

He firmed his grip on her. "Why, Miss Loudon, I don't believe you've caught me out of my clothing." He paused. "Yet."

"You're going to make me blush." She remembered that night at the end of the year, the bride's dress riding up, the groom fumbling with his pants. And there was that very sofa where she had witnessed the scene, right in front of them.

Ivan didn't stop at the sofa. He spun her, and began to dance in place. She matched his footwork, too caught up to think. When he spun her again, she laughed, running with him down the corridor until they were out of the music's range again.

By the time they returned, the piano solo had ended and the full band had begun to play. "Ooh, a tango. Can you tango?" she asked.

He changed their hold and bent so that his cheek touched hers. "I'm a regular Valentino."

She didn't really know how to tango herself, but she had seen *The Four Horsemen of the Apocalypse* seven times. It seemed her Russian had seen it as well, for Ivan took her through many of the same steps she remembered from that four-year-old movie. She kicked with him, knelt, touched toes. They moved completely out of time with the music, laughing all the way.

But then, he pulled her to him in the move Valentino had done so deliciously. Her body weight leaned against him from the knees up. Instead of a proper hold, in naughty abandonment, she wrapped her left arm around his neck, feeling his pulse beat an exquisite rhythm against her skin. Her head fell back into what seemed like a perfect kissing position.

His mouth came down on hers, hard and soft at the same time. He plundered the inner recesses of her mouth with his tongue. One hand still held hers, but the other, high up on her torso, slid until it touched the lower slope of her breast.

She gasped and pulled back, the skin of her breast tingling. The rest of her body had gone liquid with desire. She couldn't close her mouth; it felt too swollen with his kiss.

"More," she groaned softly, and wrapped both of her arms around his neck. His hat fell to the carpet. He pushed her up against the wall and took her mouth again. This time, she tried to match him, caress for caress. He stroked her tongue and she touched his delicately, making him moan in return. She was damp, needy, desperate, a woman desired by this man.

She felt heat against her belly, and knew nothing more than the need to get him out of his coat. *His coat.* He was on duty. She could cost him his position.

The thought acted on her like cold water splashed over her head. Her hands went to his shoulders and pushed. She realized the music was out of hearing. Blinking, she saw they were out of the service corridor, nearly into the main lobby of the hotel. And people were there, passing by. She stumbled back, wondering what might have been seen.

"I'm so sorry," she said. "We never should have tangoed."

He wiped his mouth, touched his tousled, overlong hair. "It does stir the passions."

She backed up and he followed her, a dangerous glint in his eye. Was this what her grandmother had warned her about so many times? The male beast, once aroused, becomes unpredictable, and this was why such things were best saved for after marriage.

Her grandmother hadn't been talking about the tango. She should have been.

"Did you like tangoing with me, Miss Loudon?" he asked, staring hard at her mouth.

"Are you asking me about the dance or the kisses?" she asked, still backing up.

He bent down and picked up his hat in one graceful motion. "Both, but then, we've kissed before."

"You're a dangerous man, Ivan Salter."

"Why?" He was breathing hard.

"You make me feel things I never have before," she whispered.

"Surely you've felt like this, even if only when watching a Valentino movie."

"I feel twitchy and excited and desperately uncomfortable," she admitted. "I don't know what to do about it."

He curled a finger under her chin and lifted it up. "That's desire, my dear jazz baby. You want to go to bed with me."

"I do?"

"I want that too."

"You do?" What a stupid thing to say. As soon as he'd said it, she knew he was right. He wanted to put his man part into her woman part, and that was right where she ached and tingled the most. She was wet through her clothes. Oh, she wanted to stamp her foot in frustration. She needed to know more and he was the wrong person to ask.

He smiled, a curve of those full, perfect berry lips, so knowing, so exciting, so lethal to her senses. She wanted to wrap her arms around him again, but instead she drew her battered sense of self around her like a shawl and pointed to his coat.

"You are still on duty," she reminded him.

"I'm off at eight A.M. I could come to your room."

Dark spots flashed before her eyes. The mere thought utterly overwhelmed her. "My room is right next to Richard's. If he heard anything, I could lose my job. I'd have to return to Bagshot immediately. I've less than a month's pay."

"Don't panic." He took one of her hands and squeezed it between his. "You aren't ready. I understand. But there are plenty of nooks and crannies in this hotel. When you want to make love with me, I'll find somewhere completely safe."

She found her mouth had fallen open and she snapped it shut.

He frowned. "It does trouble me though, that you don't feel your bedroom is private. Which one is it?"

"The valet's room for Richard. Sybil's maid has the other room."

"You keep the interlocking door bolted, right?"

"At night."

He nodded.

"But they knock if they need something. I can be up quite late mixing drinks if they have friends over."

"I can always find you here."

"You must not always be looking, because I'm upstairs at this hour a couple of times a week."

"And at eight? Where are you then?"

"Dragging myself out of bed."

"And Richard Marvin? Where is he at eight?"

"Asleep. He rises about nine. Sybil an hour or so after that."

"Then we'd be safe at eight." His lips curved.

She narrowed her eyes. "I won't risk either of our jobs. I'm not prepared, besides. I could have a baby. What about that?"

"There are ways. Haven't you heard of the book *Married Love*?"

She shook her head.

"Ask Sybil. She's never had a baby. I'm sure she knows all the ways."

Outrageous. "I'm not going to ask my employer how to, um, you know, not have a baby."

"Don't you have that kind of relationship? I thought you had that sort of intimacy."

"On her side perhaps, but not mine."

"I wish you had a friend you could talk to about these things."

"It won't be Sybil Marvin," she said piously. "They hired me to be a secretary, not, well, a private citizen."

He looked amused at that. "I know, you can ask Miss Plash. She'll definitely know how to get you what we need. I can take care of it too, to be honest, but you ought to know the options."

Unease crept over her. "Why, so I can take a plethora of lovers?"

"I wouldn't want you to do that, Miss Loudon. But think about it." His voice lowered to a purr. "You and me, doing a sort of delicious tango together, between the sheets. My hands on you, your mouth on mine, my body on yours. Our flesh together, all that lovely friction. You probably have no idea of what I speak."

"Have you had many lovers?" Her voice squeaked.

"I'm no virgin," he said. "Back in Russia, I admit there were more than kisses going on in the barns of the neighboring estates."

She was jealous. "It sounds like a fun, careless time."

"We were so young," he agreed. "So incredibly young."

She couldn't resist asking, "Do you remember how? I mean, to tango between the sheets?"

"I've never done it between sheets, exactly, but I want to try."

She giggled. "Why me?"

He cupped her cheeks. His gloves were hot against her skin and she wished she could pull them off, but then she'd want to kiss his hands, suck his fingers.

"You have to stop looking at me like that. I'm going to explode," he said in a curiously strangled tone.

"How?"

"Oh, you know how, don't you?"

They stared at each other. She wanted his kiss like she wanted air, but she really didn't know what he meant. She'd grown up in a vicarage.

A whistle sounded.

He didn't move for a moment, then cocked his head. "Those Gypsies," he said slowly. "Oh, forgive me, those Gypsies. I have to go help."

He let her cheeks go. She kissed the tips of his fingers as they brushed her lips.

He spoke quickly. "Can I come at eight?"

"Not until I know about, I mean, more of, *Married Love*." Her thoughts were jumbled.

"Talk to Miss Plash," he said. "I'm sorry, I have to go."

She stepped back until she was against a wall. Her head knocked against the edge of one of the Russian paintings. Ivan moved fast. Then he was gone. She was left alone with thoughts that made no sense to her. So many hungry thoughts. Sheets and bodies and some kind of mysterious apparatus that stopped babies from coming.

How had the vicarage wrapped her so completely in cotton wool all these years? She was twenty-two and he was right. She was just a baby. But a jazz baby, that was something else. It implied makeup and short skirts and high heels. Kicking them up and dancing all night long. Some of that dancing might very well take place between the sheets. And Ivan, who had been a libertine, and wanted to be one again.

But what did she want? She'd come to London hoping to be a flapper, and had found herself the same old dull girl. Ivan held out a hand to her, a promise of a different kind of life, but what kind of a future did that hold?

Unlike Sadie, she was a thinker. All she had to do was remember how good it felt to be held by Ivan. Wasn't that enough? Why couldn't she worry about that and nothing else?

Ivan didn't come to her room at eight that morning. The chambermaid who came to clean the rooms said there had been a lot of drama with the Gypsies. Police had been called; a chase ensued. Ivan had probably been run off his feet.

If he'd come later, Alecia wouldn't know. A bellboy had arrived at nine to announce that Max Parker wanted a word with the Marvins. She'd woken both of them and a flurry of preparations had begun. Twenty minutes later, Max had swanned in with a bottle of champagne.

"Darlings!" he said, with a flourish of his free hand. "I bring exciting news!"

"What is it, Max?" Richard said, a yawn exposing the gold molar in his lower jaw.

"*Anna Christie*," Max said portentously.

"Pulitzer Prize–winning *Anna Christie*?" Sybil warbled, staring hard at the champagne.

"Yes, my love. No more fighting for *No, No, Nanette* for you."

"What is the part?"

"Why, the lead, of course."

"Isn't she a prostitute?" Richard said, with an arch of his brow.

"What theater?" Sybil demanded.

"Alecia, my love, some glasses?" Max said.

Alecia went to the drinks cart and found some suitable flutes, and delivered them as Max popped the bottle. Sybil squealed as Alecia neatly caught the spray of liquid and bubbles in a glass. She handed out the glasses, then Max held his up in a toast.

"To the West End you go, my darling! Our star is back!"

Everyone drank, then Sybil began to fire questions. Richard had thoughts as well, but became more and more silent as the conversation progressed.

The play was due to open in March, in some smallish theater in a good location. Sybil would be very busy from now on. Alecia wondered if Sybil's affair had really begun, and how it would fare with her so busy. On the other hand, she had the excuse to be gone all hours now. Still, her own secretarial employment should be secure.

"But this isn't all my news," Max said.

"No?" Sybil said, her eyes glittering with excitement.

"Richard," Max said, trying to regain his other client's attention.

Richard had finished off at least half of the bottle on an empty stomach and already looked bleary eyed. "What?"

"Gainsborough Pictures is terribly eager to have you do a screen test for them. You only have to go to Shepherd's Bush, which is where they do the quality stuff. They are considering some Shakespeare and your name is at the top of their list, of course."

"A film?" Richard frowned.

"Precisely. They'll light you and put you on camera for this screen test. Just half a day or so of your time. You aren't in competition for a part. You won't have to sit around and watch others."

Richard rubbed his eyes. "If they treat me with the dignity a star deserves, I don't mind it. I would like to see how I fare on camera."

"Oh, Richard, we're purists," Sybil said.

"The Bard, my love," Richard responded.

Sybil sighed theatrically and rearranged her peacock-blue dress. "Oh, very well."

Alecia was merely happy good news had come for both of her employers at the same time. The busier they both were, the less she'd have to manage their emotions and personal dramas and the more she'd be a real secretary. "Congratulations!" she said quite sincerely.

Max upended the bottle into his glass and found it empty. "I should have brought two. Shall we order up some more?"

"My dearest, I have a hair appointment," Sybil said, rising. "I forgot all about it. Alecia, please call Ethel to help me dress so I can leave quickly."

"Yes, Sybil," Alecia said, glad she'd risen earlier and broken her fast. The morning had become a whirlwind and she wouldn't want to get through it with a clumsy head.

In her room, Sybil sat down at her dressing table and began opening jars. "Can you lay out a suit? Something simple. I really am having my hair done." Ethel entered with fresh underclothes.

"Of course." Alecia went to the wardrobe and hunted for something suitable.

"I saw you last night when I was coming in," Sybil said.

"Where?"

"Downstairs, darling. You were in a heavy petting session with that beautiful night watchman."

Alecia dropped the pair of shoes she'd just picked up. They hit the thick carpet and rolled apart.

Sybil chuckled. "It's fine with me that you have a boyfriend. It's not often I would need you at midnight. As long as you are awake the next morning, do what you like."

Ethel found a pair of silk stockings and handed them to Sybil, who already had suspenders on under her robe.

"Are you hoping to marry him?"

"Why?" Alecia picked up the shoes and checked the polish.

"I wouldn't want you to become pregnant by accident with your first lover."

"What?"

"You are such a baby, Alecia. Freshness pours off of you in waves."

"He suggested I read *Married Love*," she admitted.

"Oh, the next book by that author is much more useful," Sybil said. "Just tell the boy to get sheaths. It's the easiest for now. And if he's trying to put all the trouble or expense on you, well, that tells you he's the worst kind of flatwheeler."

"I think he wants me to understand," Alecia said doubtfully.

"You should understand your body. I have a diaphragm, myself, but I purchased it in the Netherlands."

"I don't even know what that is," Alecia said, as Ethel smirked and walked away with Sybil's discarded robe.

"It goes inside," Sybil said. "Would you brush my hair, please?"

Alecia took up her brush and began to stroke through Sybil's short, dark curls. She could see a couple of gray strands, but since Sybil was on her way to a hair appointment, Alecia decided not to mention them. They'd be taken care of.

She decided to match Sybil's frankness with her own. Talking to Emmaline Plash seemed so outrageous. "He wants to come to my room," she admitted.

"Richard wouldn't like that," Sybil said. "Doesn't he have a place of his own?"

"He lives with his sister in Poplar."

Sybil frowned, then quickly blanked her expression and picked up a powder puff. "That's unfortunate. Such a handsome boy, too. He probably has a great deal of experience in the bedroom. But don't have him here when Richard is in his bedroom. If we both become busy with roles, you'll be able to sneak him in. Just be patient."

Alecia nodded and set down the brush. Patience was a virtue. She had it in spades, but did Ivan? Or would he move on to the next girl while they waited for Richard to be occupied?

Chapter Nine

Alecia went downstairs with Sybil when she left for her hair appointment and picked up the mail at the reception desk. She wondered how the relationship with her employer would change now that Sybil knew a secret about Alecia's nights. And that she wanted to lose her virginity to Ivan.

She regretted telling her employer so much about her life. If only she had a decent confidante. She missed her sister. This was the first time she'd tried living without someone to talk to about absolutely everything. The problem was, Sybil had too much power over her already. She wouldn't feel secure until she had built up at least a couple of months' savings. Her salary was low, given her inexperience and that the position included room and board. When she'd taken a job that offered no real privacy or days off, she hadn't thought twice. She'd simply wanted a fresh start and to leave Bagshot. Now, she could see the job would only be tolerable long-term if the Marvins were gainfully employed and therefore busy. She sent up a prayer that Richard would pass his screen test and begin work in film as soon as the Scottish play had been performed.

Mr. Russell, the concierge, offered her a big smile when she asked for their mail. She smiled back tentatively, not sure why he had noticed her.

"Letter for you, Miss Loudon," said Hugh Moth, the reception desk clerk. "And an assortment for the Marvins." He located their cubby and pulled out the mail.

"Thank you." She saw her letter was from Sadie, the first she'd received in the New Year.

She turned away from the desk.

"Just a moment, miss, if you don't mind," Mr. Russell said, flipping up a hinged part of the front desk and stepping through.

"Yes, Mr. Russell?" She sorted the letters into a neat pile.

"Frank," he said. "I had a question for you, miss."

Bemused, she asked, "What is it?"

"Olga is the chambermaid on your floor, isn't she?"

"Yes. Very nice girl."

He grinned. His smile creased his face all over, yet also displayed how young the concierge was, with his neat, even teeth and freckled cheeks. She had yet to see a hotel employee over thirty. "I wonder if you might know when she takes her break? Have you seen when she goes into the den on your floor?"

"Sweet on her?" she asked softly.

His face reddened as he nodded. "Yes, miss."

"Well, Frank, I have no idea, but I shall figure it out and report back to you."

"Thanks! I'll owe you one."

She smiled and walked away. Having the concierge in her pocket could be a good thing. Rather than returning to her room, she ventured into the Coffee Room and helped herself to a cup of coffee from the urns and a healthy dollop of cream, then sat down with the thick envelope from her sister.

Her eyes widened as she read. Sadie had thrown over her curate suitor. That minx. Their relationship had been on tenterhooks for a while over the past summer, because Sadie had actively thwarted the curate's attempts to court Alecia over the previous year's holidays, then had made a move on him herself. And now she'd given up on him. How irritating.

Not only that, she'd left the vicarage due to the resulting tension with their grandfather. Alecia dropped the letter to the table and put her forehead into her hand.

"Bad news?"

She glanced up to see Peter Eyre standing next to her. He indicated the chair beside her and she nodded. He sat down, sending the scent of cigarettes, hair pomade, and lavender past her nose.

"It's a letter from my sister. She's broken her engagement and left our grandfather's home."

"You seem tense. Is she in danger?" He set down his cup of coffee.

Alecia considered this. "She's taken a position at an inn just outside London, between here and Bagshot."

"Doing what?"

"Chambermaid."

"You must have her work for us," he said, taking out a fancy cigarette case. "If she's as pretty as you, she'll be an asset here."

"Much prettier," Alecia said.

"Don't look so glum. I don't believe it for a moment," Eyre declared, holding out his case to her. She shook her head. "How old is she?"

"Nineteen, almost twenty."

"Older than you?" He put a cigarette to his lips.

"Don't tease. Younger, by more than two years."

"Not teasing. Your fresh face gives nothing away," he said. "How are you managing with the Marvins?"

"Very well. They both have new opportunities. We were just celebrating."

"I can smell the champagne on you. I did wonder." He winked.

"I don't usually drink so early."

"I didn't think you did, especially since you are a night owl." They traded glances.

"Does nothing escape your eyes, Mr. Eyre?"

"Not much." He took a sip from his own cup. "Do you like our coffee? You've barely touched it."

"It doesn't mingle well with the champagne," she admitted.

"I'll find you some toast," he said.

"You don't have to do that."

"It's not a problem. I'm peckish myself. Just sit and finish your letter." He walked away, lighting his cigarette.

Alecia wanted to feel pleased that Mr. Eyre was flirting with her, but she had to admit she was hung up on old feelings of sibling jealousy. Did she want her sister to work at the hotel? One thing was for certain. She'd have to make sure her relationship with Ivan was secure before letting her sister anywhere near the Grand Russe. Her sister could have Peter Eyre, if she could manage him. Alecia knew herself to be hopeless around such a sophisticate, but Ivan, despite his background, seemed to want to give her a chance. And she felt the same way.

Eyre returned with the toast and an ashtray, and asked a number of questions about Sybil's new stage role. Alecia couldn't tell if he was asking out of interest, or if he was attempting to learn about his new lover's availability. She had no idea if he and Sybil had ever been together, but she suspected Sybil had at least spent a day with someone.

She hadn't seemed upset at having a new role, though, so she must not be too carried away with her new lover. Alecia, on the other hand, found it difficult to put Ivan out of her mind for more than a few minutes at a time, even though they weren't lovers.

"Woolgathering?" Eyre asked.

She smiled. "I am. It must be the champagne."

"Let that be a lesson to you." He smiled. His expression was sophisticated, urbane, nothing like Frank Russell's farmer-boy grin.

She nodded. He put his hands on the table and stood. "I look forward to meeting your sister. Tell her to come into town on her first day off and fill out an application. I'll hire her on your word alone."

"For which floor?"

"One of the lower ones," he said. "We have a clear hierarchal system of floors. The higher up you stay, the more important the customer."

"Six residential floors," she said. She knew the building was taller than that, but it seemed some of the floors weren't used for guests. "And we're on the fifth floor, or the fourth residential floor. I suppose that means Olga is quite a trusted employee."

He looked at her with amusement crinkling the corners of his eyes. "Yes, it does. I keep meaning to give her a proper management title. Chambermaid supervisor or such. I'll start your sister on two through four, wherever there is an opening."

"Thank you. I'll write her."

Eyre smiled at her and walked away, leaving his ashtray holding the remains of his cigarette. A thin trail of smoke curled up from it. She returned to her letter. The last few lines made her sit up straight. Her grandfather was coming to London? On Friday? Here? Thoughts warred between pleasure at the idea of seeing him and irritation that her resolve to pursue Ivan would have to be put aside for now.

The last thing her grandfather needed to see was his responsible oldest granddaughter behaving like a *flapper*. She hiccupped, tasted champagne. Maybe she'd become more of a modern girl than she realized. She reached for her toast.

"Wake up, sleepyhead." Ivan heard his sister, speaking English in her thick accent, distantly. He moved his hand and discovered he'd placed a pillow over his head at some point. He'd attempted to block out the sound of her doing dishes at midday.

Vera put a cup of tea on the crate that served as her bedside table. He sat up on her bed, not the easiest thing to do on the old, sagging mattress, instantly suspicious. She'd been with her friends when he'd come home again, so he'd hidden in the bedroom and fallen asleep, too tired to care about the noise.

Gesturing to the tea, he asked, "What is this for?"

"You look at it as if it was poison." She tossed her hair back. Her black locks were longer than the average flapper hairdo and hid her thin neck.

"Do you blame me?"

"We need your help. The best way to finish off Georgy for once and for all is a bomb. Pavel knows someone who can make it. All you have to do is put it under Georgy's chair before the performance."

His throat went dry. He picked up the tea and drained the cup. The leaves had been used before, and he missed the smoky taste of the tea back home. Why now, when samovars and Russian tea had been lost to him so many years before?

"You would risk my life, carrying a bomb, to kill our cousin?" he asked.

"The bomb maker is a professional. There's no risk to you."

"There is always a risk." Surely she understood that.

Her eyes glittered. "We must have revenge."

"I won't be scheduled to work during the time the performance is being set up," he said, moving to practicalities, something more real than bombs.

"You could change your shift."

He put his hands to his eyes. "My day off, perhaps, but not my hours from night to day."

"You can go in to visit a friend," she suggested. "I know you have friends in the staff."

"I have people I converse with, but they work at night as well."

She stomped her foot. "We need to put the bomb under his chair."

He didn't like the out-of-control emotion she displayed. "How many people will that kill?" he asked. "How many innocent people, like our parents, do you want to die?"

"And our sister," she shot back.

"Catherine wasn't innocent. She was involved with Fanny Kaplan and her group."

"Lenin needed to die."

"So Trotsky could take his place? Or Stalin? Once the tsar was gone, Russia was always going to go to hell. Swapping leaders does no good."

"We must avenge our parents!" she shouted.

"Not at the cost of innocent lives," he said. "A bomb is not the answer. You used to know right from wrong, Vera. Remember our parents. They would not want this."

She stiffened. "Our family honor is at stake."

"No innocent lives," he repeated.

She put her head on his cheek. Her skin felt cold. "Don't you want Russia to be free again?"

He thought of Alecia. "I'm British now. I don't care about Russian oppression."

She poked him with her fingernails. "That is a lie. You love our country."

"I'm never going back. We fought too hard to have a life here."

"At least come to our meeting this afternoon. Help us think of a way to kill him without risking innocent lives." She chewed on her lip. "I hadn't thought about you working nights and not days. Maybe we need another Russian employee in our circle. There are Russians on the day shift at the Grand Russe. Can you make a list?"

"Yes, I can do that." If they could get someone to join, he ought to know. Bad seeds could be weeded out from the employees. He'd turn himself into an informer to survive, like many of his people had.

"Thank you."

He wondered who their insider was, this person who knew facts about the command performance yet had no ability to bring a bomb into the room, wherever the performance ended up being held. Maybe that person wasn't at the Grand Russe at all, but in the prime minister's office. Or among the Russian diplomats. But he remembered the brooch.

"Vera, do you remember a brooch of Mother's? Mother of pearl, in a bird shape? Rather cunning, really. There's a baby bird in a nest with eggs and the mother is feeding it?"

Vera nodded. "Yes, she had a set of three, with different gemstones. I liked them when I was a child, but I didn't have any of them with me when we went to the wedding."

"Did the kitchen maid who brought us things after Mother's death bring us any of the brooches?"

Vera shook her head. "No."

"Would Mother have given one to an actress after a performance?"

"Goodness, what a question. No, I shouldn't think so. Father might have, though, if he didn't think Mother would miss the piece. He did like actresses."

Ivan's eyebrows lifted. "He did?"

Vera nodded absently. "I must go. I have to meet Sergei." She walked out of the room without looking back.

Ivan dropped his head into his hands as he realized how little he knew about his own parents. He'd never had the chance to know them as an adult, but he found it hard not to judge a man who might have given his wife's jewelry to an actress. Unless Vera was lying.

Alecia stared glumly into her wardrobe. The day before had been such a busy, flustering one, with Sybil dragging Alecia in her wake all afternoon as she searched for the perfect dress to wear to her first meeting for the play *Anna Christie*. Sybil had returned from her hair appointment positively buzzing with ideas for a tawdry, modern dress, something that made sense for a prostitute to wear.

Alecia had lost any innocence she still maintained about scanty underthings during the excursion. For years, she'd knitted her own underclothes, but now she discovered an erotic, delicate world of satins and crepe. Sybil wanted corselettes to smooth out her shape, but Alecia, after viewing the offerings at a high-end shop, wanted to make a set of step-ins for herself. So elegant, but she couldn't afford a new dress, much less fabric for underclothes. If she ever had an opportunity to undress for Ivan, he'd have to accept her underthings as they were. In some cases, she suspected her hand-knitted camiknickers were nicer than her dresses. She'd made a couple of new sets of underthings in November when she wasn't working.

She had drooled over the black lace negligee Sybil bought herself as a gift. The V-shaped waist and voluminous all-lace skirt took ten years off of Sybil's figure, making her look positively girlish. Alecia wondered if Richard would see it, or Sybil's still mysterious lover.

After Sybil dropped the equivalent of three months of Alecia's pay on underclothes, they went to an exclusive dress shop owned by the daughter of a Peer. They found a black-and-white checked dress with an all-white bodice. Sybil said the fabric looked cheap, which was exactly what she wanted. With white stockings and gloves, she would feel her new character coming to life.

Next, they went to find a hat, though, thankfully, Sybil wore out before she had the idea of looking for shoes. She'd spent over an hour in the milliner's shop alone, and never thought to stop for tea. Alecia suspected that Sybil would be watching her figure very carefully from now on. No more cream teas in the Chinese Suite.

After all that, and nothing but salad and wine for dinner, Alecia did such a rare thing. She fell asleep, clothed, on her bed, at eleven P.M. At the time, she'd planned to look through her small wardrobe and pick out something nice to wear to meet her grandfather, as if such a thing existed. She was beginning to hope Sybil would dump her wardrobe and buy new, but of course, Ethel, Sybil's maid, would get those clothes, not Alecia. No, she was forced to rely upon herself for clothing. And she wouldn't be paid until Friday, the same day her grandfather would arrive. Not that he'd expect to find her looking smart. He'd probably rather have her money for the church's roof fund. But she wasn't going to give him one shilling. She needed new clothes. Shopping with Sybil wouldn't bear any fruit for herself, however. She needed a more modest type of store.

With her head spinning along these lines, she'd relaxed her head against her pillow for a moment, before starting her foray into her wardrobe. Her eyes drifted closed and she'd lost her chance to see Ivan that night.

Today had been quieter. Sybil had drifted off to her meeting with the producers, and Richard had been busy with calls after dictating several letters. He'd sent her to a costume shop in the afternoon, but she'd been at liberty after that. Sybil had never returned.

She'd had a hearty meal with Richard, with Sybil gone, then returned to her room since he didn't seem to require company. Often, in the evenings, she'd be mixing drinks for callers, or, if they were alone, playing cards or games like chess and backgammon.

She tidied her dismal wardrobe as best she could, tightening buttons and fixing a sloppy hem. Then, at ten, she considered her meager finances. As soon as her grandfather returned home, she planned to do some shopping of her own. Should she buy a dress pattern and make her own, or buy something ready-made? She'd have to hand-sew, but it would keep her busy, and she liked to have a project for the evenings.

At eleven, she fought back a yawn and went downstairs to hear the music. Even if she beat the trouble of falling asleep, the nightmares came, four nights out of five. The ten-year anniversary of her parents' death was in May. When would she be able to let the tragedy go?

Ivan's broad back in his magnificent red coat was moving away from her as she stepped off the lift. She wanted to call his name but didn't want to make a fuss. Who knew how many people had seen them necking the other night? Instead, she turned down the corridor to the service corridor and went to the nightclub's back door.

At first, she wasn't the only one there. A courting couple sprang apart on the sofa in the corner when she came into view. This was her spot though, and she wasn't about to cede it to them. She simply pretended they didn't exist and focused on the music.

Ivan must have been at the start of his ground-floor round, because he appeared about twenty minutes later. By then, the female half of the courting couple had spoken to her, and she'd ended up sitting with them on the sofa, chatting about music. After a while, they'd danced to the music together.

Alecia stopped midstep, out of breath and laughing, when she spotted him.

"What's this?" Ivan asked in a stern voice.

"Miss Waters is teaching me a new dance called the Charleston. Her friend Mr. Perry is this gentleman."

"She has only stepped on my toes twice," said Mr. Perry cheerfully. "Are you going to order us to disperse now?"

"No," Ivan said. His face transformed. "I want to learn the dance too."

Miss Waters jumped to her feet. "I'll teach you! Step forward left, step back and tap." She repeated this several times, watching Ivan. "Now we add swivel motion and arm movements to have you dancing."

Ivan watched her closely, imitating her until Alecia giggled. He had rhythm, but he was a large and imposing man, and his version of acting like a dandy, with the head wiggling Miss Waters taught him, came across as very comical.

The four of them danced through three of the band's numbers, trading partners and dancing in a line. Ivan and Alecia kept up with the other two, picking up the simple moves they demonstrated.

"Ugh. I think the band is going on break," Miss Waters said with a pout, when another number didn't start. She adjusted her silver headband.

"Why don't you go to the club?" Ivan said. "You'll be able to teach the dancers in there a thing or two."

"No money for it," Mr. Perry said. "We spent it all on dinner. Lovely night though."

"He's such a big-timer," Miss Waters said, patting her hair.

Ivan reached into his pocket and handed him two tickets. "Passes to the club, with my compliments."

"Oooh," Miss Waters squealed. "Really?"

Ivan smiled. "New dances keep a club hopping. I wouldn't be doing my job if I didn't suggest you go in. Do you know where the entrance is?"

Mr. Perry nodded enthusiastically. "I never thought I'd like a Bolshie, but you, sir, are the bee's knees."

"He's not a Bolshie," Alecia said. "Not at all."

"My apologies then," Mr. Perry said. "Maybe we'll see you around some night."

"Oh, let me take you shopping, Miss Loudon," Miss Waters begged. "As soon as your grandfather is gone, ring me up. I'm in the book under my father. Reginald Waters."

Alecia smiled. "I would love that."

"I know all the best fabric stores," Miss Waters cooed, taking Mr. Perry's hand. "Toodle-oo, darlings!"

The couple ran off, full of energy. Alecia grinned at Ivan. "Now that's why I came to London, for a night like this."

"It's a fun dance. We might be the first nightclub to learn it," Ivan said.

"I didn't know you had passes." She gave him a mock pout.

"I couldn't send you in unescorted."

"Oh, I didn't mean you should have offered me one," she assured him. "Not at all. I think it's wonderful that you could offer it to them, though. I'm resolved to have a dancing dress soon."

"I'd love to take you dancing," Ivan said.

She wanted to squeal with pleasure, but restrained herself. Her hands clutched. "First though, as you heard, my grandfather is coming to town. Tomorrow, in fact. Would you come and have tea with us, here at the hotel? I hope that's late enough in the day that you won't have to give up your sleep."

"Of course. I'd be honored to meet the vicar." He hesitated. "Do you think he'll call me a Bolshie too?"

"He'll ask questions. He's a provincial, you know. Not like my parents. But he's a fair man, and of course, you've had no part in anything bad." She saw him wince. "It's not your fault, what your sister did, and besides, who can say what she did was wrong, really."

"It didn't do much good," Ivan said. "And it destroyed our family. I don't have any answers about this complicated business of revolution."

"You aren't political?"

His cheek twitched. "I'm a survivalist. My sister may flirt with ideals, but I'm the one making sure she has a roof over her head, and all too often, I feed her friends too."

"There have to be men like you supporting those with ideals," she said. "Everyone has to eat."

"Very true." He smiled suddenly. "I've missed you. Where were you last night? Working?"

They sat on the sofa together and she told him about her night, resting her head on his shoulder. Eventually, his fingers found his favorite spot under her chin and tilted her head so their mouths could meet. He kissed her tenderly, and separated from her far too soon. She wanted to pull him back. She wanted him to court her in earnest.

"I'm being negligent of my duties," he said. "I need to return to my rounds."

She nodded.

"I still want to come to your room some morning."

She waved her hands. "My grandfather."

"I understand. I can wait. Just don't forget."

"Sheaths," she said impulsively. "Sheaths are the easiest."

He nodded. "I can get those. But I wanted you to decide."

"For now." She blushed. They could try other things later, if she really did proceed with him.

He smiled and kissed her again, lingering at the corners of her mouth and the bow of her lips. "I like the sound of that. I can't wait to show you everything I feel. But tomorrow I will be as proper as a doting grandfather would wish."

She kissed his cheeks, his chin, but he pulled her away, in the manner of removing a clingy cat, before she could touch her lips to his neck.

"This is hard," he murmured. "I have to go but I'll see you to your room first."

"Better not," she said, feeling heavy with longing. "I might invite you in."

He shuddered. "Then go. I'll watch until you're safely on the lift."

She walked away, feeling his gaze on her, elated by the way he'd reacted to her brave words. Would she have actually done it? She rather thought she might have.

The next afternoon, she tried to force her thoughts into the purity of freshly fallen snow as she waited outside the Coffee Room for her grandfather. Cream teas were served in the room in late afternoon for an outrageous price. Her grandfather did like the best in comestibles, and even when the Grand Russe was called by another name it was known for its tea service.

Her grandfather still hadn't arrived when she saw Ivan, somewhat shabbily dressed in his daytime clothes. She wanted to take his coat off and fix the buttons. Didn't his sister take the time to care for his wardrobe?

He saw her and removed his hat and gloves, then came toward her. She wished she could run up and kiss him, but that was behavior for midnight in a service corridor, not here and now. Besides, she saw her grandfather some three yards behind him, distinguished in an old-fashioned top hat, his gray handlebar mustache marking him firmly in the Victorian mode.

Ivan grinned at her. She nodded solemnly at him as he reached her. Thankfully, he was as controlled in his impulses as she was, in the daylight. Quickly, she took Ivan's arm, then turned him around so they greeted her grandfather as a unit.

"Grandfather," she exclaimed, as he reached her.

When he saw her and smiled, she stood on her toes and kissed his cheek, already sandpapery. He smelled like citrus, a scent she always associated with him. He must have eaten an orange on the train.

"Good journey?" she asked.

He patted his chest. "Yes. I've checked into my hotel."

"You are always so organized." She realized she was still holding Ivan's arm and dropped it quickly. "I'd like you to meet my friend Ivan Salter."

She turned back to Ivan. "Mr. Salter, this is my grandfather, Harold Loudon."

"Father," he said, offering his hand.

"Mr. Salter," her grandfather said gravely as they shook. "Russian, are you?"

"Yes, sir. I've been in London for three years."

"Should we go in? We don't want to lose our reservation," Alecia said.

The men nodded and she gestured to the hostess, who handed three handwritten menus to a waiter. He took them to a small table in the area where the quartet played at night.

"Where were you raised?" her grandfather asked Ivan after they were seated.

"My parents had a house in Moscow but we mostly lived in the country in our dacha."

Her grandfather picked his napkin out of its fancy knotted shape. "In the Great War?"

Ivan echoed his gesture. "Too young, sir. I'm twenty-six."

Alecia winced as she saw the direction this conversation would take. She spread out her own napkin and searched for a way to change the conversation.

"I see. Lost two sons in the war," her grandfather said. "Alecia's uncles."

"And her parents, I understand."

"On the *Lusitania*, yes. Dreadful business, the war. I can't pass by the war memorial even now without stopping for prayer."

"Let's not talk about anything unhappy," Alecia urged. "We're just getting to know each other."

"He cannot be such a recent acquaintance if you are introducing us," her grandfather said. "I thought I'd be meeting your employers."

Chapter Ten

Alecia was caught off guard by her grandfather's intent to meet her employers. In her mind, actors and vicars did not inhabit the same space. "They are in meetings, sir. Mr. Marvin is blocking scenes for the play he is doing here, and Mrs. Marvin is meeting with the wardrobe mistress for a new play she's been cast in."

"So they are both working? I am happy to hear that. I was concerned they might not have the money to pay you." Her grandfather angled the menu away from him so he could read it.

Alecia went stiff at the mention of money. She didn't want to tithe her wages to her grandfather's church. Her wardrobe was a disgrace and she had no savings since she had used her first week's pay for Christmas gifts. Her second week's pay had gone to replenishing toiletries and other small necessary items. She should receive last week's wage sometime today.

"I think the Marvins are secure for now," she said, shifting uncomfortably. "They always had the command performance, and now Mrs. Marvin has a solid new part and Mr. Marvin has opportunities as well."

"I didn't quite understand what you were saying with all the theater jargon, but have they decided where to hold the command performance?" Ivan asked.

"Yes, on the first floor. Some of the conference rooms can be opened into one larger room, I understand. They don't need anything as large as the ballroom since it is a dignitaries-only audience."

"Are they going to build a stage?"

"One of the conference rooms has a higher floor than the other for exactly this reason."

Ivan nodded as their waiter appeared, to take their order. "I didn't know that. Fascinating how they plan these things."

"I remember when this hotel was first opened," her grandfather said. "Under the old name, of course, before the scandals. I was quite young then."

"The nineties, wasn't it?" Alecia asked.

"Yes. A rather famous family was involved. Aristocrats and wealthy merchants."

"I have wondered who Peter Eyre is, Grandfather," Alecia said. "He's the hotel manager and much too young for the job, plus he has such an air of mystery. Just the sort of person you'd twig for a secret earl or millionaire."

"And here he is," Ivan said with a faint air of distaste.

For the first time in her life, Alecia had that thrilling feeling of being caught between two suitors, as Mr. Eyre approached the table. It was hard not to contrast the two men. Ivan with his bold, foreign, dark good looks and shabby clothes; Eyre, the consummate Englishman with the fashionable clothes, golden hair, and narrow face that sounded the bell "aristocrat" to her.

Even their sexual styles were different. Eyre had a mistress but seemed to always have an eye on the next conquest. Ivan boldly propositioned a mere secretary but, for now, left the game in her hands.

"You look very cozy today, Miss Loudon," Eyre said, smiling genially at her.

"This is my grandfather," she said. "And you know Mr. Salter, of course."

"Mister Dean," Eyre said, taking her grandfather's hand.

Alecia, startled by the fact that Mr. Eyre knew how to address her grandfather properly, exchanged a glance with Ivan. How did Mr. Eyre know her grandfather was the most senior priest in his diocese?

The hotel manager exchanged a few inconsequential remarks with her grandfather and winked at Ivan before drifting to another table. She hadn't realized he policed the Coffee Room even in the daytime. He was like a ghost attached to one part of the hotel.

"You must know all the stories about this hotel, Grandfather, since you remember it from when it opened. I haven't had time to look into it much."

"I wish there was a scrapbook," Ivan said. "A history of the hotel? But if there is, it's not available to the employees. People ask me questions I don't know how to answer."

"That may be for the best, young man," her grandfather said. "This hotel gave Sodom and Gomorrah a run for its money just after the war. They say when you stayed here, you didn't even need to go to the Chinese for drugs. They'd be delivered right to your door."

Two waiters arrived, one with a tray of teapots, and the other with tiered silver trays holding finger sandwiches, scones, lemon tarts, and some kind of chocolate treat. Alecia was glad she'd skipped luncheon.

"And those famous murders?" Ivan asked.

"Theatrical people," her grandfather said. "When do they ever come to a good end?"

"I wonder that you allowed Miss Loudon to take this position with the Marvins, especially here at the hotel."

"You misunderstand, young man. She didn't ask my permission. That's the sort of modern girl she is. She and her sister both. They don't listen to their elders."

Her grandfather said this in a measured tone, but she saw a twinkle in his eye. Somewhere, beneath the starch, he enjoyed his granddaughters' independent ways. To a degree, at any rate.

The conversation moved on to Russian politics and a discussion of a British-Russian trade conference in London in the spring, which Ivan didn't know much about. Alecia wasn't sure politics were better than talking about the war, but she couldn't expect her grandfather to engage in a conversation about dancing or dresses. Ivan spoke lyrically about his childhood though, extolling the virtues of Russia's natural beauty. How he'd ended up in a large city she'd never know. He made himself sound like a country boy. Maybe it was his somewhat mysterious sister who insisted on city life.

Finally, both her grandfather and Ivan revealed they had dinner arrangements, and she realized this was Ivan's day off, and once again, she'd made him spend part of it at his workplace.

"Thank you both so much for coming. Will I see you tomorrow?" she asked, as they left the Coffee Room.

"I'll see you during my rounds," Ivan said.

"I will call for you at midday and take you for luncheon, if that is acceptable to your employers," her grandfather said.

"I'll meet you in the Grand Hall tomorrow. I will telephone your hotel if I learn otherwise," she promised.

When she went upstairs, she didn't go straight to her room. The early evening was peaceful and the suite's parlor had much better furnishings than her small room. She found a copy of the O'Neill play Sybil had been cast in and began to read.

Richard came in at eight, when she was just finishing reading it. He noticed and came over to her. "Not your sort of life, eh?"

"I wanted to understand the part in case Sybil needs any assistance," Alecia told him, closing the script. "Did the blocking go well?"

"I should have had you there to make notes. We'll forget half of it."

"I'll retrieve my notepad now and you can tell me everything you remember so it won't be forgotten." She stood up, discovering too late that this made her bump up against him. He'd been standing over her and she hadn't realized how close his feet were to hers.

The next thing she knew, he had his arm around her and they were back on the sofa. She stared up at The Chinese on the wall, stunned. Scooting to the edge of the sofa, she said, "How clumsy of me. I'll just gather my things."

He slid his arm around her more, trapping her. "Where is my wife?"

"At her meeting still, I suppose. No one has delivered a message from her."

"I wonder if she'll come back tonight. Slipping through the net, she is."

"I imagine it is a great deal of work, starring in a play," she ventured, trying to separate herself, inch by inch.

"You have no idea. A great deal of responsibility. And here you are, to make our lives easier."

"Yes, and I want to do that by helping you to remember your blocking. Next time I'll know to come with you."

"Do you know, that's quite a naughty thing you said." He nuzzled her hair.

She could smell lemon and alcohol on his breath. He'd stopped his blocking for cocktails at some point, and would have been drinking without eating much, either, since he was reducing as well. She knew dieting and drinking together meant he was likely to behave irrationally. "I do not know what you mean by that remark, sir, but I think you should go to your bed."

"Why don't you come with me? I could show you a few things."

"Nothing I'd like to know, with all due respect."

He tilted his head back. "Why, a kitten with claws."

"I think you are not at your best, Mr. Marvin, and may regret this in the morning, so I will go to my room." She debated the wisdom of passing through his room to get to hers, or going out into the hallway. That seemed the wiser course.

"When did I stop being Richard?" he asked, his tone going soft.

"When it became unacceptably intimate to call you that," she snapped.

"Come now, I was just having a little fun. Order me a steak and chips and we'll get to work."

She contemplated him. Were the cocktails wearing off? "I think your wife would say we were done for the evening. Good night." She left the suite, remembering just in time to reach for her keys, and ran for her room, wanting to make sure she was inside and the connecting door was locked before his alcohol-slowed impulses allowed him to attempt to reach her bedroom.

In the back room of Boris's pawnshop, Ivan leaned over his plate of sausages and sauerkraut to reach the bowl of lentils in a sour cream dill sauce. "I do love coming here to eat. You're a better cook than Vera."

"What does your sister do all day?" Boris asked, cutting a piece of dark rye bread from the loaf on the table.

Ivan wondered if his friend had made the bread too. He could have been a professional cook, but instead, food had become his passion while he traded in used goods. "She intrigues, I suppose."

"I don't think catering should be her profession if I am a better cook," Boris said.

"You are the best cook. There is no comparison," Ivan said with a smile. "She does well enough, and cooking for parties is less sophisticated than cooking for friends."

Boris's chest puffed. "Is there enough work for her around here?"

"No, and that's why we purchased the gramophone, so she'd have something else to offer. Even people without a lot of money are going to want to dance after dinner. For a few shillings she can rent out our gramophone and seventy-eights."

"Not a bad plan." Boris forked up an overlarge piece of sausage and chewed reflectively for a moment. "Is that Sergei ever going to marry her?"

Ivan wiped the corners of his mouth with his napkin, then dug in again. "How could they afford to live? I'm not going to share a one-bedroom flat with a married couple, and pay the majority of the bills besides. As it is, I feel like I'm feeding half of the Whites in London."

Boris winced theatrically. "Surely not half. You don't have the dispossessed aristos at your table."

"No, only the people who have nothing to gain under any regime," Ivan said, picking up his wineglass and draining it.

Boris smiled. "You'll never be one of them, my boy."

Ivan tipped the wine bottle over his glass. "I never wanted to be. I won't be involved in this bomb mess."

"Bomb?" Boris's shadowed eyes opened in alarm. He set his fork down and repeated the word. "Bomb?"

Ivan nodded. "They had an idiotic notion that I would be willing to carry a bomb into the Grand Russe and plant it for them, in the room where *Macbeth* is to be performed for Ovolensky."

Boris ground his teeth and swore in Hebrew. "So you were to die for a cause you don't believe in, while they huddle next to their samovar miles away?"

That image reflected exactly what Ivan believed, for some of them at least, and they would feel no shame in not carrying out their bombing themselves. "It's not a cause for Vera, it's revenge for our parents' deaths. Which I don't mind. Making Ovolensky pay, some-how. However, I am not going to ruin the hotel that puts bread on our table, and I would never risk Miss Loudon's life."

Boris's eyes took on a speculative gleam. "So you'll allow your sister to risk her life, but not Miss Loudon's?"

Ivan made a flicking gesture with one hand. "My sister is a fool. I can't even tie her to a chair until she sees reason, because I am not home enough hours. She has all these fellow fools who could rescue her. But Miss Loudon is completely innocent. She took a position with those actors so she could come to London. A vicar's grand-daughter, and the old gent is very nice."

Boris took up his fork again and expelled a long sigh. "You might want to spend more time thinking about how to protect your sister from her so-called friends, and less about how to protect Miss Loudon." Boris paused. "Unless, of course, you are in love with her."

"Love?" Ivan said it again, softly, under his breath. "Love. What do I know about that?"

"You may be in the uncomfortable process of discovering exactly what you know," Boris observed.

Ivan considered that, then shied back into practical matters. "I know I can't have any part in the attempt on Georgy's life, not if it risks Miss Loudon or any other innocent party. I don't want to help this plot along at all."

Boris swirled sour cream through his lentils. "I think it is time for a man-to-man talk with Sergei. Insist they marry and pay for their own bread. You can stay with me while it all shakes out. I imagine you'll let your sister keep your furnishings."

Ivan pounded his chest where it felt like an entire sausage link had lodged. "They are too busy trying to kill Georgy to marry."

"Then they will soon be dead, or in police custody," Boris said, forking his last piece of sausage into his mouth. "A pity. Your sister would have beautiful babies. Have you thought about finding her a nice Englishman?"

Ivan drank deeply, trying to dislodge the nonexistent piece of sausage. "I don't think she cares about any of that. My parents' deaths are a cancer eating away at her. She cannot let them go. She's lost faith in me. She'd never let herself be courted by someone of my choosing." He was struck by a stray thought, that of Miss Loudon pacing the halls at night, tortured by nightmares of her own parents' passing.

Boris leaned over his plate. "What is it?"

Ivan winced. "Miss Loudon is not over her parents' deaths either, but I never hear her cursing the Germans over it."

"It is more impersonal, sinking a ship versus a firing squad."

"They are no less dead."

"That, boychick, is philosophy." Boris sat back and poured the last of their wine into his glass.

Ivan reached for his glass again and saw it was empty. Time to drink water. "Do you think, if I introduced Vera to Miss Loudon, that it might have some effect?"

"It depends on how deep she's gone. How nihilistic she's become."

Ivan nodded. "I would like Vera to put a human face on this command performance. If she sees who she might kill in the process, maybe she will relent."

Boris smiled sadly. "Vera is not the ringleader."

"Maybe not, but one step at a time. I can't save everyone."

"You shouldn't spare a thought to help the others, unless you mean Sergei. Just try to minimize the damage they can do to your sister."

"Wise words, my friend. I did speak to her about the brooch. It sounds like it once belonged to my mother."

His friend shook his head. "A pity. It's a very expensive piece."

"I know. I have no claim on it."

"I wish I could afford to give it to you, if the present owner fails to claim it."

"No." He thought about what Vera had said. "I wouldn't want it."

Boris covered his mouth as he belched. "We'll have to break out another bottle, or should we just move on to the vodka?"

Alecia took her grandfather to the café where she had dined with Ivan, since she didn't know of anywhere else.

"This isn't what I expected Londoners to eat," he said, breaking his plate of eggs into bite-sized portions.

"This is simple workday food for office people," she said. "I don't know London yet. I spend most of my time at the hotel."

"I was afraid the Marvins would be taking you out at night, forcing you to live a decadent lifestyle."

Alecia recalled New Year's Eve at the nightclub. She'd be willing to go out every night if she could listen to music, but the Marvins weren't like that. They let Max Parker visit the parties and hot spots for them, while they had small parties of equals in their suite. "No, it isn't like that. I expect my evenings to grow even quieter when Mrs. Marvin's play opens."

"What about Mr. Marvin?"

Her grandfather seemed to have intuited some piece of the truth. She couldn't not ask him for help. "Mrs. Marvin isn't spending very much time with him. Everything is fine generally, even if he and I are alone working. They are genuine professionals."

"Generally? Something has happened?"

She let her chin drop toward her chest. "He made advances last night. I don't know where his wife was."

He frowned at his eggs. "Do you think she expected it?"

Alecia thought back. "Yes. But she told me some time ago not to trouble myself. She didn't expect me to comply with his demands."

"I should think not." Her grandfather's shoulders straightened and his cheeks seemed to have moved toward his nose, making fierce lines down the center of his face.

A shiver passed down her back at the memory of last night. "Do you think I am in real danger from him? He had been drinking and he didn't pursue me when I refused."

"This may sound like a separate issue, but it isn't. The fact that you introduced me to Mr. Salter tells me that he is important to you."

"Yes, Grandfather, he is." She hesitated. "Of course, I've only known him two weeks, really."

"You've been here a month."

"I never spoke to him until just before the New Year."

"Do you think a proposal is forthcoming?"

"Oh." She was taken aback. "No."

"No?" he repeated.

Ivan wanted to be her lover. Did he mean for that to move into a commitment? In her sheltered life the answer would be yes. In fact, she'd never known a girl to be her fellow's lover until she was properly engaged, though some anticipated the wedding date. Who had the template for correct behavior in these modern times?

"I'm not sure."

"I would want better for you than a night watchman, but Mr. Salter seems to have the eye of the manager, so he has prospects."

"He's very intelligent," she enthused. "And think of what he's come from. A privileged background. He escaped Russia because he was close to Finland with his sister when his family was killed. He was on the run from one country to the next for about four years before coming here. So his career now doesn't reflect his true prospects, because he's been a refugee."

"He might not ever catch up. So much success is in who you know. Where does a Russian like him fit into our class structure?"

"I believe his family was gentry."

"That was in Russia. I don't know what your life would look like as his wife."

"I don't either, Grandfather. Nothing seems real inside the Grand Russe. It's so outside of what my experience has been. The very air is opulent." She swallowed hard. "But Mr. Salter, I've been outside the hotel with him. He no longer feels like a part of a grand hotel dream."

"Would you like to come home? I don't want you risking yourself with this Mr. Marvin."

"I don't plan to." She said the words with firm intent and meant them. While she might lose her virginity, and soon, it wouldn't be to Richard. "I'll investigate other options."

"Such as?"

"I'll speak to the hotel manager." She picked up a piece of toast.

"You've one month's experience as a secretary and about three months' experience as a nurse trainee."

She gestured with the butter knife. "I have more secretarial skill than that. I worked for you for years."

"You'll need a good reference from the Marvins," he warned.

"I'm sure Mrs. Marvin would give me one if I explained."

"I'd rather you came home, especially now that Sadie has run off." He took off his spectacles and rubbed the bridge of his nose.

Her dratted sister. "I'm sorry neither of us is taking care of you."

"You have to make your own way," he said. "It's a new world and you both want to be a part of it. I understand that, but I want you safe. I want the pair of you to have the right sort of husbands."

"I'm running out of time to find one. I'm twenty-two."

"Then you had better stay and see how serious your Mr. Salter is about you. But don't let a year pass by while you sort it out with him."

"No, sir."

They finished their lunch and then went in opposite directions on the pavement after shaking hands goodbye. He needed to return to his hotel and pack for his train. She wanted to see if she could speak to Mr. Eyre before she returned to the Marvins. But before she crossed the street she watched the beloved, slightly stooped figure of her grandfather walking away. He was not a demonstrative man, but she knew he loved her and wanted her protected.

Upon her return to the hotel, she went to the front desk and asked Mr. Moth if Mr. Eyre was available. Less than five minutes later she was being ushered into the manager's office.

Peter Eyre ground out his cigarette as she entered. He was dapper today in a dark pinstriped suit, and very appealing as he smiled in a rather sleepy fashion. "What brings you in today, Miss Loudon? The business of the play?"

"No, sir."

"Sir? So formal today."

She nodded. "It's only that I wanted to speak to you about professional opportunities."

"For your sister again? I haven't changed my mind. We'll hire her."

"No, but since you've been so generous with her, I thought you might consider me for a position as well."

He came around his desk and leaned against the front. "You? Trouble in the Chinese Suite?"

"Visiting with my grandfather has reminded me that I am a vicar's granddaughter and I'm not sure it is suitable for me to continue living in a man's valet room."

"You understand that if you had a position here, you wouldn't be able to live in. That throws you into the London housing market."

Alecia remembered where Ivan had to live, near that pawnshop. But then, Sadie would need a place to live too. They could find a flat together. She would have to room with her sister. "I understand."

"I'm afraid we don't have any secretarial positions available. I don't imagine you want to be a chambermaid."

"I might," she told him.

"I wouldn't want to hire you for that. You know how to type and write letters. Those skills pay better. I'll certainly let you know if we have an opening. But if you do leave the Marvins, I'd suggest looking for work as a secretary, or at least a typist."

She didn't want to whine, but she didn't want to give up, either. "It's hard to find work."

"I know, but at least you are in a large city. If the situation becomes intolerable, I do hope you'll speak to me. Is there anything I can do for you now?"

She wanted to tell him to stay away from Sybil, if he was indeed Sybil's lover, so that she'd spend more time with Richard. But she couldn't say that. "No. Thank you for your time."

"Of course." He frowned and pulled his cigarette case from his coat. When he saw she was still looking at him he held it up. "Cigarette, Miss Loudon?"

"No, sir. Good afternoon." She stood, and tripped over a chair leg when she moved too quickly. A very firm hand clasped around her upper arm, holding her steady. "So sorry."

He let her go almost before she registered their proximity. "Not at all. You do seem agitated, Miss Loudon."

"No, I'm merely sorry to see my grandfather leave so soon. I'll sort myself out." She forced a smile and opened the door, walking out without looking back.

Ivan left his flat a little before seven P.M., planning to buy something to eat from the corner pub before going to work. He walked through an icy drizzle, whistling one of the jazzy tunes he'd heard a few times through the nightclub's rear door. A newsboy shouted out some sort of commentary about the inevitability of another war in Europe. There had been a time when Ivan's English had not been good enough to understand such a boy's accent and the news he shouted. Now he understood perfectly, but he hoped that piece of news was wrong. He had traveled for years through Europe after the war and never wanted to see such devastation again in his lifetime.

He opened the door of the pub and went up to the bar. A copy of the *Evening News* was right there, so he sat down, deciding then and there to eat in the pub. He ordered a plate of bread, cheese, and pickles, plus coffee, and opened the paper.

Once his food arrived, however, his thoughts began to drift. He couldn't focus on the paper, so he set it aside and let the voices in the pub act as a soothing balm while he collected his own thoughts. Did he love Alecia Loudon? Could Boris be right? He'd thought he was simply trying to get a pretty girl into bed. Now, though, he'd met her grandfather, a very proper sort of old gent, and he'd learned that her sister was moving to London. Family complicated the kind of arrangement he'd suggested. At least it might. What did he know? Could he really take a vicar's unmarried granddaughter to bed in her hotel room?

Frankly, he suspected he could, but he'd feel guilty about it later. If she indicated her willingness, he wasn't about to resist her, but was that because he loved her? His thoughts all but shut down at the mere thought, as if he'd lost the English he forced himself to think in most of the time.

When he heard his sister's voice behind him, he frowned. She'd better not be spending money in a pub when she was meant to be drumming up more work for herself. Still, he wouldn't admonish her in public. There was a small chance Sergei was paying.

When he turned around, he could not believe the evidence of his own eyes. His sister was sitting across from Richard Marvin, Miss Loudon's employer. How on earth had they met? Was he the missing link between the conspirators and the command performance? Had Vera lied about the brooch?

Chapter Eleven

Ivan's feet didn't feel as light as they usually did when he made his service corridor check just before midnight. Once he'd been looking for petty thieves and naughty Bright Young Things necking in the halls. Now he only hoped to find Miss Loudon. With her distractions, he'd probably lose his position if not for the official sanction to pursue her.

His sad heart lightened when he saw her, her hand splayed against the wall as she listened to the music. He came up behind her. "May I have this dance?"

She turned around slowly, and he was shocked to see the gleam of tears in her eyes.

He put his hand to her cheek and gently wiped one tear away. Her cheek felt cool under his fingers. "What is wrong? Or is it just the music making you emotional?"

She wiped her other cheek. "I'm feeling homesick, I guess."

He pulled out his handkerchief and gave it to her, then leaned against the wall and glanced in her direction. "But you love London."

Her lips pursed, then relaxed. She shook her head slightly. "I'm going to have to leave here."

He felt stupid, stuck in short sentences. Strands of hair drifted around her face. She normally looked more put together, even at this hour. "But your sister is coming."

She blinked. "I don't want to be a chambermaid."

He sighed. What was wrong? Was there anything he could fix? "Miss Loudon, I don't understand."

She pressed her palms together and raised her fingers to her lips. "I asked Mr. Eyre about a position, but that was the only thing available."

No wonder he was confused. The most important part of the story was missing. "Were you sacked?"

She shook her head. "No, but Mr. Marvin made advances. He drinks too much. What if he gets out of hand?"

He took a moment to process that, putting it with what he'd just seen at the pub.

"Ivan, what are you thinking?" she asked, when he didn't immediately respond.

"I think Mr. Marvin has a lot on his mind. I don't think he will bother you again," Ivan said, reliving the unwelcome sight of Marvin with Vera. He'd whipped around on his stool, fists clenched, ready to confront them, then realized he was almost late for work. He'd had to run for the bus, unnoticed by the pair, and made it to the hotel's basement only a minute before his shift began. Figuring out what the connection was between his sister and Mr. Marvin had not been on the day's menu.

For sure, he needed Miss Loudon to stay in her position so he could find out what was going on. He stared intently at his teary-eyed innocent. "If you go home, we won't be able to see each other."

A tear leaked down her cheek. He lifted a thumb and wiped it away again. "Do you really think you're in danger from him?"

"No. He didn't pursue me when I walked away. That's a good sign. It's merely an issue of discomfort."

He nodded sharply. "Good. I don't want to say goodbye to you. Do you think Mr. Eyre might be willing to speak to him on your behalf?"

She put her fingers to her temples. "I need to be able to fight my own battles."

He made his voice low, urgent. "I need time with you. A lot more time." When he said it, he knew it was true, for many reasons.

"I want the same thing," she whispered.

He slid an arm around her and pulled her close until her head rested against his shoulder. "You could talk to Mrs. Marvin."

"She's basically disappeared. Her maid, Ethel, is the only one of us who sees her."

"The new acting role is keeping her busy?"

"I think it's more than that. But I have no idea where she's spending her time. I have a very strange position," she admitted.

"You're spending too much time with Mr. Marvin." The sweet scent of her hair alone was enough to make him harden.

She sighed. "I know. I think Sybil knew something like this would happen if she strayed, but she did it anyway."

"She has a lover?" What a complicated couple.

"She thought about it, mentioned it to me, then started disappearing."

Richard Marvin with Vera. Sybil with who knew who. Ivan could hardly keep track. "You don't think you were hired to be his mistress?"

She blanched. "No."

"Why not?"

She considered for a moment, then said, "I came to the hotel with them. They arrived in London on the first day I was employed. She didn't seem to have her eye on Mr. Eyre. Possibly she'd never seen him before then."

"Mr. Eyre?"

"Yes. What do you think? She wanted to have an affair with him."

He couldn't see that as a possibility. "I think he's seeing Miss Plash."

"Still?"

He nodded. He'd seen them together again. "Yes, still."

Miss Loudon chewed her lip. "Would he see both of them at once?"

"He's no fool. Seeing two women who live on the same floor would lead to disaster before long."

"So he probably turned Sybil down when she made the suggestion," Alecia said. "If that's the case, who is she with all the time?"

"I don't know, Miss Loudon. I haven't seen her with anyone." But he'd be keeping an eye on both Marvins.

"I wish you would call me Alecia. Miss Loudon seems so formal, now."

"After all our kisses?" He smiled.

"Rather, after two weeks of friendship. I do hope we are friends."

"Please stay, Alecia." He stared into her eyes. "I will be very sad if you go."

"Mr. Eyre said to look for a secretarial position somewhere in the City."

He cupped the back of her head, drinking in her lovely face. "He doesn't know how I feel about you. If you go, then what? I will only see you one day a week. It isn't enough."

"Every night isn't enough." She wrapped her arms around him and nuzzled close as the piano player in the nightclub tickled the ivories with a dreamy version of "Spanish Love."

Ivan swayed to the music and Alecia moved with him, as if they were one body. "This is what making love to you will feel like," he whispered.

"We aren't even kissing."

He nuzzled her hair. "There's more to it than lips touching."

"How is it that the same thing can seem so beautiful or so tawdry?"

He slid his hands down her hips. The desire to touch her everywhere warred with the knowledge that he could scare her away. She had little knowledge of life's realities. Such a sheltered, pretty, dear girl. "Emotion? Intent?"

"Don't you think you should be in love first?"

He thought about all those girls in the barns of Tver's dachas, so many years ago. Fervent couplings against trees just above the grassy banks of the Volga. He'd been in love with the touch of young, firm bodies and the passion of fearless youth. "In love with life? In love with possibility?"

"Really?"

What had happened to those careless girls? Were they married now, dead? Hollow-eyed with want from ten years' privation, or were they with the likes of Ovolensky, moving up the ranks of the new government?

"Ivan?"

He looked down at her, somewhat surprised.

"You look tired." She released her arms from their tight hold around his back. "I should go."

"It is late." As if to mock his words, the full band blared to life, trumpet in the lead. "Some night we'll have to sneak into the nightclub."

"Do you have the keys to this door?"

"I can get them."

They smiled at each other, coconspirators.

"Promise me you won't leave without coming to me," he said. "Or, if you must, go to the pawnshop and ask for Boris. He'll find me for you, if I'm not here."

She nodded. "I'm sure nothing will happen. I'll mix weaker drinks for him. And try to find out what is going on with Sybil. She needs to rehearse for the command performance anyway. I'll remind her about the rehearsals."

He took her slender white hands in both of his and kissed them fervently. "My *myshka*."

"To think I thought that word an insult at first." She put her hand to her mouth, kissed it, then pressed her fingers against his. "Goodnight, Ivan."

She ran lightly down the corridor. As he watched, he realized she'd lost weight since he'd seen her. Those horrible dresses were even baggier than before. She wasn't thriving here at the Grand Russe. Hotel life wasn't for everyone.

Alecia rolled over in bed and rubbed the sleep out of her eyes. She'd felt incredibly unsettled when she'd returned to her room the night before. Her body tingled from Ivan's caresses, while her ears nervously listened to her walls, afraid a scratching would come at the door between her room and Richard's. She only fell asleep after resolving, however impossibly, to insist that she be housed elsewhere in the hotel.

The next day she realized the idea was silly, now, in the daylight. Richard couldn't access her room unless she unlocked the door in between. She was as safe here as in any room in the hotel. Her thoughts were jumbled from sleep deprivation.

It had been a big night. She and Ivan had come one step closer to agreeing to become lovers. But she still didn't know how he felt about her. Surely if he loved her he'd have said so, instead of drifting into the privacy of his thoughts. She preferred honesty, remembered her mother warning her that boys would say anything to receive what she called "the privileges of marriage."

She'd given that advice before the war. Everything had changed now. War would come again, some people said, with the knowledge that their dear boys could die in battle. Others said war would never come again, but that number became fewer every year.

What was there to do now except live? As long as they took precautions, what was the harm? She didn't want to marry a vicar. No, she wanted to be the girl a boy took to nightclubs before it was too late for her.

She poured water from her jug into her basin and washed her face. Was Ivan too different from her? Could she ever understand the heart and mind of a Russian? Could she trust that the impact she put on his words matched how he really felt? Which was a bigger distance—boy to girl, or Englishwoman to Russian? She wondered if the Marvins would have any advice, since they had been to Russia. The idea of confiding to either of them any more than she already had seemed nonsensical, though.

She finished washing, then checked the drawer in her wardrobe to make sure her pay was still there. Her grandfather had received none of it, and now she could afford a new dress. She couldn't wait to review the papers and see what stores would have sales during the week.

An involuntary yawn distracted her, a reminder of how few hours of sleep she'd had the night before. Should she try to go back to sleep? She had at least an hour before Richard rose, more before Sybil did, if she'd even come home the night before.

Her threadbare dressing gown came off without her making a conscious choice to remove it. She bent over her bed to pull the blankets down, ready to crawl under them. A knock at the door stopped her.

She whirled around. Richard? No, it had come from the door into the corridor. The chambermaid wouldn't be trying to clean the room so early. She picked up her pocket watch and saw it was 8:10. Her heartbeat picked up speed. Ivan's shift had just ended. Had he decided to join her in her room?

She grabbed her dressing gown and pulled it on, still tying the belt as she opened the door a crack.

"Good morning," Ivan said. His eyes looked red, but otherwise she'd never have known he'd worked through the night.

"Hello." She checked her belt, forgetting she had just tied it, her heart pounding.

He craned his neck and peered over her head. "It's a very small room."

She glanced around him into the corridor. No one could see him here. "You'd better come in."

He nodded and stepped forward as she backed up, and then closed the door behind himself. "Thank you."

"Are you even allowed to be up here? Could you be sacked?" she asked breathlessly.

"No. It's fine." He took off his watchman cap.

"Really? I'm surprised."

"This is the Grand Russe, not some regular sort of hotel." He winked.

She chuckled. "Scandal is permitted?"

"Something like that."

She lowered her voice. "Scandal is preferred?"

"To a certain degree." His lips curved. "But there are limits. May I kiss you?"

She put her hand to her cheek. "I'm half asleep."

"A sleepy kiss is divine." He bent forward and touched his lips to hers, sweetly, without touching her anywhere else.

She caved first, wrapping her arms around him and intensifying his sweet offering. Her breasts felt full as they pressed against him, her nipples tightening into sharp points. The rest of her softened. If he leaned back it would be like they were doing that tango move Valentino had perfected.

Ivan's arms went around her waist. Her skin heated underneath her nightgown, everywhere his warm body touched.

"You must be exhausted," she murmured against his mouth. "I was thinking about going back to sleep myself."

"I'll leave in a moment," he said, after he broke this kiss. "I just wanted to tell you something."

She blinked. He didn't want to make love to her? She looked at him again. He really did look tired, and he was only two days into his work week. "What?"

"I traded my day off this week for tomorrow." He squeezed her waist.

"Oh?" Did he want to go on another date before they became lovers?

"Yes, it's Vera's birthday. My sister? I'm having a small party." He looked rueful. "You'll only know Boris, but the food will be good and there will be dancing. Would you come?"

"Tomorrow night?"

"Yes, at my flat. I know it's not a good neighborhood, but if you come by taxicab I'll escort you in from the street, and back again. I'd tell you I'd come pick you up, but I'll be over at Boris's flat cooking all afternoon."

"You cook?" She couldn't imagine those big hands finessing food.

"No, he does. He's very good. I'll be doing whatever he tells me."

She squeezed his arms, enjoying the firm biceps under her fingers. "It sounds like fun. I'm sure I can come to the party, but I don't think I could have the afternoon, too."

"It will be wonderful if you can come for the evening." He released her and stepped back.

She supposed he really was going home. If she asked him to stay, well, she courted disaster. No wonder she needed to be the one to take care of preventing pregnancy. Lovemaking opportunities came about when you least expected them. She tingled all over at the possibility. "Do you have enough records? I could borrow some of Sybil's."

He nodded enthusiastically. "Oh, could you? We'll be playing the same five records over and over again, otherwise."

"I'll manage it. I can't wait to try Russian food."

They smiled at each other, but the distance between them had grown to two feet. "Thank you. I hope to see you tonight."

"The usual place, and an entirely different one tomorrow."

"Yes. Oh." He fumbled in his coat, then held out a scrap of paper. "My address. Do you have money for the taxicab?"

"Yes, I haven't spent a penny of my pay yet. Maybe I'll have a new dress for tomorrow. I plan to shop for one."

His gaze raked her body. "How exciting. I can't wait to see it." He yawned.

She held out her hand to the door and picked up his cap. When he nodded and took it, she opened the door a crack and peeked into the corridor. "Out you go."

He kissed her cheek as he passed by her, then he was gone. She closed the door and turned to stare at her bed. Now she was awake, and fidgety. Maybe she'd go to the Coffee Room and look at newspapers.

Downstairs half an hour later, she found a C&A advert illustrating the various outfits a woman might wear over the course of the day. She liked the satiny pink dress the model wore for evening, though of course, it was just a line drawing. The pleated skirt floated at the knee. She couldn't discern the shape of the top because a matching cardigan was worn over it, but it was probably loose and sleeveless.

"Here's my best darling," Sybil cooed, appearing in the doorway of the Coffee Room in a dropped-waist satin dress most women would wear in the evening. She'd topped it with a voluminous brown fur coat, no hat.

Alecia smiled at her. "Coming in? Going out?"

"Oh, I couldn't stay in the suite this morning. Stuffy upstairs today, isn't it, darling?" Sybil opened her purse and found her cigarette holder, then opened her cigarette case.

Alecia took the offered lighter and held the flame to Sybil's cigarette. "It's not stuffy down here, but chilly."

"Yes. You need a fur coat, darling." Sybil blew smoke from the side of her mouth.

What could she say to that? "Shall I fetch you some coffee?"

"Black, darling, and a naked little piece of toast."

Alecia hurried to do as she was bid. It didn't take long. She placed the items in front of her employer, then reseated herself.

Sybil touched the advert with the tip of a perfectly groomed nail. "Planning a shopping trip?"

"I've been invited to a birthday party tomorrow night, if you don't need me."

"You can go if I can take you shopping. That's some appalling viscose number judging from the price, darling. It will never last the season, with London's damp."

"I can afford it, though." Alecia frowned at the newspaper.

"We must not be paying you enough," Sybil mused.

"It's not every secretary who can stay at the Grand Russe," Alecia said.

"Yes, but it's taken out of your wage, really." Sybil took an antlike bite of her toast. "You must have a silk dress. Are you set on pink?"

"It suits my coloring."

Sybil nodded. "Not mine. I must have red for evening, if I'm trying to be sexy. Is this party for your Russian?"

"He's the host."

"We could try you in red. Save your money and wear something of mine."

"Won't I look too fancy for a party that is probably full of Russian refugees?"

"It's never wrong to be the best-dressed girl at the party. Especially when you are connected with the theater. No, let's buy you an evening coat and save your dress money. We'll try that new dress shop by my manicurist. The girl who owns it is the daughter of a baronet and knows *nothing* about business. She'll be so star struck by me that you'll have it for a song."

She hoped Sybil was right. "I could use a new coat."

Sybil nodded. "Let's have our nails done, then to the dress shop we'll go."

"What about Richard?"

"We'll stop at the front desk and leave him a note. I have to spend all afternoon with him rehearsing anyway. Such a bore." She rolled her eyes. "As if I don't know my part perfectly. I've played Lady Macbeth dozens of times."

"Can I help?"

"Oh yes, you should be in the room with us. Script prompts, if anyone needs them. I don't know who Richard has hired for the other roles. Poor darling, so much for him to do. I much prefer to act than tend to all the business he does."

"He's been very busy," she said cautiously.

"As have I," Sybil said. "Now run along and retrieve that ratty old coat of yours. I'll meet you at the reception desk in a few minutes."

Alecia couldn't wait to take off her tired old coat and dance in the silk and velvet dress she'd borrowed from Sybil. They had considered, at length, a beaded silk dress, but Sybil was just a little taller than Alecia, so the beautiful red dress seemed matronly on her. The sleeveless dress with the high-low hem that she wore now had a pink silk lining that showed behind her legs, and embroidered flowers across the waistline. The top part was stark black, perfect for a rope of pearls, if she'd had one. Her mother had owned beautiful pearls, but they'd gone down in the *Lusitania* with her.

She wouldn't think about that tonight. While she hadn't come home from her shopping excursion with a new coat, she had fixated on a pair of pale pink leather T-strap shoes with a rhinestone button that made them work for evening as well as day. With the purchase of them, she had just enough room in her budget for a dress pattern and some fabric. She'd make herself a new dress to wear with her shoes eventually, but tonight, she'd dance in borrowed finery.

She paid the taxicab driver and stepped onto the cracked pavement, holding her bag of records. In this part of town, she might be safer wearing her old coat. It didn't smell very nice here either. She hoped she didn't ruin her new shoes.

"Alecia!" A figure peeled itself from the wall of the residential building.

She recognized Ivan's voice and trotted to him, careful to watch where she stepped. "Hello! Did you finish your cooking?"

"Yes, wonderful things. Potato dumplings, my sister's favorite lemon dessert, pancakes, some beautifully spiced lamb from Boris's secret recipe. A fish soup, too." He stepped forward.

"It sounds like a real feast," she agreed.

He picked up one of her hands and kissed the back of her glove. "A feast for all the senses, just like you."

She blushed, forgetting the night's cold. "You are sweet."

He tucked her hand around his arm. "Now, we must go in so you can meet these crazy Russians. You may hear things you'd prefer not to, but hopefully, they will be speaking in Russian and not English."

"Are they trouble, your friends?"

"My sister's friends," he corrected, sounding stern. "Let us go in."

Alecia wondered what she had landed herself in as she climbed the stairwell behind a greengrocer's. The truth was she was simply happy to be spending time with Ivan. Since he had only one day off a week, they wouldn't be able to have another date soon. She thought he might just be too tired after his shifts to pursue her in the morning hours, whatever he hoped.

He ushered her in through the door at the top of the stairs. She saw an assortment of bushy-bearded men in the small room. It must be the fad among Russians. Most people looked to be about a decade older than she was. She recognized Boris Grinberg from the pawnshop, presiding over a tureen of soup. By the far window she saw the clerk who worked at the pawnshop. A woman with a wedding ring sat on an ancient sofa pushed against the wall. She hoped Ivan saved most of his money instead of paying it in rent. These damp walls scared her. No celebratory cheer was present.

On the other hand, she'd never seen a gramophone like the one on the table in the center of the room. The sight of it instantly made her happy. The sound was good, however primitive the machine appeared to be. "Are we dancing already?"

"No, but Vera loves music almost as much as you do." He indicated her bag. "Did you bring records?"

"I did." She opened the bag and showed him.

He clapped his hands with pleasure. "What's in the wrapping?"

"A gift for Vera. It's a new recording by the Wolverine Orchestra."

He shook his head. "Oh, you didn't need to bring a gift. I didn't expect that."

"I wanted to. After all, she's a music lover like me." She wanted Ivan's sister to like her. "There's beautiful cornet work on it."

"I heard the Piano Suite on the seventh floor is empty tonight. Maybe we can go back to the hotel later and you can play for me?"

She blinked. She had mentioned to him that she knew how to play the piano a little, but hadn't expected the opportunity to do so. "My goodness. You can do that? The seventh floor?"

"Yes, I can get the keys. I'm a watchman. I have to be able to respond to emergencies."

She noted the pride in his voice and liked it. Did she want to go to a hotel suite with him late at night, alone?

In a word, yes. Whatever happened.

Chapter Twelve

After Ivan had made his suggestion and she'd agreed, the party became torture. Alecia's first priority was making sure her borrowed recordings were played, so that she could take them with her when she left. Ivan found her a plate and Boris gave her a mouthwatering selection of his culinary specialties. Then, while Ivan talked to a thin man in his early thirties, introduced to her as Vera's fiancé, she sat with the married lady on the sofa. Actually, the woman was a widow, the sister-in-law of a man named Anatoly, who she never heard speak to anyone during the hour and a half she stayed at the party.

Vera had come up to her after about twenty minutes. Her English wasn't as good as Ivan's, but they talked about music and Alecia felt like she'd done well, though she didn't feel as if she'd made a friend. Vera seemed nervous and vague.

Then, very soon, Vera had unwrapped her presents and settled into the business of serious dancing with Sergei, who probably stayed so thin by vigorous exercise. She'd never seen two people move their feet so fast when they danced. Boris asked her to dance once, but the Russians gave her a wide berth. Ivan was kept too busy pouring drinks to dance more than once with her either. When he signaled her, she put Sybil's records back into the carrier bag and slipped out with him.

"I have a taxicab waiting," he said, as they went down the stairs.

"I'm sorry, I didn't realize you had left."

"The music had you swept away." He grinned at her as they went out the door of the greengrocer's shop.

"I need my own record player."

"You'd never leave your room," he teased.

"I would." She grinned. "To buy more records."

The taxi was at the corner and they scurried toward it. The temperature had dropped dramatically. Alecia could see her breath in the night air. Ivan kept his arm around her the entire way to the hotel, only letting her go when they walked into the Grand Russe.

The temperature change upon entering made her teeth begin to chatter. "It will be quite warm in the basement," he promised. "We'll get the keys and then take the service lift up to the seventh floor."

"I can't wait. What's the Piano Suite like?"

"Very musically oriented. It's done in white and gold, with photographs of American musicians on the walls. Pure luxury."

She followed him through a door off a corridor by the Reading Room that she'd never noticed before, and through another door that he needed a key to unlock. Then they moved into an industrial part of the hotel, down a flight of plain wood steps, the walls painted white but marred by many scrapes and even a little dirt along the baseboards. A low hum from electrical equipment picked up volume as they stepped down. Ivan unlocked another door and they walked through.

"You shouldn't be here, so stay close," he told her. They went into a long, rectangular room with rows of hooks, shelves above, for employee belongings. A corkboard dominated the wall alongside the door.

"That's where Mr. Eyre posts his memos every day," Ivan said.

Alecia glanced at the creamy sheet of fine paper, with "Peter Eyre" across the top in lettering that matched the hotel's. "Greetings from Peter Eyre" was the first line typed underneath the letterhead.

"That's yesterday's note. I don't know when he posts them. I've never seen him down here."

She read the note. "You have a plumbing problem on the seventh floor."

"Or Miss Page is exceedingly dramatic," Ivan said. "No one else complained, but the seventh floor must be perfect."

"Why aren't Mr. Fortress and Miss Page in the Piano Suite?"

"They are in the Sleeping Princess Suite. It's the second nicest in the hotel."

"I see. It sounds marvelous, just from the name alone." She waved her hand in front of her face. It was very hot down here. She unbuttoned her coat and unwound her muffler.

Ivan nodded. "I'll just get our key." He unlocked a glass-fronted cabinet with duplicates of every key that was kept behind the desk, and chose the one he wanted.

"You're certain we won't be in trouble?"

"Absolutely."

He looked stern for a moment, but she had no idea why. "Tell me," he asked. "What are the Marvins doing this evening?"

"When I went to make myself ready, they were still rehearsing downstairs. All the actors came in today for the first time. I was the script supervisor during the afternoon, but a lot of them weren't off-book yet, so I wasn't much use. They weren't expected to know their lines. Mr. Marvin didn't mind me leaving and Sybil had already approved it."

He didn't seem to be paying much attention. "Did my sister look familiar to you at all?"

"You mean, did she look like you?" She considered this. "She's tall and I think she has your build, but I saw a family photograph on your mantel and it seemed that you look like your father and she looks like your mother."

"Mother was a beauty. Vera has aged faster. A different sort of life."

"I hope you don't tell her that."

Ivan shrugged. "As long as Sergei admires her, that's all that matters."

"Will they marry soon?"

Ivan gestured to the door, and Alecia followed him out. He went the opposite direction from before, heading for the service lift. This one wasn't manned, and had blankets covering the walls.

"To the seventh we go," Ivan said, operating the controls.

Alecia leaned against the wall as they rose, feeling the tug of gravity. She stared at her shoes, glad to see they hadn't picked up any East End detritus and still looked brand-new.

"Every time I've looked at you all night, you've been staring at your shoes."

She put her hand over her mouth, trying to hide her giggle. "I know, so silly of me, but I can't believe they are really mine."

"London shoes."

"Yes, exactly! Can you imagine wearing shoes like this in a muddy rural field? What the church ladies would say if they saw me wearing them at my grandfather's services?"

The lift stopped with a shudder. "They'd say you'd been sinning," Ivan said.

He opened the door and the gate and stepped out, then held his hand out to her. She took it and stepped off.

"Am I going to sin in these shoes?" she whispered.

"I thought I'd take them off you first."

He was so beautiful, even in the faint light of the corridor, that she had to stand on her tiptoes and lean into him. Her mouth only came up to his chin, but she kissed it, that cleft there, then trailed her lips down his neck.

His breath expelled harshly, and he shifted his stance, supporting more of her weight. She slid her hands down the buttons of his winter coat, then up again, unbuttoning them as she went. Leaning in again, she felt the hot, hard length of his manhood against her belly.

He wrapped his arm around her and she could feel the key in his hand, the heavy brass fingerplate, the long, old-fashioned key. She couldn't pull herself away as he plundered her mouth, and met him in intensity, curling her fingers around his belt, rubbing against him like a cat. Every time she moved her torso, her engorged nipples sent fireworks of liquid heat through her entire body. She had desires she'd never known before. She wanted to claw and bite his clothing off.

He lifted the key to eye level between them, and broke the kiss. "I have to—" He panted between each word.

"Open the door?" she asked, equally breathless.

He nodded. His pupils looked huge in the dimness, his lips swollen. She wanted to go down on her knees and worship. Once, her sister had made a comment about what flappers did on their knees. She had no idea what Sadie had meant, but she wanted to find out.

Ivan opened the double doors of the suite and stepped in, turning on the light. She had thought she wouldn't be able to tear her eyes off of him, but the sight of the room had her dumbstruck with wonder. She hadn't realized this floor of the hotel had vaulted ceilings with stained glass upper windows. The entire space was pure white. Carpets, sofas, the piano. Even the tables were some kind of white lacquer with oriental detailing cut into the wood. The touches of gold seemed inspired. Pillows. Ornate fans in frames. Then there were the white- and gold-framed photographs of musicians dotting the walls, a mixture of dark and light faces, all in suits, often with their instruments at the ready. She wanted to go to them and read all the group names, but then Ivan stepped back into view and she was lost in him again.

"Can I take your coat?"

She let it slide off her arms, and he gathered her coat before it hit the ground, placing it neatly on a coatrack. Next came her muffler, her hat, her gloves. They both glanced at her shoes, but she'd unbuckled them before she even left the front hallway, not wanting to leave shoe marks on the immaculate carpet. He began to disrobe too, until he was in shirtsleeves and trousers.

"I've always wanted to feel this carpet on my toes," he said.

"Then you should," she said.

"There's a bearskin in front of the fireplace."

"What part of your body did you want to feel on that?" she teased.

"Why, Miss Loudon," he said. "Not such a *myshka* now."

"All those kisses took my fear away," she murmured. "Isn't it lucky that I know how to undo your tie?" She put her hands to work.

He swallowed hard. She could feel his Adam's apple bobbing as she unknotted. Then she slid the fabric away from his shirt and tossed it on the hook with his coat.

"What?" she asked.

"I brought a sheath," he said in a gravelly voice that made him sound even more Russian.

She felt her face go hot. Yes, she wanted *it*, but his words made it all so real. But she'd made her decision.

"Do you want to go into the bedroom?" he asked.

"What about that bearskin rug?"

His mouth worked. He spoke slowly. "That's a Russian dream. I've spoken English since I was a child, but I'm finding the words hard."

"Is your brain addled, Mr. Salter?" She wondered if he could see her nipples peaking under Sybil's dress.

He nodded.

"Mine too."

"We should have champagne."

She shook her head. "I have bubbles in my blood when I look at you. I don't need anything else."

His teeth showed when he smiled. "I'll take my socks off," he said. "Take your stockings off too."

She complied. "But you have to remove your shirt."

He did, staring at her. As each inch of golden sand-colored skin revealed itself, she felt like she should *ooh* in admiration. He had the lines of a Michelangelo sculpture.

"Now you," he said.

"What?"

"Your dress."

She didn't hesitate, merely reached behind herself so she could undo the back of her dress. It fit quite tightly compared to many modern fashions. When it fell open in the back she let it slide off her shoulders and down her arms, exposing her bralette. His stare held only admiration. When the dress pooled around her thighs, her tap pants were exposed. She had bought these today too, sateen instead of silk, but pretty for the price.

Ivan muttered something in Russian, his gaze full of partiality. Then in English, he said, "I have never seen a lovelier girl."

Alecia was grateful for her grandfather's abstemious dinner table, followed by the Marvins' even more dramatic diet, which had kept her figure so streamlined. Her sister was inclined to a certain amount of chubbiness that seemed adorable now, but her own face had never looked well when it rounded. "I have never seen a more handsome man," she admitted.

"I want to make love to you on the bearskin rug," he said. "I'll light the fire. You won't be cold."

She nodded and took his hand. When they reached the soft pelt in front of the beautiful white marble fireplace, they sank to their knees together, hands clasped. His lips met hers. She could taste a faint saltiness that indicated he'd dipped into the caviar before they left the party. How fitting that they'd had a lovely feast before coming here.

"I meant to show you the piano and listen to you play," he said, smoothing a hand along her hair.

"No, you didn't. You meant this to happen." She smiled to show him her enthusiasm with the idea.

"We still have clothes on."

"We should remedy that."

"Do you want to discuss the future?" he asked.

"There is no future. It's 1925 and all I need is now."

"That is how we think these days," he agreed.

She put her hands to his lips. "No more talking. I don't want to be afraid. I just want you to touch me, make me feel the things that I know you can. Love me, Ivan, before I think too hard about it."

He let go of one of her hands, reached to the sofa and grabbed one of the gold pillows. Placing it behind her, he maneuvered her back until she lay with her head against the pillow. He stayed on his elbows to keep his weight off her.

"Is it going to hurt?" she whispered, caressing his shoulder.

"Not if I can help it." He kissed her tenderly as he removed her bralette.

She felt his gentleness in the way he contained his strength. When his mouth moved to her neck, she shuddered a little. He roved toward her clavicle, then for the first time, a man's mouth touched her breasts. She arched into him as his tongue found her nipple, not afraid in the least. All she wanted was more, more, more.

It couldn't possibly be any better than this, the gentle suction of his mouth on her breast, the way his strong arm wrapped around her hips. Fingers rolled down the top of her tap pants, her only remaining clothing. He kissed the indentation of her belly button, then ran his tongue along the curve of her hip bone. When he lifted her infinitesimally and pulled her pants completely off, she writhed, her legs falling apart. How gentle his fingers were as they drew patterns through her curls, then slid into the moist heat he'd created between her thighs.

She didn't expect his mouth to go there too, but his entire body moved lower, and he devoured her. Or at least, that was how it felt. His fingers slowly moved into her most private place while his tongue tortured some spot that made her lose her mind. She knew she was speaking, begging even, but had no idea what words came out of her mouth. The pleasure coiled and spiraled then broke free. As the tension in her body fled, she found his dear face above her again.

He kissed her forehead. "We're joined, you and I. Isn't it marvelous?"

She turned her head one way and the other, realizing it wasn't his fingers inside her, but something else, that long, hard, masculine part of him. She hadn't even been aware. "I'm not a virgin anymore?"

"No, my pretty darling. You're mine." He rocked his hips against her, making her gasp. Little black dots danced behind eyelids she hadn't realized she'd just closed.

She smiled and feathered her fingers into his thick black hair, then pulled his mouth to hers. He tasted of dark things, the recesses of her own body, her passion. He tasted like heaven and felt even better.

Seated behind his desk, Peter Eyre lifted his teacup to his lips and enjoyed his first sip of smoky tea made in a traditional samovar. He'd ordered it for the Ovolensky visit, only four days away now, and had it set up in the Coffee Room. The hall porter had just brought him the first official cup. He could see it would take some getting used to, but he liked it nonetheless, and the samovar was a beautiful one. He'd found the silver and blue enamel piece at an auction house. The matching cups had been missing, but they'd have been stolen soon enough anyway.

His door burst open without even so much as a warning knock. *Emmeline.* No one else dared be so informal with him.

"She's missing again, the old cow."

His lover's face had aged a decade since he'd seen her the night before. She had bags under her eyes, and without her expert application of lipstick he could see how thin and colorless her lips really were. She was much more beautiful with makeup, sad to say. And her dark roots were showing. It wasn't like her not to find time to go to the salon. She must be running low on funds again, despite his covering her hotel bill.

"Mrs. Plash?" he said mildly, setting down his serviceable white tea mug.

"Obviously. Her behavior is going to send me to the lunatic asylum one of these days. Just you wait and see, Peter."

I'm not planning to wait long enough to see. "Mr. Russell should have just come on duty. He'll alert staff." He stood and walked around his desk. As he passed by her, he noticed the cigarette ash ground into her glove.

He snapped his fingers at Mr. Moth. "Call Mr. Russell and the hall porter in here."

Within two minutes, both men were in his office, listening to Emmeline's description of what her mother had been wearing to bed. She thought her mother was still in night dress.

"We'll find her," Mr. Russell assured her. "We always do."

Peter shut the door behind them. "Look Emmeline, this isn't working. Your mother needs to be somewhere more manageable. Larger than a hotel suite but smaller than a grand hotel."

Emmeline forced a sugary smile. It looked obscene on her un-painted face. She danced her fingers up one of his immaculate sleeves. "Look, darling, I know she's a challenge, but I'm worth it, right?"

"When I said you could move in here, I wasn't aware you had an ill mother in tow. It had been years since I'd seen her. I've been patient for a month now, but it isn't getting any better. This is the wrong sort of establishment for Mrs. Plash."

"What about me?" She squared herself off with his body, then pressed her chest against him.

He had the feeling she hadn't bothered to put on underclothes beneath her loose red sweater and skirt. She smelled like last night's sex, old perfume, and even older cigarettes. "Your mother has money and so do you. Not grand hotel money, but something. I'll have your things taken over to the boardinghouse where Olga Novikova lives."

She gasped. "You must be joking. She's a chambermaid."

"She was a princess, in the old days, before the imperial government fell. Still has some lovely things. Authenticated my new samovar for me."

Her lips pressed together, wobbling dangerously. "How dare you!" She made fists and pounded them against his chest. "A boardinghouse fit for a chambermaid?"

He grabbed her wrists and held them away from his body. "It isn't going to work here. You're disturbing my concentration. I need to focus on the hotel, not your mother."

"Peter!"

"And not your drama. I've had enough of it."

He pushed her wrists toward her and dropped them. She rocked back as if he'd put real force behind the gesture. Tears began to spill from her eyes, drawing the remnants of last night's mascara down her cheeks in black trails.

"Go pack, or I'll have Olga do it for you." He turned toward his desk. "Focus on your mother instead of men, for once. She deserves that much."

She hit him with enough force to bend his body at the waist, then locked her arms around his neck as if to strangle him. He called out sharply, then attempted to save his breath as he fought to pull her arms apart without bruising her. He bent forward, trying to breathe, but only managed to lift her entire body off the floor. He kicked back with one leg but made contact with nothing. Time to stop working so hard and take some exercise beyond lifting a cigarette or a glass of champagne to his mouth.

Just as he thought he had no air left, he heard men coming into the room. Emmeline screamed as her arms were wrenched off his neck. Hugh Moth and the newest night watchman, Swankle, held her by the arms as she shrieked, spewing spittle.

Peter coughed and pushed the wings of his hair back into order before turning around. "Lock her into her suite. No, wait, better not do that, in case her mother returns. Do we have any rooms open?"

"Just the Piano Suite."

He nodded and wheezed. "Lock her into the bedroom. Just the bedroom, mind. I don't want her damaging anything. And take her shoes so she doesn't mark the carpet."

"I'll piss on it!" she screamed. "I'll destroy it."

"Then we'll call the police and you'll go to Holloway. Your mother will be alone then. Is that what you want?"

Her eyes were wild, but she didn't respond. She wasn't as far gone as she pretended. No, Emmeline Plash was a calculating bitch.

"I'll go quietly for five thousand pounds," she said.

"Oh, please," he said, reaching for his cigarette case, pleased to see his hands weren't shaking despite nearly being suffocated.

"You owe me."

"Not even if you were a full-blown whore, would you be worth that much after a month."

Swankle's eyes widened, but he said nothing.

"Take her upstairs. Use the service lift. Don't say anything to anyone, then go back to searching for her mother."

"I have to be at the desk," Mr. Moth said, as Mr. Swankle said, "My shift ended, sir. Do you want me to stay over?"

"Right, then." He lit his cigarette. "Of course you must return to the desk, Mr. Moth. I will wait on our guests myself until you return. As for you, Mr. Swankle, if you'd like to pick up extra pay, I would appreciate the help until Mrs. Plash is found."

"Yes, sir," Swankle said with a happy smile.

"Very good. Off you go." Peter blew out a long stream of smoke as the men dragged his mistress out of the door between them.

Alecia heard a disturbance outside her room. Was Richard throwing a fit about something? She sat up in bed, and discovered she was naked. Naked was not her bedtime routine. Then she realized Ivan was next to her on his stomach, his hands tucked under the pillow. Simultaneously, she felt a soreness between her legs that reminded her what she'd done three times over the course of the night. She touched his smooth back and reminisced sleepily.

They hadn't closed the curtains. Winter's faint early light hadn't awakened them, though whatever time it was now offered enough light to see clearly. In fact, there was enough light for her to see the doorknob turning.

"Ivan!" she cried, instantly wide awake, pulling the covers over her head and ducking down.

She heard a rustling as he sat up.

"Swankle," Ivan exclaimed.

"Uh, hello, Salter," came the voice of another man. "Mr. Eyre gave orders to have Miss Plash locked up in here."

"I see," he said. "Could you wait in the hall for a moment?"

Alecia lay still, petrified, as another woman screamed invectives.

"I really don't think so," said a voice she recognized as belonging to the front desk clerk. "A bit out of control, this one."

"Right, well, we'll take the blankets with us." He put his head under the blanket and, all business, helped Alecia pull the sheet from the bed and wrap it around her body. Then he pulled the blanket over them both and helped her to stand. They shuffled out of the open door into the parlor and shut it. The sound of Miss Plash's venom disappeared.

Ivan dropped the blanket to the floor. "I apologize. I didn't expect that to happen."

"You'll be sacked," Alecia said, frantic.

He patted her arm. "I don't think so. The room was empty for the night. But we have overstayed our welcome. I didn't expect us to fall asleep."

She blushed. "We took a lot of, err, exercise."

He grinned, losing his professional bearing. "Why, Miss Loudon, how you do go on." He bent for a kiss.

She threw caution and stale morning breath to the wind and kissed him back enthusiastically. "The Marvins are never awake at this hour, so I'll be fine. It's you I'm worried about."

"I haven't slept this well in weeks," he declared, scratching his broad chest. "I'm equal to anything."

Alecia baby-stepped toward the bearskin rug, almost defeated by the mummy wrapping Ivan had woven around her with the sheet. Much more awkwardly than the night before, she knelt down and scrambled for her tap pants, then unrolled the sheet enough to pull them on. She tossed Ivan his underclothes and reached for her bralette.

She had yet to fasten it when the door opened. "Hey, Ivan," Swankle said.

She ducked behind Ivan as he answered. "Yes?" Ivan asked, calmly pulling his undershirt over his head.

"Mrs. Plash is missing again. I'll keep my mouth shut about this if you help me find her."

Ivan nodded equably, despite his assurance that his position was in no danger. "I'll take the fourth and fifth if you take the sixth and seventh."

"Well done. I'd better stay near to this," Swankle said, gesturing behind him. "I'm getting overtime. You can put in for it too, I expect."

Ivan raised his eyebrows, and Swankle's gaze drifted to Alecia. "Oh my. Lucky bastard." Swankle shut the door quickly.

"Can you help me with my dress?" Alecia asked, attempting to ignore her humiliation in the interest of a speedy exit. "I don't know where my stockings are."

"In the foyer. We wanted to be barefoot on the rug."

"Right." Alecia tried to react as if this sort of thing happened to her all the time. "Since you are going to search the fourth and fifth, do you want me to check the basement? That bathroom you said she likes? Miss Plash won't calm down until her mother is found, I expect."

"You want to help?"

She forced cheer into her voice. "Absolutely."

"Brilliant plan, then," Ivan said. "I expect you are right, unless she is hiding behind that fern again. You can reach the basement bathrooms down the public staircase."

They dressed quickly. Alecia desperately wanted her hairbrush and toothbrush, but at least she could tidy up a little in the downstairs bathroom, even if Mrs. Plash wasn't there.

"I'm sorry our night together ended so abruptly," he said, helping her pin up her hair.

"Nothing more to be said about that."

"Alecia."

"I should bob my hair," she said. "It's so old-fashioned."

"No, I love it." He handed her another pin, then pulled on his shoes. "Look, I know this was your first time. It should have been more romantic."

"It was very romantic, until just now. Don't worry. It isn't your fault." She pushed her toes into her beloved new shoes and fastened them, then hefted her outerwear.

"I'll see you downstairs tonight," he said. "A kiss for luck?"

She smiled. "Always. But you can't leave me yet. I rather take the service lift to the basement."

Chapter Thirteen

"If anyone asks what you are doing on this lift, just tell them what is going on. The more people who are looking for Mrs. Plash, the faster we'll find her," Ivan said as he opened the gate on the fifth floor.

"I will." Alecia moved toward the control.

He took her hand and, staring into her eyes, kissed her hand in a very continental manner. "Last night was beautiful," he whispered tenderly. "My *myshka*, you were a wonder."

She smiled, but it felt bittersweet. In the hard light of day, she realized a night like the magical one before should have been a wedding night, not a night snatched out of ordinary life. Today they didn't start their new life together, just continued to go on like nothing had changed. Yet everything had. The truth had to be faced: She was no flapper. She wanted a husband. But she'd only known Ivan a few weeks.

Ivan shut the gate. She'd watched closely enough before to know how to operate the lift herself and made it down to the basement with no trouble beyond a rather rough, jerking stop. Once she exited into the dank, dim corridor, she had to think hard to remember where the bathroom was. She could really do with a cup of tea and a bun.

After a couple of wrong turns, she found the corridor where the four bathrooms were and opened the doors, one after another. They all seemed to be empty, but then, as she hesitated in the last one, she heard breathing. She darted deeper into the room, wondering if there were hidden recesses. It was only then that she saw Mrs. Plash, huddled down in the deep bathtub, still in her dressing gown.

"Oh, goodness," she cried, bending down. "Mrs. Plash."

"They were yelling," the old woman whispered. "I do hate yelling. Emmeline has such a temper."

"You can't stay here, Mrs. Plash." She reached out her arm. "Come, I'll bring you back upstairs. Your daughter is beside herself."

"Butter wouldn't melt in her mouth," Mrs. Plash said, the deep grooves around her mouth deepening into shadow.

"Be that as it may, you need each other," Alecia said briskly. "Give me both of your hands as you climb out."

The woman complied somewhat shakily. She overbalanced as she lifted her second foot out of the tub, but Alecia kept her steady.

"We both need some breakfast," Alecia said when they were safe. "Perhaps we'll call for two trays when we are upstairs."

"Very kind of you. I would love a visitor. You're such a nice young girl."

"Thank you." Alecia patted the age-spotted hand, then guided her back to the service lift.

"We aren't supposed to be here."

"No," Alecia agreed. "But I don't think you are a stranger to it."

Mrs. Plash's face took on an expression of girlish defiance. "I came here as a young matron, you know, with my husband. We loved to explore the place. Mr. Plash was very friendly with Mr. Eyre's father. We went to his house a number of times for dinner parties."

Alecia half listened to the woman ramble as she closed the door and started the lift. So, Mr. Eyre didn't spring directly from Zeus's head. And it did sound like the senior Mr. Eyre was involved with the hotel. Maybe the rumor was true and Mr. Eyre was not just the manager, but the owner.

The lift didn't jerk quite as hard when she stopped it this time. She escorted Mrs. Plash out. The older woman fished her key out of her dressing gown pocket, but they didn't need it. Her door was already open. Olga, the chambermaid, was inside, packing dresses into tissue paper and putting them into a trunk.

Mrs. Plash faltered at the door and stopped moving. Alecia had to peer over her shoulder.

"Olga?" she asked.

The beautiful Russian woman whipped around. "Oh, Mrs. Plash!"

Mrs. Plash's lips trembled. "What is going on?"

"I—" Olga started then stopped. "I'll step down to Mr. Eyre's office and let him know you have returned, yes?"

"Could you arrange for food to be brought as well?" Alecia asked. "Mrs. Plash is hungry."

"Oh, miss, there is already a car waiting outside. I'm only just finishing the packing."

"It hasn't been half an hour since I went to search for her," Alecia said.

"I had help at first," Olga said. "But she had to start cleaning the rooms on this floor."

Alecia felt a hand on her shoulder. Ivan looked down at her, the dark stubble on his face only emphasizing his beautifully cut jawline. "What is the news? Oh, you found her. Excellent!"

"You can't let them send her away," Alecia said. "She'll be even more confused in an unfamiliar place. We've had church families go through similar experiences."

Ivan drew her aside as Mrs. Plash wrung her hands. "Mr. Eyre won't have her in the hotel any longer, because Miss Plash attacked him."

"What?"

"Physically attacked him," Ivan confirmed. "You heard her upstairs. She's a lunatic."

"I don't think they should go. What does Mr. Eyre think, treating a woman like that? He's flirted with me in front of Miss Plash. He's not a nice man."

"He's my employer," Ivan said. "Please don't speak about him like that, especially here."

"I'm hungry," she said. "Instead of a quiet morning, you know what I had. Embarrassment, no privacy, and another ramble through the basement. I want a cup of tea and for Mr. Eyre to behave himself." And a husband.

"I'll go down to the Coffee Room and get tea and toast for you both while Olga finishes the packing."

Olga spoke up. "I was going to go downstairs myself." Then she muttered something in Russian.

Ivan rolled his eyes. "I'll do it. Finish your task."

Ivan took the steps from the fifth floor to the ground floor. He needed time to gather his thoughts. While he was grateful Mrs. Plash had been found, his entire existence felt muddled. Alecia wasn't the only person to have been denied her morning cup of tea. When he touched his chin he could feel the stubble. He didn't like to present himself in this unwashed fashion. Not only was it against the employee handbook, it just didn't look right in such an upscale establishment.

He went directly to Mr. Eyre's office.

"What?" the manager barked.

"Miss Loudon found Mrs. Plash. Olga is almost finished with the packing."

"And Miss Plash?"

"Half an hour ago she was still hysterical." Ivan shrugged.

Eyre glanced up. "The Grand Russe may be at sixes and sevens this morning, but I do recall you are a night watchman, not day staff. Why are you here, Salter?"

"I spent the night with Miss Loudon in the Piano Suite," he admitted.

"You cad," Eyre exclaimed. "Did they walk in on you?"

"Yes, sir." He lifted his gaze to the ceiling.

"Have her confidence now, do you?" Eyre mused.

"I'm not sure how important that is, sir. This situation has come very close to home."

"What do you mean?"

Ivan stared at the battered old ashtray on Eyre's desk. "I saw my, err, someone from my neighborhood with Mr. Marvin."

Eyre frowned. "Mr. Marvin? I can't imagine he wants Ovolensky dead. Have they ever met?"

He straightened. "I wouldn't know, sir."

"Any legitimate reason for Marvin to speak to this person?"

"The person is a Russian caterer."

Eyre shook his head. "No, that won't do. Marvin isn't in charge of catering for the command performance."

"There is a banquet scene in *Macbeth*."

Eyre's eyebrows relaxed. He reached into his coat for his cigarette case. "Maybe he is staging the play Russian-style. Find out from Miss Loudon."

"Very good, sir." He was glad Eyre didn't seem to mind about the suite. Just as he'd expected from such a worldly sort.

"We're moving the Plashes to the boardinghouse where Olga lives. Do you know it?"

"Yes, sir." Where everyone lived had come up in conversation when all the employees started work.

"Help with the transport, will you? You can add all this to your time card. Except the time with Miss Loudon. Although, now that you've become intimate, I wonder if you can ask her more direct questions. Have her find out more about the play, for instance."

"I'm sure she knows about it already."

"Find out for us, then. Where is she now?" Eyre asked with an air of impatience.

"With Mrs. Plash."

"Excellent. You can answer the banquet question right away. I'd hate to think Mr. Marvin is involved in a conspiracy, but if he is, we might be able to stop it right here and now."

Ivan nodded. He walked out, despairing. One night of singular beauty and now it had turned into an act of spy craft or commerce. And Alecia was cross with him. He knew her well enough to tell.

The day continued in the same fashion. Alecia had scarcely spoken to him during the transporting of the bags and the Plash women to the boardinghouse. Ivan didn't blame her, because he and Alecia had had absolutely no privacy and both women were completely distraught, Miss Plash by her failure to secure her man, and Mrs. Plash by contrition. The confused elderly woman was convinced she was to blame for the removal and apologized repeatedly. Alecia could calm her down for a minute or two, then the speech would begin again, as if Mrs. Plash had not said it two minutes before. No wonder Miss Plash had thrown herself into a frenzied lifestyle. The strain of dealing with her mother's condition must be acute.

Alecia didn't seem to mind, however. She was patience itself. If only she looked at him with the soft eyes of love, instead of daggered expressions that made it clear she had not forgiven him for the way their night had ended, and his complicity in removing the women from the Grand Russe.

And she didn't even know about the assassination plot.

He walked to the service corridor at nearly midnight, his feet dragging a bit. Very little rest and a great deal of mental strain over the previous day had taken their toll. He felt a little like he had during those days in Helsinki when he'd been mourning his dead family and trying to keep food in Vera's mouth. Now Vera was the one causing him pain by her refusal to let go of the past.

He saw Alecia sitting on the sofa in the corner where the nightclub back door was. Normally, she leaned against the wall to hear the music better. When he reached her, he realized she'd fallen asleep. Her eyes were closed and her lips were slightly pursed, as if she were ready for a kiss.

Should he carry her up to her room? As he puzzled this out, he seated himself next to her, and realized his feet ached. Surely at twenty-six he was too young to feel like this. His body felt as weighed down as his heart. But looking at this beautiful woman lightened him. He remembered tracing the line of that cheek with his tongue. Now he knew that slim, youthful body under her clothing, how her hips jutted out softly, how her belly gently rounded, how her nipples pointed up slightly. Those sounds she made when he licked her there. *Heaven help him.* He closed his eyes as his erection grew. All those girls from Russian summers had faded into ghosts, but he didn't believe he could ever forget making love to Alecia Loudon. He'd been her first.

He tucked his chin into his hand and stared at her. How often did he have a chance to memorize a woman's face? The close-ups of cinema stars were one thing, but they only lasted a moment. Alecia Loudon in repose was a treasure just for him.

Odd that he'd found peace here, while on the other side of the wall a trumpet blared and he could hear dozens of careless idlers at the nightclub, drinking their champagne, dancing the soles off their shoes, intriguing for their next romantic partner.

Alecia's head listed to the right and she jerked. Her eyelids fluttered. She placed her hands on the sofa cushions as if she felt she was losing balance, then her eyelids popped open. She stared right at him, but it only made her blink. Then she half smiled and looked as if she might fall back to sleep. An instant later, an expression of confusion crossed her lovely face. She stared down. Her hands moved over her gray skirt. Then her head turned and she perused the length of his body.

Ivan was grateful for the long coat that covered the evidence of his desire, inappropriate given that she hadn't known he was watching her.

"Where are we?" She yawned.

"Behind the nightclub."

"I fell asleep?" Her expression was one of fascination rather than upset.

"Yes." She had sleep sand in the corner of one eye. He found it shockingly intimate.

"I never do that. I must be exhausted. What a terrible day."

"It was hard to see the Plashes go," he agreed. "Poor women."

"Sometimes frivolity hides a great deal of pain," Alecia said. "I expect Miss Plash is that way. I knew girls in the village who behaved like her. They'd lost their sweethearts, fiancés, in the war. They'd get into the most shocking scrapes, girls who'd been so respectable before."

"They talk about shell shock for soldiers," Ivan said. "But I think there is a different kind for the civilians. We have our own kind of shock."

"And our own kind of loss. I can never forget how my parents died. It haunts me. Why? They could have died in a train accident, or of influenza. Would it haunt me then?"

"I don't know. I don't think any doctors do."

"No. The human mind is a strange place."

They stared at each other for a moment. "I'm sorry we argued," he said.

"As am I." She wiped her eyes.

"Mr. Eyre has the right to run the hotel the way he sees fit. I didn't mean my defense of him to be an attack on you."

"I still think he behaved shoddily," she said stoutly.

"Mrs. Plash cost the hotel a lot of time. He has to pay overtime to me and to Swankle, and others weren't able to continue their regularly assigned duties. If you look at the situation from his perspective, his actions were logical."

"It was his fault. He brought them here. He knew."

"I don't know that he did." Ivan leaned forward and took her hand. "Besides that, I'm sorry our lovely evening ended so poorly. You deserved better."

"Most of the night was better than most girls ever get to experience." She bowed her head. "I'd better go upstairs. I have a long day of rehearsal tomorrow, and if I can sleep tonight I had best take advantage of it."

He heard unspoken thoughts in her voice. What were they? "You didn't have any nightmares last night."

Her lips curved. "You chased them away."

Alecia woke on Thursday morning, later than usual, with a sick feeling in the pit of her stomach. Wednesday had been horrid. She couldn't stay with the Marvins much longer. Sybil was attending rehearsal in only the most limited fashion, before dashing off with claims that she needed to meet someone or other for her new play. Richard was sinking into a gloom and had been nipping at a flask all the previous afternoon. He'd demanded Alecia go to dinner with him in the hotel restaurant and then pawed at her all through the meal, until he was in a stupor. The night watchman Swankle had helped her take him upstairs. After Swankle left, Richard had made the most foul proposal to her, in language she scarcely recognized as Anglo-Saxon.

When she remembered how lovely the sexual act could be in the right hands, it made her want to cry. How could Richard Marvin reduce it to that? Sybil had a lot to answer for, treating her husband like discarded trash, but then, if this behavior was habitual, Alecia wasn't sure she could blame Sybil.

Would today bring more of the same? Sybil no longer told her what her day's schedule would be. Ovolensky was arriving tomorrow and the command performance would be the next week. At least Sybil hadn't been lying about knowing her lines already, unlike some of the other actors.

Alecia rose and went to her jug of water to begin her ablutions. She'd been afraid to leave the suite the night before to see Ivan, for fear Richard would become ill from his overindulgence. Ivan had apologized, so he wasn't angry with her. And she was grateful that Peter Eyre wasn't angry with him. After what they had done in the Piano Suite, she had hopes of a real relationship with Ivan. She needed to start thinking about his career over hers. If they married, her job would be to support him, not criticize Peter Eyre, who controlled Ivan's immediate future. Not that he'd offered her any hope in that direction.

After she dressed, she went into the corridor and back into the main room of the suite. A tea service had already been delivered and Sybil was seated behind it in an ornate, Egyptian-style dressing gown, her long braid dangling down her shoulder while she read a newspaper.

"You're up late."

"I hadn't been sleeping well and now I am catching up," Alecia said, sitting next to Sybil on the sofa and pouring a cup of tea.

"I had a note from Mr. Eyre slipped under my door," Sybil said. "About Richard's shocking behavior in the restaurant yesterday evening."

Alecia took a gulp of her tepid tea, but said nothing.

"I told you, darling, you needn't encourage him. Why did you allow it?"

"Allow what? Should I have said no when he ordered me to dinner? He doesn't like to eat alone."

"That is not your concern, Alecia. Don't be a child. You must have known what he had in mind."

"In a restaurant?" Alecia said. "I had to have known he'd attempt to make love to me in public?"

"He was drunk," Sybil said. "Anything could happen. Going to dinner with my husband is not part of your duties."

Alecia wanted to make a cutting remark about Sybil's disappearance, but wasn't foolish enough to risk it. She didn't understand how the night's disaster could be laid on her doorstep at all, but somehow Sybil seemed to be laying some blame at her feet. "I'm sorry. I didn't know what to do. He was forceful."

"But not so forceful that you didn't take the time to wear one of my dresses to dinner."

"It was the velvet," Alecia said. "I still had it in my room from the other night."

"Take it to Ethel now, to curb such impulses in the future," Sybil said.

"Yes, ma'am, of course." Alecia drained her teacup and went to retrieve the dress, feeling very badly used. Sybil could have Ethel clean the wine stain courtesy of Richard's clumsiness the night before. When the maid didn't answer her door, she returned the dress to her own wardrobe, and felt not the slightest bit guilty.

Ivan buttoned his coat in front of the mirror in the employee lounge just before he went upstairs to begin his rounds. At eight P.M.

the main floor would be busy with diners and Eyre's acolytes in the Coffee Room. Eventually the traffic would move from the Restaurant to the Reading Room, and the Coffee Room crowd would drain into the nightclub, but that was still a couple of hours away. He'd be diligent until eleven or so, then check the service corridor for Alecia. The hotel would probably be quiet. The Plashes were gone and the Gypsies had been scared off for now. No troublemakers had moved in. Tomorrow, Ovolensky would arrive and security would be heightened.

"Evening," Swankle said as he entered the room.

"Running late?" Johnson asked. He glanced up from the *Daily Herald*, then folded it and set it down on the arm of the ancient armchair he sat in.

"Bloody bus," Swankle said in answer, pulling off his muffler and tossing it on his hook.

Ivan went to the notice board and saw Eyre's staff note was all about plans for tomorrow. Swankle followed him, stripping off his overcoat.

"The watch staff is being increased by fifty percent," Swankle read over his shoulder. "What is Eyre worried about?"

"Lots of unhappy Russians in London."

"Not as many as Paris, or even Berlin, right?" Swankle said. "I don't understand it myself. The tsar's been dead so long. It's all old news."

"You aren't Russian. We have long memories. Besides, no one knows for sure what happened to the imperial family."

"Sounds pretty cut and dried to me. Except maybe for Princess Anastasia."

"Grand Duchess," Ivan corrected. "Forgive me for not discussing Russian politics with you, but I need to get on with the evening."

"Don't be daft," Swankle said. "I was only teasing."

"None of it was funny," Ivan said. "You'd feel the same if I made disparaging comments about Queen Mary."

Swankle shrugged. "I don't much care about the royals. What have they ever done for me? Guess I have more in common with the Bolshies than I realized."

Ivan turned on his heel and stomped out. There was a time when he wouldn't have minded Swankle's levity, but it seemed inappropriate with Ovolensky on his way. The tragic past was coming back to life.

Two hours later, he'd completed his first rounds and was walking through the Grand Hall, making sure everything was in its place.

"Mr. Salter," called the night porter, curling his fingers around the pocket watch that hung from a chain attached to his waistcoat.

Ivan walked toward him as the man gestured him forward.

"I can't leave the floor. There's an intoxicated man in the Coffee Room who isn't with his wife, if you know what I mean, but I happen to know his wife is in the Restaurant dining with her sister."

Ivan's eyes widened. "Can you keep them apart?"

The night porter's expression was pained. "I can do my best. Mr. Eyre is still in the Coffee Room. Could you take this note to him so he can be apprised?"

"With pleasure." Ivan took the note, on folded hotel stationery, and nodded at the night porter.

When he went into the Coffee Room, he found it in full swing. The high, arch voices of fashionable men said silly things; half-drunk women swayed on their high heels, tittering.

Mr. Eyre saw him and gestured him over. Ivan handed him the note, and his manager said, "Some trouble with the band tonight. Trombone player has hurt his hand."

"Can they find a replacement?"

"Working on it now." Eyre opened the note and sighed, then lifted his chin at a rotund banker-type with a black-haired vamp on his lap. "There's trouble."

"It all loves to come to the Grand Russe."

"We want it to keep coming because it makes money. But let's not tell the salacious tale to our guests until tomorrow." Eyre winked at him. "Since I have you here, can you take this to the Chinese Suite?" He pulled a creamy envelope out of his pocket as a bottle of champagne popped nearby, sounding like a gunshot.

Ivan flinched but took it. "What is it?"

"Invitation to a drinks party at Number Ten. Ovolensky, of course."

"Of course," Ivan repeated. His jaw ached from the effort of not clenching it in front of his employer. "Straightaway."

"Sorry to make you a messenger. I have this sense we are short-staffed tonight, though I don't think we are."

"Some nights feel that way," Ivan agreed. "Is it a full moon?"

"I can't remember the last time I saw the moon," Eyre said. "By the way, did you find out if the *Macbeth* banquet is going to be Russian?"

"Miss Loudon did say there were elements of Russian interest integrated into the play, including the banquet." He hadn't learned anything that made him think his sister was involved in the preparations, however.

"Very good. Anything you can learn," Eyre said casually.

"I'll take my leave." Ivan inclined his head and walked away, ignoring the frivolity behind him.

He took the service lift to the Chinese Suite and knocked on the door, but no one answered. When he pressed his ear to the door he couldn't hear anything inside, but the walls were solid. He walked down the hall to Alecia's room but had no answer there either. Should he push the note under the main suite door? He had a feeling that Mr. Eyre wanted the message delivered personally, and he knew the Marvins weren't in the Restaurant.

They could have stepped up rehearsals with the command performance coming so soon. So he went back to the lift and took it to the first floor where the play was going to be performed.

The first floor seemed deserted, which was common at this time of night unless there was an event in the small ballroom. He stepped off the lift, wondering where the Marvins—and more importantly, Alecia—were.

He decided to check the connecting rooms anyway. Swankle had this floor for rounds tonight, so he didn't waste time looking around. Not a soul was in the corridors. All the drama was on the ground floor tonight. He took a moment to stop in front of his favorite painting in the hotel. While he didn't recognize the exact landscape, the view of a river with a dacha on the banks was a memory of someone's beloved, lost home. While it reminded him of Tver, it wasn't his river in the painting. He could feel the artist's memory being employed. The work was unsigned and he had yet to meet anyone who recognized it. The brushstrokes reminded him a little of van Gogh, but more delicate. The same intensity of colors was the chief point of comparison. He had the sense that a woman had painted it.

A sound came from the end of the corridor. A chair squeaking on the floor? Something falling? He left the painting as his senses went on alert. All the doors to the connecting meeting rooms were closed, but there was nothing else at the end of the corridor. Had a piece of scenery or prop fallen? Was someone down here after all?

He pushed open the first door and found the room empty, though the chandelier overhead was still on. The divider between the rooms was half up. Beyond it was the room with the raised floor.

He heard the sound again, a dragging noise. Striding forward, he reached the room divider and bent it back against itself, folding it against the wall.

The scene was like something from a movie. Little in the way of furnishings decorated the stage; only a scarred wooden table and four chairs. A gin bottle and two glasses waited on the table with half of a sandwich on a plate, the meat curling tiredly around the bread. Richard Marvin was bent over Alecia, dragging her on the floor by her hair and the collar of her dress, which was pulled up under her chin. She coughed and struggled weakly, but her dress must have her half strangled. Richard seemed to be pulling her under the table. As Ivan ran forward, the fabric of her homemade dress made a tearing sound. Alecia clawed at the floor.

Richard bumped the table with his hip. The bottle wobbled and fell on its side. Gin poured onto the table and dribbled off, wetting Alecia's hair.

Ivan didn't think. He closed his hand into a fist and swung at the older man, using his entire torso to lend weight to the move. Marvin bowed back comically, then fell over Alecia, his leg striking her shoulder. Ivan climbed over his lover and grabbed for the man, pulling Richard away from her. Richard had lost his grip on her torn dress but still held some of her hair. Maddened, Ivan kicked and punched until Alecia had pulled herself into a ball, away from the two men, free of Richard's grasp.

Richard attempted to land a blow of his own, but only caught Ivan in the shoulder. Ivan grabbed him in his best approximation of a wrestling hold and took him down, hard, to the floor, stunning Richard into stillness.

Alecia moaned and Ivan saw Richard held a fistful of her long blond hair, pulled painfully from her head. He winced. How that must have hurt.

"What's this!" A shout rang out behind them.

Ivan, breathing hard, didn't move or look behind him. "Alecia? Are you well?"

She didn't answer. A moment later, Swankle peered over his shoulder.

"He was attacking Alecia," Ivan gasped. "Miss Loudon."

Swankle's oniony breath disappeared as the man moved away. "Are you all right, miss?"

Ivan heard Swankle kneel next to her. All Alecia could do was cough. When Ivan turned his head, he saw her holding her reddened throat.

"What happened?" Swankle asked.

"It was the scene," Richard wheezed. "Act five, scene eight. Macduff drags Macbeth's body. I had trouble with the blocking."

"Liar." Ivan tightened his grip on Marvin's shoulder and arm. "You're playing Macbeth, not Macduff."

"I wasn't trying to hurt her." Richard's reddened face suddenly calmed. "And if Miss Loudon wants to keep her position, she won't contradict me."

Actors.

Chapter Fourteen

"She reeks of gin," Swankle reported, staring down at Alecia, her legs drawn against her torso as she leaned against a table leg, coughing.

"Marvin knocked the bottle over on her. I saw him hit the table." Ivan's hand clenched around Richard Marvin's shoulder.

Marvin moaned theatrically.

"Let him go," Swankle demanded of Ivan.

"You can't believe him," Ivan said. "I saw him dragging her by her hair and dress. Look, you'll see it is torn. Her hair is in his hand."

"Miss Loudon?" the other night watchman asked.

She, still in a ball, merely held her hands to her throat and coughed.

Ivan repeated himself. "He ripped her dress. He was pulling her by her hair, Swankle. You can't believe him."

"You saw what you did, and he has an explanation for it," Swankle said stiffly. "As a guest of this hotel, I have to believe him, unless the young lady says different."

"Can you speak?" Ivan begged her.

She coughed again. Tears leaked from her eyes and drifted down her cheeks. He wanted to go to her, but was afraid of what the other man would do next.

Richard waved his hands feebly in the air.

"You have to let him up, Salter," the other watchman said. "She works for him. Let him go."

"Find a doctor," Ivan suggested. "She needs medical attention. Get Eyre."

"Not until you let him go," Swankle said in a patient voice.

Ivan's left arm trembled, a sign of how tightly he was holding the actor. With a growl of frustration, he lifted the man slightly then released his grip. He heard Marvin's forehead thud on the hollow stage as he swiveled around and went to Alecia.

"Go for a doctor," Swankle said when Ivan reached Alecia.

"You do it." Ivan knelt next to her.

"I can't trust you with Marvin," Swankle told him. "It has to be you."

"Alecia?" Ivan asked, wiping away the track of a tear. "Do you feel safe here for a few minutes?"

"He was going to rape me." Her voice was a broken thread. "I wasn't teasing him."

"I know that," Ivan told her, as Swankle's eyes widened. "You've been trying to do your job, nothing more."

She reached for his hand. He wrapped his other arm around her shoulders and he helped her sit up. "You shouldn't have hurt him."

"It was instinct. I'm not sorry," he said.

"He'll have your position." She coughed.

"I don't care."

She wheezed when she took a breath. "I'm going to lose mine."

"You can't stay with the Marvins now."

"She needs rest," Swankle said. "Stop talking. If she can stand, take her to her room, get the doctor, and send Mr. Eyre to me."

Ivan frowned as he turned to the younger man. Where had he developed such an air of authority? Swankle was more than he had seemed before. He would have to watch carefully to make sure the night watchman didn't have some involvement in the bombing matter.

Reaching an arm around Alecia's back, he helped her to her feet. "What do you think?"

She coughed, the spasm racking her thin frame. He could see her collarbone through the torn collar of her black dress. Marvin had needed to use some force to tear the serviceable fabric.

"I'll carry you," he said, bending his knees so he could slip his arm under hers and swing her up. Without a backward glance, he took her out of the room and walked toward the service lift. "Should I take you directly to the hospital?" he asked.

"I don't think it's that bad. I was in shock. He came at me suddenly."

"This had been coming for a while. Were you drinking with him?" He knew Marvin had a creditable tale. Did she?

"No. He offered, even demanded, but I'm not such a fool as that. He's been making advances. There's no liquor on my breath."

"Good." Ivan held her against him as the lift went down. On the fifth floor, there were people in the halls. A middle-aged woman looked at him with great suspicion, but he kept his head high and held Alecia close. She'd closed her eyes as if to hide from their audience.

He opened the door to the sitting room of the Chinese Suite, where the light was better, so he could examine Alecia for injuries.

Instead of peace, he heard a shriek and rushing feet. He turned his back to absorb a blow. "Mrs. Marvin!"

She stepped back, wild-eyed. "Ravisher!"

"No, ma'am. That would be your husband." Keeping his gaze on Mrs. Marvin, he went to the sofa and gently deposited Alecia there.

The older woman walked unsteadily on her high-heeled slippers. She'd obviously been drinking alone, and the room reeked of stale perfume, cigarettes, and spilled champagne. "W-what are you talking about?"

"Look at her dress," Ivan said grimly. "Mr. Marvin tore it. He dragged her by her hair, nearly choked her. I found them just in time."

"W-what were you doing there?"

"I had a note." Ivan patted the breast of his jacket, then reached in and pulled out the envelope. "From Mr. Eyre."

Mrs. Marvin's eyes crossed before she blinked and took the envelope. "For me?"

"Your husband."

She dropped the envelope like it burned her. It fell on the carpet and she stepped on it as she turned to Alecia. "I told you not to bother about him."

Alecia pulled the edges of her torn collar together. Her voice was hoarse. "He attacked me, Sybil."

"He claimed he was rehearsing the scene where Macduff drags Macbeth's body," Ivan said.

Alecia put her fingers to her eyes. "It was a lie. He wasn't rehearsing at all."

"What were you doing there?" Sybil demanded.

"He claimed he needed help moving scenery," Alecia said.

Mrs. Marvin collapsed ungracefully onto the sofa next to her employee. "You'll both lose your jobs over this. I can't protect either of you."

"Why are you here?" Alecia rasped. "I thought you were at rehearsals for your new part."

"They sacked me," Mrs. Marvin said.

"What?"

"I'm sure Richard will tell you to go, because we can't afford a secretary now," she said, slurring slightly. "You won't say anything, will you? I'll give you an extra week's pay. You can go as soon as Richard gets around to making the speech."

Alecia shuddered. "You can't think I want to be anywhere near him after what he did."

"They will ask us to leave the hotel as soon as the performance is done," Mrs. Marvin said. "So much unpleasantness. Why couldn't you stay away from him? I thought you were smart. I trusted you."

"If I understand you correctly, you've always known your husband would attempt to assault Miss Loudon?" Ivan asked. "And you thought she would be able to avoid this situation?"

"Yes."

"A naïve vicar's granddaughter? With his wife almost never around and a major performance about to happen? How could you possibly have thought she could avoid him?" Ivan demanded.

Alecia shook her head. "Don't fight. I'd like to go to my room."

"You should have a doctor," he said.

"Who would pay?" Alecia asked. "And what could they tell me? I just need to rest. It hurts to talk and my scalp is aching."

Sybil stared at her dispassionately. "You aren't bleeding, but bruises are coming up on your neck."

"Has he ever done this to you?" Ivan asked.

Sybil's eyes were bottomless pools when she turned her gaze to him. "What does that matter?"

"You won't leave him? Divorce these days isn't such an issue."

"We're the Marvins." Her eyes lost focus again.

How he wished Alecia had been savvier and had understood the risks she had taken when she accepted this position. It was so obvious now why they'd hired such an inexperienced person. She was ripe for abuse. But if she hadn't been so foolish, he'd never have met her. Or been about to lose his own position.

He bent down and picked up the envelope, then set it on the table. "Please don't lose this. Is there anything I can do for either of you?"

"Keep your little Russians away from my husband," Mrs. Marvin said. "I know all about that mistress of his."

Vera. He'd almost forgotten. When had his sister decided to betray Sergei? He bent forward and grabbed Mrs. Marvin's arm, then put his face right into hers. "What do you know?"

"She's trouble," the actress said. "And she must not be enough for Richard or he'd have left Alecia alone."

Ivan dropped her arm, fuming, and went to the desk. He took a piece of writing paper and a pen, then handed them to Mrs. Marvin. "Write Miss Loudon a character now, please. I'll keep it safe for her."

"You won't get one from the hotel, not after this."

As if he cared. "I'm concerned for Miss Loudon. I won't have her turned out without a character."

"Fine."

Ivan stood over her as she composed a brief note. "Fix the date," he demanded, when he saw she'd written 1924 instead of 1925.

When Mrs. Marvin was finished, the note was sloppy but positive. He tucked it into an envelope he found in the writing table, then put it in his pocket. "I have to see Mr. Eyre now. Are you certain you don't want a doctor?"

Alecia shook her head. "I'll go to bed, if Sybil thinks I'll be allowed to use the room."

Mrs. Marvin stared steadily ahead. "It's yours until Richard sacks you. I don't care."

"Will he hurt you when he discovers you've lost your role?" Ivan asked.

"I've called our agent, Max. He'll share the news when Richard is sober." She poured the last ounce of champagne into her glass. "It's back to the cheap stuff, I'm afraid."

"Lock yourself in," Ivan told Alecia, then helped her rise. He walked her into the corridor without a backward glance at the other woman. "I wish I could take you home with me."

"The longer I can stay, the more hope I have of receiving my pay."

"I wonder if Mrs. Marvin will remember any of this in the morning."

"She isn't that drunk," Alecia said. "But she's shattered. I wonder how she lost the part?"

"It doesn't matter. You'd have been out the door either way."

"What was that about Richard's mistress?" she asked.

Ivan shook his head. "Don't worry about that. Just make sure, however it goes, that you are on your way out of the Grand Russe before the command performance. They will probably be forced to leave right after that. You don't want to be mixed up in it, especially when you'll be lucky to get your wages."

"I'll be due my full week's wages by tomorrow day's end," she reflected.

"Take what you can get and go," he advised.

"What about you?" Her voice was creaking again and he could see it was painful for her to swallow. "When will you be sacked?"

"Might be in five minutes," Ivan admitted. "I hit a guest."

"There is my side of the story," she said.

"If I had handled it without violence, there might have been some hope," he said. "But I didn't."

Alecia's lips flattened over her teeth. "I'm glad you hit him." She touched his cheek, then unlocked her bedroom door and went in without a backward glance.

The vicar's granddaughter had some less than Christian thoughts, and he couldn't blame her. Unfortunately, the flapper's life had a dark side, and that didn't just mean jazz and revealing clothes.

Since she hadn't closed the door behind her, he followed her in and closed it. He wanted to be gone before Mr. Marvin came this way, but also needed to be convinced the adjoining door was locked.

While Alecia sat down on her narrow bed, he went to the door and tested it. "I wish it had a deadbolt, too."

"He's never come in."

"After what he did downstairs, you should not trust him in any fashion."

"He and Sybil will argue before they come to me again." Her voice went from hoarse to a dead whisper during the course of her sentence.

"You must not speak anymore. Rest your throat."

"I should pack."

"No, rest, please. I'll call for a doctor if you don't."

She sighed and leaned her head against the wall. He found her tooth mug and poured water into it, then gave it to her.

"Is there anything I can do for you? Should I stand guard?"

"You must defend yourself," she said. "Important."

"I'll bring Mr. Eyre up to see your neck. Is your scalp bleeding?"

He touched her head delicately. Blood caked a small portion of her roots, but the wound was small. He felt a sympathetic twinge in his own scalp.

She nodded and drank a sip, then coughed.

I'll let Mr. Eyre decide about the doctor. He forced a smile. "We'll be back soon. Don't open the door unless you hear my voice, or Mr. Eyre's."

"You can't promise that."

"I'll make it his responsibility. This happened in his hotel." He leaned over her and kissed her gently on her forehead, then went out the door, testing the doorknob to make sure it had locked.

As he walked down the hall, he heard the grandfather clock near the guest lift strike midnight. With each gong, he heard doom. He'd only managed to hold this position for five weeks. What would happen to him, Vera, and Sergei now? He'd have to ask Boris to take him into the pawnshop business, something he'd always refrained from doing. It was the only quick fix he had, if he left here without a good reference. At least he'd secured one for Alecia.

He wanted to take the steps downstairs, to delay the penultimate moment, but for fear of Alecia's health, he had the lift operator take him directly to the ground floor. The Coffee Room had emptied and Mr. Eyre was no longer on site, but the night staff knew what the day staff probably didn't. Mr. Eyre lived in apartments behind his office, with a secret, private entrance not unlike something out of an American speakeasy.

"I've got to see Mr. Eyre," he told Lionel Dew, at his place behind the desk.

"What about?" Dew's eyes were heavy lidded. He didn't look like he'd survive the night without falling asleep.

Under other circumstances Ivan would have offered to fetch some coffee. "Mr. Marvin attacked and injured Miss Loudon. I pulled him off her."

Dew's eyelids lifted. "Crikey. Go on through. You know how to open the door?"

"Yes, sir." Ivan lifted up the hinged part of the desk and passed the key box and guest letter slots, through to the inner workings of the business office.

Mr. Eyre's office door was locked, but Ivan had the hotel master key, so he went through, then found the eye socket on a piece of fake

Egyptian Isis statuary that was really a door knocker. Not ten seconds later a relief panel slid back and Mr. Eyre stood in the inky entryway, still in a suit and tie.

"What?" he asked.

"Mr. Marvin attacked Miss Loudon on his stage."

Eyre's expression didn't change. "And?"

"She's mildly injured, visibly bruised, will have lost her position."

"And?"

"I punched Mr. Marvin," Ivan admitted. "After I pulled him off her. I discovered them. Then Swankle discovered me on Marvin."

"Is he mildly injured and visibly bruised as well?" Eyre asked sardonically.

"I expect I bruised some part of his face. He's intoxicated," Ivan added.

"Where are they?" Eyre picked up a cigarette from a table and put it to his lips.

"Miss Loudon is in her room. I told her to open the door only to one of us. Swankle still has Marvin upstairs. We told Mrs. Marvin. She didn't seem surprised."

He lit the cigarette. "The Marvins are our guests. The situation is a difficult one."

Ivan heard footsteps rushing behind him. Mr. Dew was at his back in a moment.

"The Russians are here, sir."

Eyre slowly took the cigarette out of his mouth. He had yet to inhale. "When it rains it pours, gentlemen. Ivan, go into my office and phone the doctor on call. Have him see to Mr. Marvin, then Miss Loudon. He'll tell us if we need to bring in the police, but it must be done quietly."

The two managers walked out of the office together. Ivan picked up the telephone and asked the hotel switchboard to connect him to whichever doctor was on duty and explained the matter. Grumbling emanated from the man when Ivan had to admit he didn't know where one of the patients presently was, but, ignoring orders, he told the man to attend Miss Loudon first and then he would find Mr. Marvin.

Unwilling to see his family's nemesis in the flesh—or even worse, allow Ovolensky to see him—he went into a rear corridor and from there went out onto the street from the exit closest to the service lift to wait for the doctor. The mid-January, middle-of-the-night weather did not suit his indoors-acclimated body well, and he was shivering despite his heavy coat by the time the doctor pulled up in a taxicab.

The man was unshaven and smelled of wine, but his walk was purposeful and his voice clipped. Ivan took him to Alecia's room and announced the doctor, and then went to look for Marvin.

Downstairs, he walked slowly through the corridor to the meeting rooms. He could hear men's voices and became suspicious immediately. What could Marvin and Swankle be speaking about? They had nothing in common.

Unfortunately, he couldn't hear actual words through the thick walls. He opened the door as slowly as he could, hoping he might save his position if he heard something incriminating, but they had stopped speaking, and Swankle stepped away from Marvin as the doorway widened.

He didn't see bloodstained handkerchiefs or any other reason the night watchman might be attending the actor so closely. They looked like coconspirators. Ivan wondered if he was being paranoid or realistic. It was hard to know.

"Well?" Swankle demanded.

How differently he behaved now that his star seemed ascendant. "I spoke to Mr. Eyre, but he is occupied with Mr. Ovolensky's arrival." He stepped forward.

Marvin moved back into the shadows with an exaggerated cringe.

"Come now, Mr. Marvin," Ivan jeered. "You aren't playing Richard III. You and I both know I was saving Miss Loudon from rape or worse."

Marvin's posture changed. He stepped into the spotlight created by a chandelier. "You brutalized me and I will have your position for it."

"As long as Miss Loudon is safe, that is all I care about," Ivan responded.

The actor scoffed. "You'll trade your job for hers?"

"We've both lost our positions, I expect."

"I haven't decided that."

"Your wife has. She lost her new role tonight."

"What?" Marvin shrieked. He put his hands into his hair and made fists. "That blasted woman! If she's going to spread her knees for every director, it at least needs to count!"

He stomped off toward the door. Ivan could see he had indeed bruised the man's face. He had a swollen cheekbone on one side, but other than that, he seemed in fine fettle.

The door slammed, and he was left alone with Swankle.

"I don't think they are in the first ranks any longer, those Marvins," Ivan said.

"No," Swankle agreed. "But then, neither are you. It is Miss Loudon who loses on both counts, I believe."

Ivan noticed that even Swankle's accent had changed. He sounded educated now. "Who are you?"

Swankle shrugged, and he smiled that fatuous, young man's grin. "Don't matter to you. You'll be lucky to finish out your shift."

"Won't you defend me? You know what was happening. You heard Marvin not deny what I said about his attempted rape."

"You did more than just pull him off the girl. You and I both know that. You lost your sense of purpose here."

"You mean my sense of class distinction? Doesn't a vicar's granddaughter rate more highly than an actor?"

Swankle shrugged. "These days? Celebrity rates higher than anything below the titled classes."

Ivan saw no purpose in arguing. "I'm going to go back to my rounds. Mr. Eyre has his plate full. He can find me and sack me when he has time. But for now, I know my duty."

"As you wish," Swankle said. "It's nothing to me."

Ivan did just that, though he did stop by Alecia's room to check on her. She answered the door in her dressing gown, visibly surprised to see him still in the hotel.

"I'm sorry, were you asleep? It's after one A.M."

"The doctor told me to rest. But I'm fine."

"I'll leave you be, then. I don't know how much longer I'll be here."

"Have you spoken to Mr. Eyre?"

"We were interrupted by Ovolensky's arrival."

Alecia swallowed hard and made a pained face. "Oh dear."

"Rest. Mr. Marvin indicated he might not sack you over what he did to you, but—"

"They can't afford to keep me, and I can't risk staying," she said. "They've been arguing. I could hear it through the walls. If I wasn't so tired I'd have already packed."

"Then rest as long as you can in your room. I'll bring you breakfast at eight if I'm still here." He paused. "If I haven't come to your door by eight thirty in the morning, then I've been sacked."

She reached out, and he clasped her hand, then bent forward and kissed it like a Frenchman.

"Lock the door," he told her, then went back to work.

At eight A.M., he hadn't seen the hotel manager. He'd heard that several staff spent much of the night in the Piano Suite, bringing in everything Ovolensky had requested for himself and his staff. Two bedrooms had been locked away from other suites and opened for the Russians, making it a three-bedroom unit. Rumor had it that the rooms now overflowed with ice and caviar, prostitutes and smoked salmon. He had no idea if any of it was true and he didn't care.

As soon as the main clock struck eight, he went into the Coffee Room, poured two cups of coffee, and filched some rolls and butter, then went upstairs and knocked on Alecia's door. She'd probably still be sleeping.

When she opened the door she was still in her dressing gown, but her hair was in a night braid and looped around her shoulder. "You're still here!" Her voice was raspy, evidence of her previous night's ordeal.

"Busy night for management. Here, coffee and cream."

She took a cup and a roll. "Ivan, I think you should leave."

He didn't understand her meaning. He took a long sip of his own cup. "We need to talk."

She drank too, her eyes on him. "Every second you are here you run the risk of Mr. Eyre seeing you and sacking you. The longer you can avoid him, the better chance that everyone's temper will calm. I think you should leave right away and not return until your next shift."

"What about you?"

She shrugged. "I'm doing the same thing. Hiding. I'm so glad you brought me food."

He handed her the rest of the rolls and butter. "Then take all of these for later."

She smiled and deposited them in her pockets. "Come see me at midnight if you last that long."

He nodded, then kissed her cheek. "Sleep as much as you can to rest your throat."

"The coffee feels heavenly," she admitted. "It seems like a bad dream, last night."

"It wasn't." He drained his cup. "I'll fill this with water in the bathroom and bring it back."

He went down the hall to the bathroom used by the guests' servants and filled it to the brim, then returned it to her.

"Thank you."

They smiled at each other. "Everything is going to have to change," he said.

"We've had good times here at the Grand Russe. I've had adventures worthy of sharing with grandchildren," she said.

Me too. Would they be shared grandchildren? He wanted to kiss her again, but she held both cups of liquid and she needed to drink them. Instead, he stared at her for a long moment, then left to take the service lift to the basement and hopefully get his overcoat and leave before anyone saw him. If he could get home and return again, at least he'd probably be paid for one more night's shift.

He waited ten minutes at the service lift. It never came, thanks to being in use elsewhere. He didn't dare use the guest lift in uniform, so he went down the stairs, all six flights, his feet aching and his heart weary.

"What are you doing here?" Swankle asked as Ivan turned the corner on the first floor.

"What are you doing here?" Ivan countered. They were both still dressed for their shifts, in full uniform.

"I am still employed here. I expect you are not."

"Neither of us is on the clock," Ivan countered. "Why are you skulking in the stairway?"

Chapter Fifteen

Peter Eyre looked at his own notice on the employee board. He never came to the basement staff lounge. When Lionel Dew took over in the evenings, pinning up the notice was one of his first tasks. Tonight though, Peter had decided he needed to sack Ivan Salter in person. He'd pinned up his own notice, one that announced all Russian staff would be temporarily reassigned to the seventh floor for the comfort of their distinguished guests. All but one, that was.

Truly, Peter wasn't convinced the guests were distinguished. Oh, Ovolensky had fine continental manners, but the men with him seemed more like gangsters than diplomats. And he knew Ivan knew something about these men, not to mention something about a possible plot to kill them.

Meanwhile, however, he had a hotel to run, and guests to protect. He wouldn't choose the safety of some Russian visitors over the safety of a British citizen. Ivan had assaulted a proper British guest. Yes, he'd been provoked, and yes, Peter had to admit he'd had a hand in the situation, having encouraged Ivan to date the delectable Miss Loudon in order to learn about this supposed plot.

But here they were. The Russians had arrived, he'd never heard anything definitive about the assassination plot, and a night watchman had beaten a hotel guest for choking his secretary while he was supposedly blocking a scene for a command performance that was real, with a real dragging scene in it. Whether that was the entire story or not, who was he to judge? A little scandal was one thing, but he wasn't about to scare off his guests by calling in the authorities because of the fears of a paranoid night watchman.

He felt worse about Alecia Loudon being injured. He'd had his eye on the shy secretary as well, and he knew she'd sensed the end coming. Richard Marvin's wife wasn't spending any time in the marital boudoir. She'd made a sexual overture at the start of the month. Peter hadn't been tempted. The woman was about fifteen years older than he, and the years showed. She had no more refinement than Emmeline, nothing to offer that he couldn't get at a dozen other places, and with a husband in tow, wouldn't even be that convenient. No, she'd been easy to brush off. Of that trio in the Chinese Suite, he'd only have been willing to play with the secretary they'd victimized.

A steady stream of people began to enter the lounge, leaving their outerwear on pegs, signing their timecards. The clock slipped forward to 7:59 P.M. Swankle and Johnson had come and gone, so where was Salter? He hadn't seemed to be a coward.

There he was. He came in the door at a jog, unbuttoning his coat. Peter stepped forward. "You are risking being late."

"The clock hasn't gone eight yet," Ivan said, then he glanced up, saw who he spoke to. His hands stilled on his buttons and his back straightened.

"I'm sorry, Ivan," Peter said. "But I'm going to have to let you go."

"You need me," Ivan said. "To prevent disaster."

"Last night, my boy, you were the disaster. I can't keep you here."

"You'll regret it," Ivan said. "He was going to rape her. I ought to be a hero."

"You used too much force." Peter pulled out his cigarette case.

Ivan stepped forward, his jaw mulish. "You'd have done the same, if you'd seen a man brutally attacking your lover."

Peter opened his mouth to speak, but Ivan held up his hand. "You know why she's become my lover, you know what is at stake. I may have fallen in love with her, and that's got nothing to do with you, but I was attempting to protect this hotel, both the buildings and the guests, when it all began, and you know that."

"Ivan." Peter opened his case, then closed it again.

"Perhaps you do not know this yet, but Mrs. Marvin has lost her new part, and Miss Loudon hasn't received the impression that Mr. Marvin's screen test went very well, so they are both out of work as soon as the command performance ends. Which means neither of them is going to be in residence a week from now. You'll have sacked an excellent employee and risked people's lives for the sake of a week's public relations with unimportant guests."

Peter had never liked to be told what to do. Staff had no business speaking to him like this. "I have wasted far too much time considering these things," he said. "I know you are good at what you do, and man-to-man, I understand how provoking the scene was for you. But all I can offer you is pay and a character." He reached into his pocket and pulled out two envelopes. "You'll be pleased with the letter. It should help you find another position soon."

"There are so many positions available," Ivan said bitterly.

"I'm sorry," Peter said. "But my hands are tied. You are right, public relations is too much of this, but our reputation is decidedly fragile. The best news for us is none right now, until we are reestablished."

"What about your reputation as a man? You are defending a rapist."

Peter's fingers tightened around the letters. "You go too far." He shoved them in Ivan's direction before he crumpled the contents.

"You're dooming the Grand Russe," Ivan said, tucking the envelopes inside his coat. "When those Russians die, and well they deserve it, the bastards, they will kill this hotel with them." He turned around sharply, the back of his coat flaring out.

Peter had never noticed the military cut of Ivan's old overcoat before. It must be something scavenged from a Russian soldier, long ago. It suited the now former night watchman. He was sorry to watch him go. Ivan had the instincts of an Englishman.

"Here is Mr. Smirnov," Lionel Dew said, coming into the lounge a minute later with an obvious Russian type.

The night manager must have waited for Ivan to leave before he entered. Peter took a long look at the new night watchman. He didn't like Smirnov's eyes, they were set too closely together, but they'd had his application before the hotel ever opened, and he'd checked out. Someone had to be on duty; they couldn't afford to leave the position open.

He nodded. "Mr. Dew will find you a uniform and be with you as you perform your duties this evening. You'll have an easy time of it. Every employee who speaks Russian is working on the seventh floor for the next couple of weeks."

"You have distinguished guests from Russia," Smirnov said slowly. His accent was much thicker than Ivan's, and his voice sounded rusty and unused.

"Yes, a government delegation," Peter confirmed. "Keep a close eye on the Piano Suite. You need to know who belongs on the floor. Mr. Dew will share the guest list with you."

Smirnov nodded. "Very well. I will keep the floor safe."

Peter nodded sharply and left the lounge, fumbling to open his cigarette case. Something about the man unnerved him, whereas Ivan, only a few months younger than he was, felt like someone who might have been a friend if he'd stayed a wealthy, cultured Russian, instead of being thrown to the four winds because of the revolution. But, he was only a pawn in a bigger game now, not a player.

As Peter lit his cigarette, he wondered if the other pawn, Alecia Loudon, had been sacked yet, or if she was still on the board.

Ivan unlocked the front door of his flat, hoping Vera and Sergei were out. It was too much to hope that his sister might be working.

Unfortunately, Vera and Sergei were in the parlor, along with their coconspirator, Pavel. Sergei had been growing his beard out, claiming he needed it to protect his face at work, but he had started to look like his friend.

"Here he is," Vera sneered. "Lost your job, did you?"

"How did you know that?" Ivan asked, shivering as he took off his thin old overcoat. He'd had to leave his watchman's coat and cap behind at the hotel.

"They hired Anatoly to take your place," Sergei said. "He started tonight."

Ivan shook his head. They'd put a fox in the henhouse after kicking out the rooster. And all because he'd been stupid enough to attack Richard Marvin. "So he's going to bring in the bomb, is he?"

"It's none of your concern, coward," Vera said icily.

"How good it is for you to eat my food and rest comfortably under the roof I paid for, plotting to destroy the very lives that gave me my work."

"You are so enchanted by the bourgeoisie," Pavel said, shaking his head sadly. "What must be done to open your eyes, and make you see truth?"

Ivan stepped next to Pavel, who sat on a chair pulled away from the kitchen table, and knocked the cup from his hand. The handle cracked off. The cup rolled on the floor, spilling tea. "I'll become disenchanted when the bourgeoisie stops providing jobs for the working class. Or possibly when you stop eating the bread others toil for. You are nothing but a parasite, Pavel."

"The bourgeoisie do nothing but live off the sweat and tears of the proletariat," a man Ivan had never seen before said, stepping through the door between the parlor and the bedroom. His skin looked young, but there was gray in his sandy beard. "They do not deserve their lives."

"I'm confused and troubled," Ivan said. "You are talking like New Soviets instead of supporters of the late tsar. We were the bourgeoisie, before the revolution, Vera. Where is this new element coming from?"

"We aim to strike at the current government together," the stranger said. "Through its vessel, Georgy Ovolensky. We are the true Marxists. We do not believe in the elitism of political leaders."

Ivan turned to Sergei. "Who is this?"

"The bomb maker," Vera's fiancé said solemnly.

"I think you're being set up," Ivan told him. "No bomb maker is going to casually come to someone's home and chat about it. You're building a criminal conspiracy, not having a tea party."

"You are too much of a coward to give us away," Vera said, smiling in the self-satisfied way Ivan remembered from when she used to take the largest slice of cake from the tray when she was a child.

Ivan pointed at the stranger. "I meant him. He might be a plant."

Pavel bared his teeth. "How dare you."

"You are still a spoiled brat," Ivan said to his sister. He pushed past the so-called bomb maker, attempting to memorize his appearance, and went into the bedroom to pack a bag. He couldn't stay here. All of them, including his sister, were going to end up dead or in jail soon. He would not be a part of that. He owed some piece of his life to Alecia now.

Less than five minutes later, he had folded the majority of his clothing into a sheet and tied it into a bundle. He walked through the parlor without speaking, ignoring Vera's childish insults, hurled at his back in their native tongue.

He didn't yet know how to rescue her from this mess, but he knew clarity would only come after he saved himself.

Alecia spent Friday resting as much as possible, and stayed in her room except for a brief trip downstairs at midnight to see if Ivan waited for her. She hadn't seen him, and the music coming in through the cracks around the nightclub's rear door didn't hold the magic it usually did for her. After she sneaked into the Coffee Room to pocket a little of the stale food left over from the night's revelry, she went back upstairs and tried to sleep through the night.

Oddly enough, the nightmares that troubled her had nothing to do with her parents' deaths, but of Ivan fleeing Russia with his sister. She could scarcely imagine the hardships they must have faced together, two pampered young people in foreign countries. Ivan had told her they couldn't speak a word of German, during a particularly difficult phase of their travels. Luckily, he'd managed with his Russian, English, and French.

When the knock came at her door at ten A.M. on Saturday morning, she was prepared. Her throat still hurt and the bruises were vivid, but she'd found the energy to pack her single cheap valise.

Sybil and Richard stood together, united, in the doorway when she opened it.

"As you know, I have lost my new role," Sybil said.

Richard didn't look at either of them.

"We won't be able to keep you on," Sybil said, thrusting a handful of bills at her. "Here is your pay, plus a little extra for train fare, and you can keep any of the clothing of mine that you've borrowed, if it is still in your room, that is. You need to be out before noon."

Alecia looked in her hand and decided that, yes, she did need to count the bills. She did so, while they stood there impassively. They hadn't shorted her, and the extra would pay for a taxicab and train fare back to the vicarage. She nodded at Sybil.

"I wish you the best, Alecia," Sybil said.

"I should press charges," Alecia said in return, touching her throat. "And you should divorce him, before he does the same to you."

"Go back to your grandfather," Sybil said. "You have your character, and your pay. I'm sorry we couldn't keep you on longer."

Alecia shut the door in their faces. What she didn't understand was why Sybil had come to the door with Richard. Was he meant to frighten her into leaving her room? She was happy to go. Ivan had obviously been sacked even before she had.

It was only when she sank to the bed that she realized what a pickle she found herself in. When her grandfather saw the bruises around her neck, he'd be livid. He might never allow her to leave the vicarage again. And he needed her, didn't he? With Sadie gone.

Sadie. Her sister hadn't yet turned up to work at the hotel. She shook her head, staring at her packed bag. While danger was unlikely for her sister here at the Grand Russe, it would not be an adventure they could enjoy, as sisters, together.

She tucked the bills safely away, then opened the wardrobe again and pulled out the velvet dress Sybil had lent her. She'd meant to leave it there, but it was hers now, the beautiful dress that went with her dearly bought pink leather shoes. Why hadn't she been more practical? So much had changed in her life in only a few weeks. She hugged the dress and thought about her magical night with Ivan, then stuffed it into her valise. Music started somewhere in the back of her thoughts, an Irving Berlin song that had the word "valise" in it.

With a spring in her step that did not match the soreness of her throat, she picked up her bag and took one more quick look around the room that had been her home for more than a month. She walked slowly out of it, down the hall, saying goodbye to everything. The Grand Russe was not a hotel for the likes of her. She'd probably never be inside it again.

The lift operator asked, "Where to?"

She smiled. "The ground floor, please. I'm moving out."

"Sorry to hear that, Miss Loudon," he said in his lilting Indian accent. "Life here simply didn't agree with you?"

She touched her throat. "Keep an eye out for the next secretary, will you? I wouldn't want what happened to me to happen to anyone else."

"Does Mr. Eyre know?" the man asked, looking more closely at her neck.

She nodded.

"Then they won't be staying here long," he said, anger flushing his brown cheeks with red. "Just until those Russians leave. We don't like girls being injured in this hotel."

"And yet they have been. They've even died here." She wondered if her story would be told in the same vein as the Starlet Murders someday, when her very name had been forgotten.

The man clucked his tongue. "It's a grand hotel. Bad things will happen."

"I'm sorry to be going, even so." She bit her lip.

"There's nothing like the Grand." The lift jerked and rattled as it reached the ground floor. "Here you go, miss."

She smiled at him and walked into the Grand Hall of the hotel, feeling like a waif with her suitcase. The elegant surroundings, all shiny finishes, bold colors, and buffed floors, dwarfed her. Around her, Londoners and travelers abounded. She saw the movie star Miss Page walking into the hair salon, followed by a maid carrying a small dog. A bellboy dashed by, holding a basket filled with flowers. The concierge nodded at her as he walked toward the lift, some important mission in mind.

She went to the door and walked outside into the chill January day. Fog kept everything hazy, though the cold bit at her exposed skin. She decided to walk to the train station to conserve her money. If only she knew where Sadie was, she could visit her first, before she went home, but she had no idea where to find her.

"Alecia?"

The fog parted long enough for her to see Ivan, back in his shabby suit and shabby overcoat, standing near the taxicab line. "I didn't know if I'd ever see you again," she said. Her voice broke. What had she been thinking? Just to leave without seeing him? Her brain was as foggy as the landscape. Those nightmares had prevented restorative sleep.

He coughed. "I've been wandering out here, waiting for you. I've left my sister, and Boris has taken me in."

"What happened?"

"My sister. I need to tell you what is happening."

"You look terribly serious."

He nodded. "I have bad things to tell you. Can I take you to Boris's house so we can talk privately?"

She had a feeling that they weren't going to be discussing their courtship. "Very well. My grandfather is not expecting me."

"I'll keep you safe, I promise." His gaze was solemn as he said it, and her heart broke for him. How proud he was, and he'd lost his position, his right to protect the hotel, because of her. She should have left as soon as Richard Marvin made his first pass at her, and now she'd ruined both of their lives.

"I know you will," she said. "You're a good man, Ivan. I trust you."

"I'm not sure you will after this. I've kept a terrible secret from you." He turned in the direction of the East End and began to walk.

"I have taxicab money," she said.

"I'd rather take the bus, but let me carry your valise." She gave it to him, thinking he might need the time spent traveling across town to gather his thoughts.

It didn't take quite as long as she expected, because Boris Grinberg didn't live that close to his pawnshop, but about three miles west. Ivan escorted her into a late-Victorian block of flats, well maintained for the East End.

"It has two bedrooms," he said, after he'd ushered her in and shut the door. "Boris keeps the second one as a study, but there is a cot I can use for now."

"I'm glad you have a place to go, under the circumstances, though I don't understand entirely what those are."

"I'll make us tea," he said. "And then we can talk."

She had always thought that being someone's lover meant you'd feel comfortable in their company. But he hadn't even touched her, and she hadn't rushed into his arms either. Were the blows to their respective career hopes too much for either of them to handle? She wanted to take comfort in him, but all he had to offer were ominous comments, and he'd had a crease between his eyebrows during the entire bus ride here.

She wandered around Boris's parlor, which had furnishings that appeared to be about the same age as the flat—dark, heavy wood with deep red brocade upholstery, some Victorian matron's castoffs. The paintings in the room were all delicate and pastoral, nothing like the bright jewel tones of the Russian art at the hotel. On the mantelpiece were a few old photographs and a curious multi-pronged brass candelabra that looked ancient.

One framed piece of art on the wall looked different from the others. Hidden in the corner to the right of the fireplace, she saw a charcoal drawing, delicately overlaid with watercolor. The little girl had the round cheeks of youth, but her eyes were deep set and shadowed. A hopeful smile was bracketed by dimples, yet the drawing seemed so sad.

"Boris's daughter," Ivan said, coming up behind her. "She died when she was eight."

"How sad. Is he the artist?"

"His sister, I think. She'd never been photographed, so this is all he had."

"How long has he been in England?"

"About fifteen years. Much longer than me. I attempted to pawn my coat right when we came here. For some reason, he wouldn't let me. I don't know why, but we've been friendly ever since."

"It's good to have a friend."

"Do you have any?"

"Not in London." She sighed. "I'm worried about my sister. Why didn't she ever come to the Grand Russe? It's been a week and a half since Grandfather was here."

He patted her arm gingerly. "I'm sure she'll turn up. Meanwhile, I wouldn't suggest anyone spend time at the Grand Russe."

"Why not?"

He clenched his fists. "That's what I need to tell you."

She seated herself next to the tea tray he'd prepared and poured for each of them. While she didn't usually take sugar, his tone made her want to fortify herself. She added liberal amounts of cream and sugar to both cups.

"Thank you," he said, taking the sturdy brown pottery mug from her. "I like these. They are strong and practical like Boris himself."

"Tell me," she said, picking up her mug.

He took a deep breath. "My sister, the one who died, was a revolutionary involved in an assassination plot against Lenin. She was killed by firing squad. It was a fair death in that she was truly involved in the plot. But none of the rest of my family was involved."

"This was Catherine, right?"

"Yes." He stared into his cup. "Georgy Ovolensky is a cousin of ours. A third cousin, and more closely linked to the gentry than we are. No title, but less removed from one. He was always a sneaky boy, what you call a brown-noser, I believe?"

She nodded.

"He would have been more at risk than my family from the Bolsheviks. He informed on my parents to protect himself. They were killed. I fled to Finland with my sister when I heard, as you know. Ovolensky's career began."

Ovolensky, the diplomat staying at the hotel. "And now he's come here."

"Yes, and my sister hates him. She's been mixed up with political types along with her fiancé. They and their friends want him dead. For her, it's personal, but for the others, it is political."

"Of course."

He drained his cup. "They have an idea to kill him in the hotel. I had no idea how far along they'd come in their conspiracy until last night when I came home and discovered they had taken concrete steps toward violence. Usually Vera's friends are nothing more than big talkers."

The way he pressed his lips together told her it was bad. She leaned forward and touched his knee. "What happened?"

"They had another man with them, a real Marxist. My sister and the others were all blathering the same rhetoric, not what I've usually heard from them. I thought they were pro-tsar until now. They've banded with this man, who claims to be a bomber."

Her fingers clutched his knee. "They want to bomb the Grand Russe?"

He stared down at her hand. "At the command performance, they had planned to bring in a bomb. They wanted me to do it."

Shakily, she put her other hand to her forehead. "I'm so confused. Why then? Because there will be British government people in atten-dance? The Bolshies want England to be their playground too."

His fingers came down on the hand she'd placed on his knee. "I am as lost as you. I agree that your idea makes sense, but it never did before. I wonder if they claimed to be pro-tsar in the hopes that I would get involved, and when they gave up on me, their true colors emerged."

She shuddered. "My former employers will be killed. I would have been killed too."

"I don't know. I saw my sister with Richard Marvin, Alecia. Near our flat."

She poured more tea into their cups, feeling the need for some-thing warm, and handed his mug to him. Anything bad about Richard, she wanted to believe. "Then he might be involved in some way."

"I was so angry. And then I saw you being attacked by him." He took a sip of tea and then began to cough.

She set down her mug and pounded him on the back.

"I don't know what to think, what to do," he said, when he could breathe properly again.

"You have to stop it."

"I tried, at least as much as I could without involving my sister.

When they sacked me, Peter Eyre was foolish enough to hire one of the conspirators to replace me."

She saw the desperation in his eyes. They had to take some kind of action. "You've got to get back into the hotel, Ivan. You recognize these people. No one else does. You have to be a bigger man than Mr. Eyre."

Chapter Sixteen

Ivan squeezed her hand. "I can't let my sister be arrested."

"You can't let good people die either." Alecia knelt in front of him on the rug in Boris Grinberg's flat. "You can't, Ivan. I know the situation is so difficult, but we have to figure out how to stop this."

"We were both made to walk away from the hotel," Ivan said, his gaze intense and focused. "We've been silenced."

She shook her head. "I'm not walking away if there is any chance my sister will be working at that hotel."

"You don't have any money to stay in London. You have to go back to your grandfather. I can't take care of you and I can't ask Boris to shelter you too. It's not proper."

"I hope my grandfather knows where Sadie is," Alecia said. "We're lucky to have people who care for us."

Ivan rubbed his forehead. "We don't seem to be very good at managing for ourselves."

"We did just fine until we had trouble with Richard Marvin. How dare they sack you for rescuing me?"

"I did use unnecessary force." He said it dully.

She snapped back. "There is no such thing in regards to a rapist, if you ask me. If he hadn't been drinking he might have succeeded in subduing me before you arrived."

Ivan curved his hand around the back of her skull and leaned forward. "It's worth anything for you to be safe, *myshka*. I love you."

Her lips parted in surprise and his mouth was on hers before she could say anything in response. She pressed both of her hands into his thighs and kissed him back ardently, tangling her tongue with his. He pulled her between his legs and she pressed her torso against his.

Now that she knew what could happen between them, she had no shyness left. She found the lapels of his coat and began to undress him.

His top half was nude and her hands had moved to his trousers before he clasped them in his and stopped kissing her. "We shouldn't do this here."

"In the flat?"

His kiss-swollen lips curved. "In the parlor. My bed is small, but I don't think we'll mind."

He helped her to her feet and then wrapped one arm around her waist, holding her close while they walked the few feet toward the study, where his bed was. Once in the room, he turned the key in the door and toed off his shoes.

Before she could touch her own, he knelt before her to unbuckle her shoe straps.

"I'm dressed in such ordinary clothes," she said.

He ran his fingers up her calf, trussed in sturdy, handmade wool stockings. "Nudity needs no decoration. Particularly with such beauty."

"Ivan," she whispered.

"I've never seen a painting, a sculpture, a landscape, more lovely than you." His fingers roamed up her leg until they found the garter holding her stocking over her knee. He pulled it down and the stocking sagged. Slowly, he removed it, then kissed the outside of her knee.

"I wish I could dress you in silk stockings and shoes even more beautiful than your new pink ones." He kissed the inside of her knee. "But you don't need beautiful things to make you look good."

His mouth moved up her thigh while his hands were busy with her other garter and stocking. Her inner thighs were damp with desire. She wanted him to fill her, give her that perfection of friction and heat, his weight on her body, his mouth on her throat, his hands in her hair and stroking her breasts. That long weight of him rocking in and out of her core.

He kissed up her thighs until he found the edge of her mended cotton underthings. She felt his warm breath against her womanly curls as the pants slid down her legs. He was under her skirt, and the room was so tiny that all she had to do was lean back and find the edge of the bed with her hands. He helped her sit down, her legs spread for him, then his tongue was tracing her tender, damp lips. She shuddered when his tongue found the place that made her gasp, cried out when he inserted his finger into her channel. Then she was nothing but an instrument that he played, a keyboard that had the same notes pushed over and over, faster and faster, until the tune was a crescendo of orgasmic noise.

His fingers made a sucking sound when he pulled them out of her. She put her hands over her mouth, embarrassed, but he didn't seem to notice, perhaps because, when he stood up, his erection pushed his trousers out. At the virile sight, she forgot everything and reached for his zipper. While she undressed him he fumbled for a sheath in a drawer by the bed, then she was lying back, still in her crumpled dress. He knelt between her legs and pulled her hips to meet him, then slid inside her wet core. They both gasped with pleasure before he paused to pull off her loose sack of a dress, then her camisole.

Nothing mattered but the feel of him against her, inside her, all around her. She knew only him. The size of the space, the lumpy mattress on the sagging cot, the smell of ink and paper and books, they didn't matter as she took this man who'd said he loved her deep into her body. Such a tiny thing, but so monumental, words of love. She craved them.

"Tell me again," she said against his ear. "Tell me."

"What?"

"Tell me what you said."

"You're lovely." His mouth was open slightly, his exertions making him pant.

She ran her fingers down his back, dampening with sweat, then sank her fingers into the flesh of his buttocks and pulled him tightly against her. "The other words."

He smiled in an unfocused way. "I love you, Alecia."

"That." She put her mouth against his. "Oh, that." She rocked her hips, losing herself in the sensations his body created.

Falling. Ivan woke up with a jerk, only keeping himself from rolling off the cot by catching himself with one hand on the floor. He blinked hard and tilted his head to see a naked shoulder in the center of the bed. Alecia must have rolled over, pushing him off the narrow space. He'd never slept with a woman before Alecia, and was amazed by how deep and dreamless these experiences had been. Next time, however, he'd prefer to do it in a bigger bed. Slowly, he slid off the edge, trying not to jostle her, and dressed.

Outside, the sky looked gloomy. It had to be around three P.M. They'd slept the day away and he needed to put her on a train.

"Alecia." He kissed her shoulder and was rewarded by a slight movement. Caressing her arm, he said her name again. This time she opened her eyes a slit. "Time to go to the train station."

She sat up, looking tousled, sleepy, and delightful. He hardened and, for a moment, forgot his purpose.

"Could you hand me my clothes?" she asked, recalling him to sense.

"Your dress is crumpled against the wall. We might have used it as a pillow, I'm afraid."

She reached above her head for her dress. One beautiful small breast popped out of the covers. He salivated. She took one look at him and hastily covered herself with her clothes.

He cleared his throat. "I'll find the rest." He wandered around the room gathering her stockings. By the time he handed them to her she had her dress on.

An hour later, the sky was almost dark, but they'd made it to the train station. He waited with her on the platform at Waterloo.

Puffs of smoke announced the train coming in. He stood silently, feeling an increasing sense of horror. Finally, just as the metal beast came alongside them, he said, "I don't want you to go."

"What does that mean?"

He put his hands on her shoulders, feeling her fine bones under the old coat. "I want to marry you."

Her lips parted. "You do?"

"But please tell me, how can I with no job? And you not working either?" The brakes screeched as the train chugged in. He felt a warm blast of air just as it passed by, slowing down. When it jerked to a stop, the doors opened and people began to pour out almost instantly.

Alecia put her hands on his chest. "If you want to marry me, that's good enough."

A man in a black bowler and fur coat pushed Ivan's shoulder as he stepped by, too self-important to move around. Ivan was distracted for a moment, then realized what she'd said.

"Is that a yes?"

She grinned and nodded.

He bent his head forward. Was he looking at the woman who would someday be his wife? His chest constricted with emotion. "You have to say it."

A dog barked at elbow level. A woman passed by holding the yappy pup in her arms. Ivan saw Alecia's lips moving but couldn't hear. "What?"

"Yes!" She shouted, then clapped her hands over her mouth.

"We're engaged?" he said carefully.

She nodded again, then threw her arms around his neck. The bulk of her, heavy with winter coat, muffler, and gloves, knocked him into a man with a gray mustache and nicotine-stained teeth.

"Sorry," he said with a laugh. "She just agreed to marry me!"

The older man chuckled and said "Congratulations" before he continued on.

"I have an idea," she said in Ivan's ear. "Let's take the train together to seek my grandfather's approval and counsel."

"You want me to leave London?"

"Just for a day or so. What is going to happen won't be until the command performance, right? We have a little time."

"It's Saturday night. We have until Thursday."

"Very well. Grandfather is terribly busy on Sundays, of course, but I'm sure we'll be able to come back to London on Monday."

"What about the cost of the train?" He glanced up at the darkening sky. Though it was only late afternoon, night came early at this time of year.

"I have two weeks' pay."

"I have my pay too, but we need lodgings."

"We'll figure it out with his help. He's a very smart man."

"I haven't had anyone but Boris to counsel me in years," Ivan admitted. "I'm not used to asking anyone for help."

"This is what Grandfather does," Alecia said. "We can trust him."

He nodded. "Then let's go. I'm sure the conductor will sell me a ticket and you already have yours."

They boarded the train as soon as it emptied, and found third-class seats. In less than two hours, they'd arrive in her village.

It wasn't until Sunday night that Alecia had enough of her grandfather's attention to share their news and ask for counsel. He'd been at his church until late Saturday night, and she'd had to settle them into the house. Then he was up before they rose, she asleep in her room and Ivan in Sadie's, to return for Sunday services. Now they were cozy in her grandfather's study, still lit by gaslight and the fireplace. Candles burned on the mantel, just like always, when he relaxed at night. Grandfather and Ivan had brandy in snifters, and were seated in armchairs before the fire. They both wore heavy sweaters that Alecia had knitted. Her grandfather always wore his until they were in tatters. She'd discovered he'd never worn his last two Christmas sweaters, which meant Ivan could have one.

She leaned against the wall, seated on a footstool she'd used since she was a child.

Ivan finished his story of the bomb plot. "So you see, sir, lives are at risk."

"I'm not sure how much of this Mr. Eyre understands," her grandfather said, "from what you are saying. It sounds to me that the hotel is completely unprepared for this disaster."

"He doesn't know he's let a wolf into his henhouse, in the shape of Anatoly Smirnov. I wonder if Mr. Marvin attacked Alecia in order to rid them of me, once I'd refused to bring in the bomb myself."

"Why would Mr. Marvin be involved? I understand he's a bad man after what he did to my poor girl."

"Ideology?" Ivan said. "He'd been in Russia before the war."

Her grandfather shook his head sadly. "Perhaps. The first priority is to stop the bomb from going off. The second is to figure out who the conspirators are."

Ivan stared into his snifter. "How can we do anything about the plot now, without having my sister arrested?"

"Son." Grandfather spoke in his most serious voice. "If you do not take action, you are as much a murderer as your sister will be. You must protect her immortal soul as well as your own."

"Even if she has to go to prison? Maybe be sent away from England?"

"Even so." Her grandfather nodded.

"If I go straight to the police, it is over for my sister. There must still be some way to save her and stop the situation from moving forward."

"You know your sister has a connection to Richard," Alecia said. "Which of them is the instigator?"

"I need to get back into that hotel," Ivan said.

"Go to Mr. Eyre and be completely honest," her grandfather advised. "Meanwhile, Alecia needs to find her sister. I am equally troubled by the lack of communication. She did telephone me last Sunday night as we agreed, but she hasn't rung today."

Alecia rubbed her twitchy right eye. "I hope she isn't in some kind of trouble."

Ivan drained his glass. "I'll go to Mr. Eyre tomorrow and tell him everything I know."

Alecia sat up straighter as an idea struck her. "I'll attempt to see Sybil and tell her about Richard seeing your sister. Maybe that will stir something up."

"Don't go near her if Mr. Marvin is nearby," her grandfather said.

"I won't. But I might help by seeing her."

"I agree," Ivan said. "But, sir, there is one more topic of discussion. I wonder if I could have a private word?"

"Will you take this note to Mrs. Marvin, please?" Alecia said on Monday morning, handing her letter to a bellboy. Ivan stood beside her, surveying the Grand Russe's Grand Hall automatically, a habit he'd developed during his employment. "Make sure she opens it?"

The boy, no more than fourteen, nodded.

"You'll be in the Coffee Room?" Ivan asked. He didn't want to lose her the way she'd lost her sister. "And you won't leave the hotel without me?"

"Yes, I'll wait for Sybil, or you, or both," Alecia promised.

"Very good. I'll try to get in to see Mr. Eyre."

"Good luck." Alecia smiled and kissed his cheek.

Oddly enough, the kiss made him feel more engaged than anything else. He'd asked Mr. Loudon for permission to marry Alecia and her grandfather had agreed, assuming he had the means to support her. But that was nothing compared to a simple, wifely kiss. He wished she still had a room so he could whisk her upstairs.

Instead, he merely said, "I'll see you in a bit, darling."

Her face lit when she heard the endearment. She squeezed his arm before walking away, but, sweetly, she looked back. He nodded at her, then whistled as he went to the reception desk to plead his case.

"Mr. Moth," Ivan said, spying the front desk clerk, who sorted the post for the guests at the rear counter.

He turned around and grinned. "Mr. Salter! I didn't expect to have the pleasure of seeing you again."

Ivan nodded, feeling too solemn now to smile. "I wondered if I might have a word with Mr. Eyre? It's important."

Mr. Moth put his hands on the desk and folded them. "He is in this morning. I'll speak to him for you. Problem with your pay?"

"No," Ivan said.

Moth stared at him for a moment, losing his smile. "Very well. None of my business." He turned and opened the door into the inner recesses, then disappeared.

Teddy Fortress, the film star, came up, whistling and rubbing his gloved hands together. "Dreadful weather, what, what?" he said in the manner of an Indian Army major from the previous century. "Think it will blizzard?"

"No, sir," Ivan said. "I do not."

Mr. Fortress chuckled. "Not going to humor me? You're one of the Russians?"

"Night watchman."

"Yes. I've seen a new one prowling around here. Very close-set eyes, like a film villain. He ought to take a screen test."

"Is he behaving suspiciously, or is it just his appearance?" Ivan asked.

Fortress shrugged. "He's a watchman. He watches. I'm a night owl, always have been, and he's poking about every time I turn around, it seems. Not the worst thing for a watchman."

"No, but we have our assigned floors. If you're keeping your wanderings to one or two floors you would see him a lot. Otherwise—"

"So you're saying, old boy, that I shouldn't see this watchman on every floor?"

"Correct. Are you?"

Fortress nodded, concern narrowing his eyes. "Exceeded his brief, I take it."

"He's new," Ivan said as the concierge gave Fortress his key and a package.

"Ah, this must be the new scenario. Thank you." Fortress nodded at the concierge. "Listen, Mr.—"

"Salter."

"Salter, then. You tell your guv about the new watchman, will you? I don't want to make enemies among the staff."

"Of course, sir."

Fortress walked away, swinging his cane jauntily. Hugh Moth looked alarmed when he returned from the back room.

"Did Mr. Fortress get what he needed?"

"Yes, Mr. Russell handed him his key, but he gave me a message for Mr. Eyre."

Moth laughed. "Working every angle, Salter? Very well, you can go back."

Ivan took that to mean he already had permission, but a little extra insurance never hurt. He lifted the partition and walked through, trying to saunter more calmly than he really felt. He wished he had a prayer rope to worry at. His mother's grandfather had fiddled with one constantly when he was a child. He hadn't thought of the man in years. A pity. He'd been a very old man when Ivan was a child, dying close to twenty years ago now.

Ivan straightened his back, remembering all the years of good breeding behind him, and walked into Peter Eyre's office.

Eyre was, as always, lighting a cigarette when Ivan entered. Ivan noticed a jeweled box on top of a wood file cabinet, winking in the light streaming in from a dormer window. The box was of Indian design. Come to think of it, Eyre's skin had a dark flush not common in Englishmen, despite his blond hair and aristocratic mien. Had he a touch of foreign blood?

"What do you want, Salter?" Eyre asked, picking a fleck of tobacco off his lip.

"I just spoke to Teddy Fortress. Sounds like Anatoly Smirnov is casing the place more than watching it."

Eyre leaned back in his chair, clearly on alert in a lazy, panther-like way. "How did you know your replacement's name?"

"He's involved in the plot against this hotel. I'm the only one who can recognize these people. You're letting death enter your hotel."

"My hotel?"

"I think I know who you are." Ivan gambled as he pointed at the box. "You're related to the family, right? I remember one of the owners of the old hotel had a half-Indian wife."

"No one thinks I have foreign blood," Eyre said, blowing smoke out of the side of his mouth.

"I do," Ivan said. "And I don't care. I'm an immigrant myself. You want to keep your secret? That is fine with me. You want to mistreat your mistress? That is fine with me. But I don't want this hotel to die. It's too important to the hard-working, honest Russian community."

"You damaged Richard Marvin's face."

"You and I both know that the Marvins will be leaving the hotel as soon as the command performance is over. They can't afford to stay, given Sybil's career misfortune. But if Ovolensky dies here, it will be a disaster for both the hotel and the British government."

Eyre set his half-smoked cigarette in his old ashtray. Gray smoke drifted in a thin line across his desk.

The room reeked of old ash. Normally it was aired daily, but Eyre must have been spending too much time in here for it to be cleaned, a sign of trouble.

Ivan leaned forward and put his forearms on the desk. "Let me help you, man. I can see the strain you are under. I'm the only one who can help."

"Why?" Eyre's narrow face seemed to be nothing but his startlingly clear, hazel-green eyes.

Ivan's jaw twitched, but he spoke without emotion. "Because my sister is involved."

Eyre sat back in his chair and lifted his face to the ceiling. "Bloody hell. The threat against the command performance is real?"

"Indeed."

"Man-to-man, you and I have very complicated families," Eyre said, then smiled suddenly. "I'm almost glad for this, you know, Ivan? I like you." He stood and extended his hand. "Welcome aboard."

Ivan stood and took the proffered hand. "Thank you, sir."

"Smirnov is on your own shift."

"But he's wandering the hotel instead of staying to his assigned floors."

Eyre scowled. "I'll say I hired you back for an extra patrol on the seventh. That way the staff knows I expect you not to run into Richard Marvin."

"Brilliant." As long as Georgy didn't see him. He'd have to be careful.

"But that is not your brief, of course. You need to watch Smirnov." He hesitated. "I'd like to sack him, though. I can, given what Teddy Fortress told you."

"Might be best to keep our enemies close for now."

"What is our best defense?"

Ivan thought quickly. "A last-minute change of location for the command performance. If we come to the end game, we need to clear the first floor and do the performance somewhere else."

"Any ideas?"

Ivan smiled. "The nightclub. It's perfect."

Eyre nodded. "After this is over, if we both survive, we'll have to discuss your career prospects. Underneath that thick accent you have a sharp brain."

"Thank you, sir. One more thing, if you don't mind."

"Yes?"

"Do you know if Sadie Loudon ever arrived at the Grand Russe to start the position you promised her sister?"

"Not to my knowledge," Eyre said. "Check with Olga to be sure. Why?"

"She speaks with her grandfather every Sunday, but she didn't yesterday. The family is concerned."

Eyre fiddled with a small elephant figurine that always stood next to his battered ashtray. "Unfortunate, but she is young. I'll let you know if I run across her."

"Thank you. I won't take any more of your time." He rose, surprised that Eyre did as well, and offered his hand. They shook, then Eyre leaned forward, still holding Ivan's hand.

"Keep my hotel safe, Ivan," Eyre said, his voice low with passion. "You are now as responsible for it as I am."

Ivan slowly pulled his hand away, matching the other man's gaze. "I understand."

He walked out of the office, for the first time feeling like the soldier he'd never been.

Alecia anxiously scanned the door of the Coffee Room as she drank her coffee. The room seemed so decadent to her now. Despite the refurbishment, it had a hint of fin de siècle to her, now that she knew the hotel was at risk. When Sybil appeared in the front door, carefully framing herself in the doorway in a triangular fringed dress, nostalgia blew through her.

Sybil Marvin, who'd seemed such a vision to her a month ago, looked tired and haggard. She saw Alecia and firmed her mouth. Her shoulders straightened. Alecia could see the woman taking on a role, and she didn't like the look of things.

Her former employer walked up to her, hips swinging. Two forty-ish businessmen at a table by the service area stared in frank amusement.

Sybil paused by Alecia's shoulder.

"Please do sit down," Alecia said in her sweetest voice. "You are making a scene and what I have to say is private."

"I should say so," Sybil snarled as she sat down. "The least you can do, darling, is fetch me a cup of coffee."

"You look more like you need hair of the dog," Alecia responded. "But I'll see what I can do."

"I wouldn't say no to champagne."

"That is more of a problem than a solution, don't you think?"

Chapter Seventeen

Alecia went to fetch Sybil coffee from the Coffee Room's sideboard. She didn't care if the woman had a headache. What she had to say would only give her former employer a fresh one.

After she'd poured coffee and placed a piece of shortbread beside the cup on the saucer, she brought it back to Sybil and placed it in front of her.

"I never eat sweets." Sybil pushed the plate away.

"Liar," Alecia said, calmly moving the plate back into place.

"I know the story now, Alecia," Sybil said with a huff. "You made advances on Richard."

"Not true," Alecia said.

"No, you did. Apparently it was all for show, because you only went so far. But you had my poor husband so beside himself that he kept going." Sybil fluttered her hands in the air. "You can't say no after you say yes. Consequences ensue. Virgins don't know this, of course."

"All of that is a lie. He attacked me, which you knew very well when last we spoke."

"Mr. Marvin has been offered a contract with the movie studio," Sybil said, staring at her coffee cup. "It's a new start for both of us."

"Since your career has fallen apart?" Alecia paused. "Why does losing this one role affect you so? You'd been offered a starring role. There will be others. Your career is far from over."

"I'm getting old."

"Self-pity," Alecia said briskly. "Too much alcohol and not enough food. Don't let Richard bully you, Sybil. If he's making a lot of money you can go somewhere and rest."

"You seem very sure of yourself now."

"I'm going to marry Ivan."

Sybil smiled sourly. "Afraid his eye will roam? I thought he'd lost his position too."

"I have a feeling he can retrieve it."

"You can't retrieve yours, Alecia. I'm sorry, whatever the truth is. I can believe both sides of the story."

"Must be a useful skill for an actress." Alecia finished off the dregs in her coffee cup, not knowing when she'd eat again that day.

Sybil's gaze lost focus. "Why don't you come to the performance? Who knows if I'll ever play Lady Macbeth again."

"Be careful, Sybil. Your husband has mixed himself up with some unsavory company."

"I know the movie industry has its downside," Sybil said. "But really, Alecia."

"I meant the woman," Alecia said, bending forward. She picked up the shortbread and broke it in half. "Here Sybil, eat this."

Sybil stared at the shortbread, then took it. "His mistress? What about her?"

"She's dangerous," Alecia said. "I don't know the full story, but it isn't good, Sybil. I'm worried about you. The tighter the rein you can keep on Richard, the better. I don't care about him, but I wouldn't want you to be hurt."

"That's very kind. I am sorry you can't stay with me. We were friends for a little while, weren't we?" Sybil stared at the shortbread, then pushed the entire piece into her mouth.

"Yes, we were," Alecia said. "I never had more fun in the shops than I did with you."

Movement caught the corner of her eye. She looked up and saw Ivan gesturing to her. She set the other half piece of shortbread back on Sybil's plate, then patted her on the shoulder and walked away.

"Did you talk to Mr. Eyre?" Alecia asked as she joined him just outside the Coffee Room's majestic two-story entrance.

Ivan could scarcely keep himself from reaching for Alecia and swinging her around. She would be so proud of him. "Yes, I have my position again."

"I'm so happy for you." She touched his sleeve demurely, but he saw her face brighten.

Now, on to the less-than-good news. "Thank you, but it isn't all good news. Your sister probably has not been here, but we need to check with Olga. She's on the seventh floor, so let's speak with her."

"What about Ovolensky?" she asked in a low voice.

He'd thought about that. "He won't be here. He'll be in meetings. I doubt they'd have maids cleaning otherwise."

"Then we should go."

Her smile looked forced as they went to the service lift. "What's wrong?"

"I'm so happy you have your position back, but I didn't retrieve mine."

"You never thought you would. I wouldn't allow it, not under the circumstances." He opened the gate so she could enter, then closed it behind himself.

"I know it's unsafe, it's just that . . ." She worried her lower lip, then licked it. He noticed they were chapped from the winter weather. Still, the unconsciously sensual gesture made him harden.

He smiled at her, then backed her up against the wall of the lift.

"What?"

He bent his head and nuzzled her ear. "I can't wait until we have some privacy again."

"When is that going to happen? We won't even be in the same city."

He deflated a bit. "We are together now."

She lifted her eyebrows as the lift jerked to a stop. "We don't have any privacy."

"I could take you back to Boris's flat."

"I have to find my sister."

Her mouth pinched. He knew he had to stop teasing and focus. "Very well." He opened the gate and stepped out, glad he still wore his old overcoat.

Olga was in Miss Page's bedroom. The centerpiece of the room was a jade and gold fireplace. Thick rugs covered the carpet and a large bed heaped with blankets dominated the space. Ivan gestured to Alecia, then closed the door behind him.

"What is it?" Olga asked in Russian, running a duster over ornate vases lining the mantelpiece. Her cap was slightly askew on her thick, shiny hair.

"If I might ask a question?" Alecia asked.

Olga gestured impatiently, then emptied an ashtray into her can.

"Have you met my sister, Sadie? Mr. Eyre offered her a position as a chambermaid here, but our grandfather hasn't heard from her in over a week."

"No. I have heard of no one by that name."

"What do you think of the new night watchman?" Ivan asked.

Olga snorted. "Intelligentsia. No work ethic, that one. Always lurking around corners, leaning on the wall."

"Did you know him before?"

"No. Why should I?"

"No reason. But, Olga." Ivan paused. "Stay away from the command performance, will you?"

Her eyes narrowed. "Why?"

"Ovolensky is a target," he said. "I'd hate for you to be hurt."

She snorted. "Ovolensky is a tool of the politburo. I have no trouble with him being shot."

"The original plan was a bomb, not a gun," Ivan said.

She swore in Russian, but the former princess had long since lost her gentility in the hard life she'd lived since. "Those fools."

"One of those fools is my sister Vera."

"That does not surprise me. I have heard of your sister Catherine."

"Vera idolizes her memory."

"Catherine did try to assassinate Lenin. I can sympathize."

"I don't know what her motives were," Ivan said. "I was still at school."

Olga pushed a stray ash-blond tendril out of one eye. "It is difficult for you. There is a pull between the struggle to free Russia and the struggle to keep your family intact."

"There is no struggle," Ivan said with complete assurance. "My family comes first."

"Very well. My staff will not interfere." She glanced at Alecia. "If your sister comes here, do you want me to turn her away in light of the danger?"

"No. Get word to Ivan. Tell her to wait in the Coffee Room if you think she'd be allowed in there."

Olga nodded. "I wish you both luck. Sisters are difficult. I don't know if my sister is even alive. She went to China and I've never heard what happened to her."

"I am so sorry," Alecia said.

"Sisters seem to be the bane of all of us," Olga said. She made a shooing motion with her hands. "Now, go. I have a great deal of work to do."

"Don't trust Anatoly Smirnov," Ivan said. "He's part of the conspiracy."

Olga nodded. "If Ovolensky is to be assassinated at the command performance, I will make sure all of my girls are far away."

"Could you do this work?" Ivan asked Alecia as they turned away.

"I'm not too proud," she assured him as they walked through the suite. "But Mr. Eyre said no when I asked. He thought I should take a secretarial position somewhere in the City."

"We'd never see each other," Ivan said. "With me working nights and you working days."

She lifted her hands, palms up. "He said no."

He turned back to nod at Olga, then opened the suite door, happy to be out in the corridor, away from the heavy smell of perfume and some odd kind of tobacco.

"Now what?" he asked, after Alecia had followed him out.

"I need to go to the hotel where Sadie was working and see what they know."

"A wise idea. I'll go with you."

"I think you should attempt to see your sister," Alecia said. "I'll be fine looking for Sadie alone."

"Meet me at Boris's house at tea time," he suggested.

"I should return to Bagshot."

"You can take the late train. I'll leave you there and continue on to work."

She nodded. "I'm going to find work in London as soon as possible."

"I do think an office is better than some kind of domestic work," he said. "What if you wind up in a situation where we can't ever see each other? If you hadn't been living in the hotel, the Marvins would have never allowed you to see me."

"I'll find something."

"I wish you could wait for me. When I'm stable again, we can marry. You won't have to work."

"That's only if you aren't supporting your sister." She ran her hand along his arm. "I don't want you to be fatalistic about her."

His stomach ached. "She and her fiancé are so easily misled."

"Hate clouds the mind. She needs spiritual guidance," Alecia said. "She needs to let your parents go."

He felt a wave of anger. "How? Have you let your parents go?"

"I'm not perfect," she admitted.

He couldn't let it go. "Would you befriend a German?" he demanded. "After they killed your parents?"

"It was wartime."

No, she couldn't do it, Ivan thought. *And if she met the captain of the U-boat that sank the* Lusitania, *she'd probably want to shoot him too.* "You befriend a German and then you can judge my sister."

She stared at him a moment. "I need to find a train out to that hotel. It's somewhere between here and Bagshot. The Richmond Inn."

"Then it is most likely in Richmond itself."

"Precisely."

They glared at each other. "The concierge will set you to rights."

"An excellent idea."

"Very well. We'll return to the lobby and then go our separate ways for now." He knew he sounded petulant.

"I can continue on to Bagshot after I go to Richmond. I'll be halfway there already."

"Don't you want to return here?"

She shook her head. "There isn't anywhere for me to stay, Ivan. We aren't married yet."

"I can't bear not seeing you."

She blinked hard. "Oh, Ivan. I'll work very hard to find a position here. As soon as you have this Ovolensky business behind you, we can plan better. We'll sort it out."

"I can't offer you a comfortable vicarage."

"It's just you I want. Only there are a few things to take care of first."

He smiled. "My parents would have liked you. My mother said I needed a girl who could stand up to me."

She kissed his cheek and went to the reception desk. He watched her as she moved. No expensive, perfectly cut clothes for her, but it didn't matter. She was the most beautiful woman in the entire hotel.

Alecia stepped down from the train at Richmond. She'd been told the inn where her sister worked was just two blocks away. The station here looked its age and the entire area seemed run-down, though she'd thought generally that Richmond, which included a royal palace, was quite upscale. She supposed tourists didn't care what the train station looked like.

She pulled up her coat lapel to hide her neck from the biting wind and walked north to the inn. While grateful to open the door and let herself in a few minutes later, she wasn't pleased by what she saw. The inn was tiny compared to the Grand Russe. Never had she been so aware that the hotel she thought of as hers had been newly renovated. Here, some of the tiles making up the checkerboard floor were cracked. She didn't think any amount of polish would make the battered reception desk shine.

"Can I help you, miss?" asked a tired, middle-aged man in a shapeless black suit, coming up to her.

"Who are you?"

"The hall porter, miss. Old Ben is what they call me. Did you need a room?"

"I was looking for my sister. Sadie Loudon?"

The porter ran his fingers over his salt-and-pepper mustache. "Ah, that Sadie."

Alecia waited as Old Ben looked to be lost in reverie. Eventually, he lifted his eyebrows. "Gave no notice, did she. Just ran off."

"Are you sure she ran off?"

He scratched his chin. "There was an incident."

"What happened?"

"One of our regular guests brings her two poodles with her and they must have eaten something that made them sick. Quite a mess she had to clean up."

"Sadie left after that?" Alecia suppressed a smile.

"Afraid so. Job wasn't for her. Can't blame her." The man shuddered. "Vile business, but that's the life of a maid."

"When was this?"

"A week ago tomorrow. She had room and board here, so I haven't a clue where's she's gone," Old Ben said. "You have a grandfather, right?"

"Yes, but she didn't check in like usual. She had another job offer but never appeared there either."

"Dearie me. Did she have a boyfriend or someone like that?"

"Not that I know of."

The porter waved his arm at the desk and a uniformed boy came over. "Can you bring Mrs. Curtis to me, please?"

"Yes, sir," the boy said, and scampered off.

"She's the housekeeper here. If anyone would know more it would be her. Do you think you'll go to the police?"

"I'm going to have to," Alecia said. "If I can't learn anything more. My grandfather and I are her only family, and she's not used to London."

"Not a country girl, though."

"No, but still. She wouldn't have had much money."

Old Ben sighed. "I hope she hasn't done anything stupid. Pretty girl like that."

A few hours later, Alecia set her utensils down and yawned. "Excuse me."

"It's been a long day for you," her grandfather said, drinking the last of his wine. "You've been subdued tonight."

"I can't believe Sadie has vanished without a trace."

"Someone will know where she's gone. Those people at the inn will talk to all of the staff now. We'll have news."

She rubbed her eyes, trying to chase the exhaustion away. "What if she was hurt? I should check hospitals, talk to the police."

Her grandfather wiped his mouth with his cloth napkin. "I will make all those calls in the morning. I'll get a better response, and you need to focus on finding a new position."

"Don't you want me to stay here and be your secretary again?"

"If I asked you to do that, how would you see your fiancé? No, my dear, you need to work in London."

She was surprised. "Do you like him?"

He gave her his full attention. "I do. He's at a huge disadvantage, being Russian, but he seems clever enough, and ambitious. I know he'll work hard for you."

She patted his hand. "I think he's a true family sort of person. He's stayed close to his sister despite a great deal of provocation."

Her grandfather nodded as he put his napkin on his plate. "I do agree. So sad about his parents. You have tragedy in common."

"It's not the only thing." Alecia folded her napkin. "I do love him. We don't need much. Just a little flat. I'm used to a single room now."

"In luxurious circumstances," he pointed out.

"Yes, but it was a valet's room. Nothing fancy for me. I thought I wanted something else, the jazz-baby life, but with Ivan I have a taste of that, and the rest is pure comfort. I think I'm a simple enough girl for an immigrant husband, but he's smart enough to know that at least one of us needs stable employment. These days, that can be hard to come by."

Her grandfather listened quietly to her speech, then spoke. "Precisely. Any ideas?"

"Read the newspapers, of course."

"What about people you met in London? The best positions usually come from people one knows. Even your work with the Marvins came because they spoke to an innkeeper's wife here in Bagshot."

"I can't expect anything from the Marvins. The hotel manager didn't want to hire me as a chambermaid. I never knew any of the employees very well, except Ivan." She thought hard. An image of the elderly Mrs. Plash drifted into her head, holding ashtrays. "Mrs. Plash!" she exclaimed.

He folded his hands across his midsection. "Well connected?"

"No, I shouldn't think so. She's elderly and confused. She needs a minder. I could do that."

"Does she have the money to hire you?"

"I don't really know, but it's worth asking about. I could write her daughter. I know where they are living." She would write Peter Eyre too, knowing how much influence he had on the Plashes.

"Why don't you write her tonight, so the letter goes out in the first post? I'm going to spend the evening making a list of places to telephone in the morning."

"I'll help you as soon as I've written the letter," Alecia promised. "We're going to have a busy day tomorrow."

Her grandfather nodded. "If I'm completely honest, I don't like either of you girls being alone in such a large place as London. If one of you is there, I'd rather have you both there."

"I understand."

He smiled. "Soon, though, you'll have Ivan, too. That will help, having another man in the family. I'm so pleased for you."

She felt her cheeks redden. "Thank you."

"I'm surprised you would show your face here," Vera said in Russian, opening the door to the flat at Ivan's knock. Though he still had the keys, he didn't think it wise to enter unannounced. Someone might knife him.

"You are still my sister."

"What do you want? Did you leave something here?"

Her face looked jaundiced and too thin.

"Has Sergei been working?"

She waved her thin fingers. The rings she wore in Russia, long sold, would no longer fit. "We are busy with details."

"Have you been eating?"

"I know how to prepare food." She glanced away.

"That isn't an answer to my question."

"What does it matter to you? You aren't working. You have no money."

"I have my position back," he said. "I start again tonight."

She thought for a moment. "Isn't Monday your day off?"

"I had the last two days off, having been sacked. I don't know what my schedule will be now."

She said something rude under her breath. "What about Anatoly?"

"He is still employed."

She snapped out her hand. "Come in."

He stepped in and she shut the door. "What is wrong?"

"You don't know who is listening. We've risked everything, becoming involved with the bomb maker."

"Even your beliefs," he said. "Why does a Bolshevik want to kill Ovolensky? At least you have revenge in mind."

"Konstantin wants to kill the British government ministers who will be there," she said, folding her thin arms around her midsection. "We've had to change. We . . ." She trailed off.

"Who are you now, Vera? You and Sergei? Don't you want children, to live a normal life?"

"This is not my life." She said this in a bitter tone.

"It's all we have now. Princess Olga is cleaning loos. We're a lost generation, but we can build our lives again, find comfort for our children."

"You are very dynastic all of a sudden."

"I've become engaged myself." He touched her shoulder. "We need to think about the future. Allying yourself to this Konstantin the bomb maker is going to ruin your life, Vera."

"Oh?" Her lips twisted.

"Killing Georgy won't bring our parents or Catherine back to life."

Her hand moved like the head of a cobra. He felt the sting of her open palm almost before he saw her move.

"Get out. You are not my brother!" she cried. "How dare you, a man, not want revenge!"

"You have the look of madness in your eyes," Ivan said, with sorrow in his heart. "May God have mercy on your soul."

Her eyes burned with no hint of tears in them. She was immersed in her revenge fantasy. Her life, Sergei's, his, all of it meant nothing to her.

As he left the flat and the building, he wondered if his parents had seen a similar level of vicious focus in his sister Catherine. He'd been too young, too self-involved to notice in those days. As much as he hated Ovolensky, he wouldn't sacrifice his happy future with Alecia to revenge. No, but he still had to try to protect Vera from herself.

He'd thought of contacting Sergei at the train station, but now he thought there was no point. He needed to find an external solution.

Alecia clutched her letter from Emmeline Plash as she stepped down from the omnibus in front of a plain brown brick house on Montagu Square. The wind battered the length of skirt that hung below her winter coat, turning her ankles to ice. A drop of what felt like ice slashed her nose as she followed the building numbers, looking for the Plash residence.

A few houses in, she could see a faded sign announcing a girl's finishing school, long closed. The building had been converted to a boardinghouse after the school's headmistress died. Olga had told her more than she ever wanted to know about the Regency-era building when she'd stopped in at the Grand Russe, having two hours to spend between coming in from Bagshot and meeting Miss Plash. Apparently architecture was Olga's passion. She'd stopped straightening the pastry table in the Coffee Room and happily talked for twenty minutes about the history of Montagu Square.

Alecia, on the other hand, could still scarcely believe she was talking to a real life princess, albeit one who worked as a chambermaid now. Olga, however, was as unpretentious as possible, and if it weren't for her background and reserved air, they might become friends, particularly after she married Ivan. Who knew? Would it be possible one day, especially since she might work for a time in the same building where Olga resided?

She knocked on the door. It was opened only seconds later by a wizened man, half bent by great old age. She was still wiping icy water from her nose.

"Yes?" he quavered.

She dropped her hand to her side. "My name is Alecia Loudon. I have an appointment with Miss Plash."

"Oh yes." The man smiled, showing a mouth with only a few teeth. "Pretty girl, what?"

"Yes, sir."

"Come in then. My old bones can't take the cold."

She noticed he wore two sweaters and had an egg stain on his tie. Poor old thing. No wedding ring. "Are you the porter here?"

"No, no, I'm Bert Dadey. I own the place." He tottered across the hall to a compact sitting room with a fireplace and an expensive Victrola.

Her spirits lifted immediately. Olga hadn't mentioned the record player. It might be worth living here, despite the dreary air, for a chance to play records on the machine. "I see."

He peered at her closely. "You're a pretty girl, too. Friend of Miss Plash, are you?"

"Thank you. I don't know her very well, but we lived very near each other for a time."

"Pity about her mother. Lovely old dear, when she isn't wandering."

"Yes, I like Mrs. Plash very much. That's why I'm here, you see. I'm hoping to care for her."

"Very good, she needs a companion," the man said.

"Should I go up?" she asked, afraid he was going to settle in for a chat if she didn't stick to business.

"If you like. Is that the plan?" he quavered.

"I think so." She actually had no idea.

"First door on the left off the second landing."

"Very good. Thank you." She paused. "Has Mrs. Plash been wandering at all?"

"No, dear, but I do hear her crying at tea time. About the time full dark sets in."

She frowned. Too much change for a confused elder. "I'm sorry to hear that."

"It's good that I'm too deaf to hear it much, but some of the boarders have complained. They won't be able to stay if Mrs. Plash continues to cause such a fuss." The man shook his head. The loose flesh around his neck wobbled.

"Thank you for sharing that with me." She glanced at the Victrola one last time, then left the room and climbed the stairs. As she went up, the smell of cabbages and onions that was prevalent on the ground floor diminished. By the time she reached the Plash's door, she could smell Emmeline's distinctive perfume. Did she spray it on the mat in front of her door?

Chapter Eighteen

A lecia knocked on the Plashes' door. The pause between her knock and the door being opened was considerably longer than the one down below.

"Good afternoon, Miss Loudon." Emmeline wore an ice-blue silk dress with a lace panel at the neckline. She didn't smile.

Alecia forced up the corners of her lips, feeling even dowdier than she perpetually did with Sybil Marvin. She hadn't dared to wear her beautiful pink shoes in this damp weather, so she was dressed every bit as badly as usual. "It is a pleasure to see you again."

Emmeline gestured her in. "I understand the Marvins sacked you."

"They didn't need a secretary," Alecia said. "Due to reduced circumstances. I have my character here to show you. My position was an experiment for them."

"It must have been hard to lose your position so soon after you'd found it." Emmeline sat on the sofa in the small sitting room. The room did not contrast well with the sitting room in the spacious hotel suite they'd been forced to vacate. There was only the sofa, a threadbare rug, and three small tables. A large, mostly empty bookcase filled the wall with no doors.

"I would have been happy to stay at the Grand Russe," Alecia admitted, removing her coat. "But I don't think the Marvins will be there much longer either."

"No, I did hear there was some drama. Peter was here for tea yesterday."

Alecia noted the familiar term for Mr. Eyre. Was Miss Plash still seeing him? If he was paying her bills, Alecia might actually have work here. "How is your mother?"

"It is a difficult situation. If I can't calm her, we won't be here much longer. Other residents are complaining."

Alecia nodded and sat next to Emmeline as there were no other options. At least she didn't see any sign of dust on the surfaces or lurking in the corners. "Olga didn't mention it, but Mr. Dadey did. He said your mother has been crying in the early evenings."

"Something about the dark frightens her."

"I've heard of that before with the elderly, a couple of times."

"Oh?"

"Yes. You hear about all kinds of troubles, growing up in a vicarage. People tell my grandfather a great deal over tea."

Emmeline looked down. "But do you have any ideas about how to fix her, Miss Loudon?"

"No, but I'd like to help you keep her more comfortable. She's a dear."

"I know she likes you," Miss Plash said. Her lips tightened. "She has the strangest ideas about me."

"Were you close when you were younger?"

"Not especially. She was one of those ladies with causes and clubs. Suffrage and all that."

"Not you?"

"Not then. I went to finishing school in Switzerland, then was busy with debutante balls and the like. The profession of finding a good husband. But I wasn't a very serious girl. Didn't find that husband, though I was engaged twice. Then the war broke out when I was about twenty-three. Most of the boys I knew died. I ran out of time to be who I was meant to be."

She was younger than Alecia had thought, by a couple of years at least. "I'm sorry. I thought I would never marry myself."

Emmeline frowned. "What changed your mind?"

She smiled. "Ivan Salter proposed."

Her eyes widened. "The night watchman?"

"Yes, the very one." Alecia allowed herself a moment of complete female satisfaction. She wouldn't be a surplus female.

"Goodness. Isn't that marrying down?"

She wanted to slap the woman. She locked her fingers together. "In Russia, he was gentry. Higher in class than me. I'm a respectable vicar's granddaughter, but no earls in the distant family tree or anything like that."

Emmeline made a purring sound. "He's a handsome devil. Very smoldering."

"Yes. I can't deny it."

"When are you going to marry?"

"I don't know. Life is rather unsettled right now."

"So it will be awhile?"

"I should think so. We need to save up some money."

Emmeline took a deep breath. "Peter seems to trust him. I assume he wasn't mixed up in that drama from a few days ago?"

"Which drama was that?"

"Something about the Marvins, I believe." Emmeline tilted her head.

"He may have been, but he's still employed." If Miss Plash didn't know the details, Alecia saw no reason to share them.

"If I may be blunt, Miss Loudon, you are looking for a roost in London until you wed, am I correct?"

"Not entirely. I do need to work." Despite Ivan's desire to support her.

"I do not want my mother to become used to you, only to have you leave."

"There is no reason for me to cease working the moment I marry," Alecia told her. "Ivan works long hours."

"I do need help, and Peter said he would pay."

Alecia knew her expression betrayed surprise for a moment, as most women would not want to admit to being kept, but she blanked her face quickly.

Emmeline smiled. "It is complicated between us. My younger brother was his best friend."

The plot thickened. "Did he die in the war?"

"At the very end." She nodded and gestured toward a series of framed photographs on the mantelpiece. "I first noticed my mother's forgetfulness a couple of years after that. She may have been hiding the truth before."

"Aging can be a slow process or a fast one. I've seen all kinds in Bagshot."

Emmeline pinched a crease into her sleeve. "You'll have to share my mother's room. Later, when you've wed, maybe the owner here will let you both move in."

"If he's still alive." Alecia snorted.

"He's feisty. I wouldn't be surprised if he lives another decade. He has that hard-baked quality."

"I like him."

"And his Victrola." Emmeline smiled. "I know about you and music. No wonder you fell in love with a night watchman."

She changed the subject away from Ivan. He was too precious to gossip about. "Have you always loved Mr. Eyre?"

"No, I thought he was a child. I was in love with his older brother, Noel."

She shied away from that. "Did he die in the war?"

"He might as well have. I suppose Peter and I came together out of grief."

"Were you engaged to Noel?"

"I ought to have been. But I was so silly. He didn't have a title, not that there was any reason for me to have been acquired by a man with a title myself." Emmeline pulled out a handkerchief and dabbed at her eyes.

Alecia waited for her to finish. "Who was your father?"

"A man with money. He had invested in the hotel when it first opened some thirty or forty years ago, though he pulled out his stake around the turn of the century. It's too bad, really." Emmeline smiled. "But I think you can see why Peter will never desert us."

"Your family friendship leads back a generation," Alecia summarized.

"Correct. So there will be money to care for my mother, even when my own funds occasionally run dry. Peter can be ruthless and cruel, I don't deny it, but his heart isn't completely black."

Alecia still wanted to visit Ivan before it grew dark and she needed to return to Bagshot. "Then, I can help you?"

"Yes. Do you want to move in tomorrow?" Emmeline didn't look at her.

"That will be fine. I have to return to Bagshot and gather my things."

Emmeline made a face. "I do hope you can improve your wardrobe. It hurts my eyes to see so much ugliness on an otherwise pretty girl."

"I hope to do exactly that, if I can stabilize my life."

"Very well." Emmeline adopted a bored expression. "We shall see you tomorrow, then? I would take you to Mother now, but she's napping."

Alecia hoped her new employer's lack of interest in the proceedings masked her pleasure in the arrangement, rather than a true absence of feeling. "Does she often nap this time of day?"

"Yes, after luncheon. And after dinner. She doesn't sleep well at night. You will have a terror on your hands."

"What will you do?" Not that it was any of her business.

Emmeline stared at her hands. "I don't know. Take long walks, I suppose. I need to sort myself out before it is too late. I've given up on marriage, on children, but not on life. Some use must be made of me."

She knew there were plenty like Emmeline, just the wrong age a decade ago. They were a surplus population, these women whose young men had gone to war and not returned. She had to school herself to be careful, to be helpful herself, and not pity the woman, when she had the excitement of planning her own wedding.

"Thank you for giving me the opportunity," Alecia said. "I shall see you tomorrow."

Emmeline rose immediately. Alecia could see she'd already been dismissed in the other woman's eyes. She suspected there had once been quite a lot of money in the Plash family, given Emmeline's behavior. They clasped hands, as if they were men of business, then Alecia left.

It was only as she went to find an omnibus that she wondered what the domestic situation at the boardinghouse was. Emmeline must have at least two bedrooms and the sitting room at her disposal. What about a kitchen? A bathroom? For sure, it wouldn't be the Grand Russe.

"Alecia!" Ivan grinned when he saw his fiancée at the door of Boris's flat and grabbed for her hand, pulling her in. Her worry about her new living arrangements dissolved when she saw his dear face. He wrapped his arms around her before she could respond, burying his face against her neck, between her coat and the edge of her hat.

"I'm glad to see you too."

He lifted his face and kissed the tip of her nose. "I have only a couple of hours before I have to go to work."

"I know, and we have so much to discuss. How did the meeting with your sister go?"

"Very badly. She is intent on her course. Or rather, she has no other option, now that they've involved themselves with the bomber."

She removed her hat and handed it to him. "Does she have any re-morse?"

He set it on a chair next to the door and helped her with her coat. "No, she wants revenge. I do not think she considers her position very deeply." Ivan touched her cheek. "Even though she is older than me, she didn't have the education I did. I even had a little time at university, studying philosophy."

"I didn't know that."

"Yes. I spent a lot of time with Nikolay Mikhaylovsky's work."

Finally, she stripped off her gloves. She flexed her frozen fingers. "Who is that?"

"He was a social philosopher, interested in the interaction between the individual and the masses. He had interesting thoughts about leadership, about peasants."

"Tell me more about that while I take my shoes off. They need to dry." She had nothing to wear closer than Bagshot.

"We can put them in front of the fire." He pointed to where a fire burned merrily in the parlor.

"Perfect."

"Do you want to borrow my slippers?" he asked, glancing uncertainly at her feet.

"Thank you, but my feet would drown in them."

"I could bring you some socks," he offered.

"After my stockings dry." She smiled at him.

As she bent to unbuckle her shoes, he said, "For instance, Mikhaylovsky wouldn't say Peter Eyre is a great man, born to lead, but a regular man, put into a position by society, where he finds himself a leader. He doesn't have to be outstanding to be where he is."

"Oh?" She had one shoe off and went to work on the other, slowly, with her stiff fingers.

"Yes, he's special because his staff makes him so, not because he intrinsically is."

"So that means the Grand Russe as a collective unit is more important than Peter Eyre." She sounded Russian even to her own ears.

He nodded. "I need to serve the organization, not just the man."

She picked up her shoes and followed him into the sitting room. "So you could also say that Ovolensky isn't very important either?"

"I'd have already said that," he scoffed. "This is a personal feud that has grown too large. I have no interest in taking down the British government. Why would Vera help someone who wants to bring the Bolsheviks to power here?"

She had no answer. "What are you going to do?"

"I've been thinking hard about my options." He took her hand and pulled her to the sofa in Boris's parlor. "Your face is chilled. I'll make you some tea and fetch you those socks."

He went into the kitchen while she placed her damp shoes in front of the fire. Hot water must have been ready because he was back quickly with a pot of tea and mugs.

"That looks wonderful," she said, watching steam rise from the pot.

"Nothing better on a cold day." He handed her the socks.

She rubbed her hands over the cool wool. "Which university did you attend?"

"I spent one year at the University of Moscow. It's the oldest in Russia."

"What were you training to do?" She wiggled her toes, willing her stockings to dry.

"I don't know. Write books or something. My thoughts weren't well-formed at that age."

"Maybe you'll become a philosopher yourself and introduce a new theory to the world."

He smiled. "I'd need a lot more education for that. I suspect my prospects have been thoroughly quashed, along with many in my generation. It will be up to our children to reeducate and move us forward. My generation of Russians is going to have to work hard to put food in our bellies and keep roofs over our heads."

She touched his hand. A hard truth, but he could be right, for now at least, with all the unemployment issues. It was hard to keep a job, and immigrants had other barriers too. Maybe someday they would be comfortable enough for him to acquire more education. "Miss Plash was telling me about her past. It's quite posh, really. She's come down in the world, but the most interesting things I learned were about Peter Eyre. Miss Plash has known him all her life."

"You don't say." Ivan rearranged shortbread on a plate. "Did she agree to take you on?"

Alecia smiled. "She did. I return to Bagshot tonight to pick up my things. Since it's Emmeline, she couldn't help but insult my wardrobe, of course, but she's hired me. Mr. Eyre will pay."

"It seems you won't really be leaving the world of the Grand Russe after all."

"No, I suppose not. It's very sad. He has an older brother who she neglected to marry when she should have."

Ivan lifted his eyebrows. "He died in the war?"

"I had the impression that he didn't. What a mysterious family."

"You don't have to be a Russian to have tragedy, not in our generation."

"You sound so fatalistic."

He smiled at her. "I'm not. We've found each other despite this crazy world. As long as we can work, we can marry and be together."

"Work is the thing we must do," she agreed.

He leaned forward and captured her mouth. His lips slid against hers. She could feel a tiny crumb of shortbread on his lip. He must have sneaked a piece in the kitchen. As his kiss intensified, she forgot she was cold. He shuddered when she wrapped her arms around him, touching his neck with her cold hands, then swept his tongue along the seams of her lips. He brought fire with him. She melted until they had both sunk to the floor of the sitting room, between the sofa and the tea table. His warm hands lifted her skirt, trailing flame up her inner thighs with each brush of his fingers. She spread her thighs apart and he cupped her through her worn undergarments.

"Oh, Ivan," she whispered. "Please don't stop."

He didn't. Half an hour later they were dozing in front of the fire, wrapped in the wrinkled garments they had both been wearing. He had her dress draped across his back and she had his shirt around her shoulders.

"When do you think we should marry?" he asked, lazily tracing a circle on her shoulders.

"I don't know how long this Plash job will last," she admitted. "It sounds like Mrs. Plash is starting to sleep a great deal. If she isn't eating either, she may not need my care for long."

"Meanwhile, Mr. Eyre said we should speak about my future once this crisis is over."

"Encouraging. If you can be promoted to a better position and your sister doesn't need you to support her, then we can speak about marriage."

He nodded. "I'm going to have to go to Scotland Yard. How it bothers me to involve the police. We wouldn't do that in Russia. They are the enemy."

"You aren't in Russia."

"No. But what are the police going to think of me?"

She shrugged. "Can you leave your sister out of it? Just tell the police about the bomber?"

"Yes, I like that idea. Without a bomb they are toothless. When Ovolensky goes, the problem should be over. Unless her friends have become men of action all of a sudden."

"You might not know until Ovolensky is gone."

He sat up. "Thank you for understanding. I must not seem like such a bargain."

"I love you, Ivan. You're a good man." But she did wonder if she was enough for such a complicated soul. Philosophy? His upper-class background? He was a toff, really, and she was so provincial. Could she make him happy as a wife? Could he be happy at all, in circumstances so different from his childhood?

And yet, he'd been living like this for eight years, more than a third of his life. He might be better off finding a woman who could bring him money and position. Certainly he had the looks to attract anyone, and his work put him in a place to meet wealthy women. Why had he chosen her?

Why did love choose any two people? She simply had to have faith in their future, in him.

She slid her arms around his neck. "Do we have time for more?"

His eyebrows lifted. "A second time?"

"I've heard it's possible." She nuzzled his neck.

He glanced down. "Oh, it is, *myshka*. It definitely is."

Ivan walked through the doors at New Scotland Yard on the Victoria Embankment the next morning, shortly after his shift had ended, feeling a little like he was walking into a prison. The striped building reminded him of a prison garment. He was surprised the building hadn't been designed with "broad arrows," which had been the sign of prison clothing until a few years ago. That was the sight that had been drilled into him as a recent immigrant to England, by Boris. The fate of a man who didn't work hard in this country was heavy, hobnailed boots that pressed an arrow into the dirt with every step. As Boris said, that was not the footprint a man wanted to leave on this Earth.

Could he escape that fate? Could Vera and Sergei? He didn't know how.

He went to the front desk and stood in line behind a frightened-looking woman. After she was passed on to a uniformed constable to help her locate her missing husband, he faced the grizzled sergeant who was screening public inquiries.

"May I help you?" said the man. He offered a kindly smile, which seemed out of place in a government institution, though Ivan was sure frightened people appreciated his pleasant demeanor.

"I work at the Grand Russe Hotel on Park Lane," Ivan said. All of a sudden, he didn't know what to do with his hands. He put them behind his back and clasped them.

"Yes?"

An angry-looking man, who looked like a banker, moved into position behind Ivan. He lowered his voice. "I believe a terrible crime will be committed there today."

"You don't say." The sergeant's bushy gray mustache swung from side to side as the man's mouth twitched.

"There is a Russian diplomat in residence, and this evening British government ministers will be at the hotel." Ivan folded his arms across his chest.

"Go on, son."

"There is a man who wants to bomb the hotel while everyone is watching a command performance of *Macbeth*." Did he sound as foolish to the sergeant as he did to himself?

The policeman's eyes narrowed. "Where'd you hear that, then? Have you spoken to the hotel's management?"

"I've met the bomber," Ivan said. "I've told the hotel manager that trouble is coming."

"Why didn't he come to us?"

"Maybe he has? I don't know. I tried to talk someone out of this but it was no good."

"Are you part of the conspiracy to commit this crime?"

"No, sir. I am not."

The man's gaze raked his. He no longer looked like a man past his prime. "You'd better come with me, son. Smith, take the desk."

A tall, skinny constable moved to the front of the desk and began helping the next person in line, the angry businessman.

The sergeant gestured him around the corner. "Take a seat here. I'll take you directly to an inspector when one is available."

Ivan sat down as instructed, staring at a sea of desks and file cabinets. Everyone moved quickly, with a sense of purpose. The smoke from a hundred cigarettes made the air almost as bad as the pea-souper fog outside. He coughed hard when a man in street clothes with a particularly heavy cigar walked by, trailing smoke, and was grateful he worked in a place with better ventilation.

Five minutes later, the sergeant reappeared. "Detective Inspector Dent will see you now."

Ivan stood and followed the sergeant into a small office, dominated by a desk. An ashtray held one thin, burning cigarette, and file cabinets took up most of the space along the walls.

The inspector, a man of about forty with slick black hair, stood and shook Ivan's hand when he walked in. A young uniformed officer leaned against a free spot along the wall, almost like a piece of furniture. He blocked a fair amount of a map of London that was pinned there.

"Detective Inspector Dent," he said. "What can I do for you today?" He had gray eyes and thick slashes of black brow, making for a slightly menacing air.

"I am a night watchman at the Grand Russe Hotel."

"You're Russian?" Dent asked as he gestured Ivan to a chair in front of his tidy desk.

"Yes, sir. I grew up around Moscow. Fled by way of Finland in 1918 after my oldest sister and parents were killed by the government."

"How long have you been in London?" Dent sat down and picked up a pen. Notepaper was centered in front of him.

"A few years. My sister Vera and I."

He kept firing rapid questions. "Why do you think there is going to be an attack at the hotel tonight?"

"My sister is engaged to a man named Sergei Bakunin. He is a White, if you understand what that means." He would sacrifice Sergei, but he couldn't help attempting to keep Vera sounding like an innocent.

"Not in favor of the present Russian government," the inspector said laconically, taking up his cigarette with his free hand.

"Yes, and he has friends who are more active than dreamers, if you know what I mean. One of them, Anatoly Smirnov, just took work at the hotel. I know he's not doing his job because he's not staying on his patch, but wandering the entire hotel."

"So you think he wants to cause trouble during this"—Dent checked his notebook—"performance of *Macbeth*?"

"I know Richard Marvin, the director of the play, has ties to this little group of Whites. But what really disturbs me is a man named Konstantin."

Dent made a note. "Who is that?"

"He's a Bolshevik. He wants the government here to fall."

"Bolshies and Whites together? That's not usual."

"No, sir."

"Is he working at the hotel, too?"

"No, but I met him, and he said he was going to bomb the hotel. He was going to prepare a bomb that Anatoly will bring in. The performance is planned to take place in a series of meeting rooms on the first floor, which can be expanded to a large open area with a stage. That's where the bomb is going to be brought."

"Why do you know all this?"

"Because they attempted to recruit me to place the bomb, before Anatoly had his position."

Dent set down his pen. "And you said no? Or perhaps you said yes?"

"Never," Ivan said with intensity. "I have a future here. I want my friends to have a future too. Good work, marriage, children. I don't chase dreams of overturning governments, righting past wrongs. I just want to get by."

"Have you informed your management?"

"Yes, and we discussed how to outwit the plot. But I don't think the manager understands that this has grown from a simple attempt to murder Georgy Ovolensky, a Russian diplomat, into the desire to kill a roomful of British people. For all I know, the bomb could bring down the hotel and everyone in it."

Dent ground out his cigarette. "How did the plot grow?"

"When it was about White sensibilities, the only concern was Ovolensky, a tool of the Stalinist government of Russia. When a Bolshevik became involved, it meant the British government became the true target."

Dent frowned. "The Whites and the Bolsheviks are enemies."

"In this they have a common cause. The Whites want Ovolensky and presumably the Bolsheviks want the British ministers. Detective Inspector Dent, I implore you to stop this. Konstantin is a very bad man. I'm not sure I should have even left the hotel today. What if he brings the bomb to Anatoly? I can identify him. I saw him once."

The inspector made hasty notes. "When does this Anatoly come on duty?"

"Eight P.M."

Dent rubbed his right ear. "We have time to find him then. Where did you first see Konstantin?"

Chapter Nineteen

"Has this chap come in yet tonight?" Detective Inspector Dent of the Metropolitan Police's Special Branch asked Peter Eyre. He had declined to sit down in one of the chairs in front of Peter's desk, no doubt to reinforce his authority.

"No, I don't imagine so. It's only six thirty, and his shift begins at eight. Night watchmen check in downstairs in the staff lounge. Mr. Dew, the night manager, has more of a pulse on evening activities than I do. I am in our Coffee Room at this time of night."

The inspector cocked his head. "Why haven't you taken this bomb threat more seriously?"

Peter stiffened. Bomb? He'd thought of guns, knives, intimate assassination attempts, nothing like this. "It may surprise you to know, but I've heard nothing about the weapon. I thought there might be an attack on the Russian, but not something that might affect the entire hotel."

The inspector rolled his eyes. "It didn't occur to you that whatever desperate act might occur, more than one life could be at risk? I can understand hating Bolshies as much as the next man, but you can't risk innocent British lives."

"I'm not planning to. We were going to move the performance at the last moment, make sure Smirnov, the night watchman, couldn't access the location. I've had a space cleared on the fifth floor and our head chambermaid, Olga, has been there all day watching the rooms. Even Ivan doesn't know this plan."

The inspector's mouth twisted. "Olga? Another Russian?"

"In Russia, this woman was a princess." He responded to the inspector's lifted brows. "Yes, you heard me, a real princess. She's not going to throw in with a bunch of Bolshies."

The inspector sighed. "I doubt this Smirnov was going to come to work, on time, with a bomb in a valise."

"How else would he do it?"

He leaned forward and spread his fingertips on the desk. "This is how bombers operate these days. They carry in small packages of explosives over a period of time, and attach them to a fixed structure in a building. In this case, perhaps in a cabinet by a load-bearing wall, or in the ceiling. Even a fireplace."

Peter's stomach rumbled queasily. "Go on."

"Then they detonate the bomb with a long cord, hoping it will give them time to escape. This could be hidden if necessary under a carpet or along a wall."

He kept his voice steady. "I see."

"Another fun trick is the forged invitation."

"What do you mean?"

"These groups want to kill as many of their enemies as possible, of course, so they might invite everyone they want dead to the same occasion."

Spots danced in front of Peter's eyes as he breathed in slowly through his nose. "We have our own invitations, and they will be checked."

"Yes, but who is going to be doing the checking? Is there a curated guest list? Is this someone who can distinguish between similar foreign names?"

"I'll do it myself. I have the guest list."

"You look exhausted," Detective Inspector Dent said, not unkindly. "Not on your game. I've no doubt these worries have had you up at night, but you should have come to us for help. This problem is bigger than you, sir."

Clearly. Even his father might have been daunted. "Now what?"

"We need to bring a team in to find the explosives. We also will want a pair of men in the staff lounge, to quietly remove this Smirnov as soon as he arrives."

"Of course."

"May I use your telephone?"

Peter nodded. He'd never had a moment yet, since the hotel had reopened, when he wished for the counsel of another. He and his older brother had been raised like prodigies by their parents and had always felt secure. Now though, he wished his parents were here, instead of in Leeds with his sister. And Noel? Oh, how he wished his brother was anywhere but in the location he was. But this was no time to consider family.

He listened as the inspector fired orders at someone on the other end of the line. He ordered three teams after he was connected to Special Branch. One to pick up Smirnov when he entered the staff lounge, one to go through the meeting rooms on the first floor, and one to monitor the actual performance on the fifth floor. Then he had a lengthy conversation with his superior.

"Another thing," Dent said to Peter when he'd hung up the telephone.

"Of course."

"Richard Marvin?"

That blasted actor again. "Yes."

"Ivan Salter claims the man is part of the conspiracy, and in fact assaulted his fiancée in the hopes of discrediting Salter."

"Lovely," Peter muttered.

"Any thoughts?"

"Marvin is a heavy drinker with an eye for the ladies and a desperate need for money," Peter said.

"Fair enough." Dent pulled a cigarette case out of his pocket. "Last minute I'm going to have for one of these tonight."

"I'll join you." Peter pulled out his own case. "Where is Ivan?"

"At New Scotland Yard. We've been picking up those members of the conspiracy that we can find, and we've needed him to identify them."

"Is he coming into work tonight?"

"He is the Metropolitan Police's guest at this point," Dent said, holding out a match for Peter.

Peter bent to accept the light. "You don't think he is involved?"

"Do you?"

The thought had never crossed his mind. Salter was secretive but honest. Peter would bet the hotel on that. "No. I absolutely do not."

Dent squinted as he quickly lit his own cigarette and waved the match out just before it burned him. "I'm not so sure. He's hiding something."

"He knows the people who are involved, from his private life." Peter inhaled blissfully, then blew a smoke ring toward the ceiling. "That much is obvious, but he has too much to lose. He loves this new fiancée of his."

"New, is she?"

"Yes. She was the Marvins' secretary, until Richard Marvin assaulted her."

"I assume she quit?"

"No, sacked."

Dent shook his head. "That's a bit of bad luck. Was she hurt?"

Peter put his hand to his neck. "Yes, but not enough to be hospitalized. A day or two in bed, though."

"And no one thought to file charges for that, either?"

"It never occurred to me. Unfortunately, Marvin had a good story. Impossible to disprove."

"You do understand that it was secrecy that brought down this hotel's previous management and reputation over the Starlet Murders of 1922, don't you? And secrecy will bring it down again. Your family has to learn to work with the police, instead of against us. We aren't the enemy, criminals are."

"We live and die by paying guests," Peter said. "Sometimes our guests are the criminals."

Dent chuckled. "Then I expect we're meant to stay enemies. Do I need to order a raid on that nightclub of yours?"

Peter shook his head. "We comply with the liquor laws. No, that's the least of it. It's a large hotel, and we have to fill the rooms. All sorts of people stay at a hotel."

Dent sighed. "After all, it's the criminal class who has the money. Like those bloody Bolshies. It was like flashing a red scarf at a bull, naming this hotel as you did." He took one last puff and ground out his cigarette in Peter's ashtray, then raised his voice to a falsetto. "Bring your foreign intrigue here."

"It's named after a ballet company," Peter said. His brother loved the ballet.

Dent shrugged. "Ballet is French, right? Nothing good can come from that."

For the next two hours, Peter shadowed the inspector as he moved around the hotel. The fifth floor suite where Emmeline had once lived with her mother was free from explosives. He'd felt his first gray hairs pop out along his scalp, however, when, at six forty-five, a police detective opened one of the lower cabinets in the raised-floor meeting room, which normally held teacups and plates, and discovered cylinders of a paper-wrapped substance.

"Dynamite," the detective said with satisfaction. "Not wired up yet."

Detective Inspector Dent checked his pocket watch. "Not leaving much time. Maybe Marvin is supposed to do it when he comes in."

"He'd blow himself up," Peter said, horrified.

Dent shrugged. "Some do, you know. Have we searched the Marvins' rooms yet?"

"They are on the fifth floor, the Chinese Suite," Peter said.

Dent gestured at a young, uniformed constable. "Get going. Tell them to move two men from the performance space to the Chinese Suite and do a thorough search for the detonator and wires."

Peter collapsed into Macbeth's throne. The scenery was still set up there, since he hadn't wanted to alert the Marvins to the room change.

Dent scratched his mustache. "What are you thinking of, Eyre?"

Peter stared at his hands. "What a fool I've been."

"You're too young to have been in the war, son. Your experience with man's inhumanity, particularly the foreign kind, is limited as a result. No, you have to leave it to those of us who know better."

"Like a Russian refugee whose own parents and sister were shot by firing squad," Peter said in a low voice.

"Who was that, then?"

"Ivan Salter. His oldest sister was part of a group that tried to assassinate Lenin."

Dent pursed his lips. "Then he's unlikely to turn Bolshie. Unfortunate that his sister fell in love with a man who did."

What? Peter lifted his eyebrows. "I'm not sure I knew he had a sister."

"We haven't found her yet. Can I use your phone again? I'd better have Salter brought here soon, so he can identify any other members of the Bolshevik cell who try to come in."

"Of course." Peter forced himself to rise, and found his legs would still support him despite the shock.

They went downstairs so Dent could call New Scotland Yard again. Peter went out to the reception desk and stood next to Hugh Moth, staring at the passing parade in the Grand Hall. The smiling, well-dressed throng seemed little more than ghosts to him, and ghosts they would be, if the police didn't sort this out. He wondered if he should evacuate the hotel, but that would be catastrophic to its future.

* * *

"Lots of police about," Lionel Dew said, coming into the room behind the reception desk at seven.

"Possible trouble with the *Macbeth* performance," Peter explained. He'd been asked to retrieve a sample of the official invitation to the performance so he could show the inspector and his men.

"Is it going to be canceled?"

"No. We don't want to damage government relations."

"Bit of sarcasm there, eh?" Dew asked.

Just then, the inspector appeared. Ivan was with him, along with two new men in suits. More Special Branch detectives, most likely.

"We'll need to send your man downstairs to get into uniform," Dent said.

"My uniform is at home, except my coat," Ivan said quietly. He had shadows under his eyes.

Peter wasn't exactly sorry the night watchman had had a rough day.

"We'll sort something out," Dew said. "We've extra clothing for emergencies."

"Go with him," Dent said, gesturing with his chin toward one of the new detectives.

Anatoly Smirnov arrived in the staff lounge at 7:20. Peter had been lying in wait for him along with the police. He was pulled aside immediately and searched in a bathroom. The constable found the ignitor for the bomb sewn into the lining of Anatoly's coat. His expression hadn't changed as he was marched out of the hotel through the basement employee door and into a waiting car. Peter wished he could punch the man, but he could do nothing but watch.

At a few minutes after seven thirty, he went to the fifth floor with Detective Inspector Dent.

"We'll search everyone you don't recognize," Dent said as they rode the lift. "Just in case there are weapons."

"Do you think the plotters have any idea that their plans were uncovered?"

Peter had taken control of the lift himself so that an operator couldn't overhear the conversation. "I'm more concerned that we haven't located this Konstantin yet. We've arrested a Sergei Bakunin, and another chap we only know as Pavel right now."

"Konstantin is the important figure?"

"Yes. He has access to the explosives. From what I've heard from the interrogation so far, Sergei is a rather pitiful character, and this entire plan started as a vendetta against the Russian diplomat, Ov-olensky."

"And Pavel?"

"A professional, as is Anatoly."

Peter frowned as they reached the fifth floor. "I can't believe we hired him."

"These Bolshies can be very clever," Dent assured him. "Good cover stories, excellent forged documents."

"Does Ivan Salter check out?" he asked as he opened the gate.

Dent went to the left, where the suite was. "His story matches Bakunin's, although neither of them is talking about Salter's sister. We need to find and speak to her."

Peter relaxed. "Then I can trust Ivan, for the most part at least. The sister has never been here asking for work. I know that much."

"We'll be using Salter at the door, but don't think we neglected to check his clothing, too, before we let him into position for checking the performance guests."

"He could have had something planted on him."

"That he could," Detective Inspector Dent said, gaze drifting across the art-covered walls. "We've checked out the man he's resid-ing with. Jewish, so not much likelihood of a Bolshie there. Assum-ing Salter's sister isn't the true mastermind, Salter is probably completely out of it."

"Do you think the sister is the mastermind?" His own mother being brilliant, Peter never discounted women.

"All this voting nonsense has women thinking they can run the world nowadays," Dent said. "Who can say? She's probably a mere hysterical cook and cleaner for the cell, but until we speak to her I won't know."

"Hello, Ivan," Peter said, arriving at the suite door.

His night watchman, pale but properly dressed in full uniform, nodded respectfully at him. "About half the guests have arrived. The stage is ready and the actors are in the valet's bedroom of the adjoin-ing suite."

"Anything suspicious?"

"No, sir. Everyone has credentials and their invitation. Wives too, of course, but they've all come with their husbands."

"Any Russians yet?"

"Neither the party from upstairs nor anyone I recognize."

"No sign of Konstantin or your sister. Those are the two we are looking for still," Dent said.

Peter watched carefully, but Ivan didn't flinch or respond to the inspector's taunting tone. The man had survived many years of hardship. He was too smart to reveal himself easily. Behind him, Peter heard any number of loud footsteps, a cough, the clearing of a throat. When he turned, he saw the Russian delegation, some dozen men.

Now he saw a response from Ivan Salter. His posture had gone rigid. As Peter watched, he tucked closed fists behind his back. He was glad the man had been searched for weapons.

George Ovolensky was somewhere between thirty and thirty-five, with dark bushy hair and a thick mustache. He looked to be impressively fit under his tuxedo, and wore an air of wealth that seemed an odd fit for a Bolshevik. Peter knew instantly that this man had come from the higher ranks of society. Why had he joined the Soviet government? He didn't look like an idealist. He had the watchful gaze of a predator.

Ovolensky's eyes widened when he took in the small crowd. Or so Peter thought.

When Dent said, "Invitations, please, gentlemen?" Ovolensky didn't even glance at him. His black gaze fixed on Ivan.

"If it isn't young Saltykov," Ovolensky said in English. He then said something guttural in Russian.

Ivan's left shoulder jerked, but his face remained impassive.

Ovolensky continued in English. "Where is that beautiful sister of yours? Dear Cousin Vera. Prettiest of the Saltykovs. Catherine had a horse face, as I recall. Better to rid the world of ugly women. Vera's looks came from your father's side. Your mother was not a handsome woman, merely wealthy."

Peter watched shock cross Ivan's face. He could tell Ovolensky as telling lies about the night watchman's family.

One of the other delegates snickered as he handed his passport and invitation to a uniformed constable.

Ivan spoke, his accent heavier than usual. "It must be interesting for your colleagues to note that Georgy Ovolensky has family here in London."

Peter hadn't thought everyone in the delegation spoke English, but now he realized he might be mistaken as attention went to Ivan.

"*Da*," Ivan said, then returned to English. "He is my late father's cousin. We were gentry, before the war. Georgy's family was wealthier than mine, better connected. If it wasn't for the fact that he had my parents murdered, I might have called him cousin."

Ovolensky's eyes bulged, and he growled something in Russian.

"My parents had nothing to do with Catherine's involvement in the plot to kill Lenin, if that was even true. If you had any idea how much Vera hated you, you'd drink yourself to sleep each night. May God have mercy on your soul, for I have none," Ivan said.

Dent stiffened. Peter wondered if he thought Ivan was going to attack Ovolensky, even though they all knew Ivan had no weapons.

Ovolensky's expression relaxed and he began to laugh. Stepping forward, he clapped Ivan on the shoulder hard, then pinched his cousin's cheek. "Such humor, this boy. You ought to be on stage, no? Are you in the play?"

Dent glanced over at Peter, and he wondered what the inspector thought about Ivan's comment about Vera. Clearly, his sister wanted Ovolensky dead. Would she try anything now? Where was she?

The constable began letting the Russians through. Behind them, Peter saw Alecia Loudon before Ivan did. She wore a black velvet dress and pink shoes. He hadn't seen her in proper evening clothes since New Year's Eve. She looked lovely and he smiled at her, but she only had eyes for Ivan, though he registered shock when he saw her.

"I'm afraid I don't have an invitation," she said. "Mrs. Marvin invited me."

"I know her," Peter said to Dent. "She used to be Marvin's secretary."

"We'll have to check you," Dent said in a fatherly manner.

"What for?" Ovolensky asked. "Such a beautiful creature should never be molested."

Miss Loudon glanced at all the men, then slowly handed her coat and purse to Detective Inspector Dent. "I'm happy to oblige."

He ran his fingers over all the seams, then glanced through her purse. "I'm afraid we'll have to examine the hem of your dress."

"Yes, sir."

Ovolensky watched, fascinated, as the uniformed constable quickly ran his fingers over the dress, careful not to touch any of Miss Loudon's skin.

"What are you looking for?" Ovolensky said.

"Detonators," Detective Inspector Dent said with relish. "You have enemies here, you know, Mr. Ovolensky."

The Russian chuckled, but his compatriots had all entered the suite, save one man who appeared from his great bulk to be a bodyguard. "We are safe nowhere, we Soviets."

"Your enemies seem to be rather more personal, sir," Peter said.

Ovolensky raised his ferocious eyebrows. "What an unpleasant remark."

"Why don't you go in, Cousin," Ivan interrupted before Ovolensky could continue. "You can find a seat for my fiancée, on the opposite side of the room from you, of course."

"Your fiancée?" Ovolensky repeated.

"Miss Loudon and I are engaged," Ivan said. Peter could hear the pride in Ivan's voice.

The Russian made a show of shifting his gaze from the girl to the night watchman. "I'll admit you are a handsome devil, Ivan, but you've no position in life. What's a beauty like this doing settling on you? Did she lose her true love in the war?"

"The war has been over for seven years," Miss Loudon said.

"Not quite," replied the Russian. "How old are you, my dear? Twenty-six, twenty-seven?"

"Twenty-two," she replied.

Peter could see what it cost her to keep her voice level. Ovolensky was utterly odious. Alecia Loudon was a youthful beauty, and barely looked her true age, much less older.

"I don't like paint on women," Ovolensky said. "It ages them, turns them into whores."

They all froze. Then Ivan broke the stillness by saying, "As loathsome as ever, I see, Georgy. Thankfully, I still remember the spider-leg-plucking, puppy-drowning boy you were, and am not surprised. I don't think I shall entrust Alecia to you after all. Mr. Eyre, would you do the honors?"

"With pleasure," Peter said, offering his arm. When she placed her hand on his arm, he tucked his hand over it and squeezed. She smiled at him and nodded, and they went into the room to watch the performance.

Despite everything that had transpired, Alecia was mesmerized by the theatrical performance. She hadn't seen many plays, and while she might have lost respect for the Marvins, they were world-renowned for a reason. However, she thought it wise to leave immediately afterward, especially when Ivan, a police constable on each side, caught her eye and tilted his head toward the door as soon as the audience began to clap.

Mr. Eyre put Alecia into a taxicab personally after the *Macbeth* performance ended. She knew she ought to return to the Plash flat and her duties with her new charge, but the woman would be asleep in the early evening hours. For herself, she knew she would not sleep a wink with all of these worries scampering through her brain like a litter of gamboling piglets. Instead, she directed the driver to take her to Boris Grinberg's flat.

When she knocked on his door and there was no immediate answer, she began to berate herself. How could she have made such a foolish choice as to come here?

Finally, the door opened. "Miss Loudon!" Boris said jovially. "I'm afraid your young man is not at home."

"He's at the Grand Russe."

Boris nodded. "You look troubled."

"Do you know what has been going on today?"

He glanced up and down the hall, then gestured her in. As soon as she stepped inside, he shut the door. "I know it all too well, my dear. The police brought me in for a chat this afternoon."

Hope surged. "But they let you go?"

"They didn't see me as a conspirator. I helpfully pointed out that Ivan came to me after his sister severed relations with him."

She blinked at Mr. Grinberg, her brain refusing to form words.

He shook his head. "Come, my dear, remove your coat. You look chilled."

Slowly, she took off her outerwear and he led her into his parlor, where she had spent very happy hours with Ivan recently. He went to a sideboard and poured from a bottle into two small cups and brought her one.

"It is kosher wine. I think you can use it."

"Thank you." She sipped it slowly. "It's very sweet."

He nodded. "Small quantities are best, I find. Now tell me what brings you here when you knew Ivan was not here. Do you need a place to stay?"

"No, I started a new position today and it includes a bed." She finished her wine and set the tiny cut crystal glass on a side table. "Do you know what has been happening? There were so many police at the performance."

"There was a bomb threat," Boris said, settling more comfortably into his armchair by the fire. "And Ivan's sister is mixed up with the group who were trying to set off the bomb."

The wine had warmed her, but her chest hurt. "Was Ivan arrested? Will he be deported?"

"I don't think so. He's an honest man, our Ivan. He was never involved in the plot. Justice will serve, eh?"

"You are from Russia, and Jewish besides. You don't really believe that, do you?"

"It is hard for any man with the wrong accent to come out ahead, I'll give you that. But I've made a comfortable life for myself here and I don't see why he cannot do the same, with you." He patted his stomach.

Alecia was exhausted, but she'd come here to learn. "What about his sister?"

Boris shrugged. "She has made her own choices. Vera is very strong willed. I don't believe a man has led her astray."

"You wouldn't consider her a victim?"

"Of course I would, but she can choose peace or violence, and according to Ivan she chose violence. She wants revenge more than a future, for herself or Ivan."

"That's terrible."

"Don't judge her too harshly. Her family was murdered. Her life as she knew it, as she expected it to be, ended in fear. I wish she had chosen to cling to the one family member she had left, even though she lost her lifestyle, but she's gone down another path, as so many have before her."

"My parents died in the war, but it doesn't make me want to hunt down Germans and kill them." She shivered, thinking about her grandfather's sermons during the war, about peace. Maybe they'd had more of an impact on her than she'd realized.

"The difference," Boris said gently, "is that she has a face to put to her sorrow: this Georgy Ovolensky. Would you do nothing if faced with the person who'd given the order to kill your parents?"

"You are not the first to ask," Alecia said. "But I could never risk innocent lives in the process of gaining revenge."

"That is where you and Ivan are different from Vera and her fiancé," Boris said. His gaze took on a haunted air, then he bobbed his head several times as if to clear old thoughts. "Why don't you rest in my study? Ivan will likely not be home until his shift is over in the morning."

"I shouldn't, but I will anyway," Alecia said. She suddenly missed Ivan. Would the pillow smell like cucumbers and birch oil? She wanted something of him. "I'm too frightened to go away and not know what is happening."

Boris patted her hand. "Mazel tov. I foresee a happy future for you and Ivan. Don't be afraid."

Ivan climbed out of the taxicab at one thirty in the morning. The icy-cold air and frost on the windows proved the point that it was January. The streets, deserted except for parked cars, were somnolent.

He walked up to the entrance to Boris's block of flats. Mr. Eyre had told Ivan to go home instead of working through his shift when he'd caught him leaning against a wall in the lobby, staring blankly ahead. He'd protested and pointed out that the hotel had lost the services of Anatoly as well, but Mr. Eyre said he wouldn't be able to sleep that night, so he might as well double as night watchman himself.

Ivan rubbed at his eyes as he went up the stairs. A part of him was still shocked that he had his liberty, after the events of the evening. He wouldn't have expected the Metropolitan Police to understand that he, a Russian immigrant, really had not been a part of the plot to bomb the Grand Russe, especially when the lead inspector himself saw the animosity between him and Georgy Ovolensky.

He had to give Detective Inspector Dent credit for being a good man.

Wearily, he stumbled into Boris's flat and took off his overcoat and shoes, then walked down the hall into the study, ready for his bed. He pulled off his clothes, wishing he had the energy to wash away the sweat that had accumulated over one of the most frightening days of his life, and climbed, almost naked, onto his cot.

A woman shrieked. He jumped back, falling against Boris's desk.

Chapter Twenty

"Alecia?" Small items fell over on the desk Ivan bumped. He could see nothing in the dark.

"Ivan?" Blankets rustled.

He recognized Alecia's voice and relaxed, then fumbled for the candle and matches on the desk and lit the candle. When he saw two framed photographs had fallen over, he righted them.

"It is you," she said, sitting up. "What time is it?"

She was in her slip and had put her hair into a braid. Clearly, she'd settled down for the night. Why was she here when she should be at the Plashes' flat? "The middle of the night. Mr. Eyre told me to find my bed."

She pushed back the covers and stepped toward him, then threw her arms around his neck. "You aren't under arrest?"

He folded his head into that soft place between her shoulder and her head, and wrapped his arms around her waist. Pure happiness. "They kept me all day at New Scotland Yard, then brought me to the hotel in case I recognized someone who shouldn't be there. Once the performance was over, the police didn't have further use for me."

She rubbed her nose against his hair. "I'm so glad they know you weren't involved."

"True, but my sister and Konstantin are still unaccounted for. Who knows what Vera will say if they catch her."

"I've been so afraid for you," she whispered. "That's why I came here. Boris assured me you'd be fine."

"He might even be right," Ivan said, his voice muffled because his mouth was on her soft neck. "Vera is where I'm vulnerable."

She put her hands on his head and gently tugged it up so she could see him. "I don't want to think about her right now."

Her lips met his. "Thank God," he whispered. "I thank God for you." Their grip on each other grew frantic. At the same moment, they both had to have each other's remaining clothing off. They fell back on the cot noisily. Ivan found himself on top, and when he touched her sex, he found her extremely wet, very ready for him. He found a sheath, then plunged into her, claiming her love as his right.

"I love you," she said in his ear. "I love you, my Ivan."

"I love you, *myshka*, I do," he whispered back, gliding into her again.

In response, she clasped him intimately, her ankles crossing high above his back, squeezing him with every muscle. He couldn't last for long, didn't, but she was right there with him, shuddering with bliss and their complete commitment to each other. He'd had no idea he could feel so happy or relaxed after such an unsettling day, but afterward, he reversed their positions so that she lay on top of him, and fell asleep.

Alecia dreamed about the Grand Russe. Ivan, in night watchman uniform, twirled her around the Coffee Room so fast that the blue-and-silver striped walls blurred into one continuous color. A drummer took up the beat of the waltz, pounding insistently. Not matching the song, either. She sat up and blinked, careful not to wake Ivan. The dream hadn't been real but the pounding was. Someone was at the front door of the flat.

She shook Ivan awake in the dark.

"What?"

"Someone is at the door. We'd better get dressed."

Ivan muttered something in Russian, then stood and relit the candle on the desk. It gave them enough light to find their clothes. As Ivan slid his feet into his well-worn shoes, he said, "Stay here. I'll find out what is going on."

He slipped out of the door, leaving it open a crack. Alecia went to the door and listened. At first she couldn't distinguish any actual words, but when she realized she was hearing a woman's voice, she decided to go into the parlor.

Mr. Grinberg had lit the fire and turned on the lights. "There you are, my dear," he said with a smile. "Could I trouble you to put the kettle on?"

The interloper in the room was a beautiful, frail woman with

Ivan's black hair and Slavic cheekbones. *Vera.* She said something to Ivan in Russian and he answered her in kind. Ivan smiled at her but Vera didn't even glance in her direction. Alecia nodded at Ivan and went to make tea.

When she returned, carrying a tray with a teapot, cups, and bread and butter slices, she heard English words interspersed with Russian as Vera spoke. Pounds. Shillings. Guineas. If she was hoping Ivan had money, she would be disappointed.

Ivan glanced at her as she set down the tray and switched to English. "Vera, you said we weren't family anymore. Why are you coming to me for help?"

"I said it in the heat of the moment," she said, twisting her hands together. A long streak of dirt marked her ankle-length gray skirt. "I'm passionate."

"I betrayed your plans to the police," Ivan said, his lips thin with disgust. "Don't you want to tell your friends so they can organize to kill me?"

"I did nothing," Vera protested. "I'm innocent."

"I don't believe that. I saw Konstantin in our flat. I saw you meeting with Richard Marvin."

"Then why didn't you betray me to the police?" she shouted.

"I thought that was Sergei's responsibility," Ivan replied calmly.

As quietly as possible, Alecia poured the tea. She handed a cup to Mr. Grinberg first, then Vera, then Ivan. Then she passed around the plate of bread and butter. Vera kept the entire plate after Mr. Grinberg waved it away, not offering it to Ivan. Alecia disliked the woman intensely. She was incredibly rude. But did that mean she was capable of evil?

"Did you see Georgy?" Vera asked.

"Yes, and he didn't seem nearly as interested in killing me as you have been interested in killing him."

"I didn't do it," Vera whined.

Ivan's gaze held an almost aristocratic level of chill. "Your friends failed. That is the truth. You'd have reveled in their success if they'd had any."

"I know where the police can find Konstantin," Vera said. "I know you don't believe me, but I am no Bolshevik. Once our plans became about killing the British government ministers, I wanted no part of it."

Ivan lifted his brows. "And Sergei did?"

Alecia could see from Ivan's expression that he didn't believe it.

"Pavel and Anatoly didn't care," Vera said, not responding to the question. "You must help me, Ivan. I am your sister. I deserve your help, just like when we heard the news about Mama and Papa and you took me to Finland." As if she were the younger sibling, not the elder.

"If you go to the police and give them Konstantin, I'm sure you will be freed," Ivan said calmly.

Vera swallowed a slice of bread. "I'll have to go to prison. I'll never work again. They'll deport me. We have no family left in Russia."

"That's not true. After all, if you weren't involved in the plot, I'm sure Georgy's family will take you in." Ivan's face betrayed no humor.

Vera's expression went wild for a moment, then she regathered her composure. "I'm certain you don't mean that."

"Help her," Alecia said, frustrated by the late hour and cold interaction between the siblings. "If she tells you Konstantin's location, I'll go to New Scotland Yard with the information while you get her away."

Mr. Grinberg shook his head and made as if to rise from his armchair. "I'll go to the police, Miss Loudon. You stay with Ivan. I don't trust her."

Vera glared, then shoved a slice of bread into her mouth.

"Where were you hiding?" Mr. Grinberg asked.

Vera's cheeks were distended. She looked at the men defiantly.

"Did Mr. Marvin shelter you?" Alecia asked.

Vera shot her a glare. *There was the hidden story.*

Alecia felt ill. This woman had a fiancé. "He did, didn't he, in my old room? You were in the hotel the entire time."

Vera swallowed, then drained her teacup. "I'm not going to tell you anything."

Alecia was losing her patience quickly. "Did you tell Richard what was going on? Or did you just use him?"

"He might have been able to stop it if he'd known the full story," Vera said. "I had orders to behave in a certain fashion. We paid him a little to look away and I kept him distracted. We thought to put real weapons among the props."

"You started this," Ivan said, his voice rising. "You started this, and then you tried to stop it?"

"I only wanted Georgy dead, for our parents, for Catherine," Vera said, matching his tone. "I didn't want to hurt anyone else. A knife, I thought. Some small explosive under his chair that would only have killed him and his bodyguards. Not something that would destroy a room full of people."

"You can ask Mr. Marvin for the truth," Mr. Grinberg said. "I don't see that she tried to stop what was happening, Ivan."

"Vera's story doesn't make sense. Marvin attacked Alecia so that I would fight him and be sacked, and Anatoly would receive my job." Ivan ran his fingers through his hair, then left it in wild disarray.

"We don't know that," Alecia said, wanting to smooth down his strands but not wanting to touch him so intimately in front of Vera. "Not for certain. I wouldn't trust him or Vera, but she's planted a seed of doubt in my mind about where Richard fits into this. For now, if she gives the police Konstantin, I think we should help her."

Ivan rubbed his face hard. "Where would we take her?"

"To Bagshot," Alecia said. "Where else? If I cannot save my sister, at least we can save yours."

Ivan frowned. "She won't be able to leave England. They'll have her name at the ports."

"Let's move her out of London first," Alecia said. "Then Mr. Grinberg can bargain Konstantin's whereabouts for dropping Vera from the investigation."

Ivan's hands went back to his hair, but at least he couldn't make it any worse. "Do you think the police will agree to that?"

"I have no idea," Alecia admitted. "But do you have a better idea?"

"No," Ivan said. "Vera?"

She huddled in her chair, looking tiny and tired. Had the fight left her?

"Take my car," Mr. Grinberg said. "There's a taxicab driver on the ground floor in the building. I'll wake him up in half an hour and have him take me to New Scotland Yard. You can be well on your way by then."

"Do you know how to drive?" Alecia asked.

Ivan nodded. "I drove a truck in Berlin for a while. Finish eating while we gather our things, Vera. And tell Boris the truth about Konstantin, or I'll drag the story out of you myself."

* * *

"What are you going to do about the Plashes?" Ivan asked Alecia an hour later as they drove toward Bagshot. Vera was slumped over, asleep in the backseat, obviously exhausted.

"I can telephone from the vicarage," Alecia said. "But I don't know if Emmeline will give me a second chance after this."

"It's Mr. Eyre you have to persuade, most likely," Ivan said. "He's paying the bills."

"So she said," Alecia admitted.

Ivan suppressed a yawn and leaned forward in the seat. Due to the fog on the lonely roads, he reduced their speed. "I was hoping we'd at least not arrive until dawn, but we are making good time."

"How did Vera travel to the flat?" Alecia asked. "The Marvins don't have a car."

"There are taxicabs outside the Grand Russe every hour," Ivan said. "Marvin could have obtained one for her. Or she walked. She was dirty."

"I see. Of course, we don't know for certain that she was there. I'd have expected that if she was, she'd have been napping all day. Nothing to do in that tiny room otherwise."

Ivan glanced at her. Was she joking? After all, Richard Marvin hadn't been busy with his play all day. "She might have been too worried. When we were on the run in '18, neither of us slept much."

"I see. It's funny, but I've slept so well these past few days. I never used to, as you well know."

"I'm glad," Ivan said. "Sincerely glad."

"Meeting you has changed my life," Alecia said. "I hope meeting me has changed yours for the better as well."

"It has," he assured her. "I know what to fight for now." Family had taken on a different meaning.

The headlamps caught the front door of the vicarage. They had arrived. Ivan pulled over and parked, conscious that none of them had any luggage, and they had a fugitive in tow. They hadn't taken enough time to confirm a story with Boris. Would he tell the police about the vicarage? Would the Plashes become involved somehow when Alecia wasn't in her bed this morning? And what about him? Would he arrive at the Grand Russe for his shift that night?

How venomous would Georgy Ovolensky be? How much power

did he wield with the British government? If he had them deported, he'd lose Alecia forever.

He stepped down from the car and opened Alecia's door, then went to the backseat and woke Vera.

"We're in Bagshot," he told her. She nodded sleepily and yawned. To his tastes, she didn't look nearly frightened enough.

Alecia used her key to enter the dark house. Ivan guessed that it was about four A.M., much too early for a non-farmer to wake. But to his surprise, as soon as they'd shut the door, the hallway lights came on and the vicar came down the steps, dressed in a dark suit and clerical collar, a bag in his hand.

"What's this?" he asked, looking both awake and composed.

"Why are you up so early, sir?" Ivan asked.

"Mrs. Johns is going, poor dear. They've asked for me."

"Of course," Alecia said.

The vicar shook his head. "Shouldn't be long, and then you can tell me what this is all about."

"I'll have a hot meal waiting for you," she promised.

He reached the bottom of the staircase and kissed the top of her head. "Until then." He nodded at Ivan, glanced incuriously at Vera, and opened the front door.

"Can I drive you, sir? The car is warmed up."

"Thank you, son, but the Johns live at the end of the lane. Very near." He stepped through the door and Ivan shut it behind him.

"So much for his help," Vera said as she took off her gloves and coat and tossed them onto a bench. Quietly, Alicia picked them up and hung the coat on a peg next to an old wool sweater. She tucked the gloves into the coat pockets.

"A dying woman is more important than you," Ivan snapped.

Alecia looked at both of them in turn. "I'll start some breakfast. No coffee in this house, but strong tea, eggs, and plenty of toast."

"We'll help," Ivan said.

"Why don't you take turns in the bath while I prepare the food? I know the kitchen," she suggested.

Ivan nodded and pointed upstairs. Vera followed him as he went up. "No more than ten minutes in the bath," he told her, pointing at a closed door. "That's Alecia's room. You can find something clean to wear. I'm sure she won't mind."

Vera glared at him and went into the bathroom.

The vicar was gone for three hours. At a little after seven A.M. he returned, his age showing in the deep grooves down the sides of his mouth. Alecia immediately fixed him tea and toast, then fried eggs and potatoes.

Ivan kept Vera in the parlor. She had curled up on the sofa by the fire and gone to sleep like a cat. He suspected she was trying to avoid all of them. Perhaps she was avoiding herself as well.

The vicar came into the parlor after he ate, trailed by Alecia with a large green teapot on a tray. He sat down in a rocking chair and said, "What's all this, then?"

"Vera may or may not be a fugitive from justice. My friend is attempting to persuade the police to lose interest in her in favor of locating a dangerous Bolshevik instead."

"Will your friend call here and let us know?"

"We didn't tell him exactly where we were going."

"Probably wise," the vicar said equably, turning his head to Vera. "Tell me, Miss Salter."

"Saltykova," Alecia corrected as she poured tea for everyone. "Vera uses their Russian name."

"Miss Saltykova." He took a steaming cup from Alecia. "What are your plans?"

Ivan poked his sister in the arm. "Stop faking sleep," he said in Russian. "I know you are."

She blinked sleepily at him. He bared his teeth at her. "What about Sergei?"

"We are no longer going to marry," she said softly.

"Why? Because he is going to prison?"

"I wanted Georgy dead. He killed Mama and Papa, Ivan, just as if he used the gun himself." A little of her old fire showed.

"He was afraid for his own life," Ivan said. "Our parents were his ticket to safety, as much as there is in Russia these days. He has no morals, but he acted to save himself."

"What about Catherine?" Vera cried, wringing her hands.

"She played the same dangerous game you did, and paid for it with her life."

Vera shook her head. "I am not a revolutionary. I wanted revenge for our parents. I wanted blood for blood."

"When has blood for blood solved anything? Not to mention mixing yourself up with revolutionaries and Bolsheviks in this peaceful country." Ivan stared down at the cup cradled in his hands.

"It went too far," Vera admitted. "That Pavel. I think he lied to us all along about who he was. He was a plant. A Bolshevik plant. We meant to give Ovolensky to Konstantin and almost gave him a dozen British politicians and their wives."

The vicar put a finger to his chin. "This man was responsible for the deaths of your parents?"

"There is no doubt about that," Ivan said, that old feeling of sickness and dread ghosting through his stomach as he thought of those days. "Indeed, I was afraid he might do something to us, if he discovered us in London. But when he did see me, last night, while his dislike was clear, he didn't seem to have any agenda."

"It might be different in Russia," the vicar mused. "Did he want anything your family had?"

"At the time, seven years ago, yes. But the new government had informers everywhere. It was terrible. People informing on their neighbors." Ivan glanced over at Alecia, who shook her head in sympathy. In peaceful Bagshot, she'd had such a different kind of life.

"Was your cousin any worse than anyone else?"

"Of course. He lied. People died," Ivan said.

The vicar nodded. "Yet here you are, you and your sister, in a free society, earning your bread with dignity. Meanwhile, this man may have material wealth, but he is imprisoned by the same society, the same politics, that made him betray his own family in order to stay alive."

Vera jutted her chin. "He is still living off his thirty pieces of silver."

"That does not make him happy," the vicar said. "If he is willing to let you go, you should let him go as well. Let your parents and your sister rest. They would not want you to suffer. Jesus counseled us to turn the other cheek, and this is what you must do."

"But he is a murderer," Vera protested.

"And so you almost became one yourself," the vicar said gently.

Tears sprung into Vera's eyes. "Sergei didn't leave Russia until 1920. He said Georgy had moved into my father's house. He'd sold our books, burned our family photographs. He obliterated the Saltykovs."

"Evil is real," the vicar said, setting his cup aside. "I don't deny it.

But you cannot allow it to touch you. You have to make your peace with the past."

Ivan had always thought Vera was the power in her relationship with Sergei. In Russia, women were considered stronger than men, a thought that seemed foreign to the British. Was it possible that he'd misunderstood, that Sergei had been the one driving this situation? He asked a question he'd never considered until now. "What did Georgy do to the Bakunins?"

Vera turned to him, her face wan and tearstained. "He informed on Sergei's brother-in-law. His sister was in an advanced state of pregnancy."

Ivan closed his eyes. He'd heard none of this. "What happened?"

"The brother-in-law was jailed. Sergei's sister went into early labor and her baby died. Sergei said she went mad. I don't know what happened after that."

Alecia spoke up. "Why not?"

"That's when Sergei's parents insisted he leave."

"He was old enough to be in the war," Ivan said. "I never understood why he wasn't a soldier."

Vera sniffed and shifted in her seat. Her eyes were red rimmed. "You know he wears glasses. He can't see well enough to be a soldier."

The vicar took off his glasses and rubbed his eyes. "When he was twenty-six, his parents told him to flee, in order to prevent him being informed on too?"

"He was a White, along with his brother-in-law."

"So there was a reason behind your cousin informing," the vicar said.

"Yes, of course," Vera whispered. "I just wanted Georgy dead, but Sergei wanted the government overthrown too. Any little bit of damage he could do to the Bolsheviks. If only he hadn't let Pavel bring Konstantin into our little group."

"I'm sorry, Vera," Ivan said. He'd misunderstood Sergei completely. "When Sergei turned up in London, I never thought he would do us harm. But you must think for yourself. Revenge made you foolish."

"It was exciting to edit their pamphlets," Vera admitted. "And cook for them while they discussed Mother Russia."

"Mother Russia has been nothing but a disappointment," Ivan said. He found Vera's words rather simplistic and disingenuous, but she'd given him more information than he could easily take in. "First, it took our brother, then our sister, then our parents and our home. I am happy to be here."

"I know you are," Vera said. "But I do not belong. I can't make a living. I can't find a decent husband. I'm almost thirty. Everything that happened has ruined my life." She put her face into her hands and began to sob.

"Are you really done with Russia?" Alecia asked.

"I am British now," Ivan said. "Whatever Vera decides. I am going to marry you and make my life here."

The vicar glanced between Ivan and Vera. "Do you know anyone in Paris? I understand there is a large Russian community there."

"Every cab driver in Paris is from Moscow," Ivan said. "So they say. We know a couple hundred people there."

The vicar took a packet of papers from his pocket. "Mrs. Johns's husband lent me her papers. Miss Saltykova can leave today under her name. Go to your friends in Paris, and stay until you know the police have cleared you."

"That's very generous of the Johns family, especially in their time of suffering," Ivan said, taking the papers.

"Are you certain?" Alecia asked her grandfather. "Won't this put you at risk?"

"We have to assume your friend won his argument with the police and that Miss Saltykova will be able to return soon. Make sure your brother knows how to contact you."

Vera put down her hands and nodded, her face still wet with tears.

"There's money for a train ticket and for passage to France. Ivan can drive you to the train station when he returns to London."

"I need to return too, to see if I still have a position," Alecia said.

"Then you should go," the vicar said. "Don't go anyplace where the police can find you until Miss Saltykova is safely out of Dover, on her way to Calais." He turned to Vera. "In return, miss, I expect you to spend a great deal of time in prayer and reflection about these matters."

Epilogue

The pea-soup fog outside didn't diminish the radiance of Alecia's thoughts as she took her place beside Ivan in her grandfather's church. Her sister, Sadie, straightened their mother's gold cross necklace, which Alecia wore for good luck, and kissed her cheek before taking her place with the other guests. While Alecia wished Ivan's sister could also be there to support them at their wedding, Vera had decided to remain in Paris. Nonetheless, Alecia and Ivan had decided they didn't want to wait any longer to start their lives together. The month since Vera had departed had felt like a thousand years, with Ivan at Mr. Grinberg's flat and Alecia with the Plashes. Once she was free of her duty to the Plashes, her grandfather had offered to buy them a license and marry them right away. They'd been thrilled to agree.

Peter Eyre walked into the church and strode directly up to them, smiling genially. "Congratulations!"

"We aren't married yet, sir," Ivan said. "The vicar was called away by his secretary."

"That gives us a moment. I had a question for you. Where does the new Salter family plan to reside?"

"My friend Boris is going to stay elsewhere for a few days and gift us with his flat," Ivan said, shaking his manager's hand. "Thank you, sir, for coming to our wedding."

"I wouldn't miss it," Eyre said with a wink. "You are the Grand Russe's first happy couple, you know. And since you are our new head of hotel security, Ivan, I would like to offer you a suite at the hotel. We're about to open the tenth floor as an employee dormitory. All the department heads will have suites there."

Alecia couldn't believe their luck. Her night watchman could give her the glamorous life after all. She clasped her hands together. "Not only did we find each other at the Grand Russe, now we'll be able to enjoy our married lives there. It's perfect."

Ivan nodded. "Thank you, sir, and I appreciate you offering my wife a position."

"It's too bad about Mrs. Plash," Eyre said, transferring his gaze to Alecia. "But at least you made her last few weeks a bit more comfortable."

"Poor thing." Alecia sighed. "I worry about her daughter."

Eyre didn't seem to hear her. "Ah, here's the vicar now."

Ivan took Alecia's hands in his, smiling warmly into her eyes. She forgot about everything but him. He looked so handsome in his new suit, his hair neatly trimmed, his tie perfectly knotted, the picture of an English gentleman. She finally had a dress for day that didn't look like a sack, one she'd sewn with Emmeline Plash during long hours in her flat. Emmeline had quite a talent for dress design.

"I love you," she whispered to Ivan. She'd learned the words in Russian, but now that she knew how firmly committed he was to being British, she'd decided to terminate her language studies. They would move forward together, bound in marriage as Salters, not Saltykovs, solid British citizens.

"And I love you, my dearest," he said. He'd ceased calling her *myshka* recently. Sometimes she missed it, but his new endearment for her made her warm inside. She really was his dearest, and nothing could make her happier than planning their life together.

Find out what happened to Sadie in *I Wanna Be Loved by You*, the next Grand Russe Hotel romance, coming in February 2017!

Keep reading for a special sneak preview . . .

Chapter One

Sadie Loudon pressed her hands down the sides of her slightly too short uniform skirt when she saw Mrs. Curtis. She'd shortened it to make it saucier, but the above-calf length created problems when she had to bend over. January was no time to have a breeze snaking up her bare thighs. However, the increased tips in this seedy inn where she was a new chambermaid more than made up for the discomfort.

"Clean up that mess in the lobby, ducks," the housekeeper said, brushing frizzy locks of graying hair behind her ears. "We'll run off our customers."

Sadie clucked her tongue when she saw the pile of paper in the middle of the small hotel lobby. "Who dumped a pile of rubbish there?"

Mrs. Curtis sighed. "No idea. We're too close to the Richmond train station for comfort."

Sadie set down her mop and bucket in the corner and went to pick up the papers. Her shoes crunched on a broken tile in the checkerboard pattern as she walked across the floor. She looked back to see Mrs. Curtis wincing at the noise.

As she picked up the first piece of cheap paper, the headline, in large, heavy type, stood out: UNITE THE WORKERS! She scanned the text: "Not a penny off the workers' wages, not a penny tax on food!"

None of it meant much to her. She had only started her first proper, paying job on Monday. No paycheck had been issued to her yet. As far as she was concerned, these labor unions trying to create unrest were merely creating labor for her.

"I'll be sorting out the reading room," Mrs. Curtis called. "Have a tidy in room 301 when you're done in here. They just went to tea."

Sadie made a face at the floor. Dreadful 301 and their nasty poodles. She hated that foul-smelling room. It took four times longer to clean than any of the others. She clenched her fist, ruffling the leaflets, then bent to gather up the rest.

She heard a slam behind her, as if a guest had opened the upstairs door in a rush. Someone hurtled down the steps. She glanced up to see a bearded man in gray trousers, a baggy black coat, and a Russian *budenovka* hat barreling toward her. Dropping the leaflets, she attempted to stand.

The running man crashed into her. She fell backwards, instinctively cradling her head. Her back hit the tile, legs going up in the air. Pain radiated through her skull and hands. She was too startled to do anything but pant.

More noise on the stairs. More crunching on the tiles. The front door banged open. Steps slowed. Another man looked down at her, this one in a slim, hand-tailored, pinstriped suit. His bowed lips curled when he saw her silver tap pants, exposed by the skirt hovering somewhere around her waist. He was clean shaven and rather young, with gray-blue eyes that regarded her dispassionately, despite the smile.

Sadie pulled her knees together and dropped her feet to the ground. "Help me up!" she begged, cautiously letting go of her head.

The man narrowed his eyes, then glanced toward the door. Without looking back, he ran after the bearded man, his highly polished oxfords gleaming from her floor-level vantage point. He pushed through the door, coatless, running into the cold after his quarry.

Slowly, she put her hands to the tiles and pushed herself up. Her back ached and her head spun. "Well, I like that," she muttered. "Such cheek." She pushed her skirt down and stared uneasily at the leaflets.

Bolsheviks were labor agitators, weren't they? And that first man was clearly a Bolshevik, with a hat like that. As much as he had frightened her, it was the complete calm in the second man's eyes that had bothered her the most. She had a sense that nothing could break through his defenses.

Shivering, she rose shakily to her feet and staggered to the battered reception desk. Old Ben, the hall porter, appeared as if from nowhere.

"Sadie, love, what's gotten into you?" Old Ben stepped up to the other side of the desk.

"Nothing," she said. "I was knocked down."

"By a guest?" Old Ben stared uneasily at the small lobby.

"They came from upstairs." She described both men.

"I don't recall either of them," he said. "I'll have to investigate. Why don't you get a headache powder from Mrs. Curtis and have a lie-down in your room?"

Sadie wanted to say yes, but she wasn't a well-trained vicar's granddaughter for nothing. "I still have work to do. After I clean room 301, perhaps."

"No, love, have a lie-down first. Half an hour."

"I will then. I do ache dreadfully." She smiled and hobbled toward the stairs. When she saw one of the leaflets, which had scattered around the floor with all of the movement in the room, she picked it up and took it with her. She had a vague sense that she needed to be better informed.

Heather Hiestand was born in Illinois but her family migrated west before she started school. Since then she has claimed Washington State as home, except for a few years in California. She wrote her first story at age seven and went on to major in creative writing at the University of Washington. Her first published fiction was a mystery short story, but since then it has been all about the many flavors of romance. Heather's first published romance short story was set in the Victorian period and she continues to return, fascinated by the rapid changes of the nineteenth century. The author of many novels, novellas and short stories, she has achieved bestseller status on Amazon's Romance Anthologies list and on Amazon UK's Romance Short Stories list. With her husband and son, she makes her home in a small town and supposedly works out of her tiny office, though she mostly writes in her easy chair in the living room. She's probably sitting there right now!

For more information, visit Heather's website at www.heatherhiestand. com. Want to stay in touch with Heather and receive exclusive information about her new releases? Sign up for her newsletter at http://heatherhiestand.com/newsletter/.

Some cravings must be indulged…

The Marquess of Cake

THE REDCAKES

HEATHER HIESTAND

His craving could be her undoing…

One Taste
of Scandal

THE REDCAKES

HEATHER
HIESTAND

First comes seduction...

His Wicked Smile

THE REDCAKES

HEATHER HIESTAND

Desire is a most delicious pursuit...

The
Kidnapped
Bride

THE REDCAKES

HEATHER
HIESTAND

Nothing is more delicious than desire...

Christmas Delights

THE REDCAKES

HEATHER HIESTAND

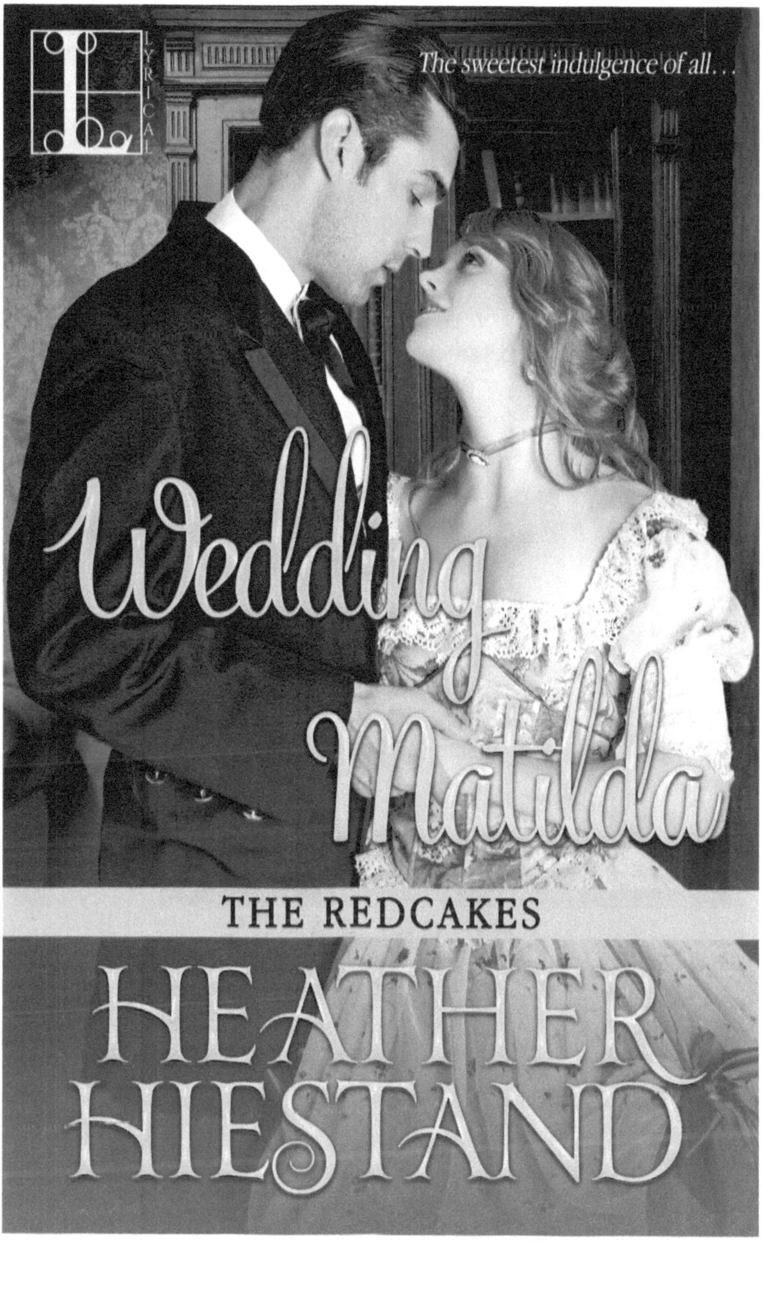
LYRICAL
The sweetest indulgence of all…
Wedding Matilda
THE REDCAKES
HEATHER HIESTAND

Trifling Favors

THE REDCAKES

HEATHER HIESTAND